GUN BARREL PLANETS 2

NEW AMERICA

BY
PHILLIP TUCKER

www.philliptucker.com.au

ACKNOWLEDGEMENT

To my family and friends. As long as a man has both, he is truly blessed. Thanks to all of you for your support. Special thanks to Steve and Diane, who helped turn an ordinary book, into something special.

COPYRIGHT © PHILLIP TUCKER 2012

Cover illustration and design copyright to Lindsey Bidwell at Bidwell Media, visit: www.bidwellmedia.com.au

This book is a work of fiction. Names, characters, places and incidents are products of the author's imagination or are used

CONTENTS

PLANET NEW AMERICA

THE YEAR 2999

"Did they see you come here, son?" Johan asked his son, as he bandaged his bleeding and burnt limb.

"No I don't think so dad, but they killed the other boys with me." He moaned, fighting against the pain of losing his friends and the ugly wound on his left arm.

"I've warned you before about going out at night looking for food on the plains son. Why didn't you listen, Benjamin?" His father spat out, more in fear than anger.

"Mum's sick and the rest of the families left in this village are starving. We all thought we could find something in the old abandoned naval base."

"Look, son, I know you meant well, but the Overmen have satellites everywhere, you know that."

"We were wearing camouflage suits with infrared jammers, they shouldn't have seen us." Benjamin pointed out. His father stared at his 15-year-old son, not knowing what to say. Since the uprising against the government that had failed twenty years ago, there'd been no peace, only bloodshed. The Overmen, as they were called, enforced the curfews, stopping anyone from leaving their homes after dark. Food was in short supply, with many of the grain producing areas devastated, in the reprisal attacks that followed the attempted coup.

Johan himself had fought in the failed coup, to try and bring democracy back from the years of military rule. They'd failed miserably, their whole plan betrayed by a spy planted inside their organisation. The Junta had come down hard. Using their spaceships, they had bombarded the planet, destroying entire cities, in their insane show of force. Cowered by the overwhelming reprisals, Johan like many others had deserted, going home. Now he lived in fear that someone might give him up for a handful of food from the Junta. With that thought, a suspicion entered Johan's mind.

"Son, how many of your friends went tonight?"

"Just the five of us dad, Cob, the foreman son at the storage sheds, became ill as we were leaving. We told him to go home; as it turns out, he was lucky he did."

"Yeah he certainly was, wasn't he," Johan answered, his right hand balling into a fist. Benjamin watching his father saw the change.

"Is something wrong dad?"

"It can wait, son. Let's check your wound, see if the blood has stopped flowing." Johan suggested, giving Benjamin a rare smile, hiding his doubts.

Both father and son spent the rest of the night awake, watching. As the sun started to appear over the hills to the north, Johan silently prayed the Overmen would be happy with the young men they'd killed. The sound of an approaching airship made him curse. He knew they'd either tracked his son home or been told where to find him.

"Get your sister Benjamin and get into the bomb shelter!" He yelled. Benjamin obeying lifted the heavy reinforced door in the lounge room floor, before running to his sister's room. He was just about to knock when his sister Marlene opened it. Telling her what was going on, she ran to the shelter, while he rushed to his father's workroom. Johan in the meantime had gone to his bedroom.

Carefully picking up his wife from the bed, he carried her to the lounge room. With Marlene's help, he managed to take her down the stairs into the bomb shelter. Placing his wife on a makeshift bed in the shelter, he told Marlene to look after her. Returning upstairs, he found Benjamin charging two laser rifles he'd taken from his workroom.

"Get downstairs with your mother and sister now!" Johan ordered.

"No dad this is my fault! I'm staying with you." His father made to reply, but the words didn't come. He was proud of his son, for what he'd done. He now stood before him as a man.

"Okay, you watch the rear and don't fire unless I say to." He smiled, taking the second rifle from his son. Checking it, making sure it was fully charged he watched his son move to the rear.

"He's head-strong just like me." He whispered, hoping Benjamin survived this confrontation; he'd make a good leader some day. Closing the bomb shelter doors, Johan was just about to move to the window adjacent to the front door, when a mind-numbing roar erupted in front of him. The aircraft hovering above them had fired a blast from one of its laser cannons.

Although it targeted the road twenty paces in front of the house the explosion was terrifying. The shockwaves from it, ripped the front door off its hinges, sending it cannoning into Johan. This caused him to be thrown backwards across the room, landing heavily on the floor. Benjamin shaking, fearing the worst ran from the rear of the house. He found his father lying face down on the floor near the crumpled front door.

Checking his father's wrist, Benjamin felt a pulse. Finding a weak but continuous one, Benjamin relieved, now knew his father was just concussed. Turning him over, he found a savage cut on his right leg and another on his shoulder. Grabbing the window curtains, which lay strewn on the floor next to his father, Benjamin ripped them into strips, using them to bandages his father's cuts. Awakened by his son doctoring, Johan opened his eyes slowly taking in his surroundings. He was just about to ask what had occurred when outside a voice boomed over the countryside.

"You inside the house, come outside and surrender, or we'll burn your village to the ground. You have one minute to comply." Benjamin, looked at his father, trying to find the words, nothing came. Standing, he silently walked to the crumbled remains of the front door.

"Don't go, son! Help me up, I'll go instead." His father cried out. Trying to stand, he grabbed onto a chair for support, before collapsing back onto the floor.

"I love you, dad." Benjamin sobbed, before turning and walking outside.

Terrified he hesitantly stepped out into the open, stopping at the edge of a huge crater, which now blocked the dirt road, which ran past their home. Staring at the hole, Benjamin knew the next shot fired would be for him. Dropping his rifle, he raised his hands above his head. Standing there, looking up at the Overman's ship, Benjamin felt a sense of destiny settle over him.

"I won't beg for forgiveness, you arseholes!" He shouted out defiantly, clenching his right hand into a fist and lowering his other hand to his side, he stood waiting his fate.

On board the Atlanta, Captain Ryan looked at Benjamin on the ship's screen. The computer using facial recognition software compared him to the earlier image of the youth, who managed to escape from the old naval base. They'd been clever in evading all the security measures around the base. Their mistake was someone loyal to the Junta had betrayed them.

"It's him, Captain, there can be no doubt," His second in command Lieutenant Hester, confirmed, waiting for the order to fire.

"He's a brave one, that's for sure." the Captain smiled. Ryan personally would have let the kid go. The area's population was starving, what else did the Junta expect people to do, just die? Unfortunately, that wasn't his call and orders were orders. Looking down he saw the young man ball one of his hands into a fist as he spoke.

"What did he just say?" Ryan asked his communications officer.

"I won't beg for forgiveness you arseholes" The Comm.'s Officer replied sheepishly, as several crewmembers chuckled.

"The kid's got guts alright." Ryan smiled. His face slowly lost the smile, as he thought about what would take place next. He was just about to tell his blood thirsty second in command to open fire when the ship's sensors sounded a warning.

"What's going on?" He shouted, as the automatic defence system, deployed their shield.

"A large object is moving towards us at high speed underwater." The operator of the sensor array replied.

"Where did it come from?" The Captain asked.

"In appeared in the area where the portals used to open." The same crewman answered, stopping all chatter.

"That area is off limits, no one uses the portal." Lieutenant Hester pointed out.

"It appears someone has Hester. Go to battle stations. Inform High Command we have a breach." The Captain ordered.

Standing below them, Benjamin's quiet moment of defiance was interrupted, as out of the ocean to his right, a giant ship broke the surface. With a heart-pounding roar, it rose into the sky, moving directly towards Benjamin's village. The ship was massive, brilliant white in colour with a slight reddish tinge. It shone in the first rays of the morning light as it rose into the air. Benjamin shading his eyes saw the ship resembled the Star cruisers the Junta used.

He knew from school that the design for these ships had come from a race called the Roax. The descendants of this advanced race were now living on a planet called Salvation, colonised by people from Earth. Their home planet New America had once been linked to Salvation, by a Portal device. His own planet's population had passed through Salvation on their way to colonise this planet.

Many years ago the portal had been destroyed; meaning space travel by rocket's engines was now their only means of moving from planet to planet. Benjamin had once seen a Star cruiser up close. It had stopped at the village to pick up grain, which was being sent urgently to one of New America's satellite planets. Looking at this ship now, he realised how unimpressive their ships were, compared to this one. Reddish white in colour now, it to him seemed to radiate power.

Watching it, he felt the thumping noise in his chest, as its engines reverberated through the very ground he stood on. For some reason, he felt a premonition of a coming cataclysm by the arrival of the mystery ship.

As if the Cruiser had finally noticed the Overman's ship, it came to a stop. Turning slightly, it faced the other ship. Standing there in the open, Benjamin couldn't help comparing the Overmen's ship to the new arrival.

Box-shaped, painted in a drab camouflage brown and green colours, the Overman's ship was nothing more than a flying gun platform. Built to keep the population inline, it had the aerodynamics of a flying brick. He'd always thought the

Overman ships large and unstoppable. Now he saw them like rabid dogs, finally confronted at last by a lion. Looking closely, he saw the cruiser had writing on its bow. Studying it, shielding his eyes for a better look, recognition hit him like a hammer.

Remembering his history lesson, he dropped to his knees in astonishment and fear.

"The Katherine" he murmured, as a huge smile crept across his face.

Benjamin as if looking at a mirage, remembered the stories of the murdering traitors and aliens from another Galaxy. They had supposedly slaughtered thousands of New American soldiers, who at the time were bravely defending a planet called Salvation. The Captain named Simon Hayes was a human, a vile creature that drank the blood of people they captured. The thought occurred to him as to why he was smiling at the appearance of these killers.

It was because he knew by their reputation, these hideous monsters from who knows where, would attack and destroy the main threat first, as after all the Overman ship was the biggest threat.

"This could be interesting," Benjamin chuckled, forgetting his fear, as a feeling of retribution for his friends' deaths, settled over the coming encounter.

Onboard the Atlanta, Captain Ryan too stared at the ship. His guts were in a knot, as around him the crew silently stared at the mystery ship of dark legends.

"It can't be the Katherine. Those murderers and traitors to the human race died fifty years ago." Hester shouted as if raising her voice would drown out the fear she felt.

"Yet there she sits. The reason why is the next question." Ryan smiled.

"Sir we're receiving a transmission." His Communication's Officer informed him.

"What's it say?"

"Leave the area immediately or be vaporised." Tense seconds passed as the crew speechless, waited for their Captain to answer.

"They don't mince words, do they? Ryan confidently said out loud, trying to inspire leadership to his rattled crew. What do you suggest Hester?" Ryan asked his second in command.

"Fire everything we've got Captain. His shields aren't even deployed." Hester grinned, looking forward to the glory.

"Any word from High command yet?" Ryan asked, looking towards the Communication's officer.

"Nothing Sir, they haven't answered".

"Move the ship away now," Ryan ordered as Hester gasped in surprise.

"But Captain!" Hester started, stopped by Ryan raising his hand.

"We are not hunting down just a group of lightly armed young criminals, Hester. The ship facing us, with supposedly no shields, shows no fear of us attacking her. That tells me that it's wise to wait until our leaders send us reinforcements," Ryan told her, putting Hester in her place, as his ship banked to the right, moving away.

Benjamin knowing nothing of what was going on above, saw a small ship leave the Katherine, as the Overman's ship turned and retreated. Continuing to watch what he took to be a shuttle, he followed its descent. It suddenly occurred to him that it seemed headed straight towards him at a rapid rate. Frozen, fearing that the whole village could become the Katherine's crews' next dinner; he looked around for a place to lead them away from his home.

He was still trying to work out where to run when the shuttle landed next to him with a thud. Knowing it was too late to flee, Benjamin rushed to his discarded rifle, as the shuttle's door opened beside him. Backing up, taking aim, he waited apprehensively for the aliens to pour from the ship, devouring all in their paths. To his surprise and relief, a young woman in her early twenties appeared.

"You can lower your weapon, we mean you no harm. We've come down to rescue you and find out what's going on." She informed him.

"The legend said you're man-eaters and drinkers of blood."

"Do I look like a drinker of blood?" The woman laughed.

"Well no, but you could be."

"Well, by the look of it, that ship meant to kill you. Sometimes it's best to go with the lesser evil, so are you going to come aboard or not?" She demanded, getting upset with him. Benjamin unsure, looked back towards his house hesitating. "Your family will be alright. But we must leave before they return in numbers." She warned him. Knowing she was right and that he couldn't stay, he took a deep breath, walking past her onto the ship.

His bravery at entering soon paled, when he came face to face with the aliens onboard. Screaming, turning to run for it, he found his way blocked by the door itself, which was now closed. Backing up against a wall Benjamin again raised his weapon, as the girl and the aliens stood looking at him, some chuckling.

"Radon it's not funny." The woman rebuked them, stopping the laughter.

"I'm sorry Kate. You've got to admit he did look hysterical when he saw us." Radon smiled.

"He's most probably never seen an alien, and he has been told we drink blood; let's give him some credit for coming aboard." Kate chastised them, the crew nodding they understood. Hearing Kate's words, Benjamin lowered his weapon. Walking up to Benjamin she placed her arm around his shoulder, reassuring him that everything was okay. She then steered him to a seat and relieved him of the rifle.

Once he was seated, the alien the woman had called Radon, dropped down into the seat next to him.

"My name is Radon; I am second in command of the Katherine, what is your name?" He asked, through two rows of small shark like teeth, offering his hand.

"Benjamin." He answered, unnerved by the close proximity to an alien. Overcoming his fear, he gripped the alien's hand shaking it. Radon as if reading his mind, nodded to him, as if understanding his predicament.

"Take us back to the Katherine, Horen," Radon shouted across the conversations going on. The helmsman nodding his understanding gripped a two-handed control rod. The ship immediately responded, rising smoothly into the air, heading rapidly back to the Katherine.

Sitting quietly studying the aliens and the young woman named Kate, Benjamin took in his situation. The aliens seemed to be of two different races. The ones like Radon seemed to have a humanoid shape. Although they were more solidly built than most humans, they had a fluid, graceful way of moving. The only thing worrying about them was their double row of shark-like teeth. Definitely meat eaters he figured, the problem was what meat did they eat?

The other race appeared more human although their facial features were more pronounced. Their skin also had a crystallised appearance. Without the protruding teeth they at least looked friendlier, but who could tell with unknown aliens. Both races, however, spoke English, better than most people on New America he observed. Looking towards Kate, Benjamin smiled, thinking how beautiful she was.

At first, Benjamin thought that she was talking to herself. A closer look revealed a small device in her ear, meaning she was communicating with someone. 'Most probably someone on the ship' he mused. Looking back towards Radon, he saw one of his men softly talking to him, before with a nod he moved towards what appeared to be a water dispenser. Coming back with a small cup of water, he offered it to Benjamin.

Thanking him, seeing the soldier being acknowledged by his superior Radon, a thought came to him.

"Radon you're not the same Radon that attacked Salvation with Captain Hayes many years ago, are you? It's just you don't look that old or does your race live a lot longer than humans?" His question brought instant silence from everyone in hearing distance.

"For a start, we didn't attack anyone Benjamin. When we returned with Simon to Salvation, we were ambushed at a reception for Simon hosted by the UN who controlled Salvation. That aside, what do you mean by many years ago?" Radon replied, as Kate to stop talking, awaiting his answer.

"Well, it must've been fifty years ago since," Benjamin, seeing their reactions faltered. "Is there a problem?"

"Best wait till we're all aboard. The others, including Simon, should hear this as well." Kate replied, an unreadable look on her face.

"My God is Captain Hayes still alive too?" Benjamin excitedly asked, as the aliens and the young woman all sat there crestfallen, no one answering.

Once on board, his courage slightly restored, Benjamin was escorted to the command deck or bridge. There he found a young man of about twenty-two, watching a screen. Looking over his shoulder, Benjamin saw at least twenty ships closing in on their position. As if sensing him watching him, the young man turned around. Looking him over, the young man approached him offering his hand.

"My name is Simon, yours is?"

"Benjamin, Benjamin Ney." He answered nervously shaking his hand. Despite his young appearance, Benjamin noticed that this Simon had a commanding air about him as if he had been born to lead men. Not incredible good-looking, he had an open, approachable demeanour, the type of man who radiated openness. It was only when an alien crewman came up and called him Captain, that Benjamin realised who he was.

"My God you're him!" Benjamin gasped backing away, more scared of this young human than the aliens.

"I got the same reaction from him, though I am an alien." Radon smiled. "It seems he's been told the murderous crew of the Katherine, attacked Salvation quite some time ago."

"That aside Benjamin, it seems someone doesn't like you. Care to fill us in on what's happening here?" Simon asked.

"You don't know?" Benjamin replied.

"Lad we don't know where we are, or what year it is, any help would be appreciated." Radon put in, as the whole room erupted with suppressed laughter.

"Since we're exchanging names, I am Kate." the young woman smiled. "The others can introduce themselves in time," she suggested, offering her hand, which he graciously took. 'She is so beautiful' Benjamin thought, already knowing her name from the shuttle. Reluctantly letting go of her hand, as he saw Simon was still waiting for his answer.

Benjamin had at first thought that Simon's question, about knowing nothing, was some kind of alien joke. Now he realised that this Captain Simon Hayes was waiting and expected an answer.

"Where would you like me to start?" He asked.

"Start with the year." Simon smiled, his eyes moving between Benjamin and the monitor incessantly. Nodding Benjamin began.

"It is the year 2999. For over fifty years the planet New America had been under Marshall Law. How the Junta had come to power he didn't know, all he knew was they were starving, while their grain was taken from them. He told them of the failed raid he and his friends had gone on in search of food and medical supplies."

"Why were you standing outside?" Kate interrupted.

"I alone survived the raid. They must've tracked me back to my home. If I hadn't come out, they were going to kill my family and the other villagers." Benjamin told them, reliving the moment.

"You are a brave human. We salute you." One of the alien soldiers exclaimed. It was followed by chest beating by the other crewmembers. This seemed to surprise not only Benjamin but Simon and Kate as well.

"I've never seen you do that before Radon. Why did you all thump your chest like that?" Simon asked mystified.

"This human displayed bravery through an unselfish act. In modern warfare, individual acts of bravery have become rare, when we carry out war from our spaceships. We still honour the old ways." Radon answered.

"We used to a long time ago give out medals for bravery. Mike had several from the war on Earth, though he never showed them to anyone." Simon informed him, taking on a faraway look.

"Yes, we have that custom too. As you said, many who win medals don't show them, as remembering the actual battle can be painful for them." Radon added as the room went into a self-imposed silence. Benjamin seeing the crew were thinking over past battles, broke the silence.

"How come you don't know what's going on?"

"Fifty years ago when I was injured on Salvation we returned to Oregarth, our home planet. From there, we travelled to an area of space usually avoided, called of all things, the Void. We entered the zone, and that's the last we remember." Simon confessed, sounding unsure.

"Why did you travel to this void place?"

"A voice spoke to me in my dreams," Simon answered distantly.

"You went to a forbidden area, because of a voice you heard while asleep?" Benjamin gave a look that suggested they were crazy.

"As stupid as it sounds we did, but on the other hand they did heal Simon." Kate put in, remembering how Simon was being kept alive by an oxygen pump, totally paralysed.

"So you don't know anything about the last fifty years?" Benjamin sounded sceptical.

"It is a mystery. I remember Kate finding my men and I hiding in the rear of the ship. Simon had only wanted Kate to go with him to the void; I decided to sneak aboard with some men as a backup to make sure they both were safe. Somehow the aliens detected us and sent Kate to get us. We came up to the bridge with her, after that I remember nothing." Radon smiled, thinking how dim-witted he'd felt when she had found them.

"Let's move on people," Simon suggested, as watching their proximity sensors, he saw at least twenty ships forming up.

"I know the memory of your planet's past is limited, Benjamin. Can you tell me instead, why you are so scared of us?"

"Our history that we're taught at school tells of your attack on Salvation. It tells us how our soldiers went there to help the planet Salvation's population fight against you. Thousands of troops died on Salvation, and the navy lost many ships when you destroyed the portal."

"What else?" Radon asked, knowing Benjamin had cut short his story.

"They said you were all drinkers of blood. That anyone who surrendered had their throats cut before their bodies were drained of blood." Benjamin looked around nervously, seeing anger and revulsion on the crew's faces.

"They are absolute lies," Kate growled, offended by Benjamin's explanation.

"Settle down Kate, yelling at Benjamin's not going to help," Simon admitted. He still remembered Benjamin's face when he found out he was Captain Hayes; no one could fake that look of horror. "

"Do you think the part about the portal being destroyed is true?" Radon pointed out.

"Yes, it's either been destroyed or Salvation's closed off the portal to New America. I'd hazard a guess and say it's the first." Simon replied, wondering what had occurred.

"We should head there immediately?" Kate suggested her voice sounding concerned, many of the crew nodding agreement.

"That will have to wait people. It looks like Benjamin's enemy ships are about to attack us." Simon warned.

"Battle stations everyone. Horen, take the ship out over the water away from the village." Radon shouted as Horen at the helm moved the ship.

"Are you going to destroy them, Captain Hayes?" Benjamin asked.

"No, not if it's possible to avoid conflict."

"But they're evil. They killed my friends!"

"Look, Benjamin, see it from my side. We appear on your planet fifty years into the future, with no knowledge of the situation here. We have only your word that what you say is true. We must be sure of what's going on before we kill the hundreds of crewmen on those ships." Simon explained.

"Okay, I can see your point, but I'd prepare for the worst. The men coming towards you will give you no other option, but to fight or die." Benjamin informed them, as the Overman's ships moved into formation, closing on the Katherine.

Benjamin watching Simon and the crew prepare knew now that their history lessons had been wildly exaggerated. If they were these monsters of the past, they would've sought to destroy the Overman's ships without a second thought. But here they were trying to reduce casualties by trying to avoid conflict. If this was true, why had they been told otherwise, he asked himself, wondering what was going on.

CONFRONTATION

Ex-Captain Ryan shook his head, trying to clear his vision. Holding his jaw, he made sure the blow hadn't dislocated it.

"Next time I tell you to move, you do it." Steiger roared, as Ex-Captain Ryan groggily tried to stand up.

Failing to act as an officer, the charge was, for not attacking the Katherine. Following his gut feeling, Ryan had moved away when first confronted by the mysterious cruiser. High Command, who he hadn't been able to contact, took his retreat as an act of treason against the Military Junta. Stripped of his rank, Lieutenant Hester had been promoted to Captain on the spot. To add to his disgrace, Captain Hester was put in charge of the coming attack.

Promising swift action against Captain Ryan once the Katherine was dealt with, Captain Hester had Ryan removed from the bridge. She had personally picked Steiger and Branson to guard him, knowing their flare for violence. She had told the whole crew, that Ryan was unfit to stay on the ship during the coming action with the Katherine. Ordering he be taken down to the surface, under guard, she told the crew she wanted him to watch the fleet's glorious victory, over the abomination from the past.

Once she assured them they had dealt with the Katherine they would return and arrange a firing squad for their former Captain. The real reason was she knew the crew respected him and she wanted no trouble from them. Now with the arrival of twenty other hover ships, Hester excitedly ordered them to follow her in an attack on the alien ship. To her surprise, the other Captains weren't overjoyed with attacking the unknown ship. Several suggested opening communications between the ship and themselves to find out what was going on. Angrily she'd pointed out what happened to Ryan. This convinced them to follow her.

Now on the surface with his two guards, Ryan standing up dusted himself off. Watching his ship sail towards the enemy, Ryan felt a sense apprehension for them.

"Well, there goes our new brave Captain. Better than the last one" Steiger smirked.

"Brave is good Steiger, but it can't bring you back from the dead," Ryan answered as Branson chopped him across the knees with his laser rifle, dropping him again onto the ground.

"You're a slow learner Ryan. You really think that ship's got a chance against the fire power of twenty of our ships?" Branson bellowed. Ryan seeing it was pointless to answer didn't. Instead, he stayed on the ground, watching the Overman's ships form a battle formation. 'Won't be long now, one way or the other,' he concluded, feeling for his men on board the Atlanta.

Above him, Captain Hester prematurely drank in her coming recognition, in being the one to rid the Universe of these traitorous creatures from who knows where. Ordering the other ships to follow her in, she involuntarily sniggered at her good fortune.

"Open fire as soon as we're in range." She ordered, resuming her blank in command face, the thought of the coming glorious victory, ringing in her ears.

Beside her at his station, Lieutenant Stuart regarded this action with great trepidation. Captain Ryan mightn't have been the most gung hoe Captain, but he was intelligent and prudent, two qualities lacking in Captain Hester. The crew respected Ryan, and although his arrest had only just taken place, already the crew was talking about freeing him. Unfortunately, he knew that would have to wait until Captain Hester had proved herself.

"The enemy ship still hasn't raised its shields, Sir," Stuart warned as they approached firing range.

"Then our attack has taken them completely by surprise." Hester put forward, watching Stuart.

"I find it hard to believe they didn't see the ships forming up Sir."

"Obviously she's somehow damaged and can't deploy her shields or spot approaching ships. I'd say that right from the start the alien ship has been bluffing. It might have worked with Captain Ryan, but not with me."

"We'll soon know Sir, we're approaching firing range," Stuart announced, as their Communications officer shouted a warning.

"Sir, the enemy has moved their ship away from the village and is now sitting over the ocean. They are warning us to stop immediately."

"Open fire!" Hester shouted. "That's their answer." She shouted, watching, as her main two batteries of lasers streak towards the alien ship. Impacting on the Katherine a brilliant flash of light lit the horizon. Beside their ship the other Captains with a sense of foreboding, fired as well. The crews on board the New America ships shielded their eyes, most were unable to look at the white sun that formed in front of them. Captain Hester chuckled insanely to herself, tried to imagine the power being projected at the enemy.

"Won't be long now?" She giggled, waiting for the enemy ship to fall from the sky as a molten lump of metal.

"Sir, the enemy ship is charging its weapons!" One of the crew screamed.

"That's impossible! With the8 weapons fire it's receiving, all its energy should be going to its shields." Captain Hester replied, sweat forming on her face forcing her to wipe it.

"What shields Sir? The enemy ship still hasn't raised them as far as our instruments are concerned. It might be best Captain to take evasive action before the enemy ship fires back." Stuart warned.

"Don't instruct me on what to do Lieutenant, unless of course, you want to join Ryan."

"I'm just pointing out the danger we are facing Sir. Somehow the enemy ship is storing our own weapons energy, to fire back at us. Why they haven't already, shows they aren't yet worried. That in itself should suggest we prepare for the worst and retreat." Stuart shouted, making the whole room grow quiet.

"You're under arrest Lieutenant. Guards, remove him from the bridge immediately." Hester ordered. To her surprise, the guards didn't move, except their commander, Sergeant Ney.

"What do you think we should do?" He asked Stuart, shocking Hester.

"This is mutiny!" Hester screamed. In one fluid movement, she dropped her arm, drawing her sidearm, as the Sergeant mirrored her movements. Pointing her weapon at the Sergeant, he, in turn, pointed his weapon at her.

"You're bluffing Sergeant?" She smiled, pulling the trigger, nothing happened, as the Sergeant did likewise.

"You should have taken your safety off when you drew your weapon, Captain." Sergeant Ney pointed out, as a surprised Captain Hester, fell backwards, smoke rising from the hole in her chest.

"Turn the ship and warn the other Captains." Stuart, getting over what had happened yelled to the helmsmen. The helmsmen, having already anticipated the order, swung the ship around diving for the ground.

On board the Katherine, Radon watched the power readings go into the red, as the ship absorbed the incoming laser fire. Like Benjamin had said the Overmen had attacked. Simon, he noticed seemed reluctant to fire back.

"We have to do something Simon?"

"They can't hurt us Radon, although the power must be released soon or we'll overload the storage system."

"They didn't know that when they attacked Simon. Like Benjamin told you, these bully boys like to inflict pain on the weak." Kate reminded him.

"Okay, target all the ship's weapon systems. Let's pull their teeth." Simon ordered, looking at Kate. "You've changed Kate. You were usually the last one to agree to open fire."

"I saw what trusting people did to you last time. I won't let it happen again."

Ryan and his two guards had watched the battle like referees at a football game of old. Comments between Steiger and Branson flowed back and forth as both tried to gauge what damage was being inflicted on the enemy. Ryan on the ground remained silent. It wasn't the flash of weapons that kept his attention, it was the time. In theory, the enemy ship should have been destroyed right away. As time went by the chances were that the enemy had survived and that was going to be a problem.

His guards were just starting to mention how long it was taking, when multiple flashes of light, burst from the Katherine. This was followed by a series of massive explosions that echoed over the countryside. Steiger looked pole-axed by what had occurred. Branson not understanding at first, continued to ask Steiger questions. Looking up, the three men in time fell silent. Spellbound they watched the twenty overman ships being pounded by laser blasts, which appeared to have no problems in going right through their shields.

At this stage, all thought of staying in a fighting formation fled, as Overman's ships dived in every direction to get away from the lethal fire from the mysterious ship of folklore. Debris ran down over the ocean, and the fields around them, as the Overman's fleet disintegrated above them. Without warning, the Atlanta that had at first avoided the return fire was hit. Having turned away, her weapons hidden from the Katherine's gunners, they had instead, targeted her engines.

Belching smoke and losing height, it rolled onto its side above them. With no engines it swiftly lost height, ploughing into the meadow opposite them. The impact of the crash landing sent both of Ryan's two guards onto the ground next to him.

"Looks like your new Captain Hester's fleet has had its first major reversal?" Ryan pointed out, as Steiger angrily pointed his weapon at his head.

"Well, you won't get to enjoy it." Steiger proclaimed as movement behind him, made him freeze. Standing above them, in a semi-circle, were at least twenty men, all armed with an assortment of weapons.

"Drop your rifles now!" a voice commanded. Steiger seeing the chances of surviving were zero, told Branson to drop his weapon, as he lowered his rifle to the ground. Now the two guards were unarmed, two of the armed men swiftly moved in, picking up the dropped weapons.

"You mud farmers will fry for this." Steiger laughed, standing up to have a better look at his captors.

"Looks like your fleet is getting that treatment right now?" Johan answered covering both men. "Frisk all of them." He continued, as the three were searched. Both Steiger and Branson had concealed knifes in their boots, Ryan being a prisoner already had nothing.

"What's your story?" Johan asked Ryan.

"Tell them nothing you traitor!" Steiger bellowed, startling the farmers, as Ryan made to answer. Johan's rifle, striking the back of Steiger's head, knocked him to the ground unconscious.

"As I was saying, what is your story?" Johan repeated making Ryan smiled.

"I'm the Ex-Captain of the Atlanta. That's my ship over in the meadow."

"Good time to be out of a job. Who are these two?"

"My guards, I was to be shot, after my replacement returned victoriously."

"Looks like your day just took a turn for the best." Johan smiled, his men laughing.

"Look, is it okay if I go check on the ship for survivors? The crash though severe wasn't too brutal." Ryan enquired, his eyes never leaving his ship.

"Okay, but tell them to drop their weapons before they leave the ship."

"There are over a hundred soldiers on that ship my friend. I see only twenty rebels." Ryan smiled.

"You forget our benefactors up there. They must know that your ship escaped that carnage."

"You're not thinking of attempting another coup? Look what happened last time." Ryan reminded him.

"The last time we didn't have a space cruiser to protect us." Johan smiled, watching as a shuttle left the Katherine, descending.

Captain Ryan ran to his former ship, wondering how badly she'd been damaged. During the crash landing, the ship had landed heavily on its side digging into the ground. Going to an escape hatch, which had been located on the roof, Ryan had no trouble reaching it now, as the ship was half buried in the soft soil. Pressing the auto release failed to open the hatch. Turning the emergency handle, he cranked it open. Inside he found a group of his crewmen, huddled on the inside trying unsuccessfully to open it from their side.

Explaining the situation, he told them to drop their weapons, instructing them to leave in groups of twos and threes. Scrambling outside they were rounded up by the armed farmers and moved into an open area next to their ship. Of the crew of over a hundred, ninety-five made it out, although many had injuries from the crash.

The rest of the Overman ships though damaged had limped away from the area, leaving the doomed Atlanta and her crew to their fate. Ryan knew if he were Captain of one of those ships, he'd have done the same thing. Looking around at the crew, Ryan suddenly realised who one of the missing was.

"Where is Captain Hester?" Ryan shouted as a sea of blank looks stared back.

"She's dead, died on impact." Lieutenant Stuart grunted as Sergeant Ney tightened a bandage on his right leg, slowing the flow of blood from a nasty gash.

"Keep some pressure on it, Sir, until it's stitched." The Sergeant told him, walking over to Ryan.

"Good to see you, Sir." The Sergeant smiled.

"You can forget the sir bit Sergeant. You know, I find it strange, that Captain Hester was one of the five fatalities?"

"Yeah, just bad luck there. Seems her weapon wasn't on safe, must've discharged as she fell."

"Will you back me up, Ryan?" Stuart asked softly.

"Of course I will, although I'm a traitor now." Ryan reminded him, as the shuttle roared to a stop, next to the downed Atlanta. "And be very careful what you say and how you react Stuart. One captain branded a coward is enough." Ryan smiled.

"I'll be happy if we just come out of this alive and uneaten," Stuart replied as both men moved forward.

The rebel farmers, like the crew of the Atlanta, fearfully watched the shuttle land. Most since childhood had heard tales filled with savage horrors, committed by the bloodthirsty crew of this mysterious ship. The stories had grown to such an extent that most expected life-sucking aliens to burst from the ship, devouring anyone who couldn't protect themselves from these invincible warriors. Many as the shuttle touched down involuntarily stepped back, ready to run if necessary.

A hush fell over the gathered humans as the door opened to show a young man of about 15, standing there with a man, aged in his twenties.

"Benjamin!" Johan yelled as Benjamin left the man, running to his father. Grabbing him in a bear hug, they both held each other, while the crowd looked on.

"I thought you were dead son?" Johan muttered wiping his eyes.

"I did too. The overman ship was just about to fry me when the Katherine turned up and picked me up." Benjamin explained. Johan overjoyed, forgot his fear and moved towards the shuttle, where the young man stood now with a young woman.

"Thank you." Was all Johan could get out, as he shook the young man's hand. A feeling of unexpected peace settled over the watching crowd at this show of friendship.

"We were glad to be of assistance," Simon replied, looking over at the crowd present and the downed ship.

The tenseness swiftly returned, as behind the young woman, several alien soldiers by their dress and weapons, appeared. They spread out on either side of the young man and woman. Even Johan moved back several paces.

"My name is Captain Simon Hayes, we mean you no harm." The young man shouted as if he sensed the returning tension.

"Tell that to our fleet!" One of Ryan's crew yelled back, as the other crewmembers of the Atlanta, shouted their support.

"You were warned what would happen if you attacked. You're lucky we reframed from destroying your ships, by only targeting your weapons." Radon shouted back, showing his shark-like teeth. The gathered crowd fell silent; intimidated by the alien's response and the fact he was the first alien they'd seen.

"Why have you come to New America?" Ryan asked moving forward, as the gathered crowd stood silently watching.

"We didn't come here intentionally, that's all I can tell you at the moment. I would now like to meet with the Commander of the downed ship and the leaders of the farm community here if possible?" The young man named Simon requested. Johan signalling to his men that he'd go handed his weapon to another farmer, before approaching Simon. Behind him, ex-Captain Ryan and acting Captain Stuart joined him.

"Can I ask something before we go up to your ship Captain Hayes?" Johan hesitantly asked.

"Go ahead, and it's Simon."

"My wife is gravely ill. Do you have a medic aboard?"

"Radon do we have a medic?"

"Yes, we do Simon. Horen, go with Benjamin see how his mother is." Without another word, one of the aliens hurried back aboard the shuttle. Moments later he reappeared carrying a bag. After a brief talk to Benjamin, they ran off together.

"How is it as Captain, you don't know who your medic is?" Ryan put in, having watched how willingly this band of supposed cutthroats had gone to the farmer's aid.

"I was seriously hurt in an assassination attempt on Salvation fifty years ago. Radon and his men boarded this ship after the incident, so I don't know many of them personally yet. Since then we have been in hibernation and have no knowledge of what has taken place." Simon told them, smiling at their reaction.

"Let's all get aboard the shuttle and return to the ship. Once we are there, we can talk about what has happened in more detail." Kate suggested. Getting nods of support she led the group on board.

Once on board the Katherine, the three men were given a brief tour, before sitting down in a meeting room beside the bridge. Simon then explained in detail, what had occurred after they left Salvation.

"And you don't know anything about the past?" Johan thundered. He'd expected this ship was here to help free them. Instead, it appeared to be some random happenstance."

"There goes your rebellion." Ryan smiled, reading Johan's mind. Johan moved to stand and take a swipe at Ryan, when a pistol tapped him on the shoulder, forcing him to remain seated.

"There will be no fighting at this meeting. Both of you settle down." Radon ordered, placing his pistol back in his holster. Stuart next to Ryan was amazed and a little scared; by the speed, Radon had shown in drawing that gun.

"You are wrong Captain Ryan. We might be here by accident, but I will not leave my people to be treated like slaves." Kate spat out, the crew stamping their feet, showing their support.

"What do you mean your people? What has it to do with you?" Stuart shot back.

"I was born on New America, Captain! I travelled to Salvation to take part in a science expedition, where I met Simon. I was also there when our military sought to kill him." Kate snapped back. Calming down she continued. "Simon and I were to be married on Salvation. The President of New America gave my mother and father, who were to be at the wedding, a present and a treaty, to hand to Simon in person. It was a bomb meant to kill us all by crippling this ship. If you think I'll now leave an undemocratic Military Junta here to rule over free people than you're seriously mistaken."

"Kate," Simon spoke out, stopping her. Sobbing she rushed into his arms.

"I'm sorry Kate. But our history doesn't mention you at all." Stuart intervened; unaware that one of the crew of the Katherine was from New America.

"Yes it does Captain Stuart, it's just been suppressed," Ryan confessed as both Stuart and Johan looked at him.

Ryan, unlike Stuart, knew a lot more than most about the action on Salvation. As a Captain of a Junta ship, he was privy to a higher security clearance. He'd seen the real information about the action on Salvation. He also knew that Salvation was a United Nations planet and New America's forces shouldn't have been there in the first place. This had led to the closing of the portal, how exactly he wasn't sure.

"I know what happened on Salvation wasn't an attack by your forces. Records show a coordinated surprise attack was launched against you; I've seen the actual files." Ryan admitted. "That aside, you have no idea what you're taking on. New America has several fleets of Star cruisers, plus many other armed vessels used between the planets we control. There is also a large fleet of the ships you encountered earlier, I would suggest you leave and take this village's population with you." Ryan suggested. Beside him Stuart and Johan sat open-mouthed, realising the Junta knew the stories of the Katherine were lies.

"Like usual Captain, you humans underestimate the power of this ship. This one ship crippled the Flax federation home fleet, and their battleships were more heavily armoured and carried similar shields to yours. When will you learn that arrogance is no match for advanced weaponry?" Radon answered getting up and leaving. With Radon's departure, the meeting lapsed into silence. Ryan after pondering the situation made an observation.

"It won't matter how powerful your ship is. The people will rise up and back the Junta against you. You're known here as killers of the innocent, drinkers of blood. You saw the reaction when you met my crew and the villagers. What do you think will happen when you approach our major cities?" This made everyone pause. Simon, in the end, broke the silence.

"You give us much to think about. We will adjourn this meeting until tomorrow. I will have Johan release your men. They can try to repair your ship. Be warned though, if you fire on the villagers I'll incinerate your ship and all your crew members." Simon warned before standing and leaving with Kate.

"Don't think for a moment he's bluffing gentlemen." Radon cautioned, from the doorway, leading them to the shuttle.

Escorted back down to the village again the three men considered the situation they found themselves in. Stuart if he fixed the ship could return to base but what would they do to them? Ryan, on the other hand, knew he was a dead man if he returned. Johan beside them saw Ryan's argument as the most likely scenario. After meeting Kate and Simon, he couldn't see them slaughtering thousands of innocents to achieve peace.

He had come to the conclusion that it was better for the villagers to leave with them he realised; thinking starting over was a better choice. The problem was, the people left behind on New America, would still be no better than slaves. What could they do to help them was the question?

Simon, Kate and Radon, collapsed into their seats feeling exhausted. Watching the outside monitor, they saw the villages gathering up Atlanta's weapons before leaving. The crew of the Overman's ship seeing their captors had left followed Captain Stuart to the downed ship. After instructions from their Captain, they broke up into groups, moving inside.

"That went well." Radon smiled.

"No one seems too happy with our arrival, do they?" Simon admitted, his mind trying to work out a solution.

"The Atlanta's Ex-Captain seems to be quite intelligent. He gave us a lot to think about." Radon added.

"Yes, no matter what we do here it will have ramifications." Simon pointed out.

"We can't leave these people enslaved because we're scared of what these bullies will do to them." Kate blurted out, worried Simon might decide to leave rather than hurt innocent people. Simon reading her mind answered.

"You are too emotional Kate. I know they're your people, but even Johan, although he quite clearly wants our help, has doubts about us."

"They've been brainwashed into thinking we're monsters. Even so, I will not leave them suffering." Kate replied, her eyes misting up.

"I think the next move must be this Juntas. Until then, we must try to work out why we're here. The Chosen must've had a reason to send us here, at this time and this place?"

"We have much to think about. I suggest we try to come up with a solution. I would also suggest we stay on the Katherine with the shield deployed, we are safer here." Radon admitted, the others agreeing.

At the village, Benjamin awaited while Horen examined his mother. Watching the alien work, Benjamin's opinion of the crew of the Katherine rose. He had been suspicious of their motives, secretly fearful the stories they'd been told, were true. After meeting Kate and then Simon he started to realise what lies they'd been told. Still, the aliens were, to say the least different, something that many on New America would have trouble with.

Seeing Horen putting his instruments away, Benjamin approached him.

"How is she, Horen?"

"I won't deceive you and say she's out of danger Benjamin. I've given her a shot of what you call antibiotics, which should clear out the infection she has in her lungs. What she needs now is rest and lots of love."

"Do you understand what love is?"

"Of course we do Benjamin. We have families and copulate, the same as humans. Because we are different does not mean we have no feelings."

"You are different from Radon. You don't have the two rows of teeth, and your skin is crystalline in appearance."

'Thank the maker for that. It must be difficult for the Oregarthians to talk, let alone eat. Our skin texture we believe is caused by our planet of our races' birth, being heavily crystallised."

"Then you're separate races?"

"Yes we are, and for a long time, we were bitter enemies. Simon brought peace to our two races, now we are brothers united in a shared duty."

"What duty?"

"To protect Simon, he is our leader and the reason why we are all alive. We owe our family's safety and the peace we all now enjoy, to him." Horan exclaimed. Benjamin at first thought he was joking, the look in his eyes warned Benjamin, his belief was fanatical. 'Maybe that's why the human planets attacked him,' he mused. Having men follow you without a second thought was one thing. To have other races pledge their unwavering loyalty to a man would make any world leader wary of such a person.

31

THE JUNTA

General Wordsworth looked over the wreck and damaged war vessels that littered the landing field. The attack against the mystery cruiser hadn't gone well he surmised. When first told of the appearance of the Katherine he'd been, to say the least shocked. Although Captain Ryan, who had sent the message, was an experienced and well-respected Captain, his assessment of the danger had been underestimated. Relieving him of command for not attacking immediately was unavoidable, but necessary.

His crime hadn't been in pulling back, it had been in doing it without orders. He had come down hard on him to discourage other commanders from thinking they too, could disobey orders. His replacement Captain Hester hadn't been heard of since launching the attack. Her disappearance was for the best, as she too had been branded a traitor for failing to carry out orders and destroy the enemy.

The other commanders involved had been put on notice. This meant that next time they had better succeed or face Ryan's fate. All round it had been a dismal day, and General Wordsworth wanted to change that. His superiors were not impressed, and his position as New America commander was in jeopardy. He knew he must do something or he too would join Captain Ryan and Hester.

"Colonel Thompson. Get in here!" He bellowed. The Colonel getting over the abrupt summons hurried into the General's office. Thompson was a career military man, following in his father's footsteps. In other words, he'd stab anyone in the back to get to the top. The General knew this, which gave him a hint of satisfaction in giving him a hard time. Thompson was well aware of this but obeyed dutifully biding his time, waiting for this fat ox to fall. This incident at the moment might be just the thing to trip him up.

"Yes Sir, can I be of help?" Thompson enquired.

"Where are our fleets?"

"As I told you earlier Sir, two of them are committed to securing the new planet G10. The other should be here in two months." The General stared at the Colonel, trying to find something to grill him over. The Colonel remained silent waiting. Giving in, finding nothing the General moved on.

"What of the Overman's ships? How many are battle worthy?"

"Nearly forty are ready Sir. Another ten from the battle may be repaired in a couple of days, seven others are write-offs."

"What is your opinion of the situation?" Thompson had waited in fear of this question. To answer, they were in trouble would be an admission of failure. On the other hand, to gloss over the day's events would be viewed as reckless. He decided on the standard military answer.

"I'm just a Colonel Sir. The strategic decisions of High Command are not for me to judge."

"Look, just for once be honest with me Colonel. What is your take on the arrival of the Katherine, off the record of course?" The Colonel for several seconds considered his answer. Throwing caution to the wind, he told the truth.

"We're in deep shit Sir. The ship, if it is the Katherine is far superior to even our latest vessels. We'll have trouble stopping her, even with the fleet's help."

"Thank you, Colonel. You don't know it yet, but you just proved yourself to me." The General smiled, dismissing him. "Maybe the backstabber has got some backbone after all." He chuckled. Looking out the window, the General thought back to the time when he had been on Salvation and participated in the attack on Captain Simon Hayes.

THE ASSIGNMENT

He'd been a young first Lieutenant fresh out of the academy, in charge of a Special Forces unit. Top of his class he'd scored the top assignment, in removing a threat to their planet. Disguised as UN soldiers, his unit was supposed to infiltrate a welcoming party for Captain Simon Hayes and the crew of the Katherine. His prime target was Simon Hayes all others were secondary.

When first viewing the plan, Wordsworth had pointed out a glaring fault regarding Simon Hayes support units. No one could tell him, how many men he'd have or what weapons they'd deploy. Asked bluntly, if he would rather have someone else take command in his stead, he'd shut up remaining quiet.

Arriving on Salvation, on board one of the three subs that secretly travel there, Wordsworth under cover of darkness landed north of New Vancouver heading inland. Arriving at the Capital Geneva, they'd remain in the forest-covered hills above the city, waiting for their targets arrival. Once word reached them that his ship had landed, they changed into their UN uniforms. Moving down to a hilltop overlooking the temporary reception marquee, his men set up next to the destroyed assembly building.

He could still remember looking down and seeing those Oregarthian armoured vehicles arrive. He knew then to attack was suicide. Radioing this new information to his superiors, he was told directly, to overcome his fear and get the job done. Talking to his Sergeant, he let him know what they were in for. Expecting anger, he was surprised when his Sergeant non-plussed, volunteered to lead the attack.

He further suggested that Wordsworth being their best shot set up a sniper position in the tree line. At first, he was dead against it wanting to lead his men, feeling that staying behind was the coward's way out. Common sense prevailed, and he accepted his Sergeant's logic.

As planned a bomb planted by their ambassador exploded at the rear of the Marquee. This caused panic amongst the diplomats and families there to welcome Simon Hayes. As they all rushed to the exit at the front of the marquee, Wordsworth men in an extended line moved down towards the confused crowd. At first, everything went to plan no one seemed to notice his men until a UN officer talking to the alien leader shouted out to his men to identify themselves.

The plan if they were challenged, was to keep moving forward, pretending they hadn't heard anything. Unfortunately, the UN officer moved his hand towards his holstered weapon. One of Wordsworth's men acting out of instinct shot him. All hell broke loose as his men and the alien forces opened fire on each other. On open ground, his men better trained might have won. Regrettably, the armoured vehicles with their heavy plated sides and heavy weapons chewed his men to pieces.

It was a slaughter as the aliens pounded the entire hill, wiping out all but two of his men. Immobilised by shame, Wordsworth frozen, lay amongst the trees feeling ashamed. Tears ran down his face, as shaking himself, he remembered his mission. Wiping his eyes, he looked through his scope, trying to cover the loss of his men with revenge. Almost immediately he identified the target, as Hayes stood up, clearly confused by the attempted assassination.

Without hesitation, he pulled the trigger seeing the target collapse back onto the ground. Focusing on the alien leader who appeared to be looking right at him, he prepared to fire again. It was then that he saw his two wounded surviving men, struggling across the field below him. Making a decision, he switched targets, firing on the soldiers pursuing his men.

Covering them till they reached the trees, he dropped his weapon running to them. Throwing one over his shoulder, he helped the other slightly injured soldier into the forest, before finding a suitable place to hide. For another four days, they moved through enemy territory, while the UN forces hunted them. Managing to lose them, they were picked up by a submarine, making their way back to New America.

It was shortly after this that the portal closed forever the reason why he wouldn't know for another four years.

When he arrived back, he found Marshall Law had been introduced. The President at the time felt there was a chance that Hayes' alien friends might decide to seek revenge for the attack on him. Peddling the line, that Hayes had launched an unprovoked attack on Salvation, the people rallied, supporting him. The UN, of course, knew the truth. Having asked for access to New America's media so the complete story could be told, the President refused. This led to the UN blockading the portal.

They warned New America that their planet would be permanently locked out if they didn't agree to tell the truth. By this time Wordsworth a national hero, had risen to the rank of

Colonel. Sent to where the portal opened they lay in wait for any breaches by the UN.

While there, a huge explosion erupted out of the ocean, causing massive damage to the coastline. Wordsworth's submarine though damage survived, limping back to base. It would be the last time the portal ever opened. An investigation failed to find what had caused the explosion. Many believed the blast had occurred on Salvation, travelling through the portal to New America.

Now being made a General, Wordsworth suspicious, asked his own team of forensic investigators to check the portal site. They located traces of radiation in the ground around the portal's exit, something the Government should've found. Further digging found that the Uranium believed used in the explosion, came from New America.

Using covert Special Forces members he had several members of the strategic weapons group picked up. It didn't take long for them to spill the beans. The President worried that the people might find out the truth, triggered a weapon smuggled into the portal base before the UN deployed the shield. Furious, General Wordsworth had called a meeting of the High Command.

Laying out all the evidence the General told them what had occurred. Seeing stunned disbelief at the stupidly of the loss of the portal, the High Command ordered the arrest of the President. Seizing power, the High Command formed a Junta to restore sanity to their world. The Junta had always planned to restore democracy, but as time passed, growing discontent over the takeover grew.

At this time the expansion into the surrounding Galaxy was in full swing. To keep the fleet and the colonised planets feed and equipped, led to many sacrifices by the people of New America. The Junta needing Marshall Law to keep the fleet's at full strength was forced to delay the transition back to democracy.

When a coup was launched, and two of the nine members of the junta were killed, the remaining generals had come down hard on the population. Wordsworth, absent at the time, had been shocked by the over the top response. Arriving back for a meeting of the full Junta, to discuss the situation, Wordsworth had asked the two generals responsible for the reprisals to be charged with crimes against humanity. Instead of listening to him, he'd been himself demoted, losing his seat at the table.

Now instead of commanding a fleet, he found himself sitting behind a desk in charge of the planet New America defences, without one space capable ship. To all intense and purpose, he was being detained, while the three fleets advanced thousands of light-years into the surrounding Galaxies. New America, although still, the Capital was now just a small part of the empire, supplying logistics and more importantly food to the ever-expanding group of planets under their control.

This expansion had not been without problem. At the moments two of their fleets had combined to face a mystery fleet of warships that had appeared from nowhere. When the planet G10 had been discovered, no indigenous population had been encountered. The initial settlement had been established with no problem, it was only after the mining for rare elements had begun that the alien ships had appeared.

Four ships, resembling oblong black blocks about four times the size of their cruisers had appeared, stopping just out of the planet's obit. The settlement at first had tried to communicate with the alien ships. Not getting any response, they'd become worried, contacting the military. The gung-ho military commander of the area, having ten cruisers under his command decided to confront the four alien ships. Firing a warning shot in front of them, he hoped a show of force would make them back off.

When no reply came, and the four alien ships raised their shields, the New America commander took this action as a sign of aggression, opening fire. Both sides lost two ships, before the alien ships retreated, the New American suffering major damage to another three. The military fearing that the alien ships would return, evacuated the settlement, as a precaution. What worried the military was the enemy's use of sonic weapons in the conflict.

Although their shields had been equal to the New America's fleet shields, their weapons appear superior to their lasers.

The Junta fearing an invasion dispatched two of their fleets, which remained stationed in the area of G10. Although since the confrontation, nothing had been seen of the aliens, deep space radio messages were being intercepted. They indicated a build up of ships in the Galaxy bordering G10.

So far there'd been no incursions, but the Junta was concerned. The arrival of the Katherine had sent tremors through the Junta, Wordsworth had gleefully noticed. It's timing, appearing through the portal just before a possible battle with an unknown adversary, had brought the memories of their last encounter with the Katherine back. True or imaginary the thought of which side the Katherine was on, filled them with trepidation.

"Colonel Thompson before you go, ready one of the ships, I am going to visit the Katherine."

"Are you joking Sir?" Thompson blurted out, for once in his life answering before thinking. Breaking his usual stone-faced look the General gave a rare smile.

"You heard right Colonel. And to make your day, you're coming with me." He chuckled, leaving the stunned Colonel Thompson unable to answer.

After the shuttle had left, Kate and Simon tired retired to their room. Both wanted time to work out what was going on? When the voice had convinced them to travel to the void to help Simon, no mention had been made of returning. Why fifty years in the future, and why return them to New America? The whys were overwhelming them, as both collapsed onto their bed. Fully clothed, they lay looking at the ceiling, soundlessly trying to figure out a way to move forward.

"Do you remember anything Kate?"

"Only a little. I remember the voice telling me Radon had hidden aboard with his men. At first, I was reluctant to leave you, but the voice insisted I fetch them back to the bridge. I remember bringing Radon and his men back here, then the next thing I was being awakened by you, warning us of the attack. What of you, do you remember anything?"

"Most is vague. I remember the constant pain and being scared of living totally paralysed, more than death. You have no idea what it's like to feel so helpless, dependant on a machine for your very next breath." Simon whimpered, his eyes misting up, as Kate pulled him to her.

"It's over now Simon, you're healed."

"Am I Kate? How do we know this is real? We could be both lying now in the Void, aboard the Katherine dreaming." Without warning, Kate reached across pinching Simon's wrist. Jumping back yelping in pain, Simon held his arm too surprised to say anything.

"Do you think it's a dream now?" She giggled.

"Very funny, that hurt," Simon answered as leaning forward he toppled her backwards onto the bed. Pinning her there he climbed on top of her as she squealed playfully. "Well I still could be in some sort of time warp, so in theory anything I do is okay." He chuckled, working her pants down over her hips.

"Don't get too creative, or your dream will become a nightmare." Kate smiled, only playfully resisting.

An hour afterwards, Simon lay next to Kate watching her breathe as she slept. With her back to him, he watched her shoulders rise and fall, her breaths coming slow and peacefully regular. 'She is so beautiful' he thought, as lying there he thanked God that he was able to move. 'Why had he thanked God' he mused? It wasn't exactly that he was religious, yet he believed now, that divine intervention had healed him.

The Chosen as they were called were just an advanced race, yet they had helped him and healed him for some reason beyond his understanding. Unlike the others, Simon had memories of his time with the Chosen. Why he hadn't told Kate or Radon, he didn't know, maybe because he wasn't sure. He remembered being on the bed in the command centre watching his pump give him another shot of air. Besides him, Kate had just returned with Radon and his men.

Looking sideways he saw one of Radon's men, a Flax Federation soldier by his appearance, fall to the ground. It was like watching a stack of dominoes, as once the first soldier fell, the one beside him followed. In the end, Simon was the only one still conscious as a bright light temporarily blinded him.

Blinking it occurred to Simon that he shouldn't have been able to, as he stared at the two figures outlined by light.

"We had the feeling you'd resist." One said as the other removed his artificial breathing system. Scared, Simon grasped for breath, finding that he could actually breathe freely.

"Relax Simon, we mean you no harm, quite the opposite in fact," the other glowing body told him, placing a small object on his head. A feeling of serenity settled over him as he watched Kate and the others seem to float away, each accompanied by a glowing entity.

"We calculated that Radon wouldn't let you and Kate go alone into the unknown, but his bringing so many men surprised us."

"Don't hurt them." Simon croaked out, trying to move his frozen limbs and stand.

"No one will be hurt young man, but you must remain still while your body is repaired." Lying still, trying to do as they suggested it occurred to Simon that he hadn't moved his lips.

"Yes Simon, we are communicating directly with you, something that your race shouldn't be capable of for another hundred years. We think it could be because of your genetic background. Your grandfather being of a different race could explain it, although we're not certain." It occurred to Simon that either of the entities could be talking to him.

"Yes, it can be quite confusing." They answered, one of the figures shaking as if in laughter.

"Will it take long?" Simon asked, worried by his condition.

"No, although the time, till you leave the void will depend on many factors."

"Why?"

"We are beyond helping outside the void, we would not survive if we left our present environment. The Universe is stable at the moment, thanks to your intervention between the Flax Federation and the Oregarthian's. When the time is appropriate you will return, until then, you will remain in suspended hibernation."

"But what if we don't want to?"

"You are in our debt Simon. It is a small price to pay to help the Universe, is it not?" Simon unable to answer, felt sleep start to take him. "Before you sleep Simon there is something else. Can you see what I am projecting?"

"Is that what I think it is?"

"Yes, Simon it's for you. Do you recognise the planet in the background?" Simon indicated he did. "When everything goes against you, remember that planet and what is there." The voice whispered fading away.

Coming out of that deep sleep, Simon found himself lying on the floor of the command centre.

"Simon, can you hear me?" The entity's voice sounded in his head.

"Yes, have I been asleep long?"

"That is not important. Your ship is about to be attacked, you must protect yourselves." Getting to his feet, Simon half asleep looked around finding the floor littered with his friends.

"Are they all right?"

"Yes they will soon recover, but you must hurry Simon. We inadvertently sent you to an approaching warzone. Time is against you, so immediately deploy your shield." The voice insisted. Stepping over several soldiers, Simon reached the defence console, deploying the shield.

"Okay, it's done. Now can you tell me what's going on?"

"For now, you must proceed with caution. All I can tell you is that your friend's futures, all hang in the balance, as does the fate of millions of other races."

"That's pretty vague?"

"We know Simon, but we do have limits to how much we can interfere with the outside worlds."

"You've interfered before when you helped me with these shields, why not now?"

"Times are changing. Other races will in time rival our superiority. For these races to grow and mature, they must be given the ability to self-govern. If we interfered every time a race did something we felt was wrong, they'd become nothing more than puppets doing our bidding. You have been sent at a critical time to help right a wrong. Other than that, I can tell you little.' The voice confessed, before fading away.

"Will you talk to me again?" Simon whispered.

"When the time is right Simon, go now and help your people." The voice implored, becoming distant as if the entity was travelling away at a great speed. Looking out the bridge's front viewing screen, he saw the Katherine break the surface of a body of water, before rising into the air.

Resigned to his fate, he shouted out 'Battle stations' as Radon, Kate and the group of soldiers strewn over the deck, rose to their feet and stumbled to their stations.

Further down the hallway in their dining room sat Radon, with his men. They were having a debriefing on what had occurred. Most remembered little, though some had memories of seeing the others fall before a light made them close their eyes. All from that point remembered nothing until Simon shouted for them to man their battle stations. Radon like the others awoke confused, unable to respond at first, he'd reacted to Simon's shouts more out of training than being awake.

Why had Simon shouted 'battle stations', galvanising the men to instantly recover from their stupor? He, like the others, had been out cold, yet Simon was already up and aware of the situation. His faith in Simon as a friend was absolute, but he had a feeling Simon knew more than he was saying. When the time was right he would ask Simon what he remembered, he knew he had to know.

Getting every piece of information, he could get out of the meeting he was just about to suggest they all get some rest when Jabo his Intel officer raised his hand. Radon signalled him to proceed with his question.

"Sir, do you remember when you drew your weapon at the meeting."

"Yes of course I do. I thought the two humans were about to become physical, why?"

"No, I'm not questioning your actions; it was the speed that I wanted to ask you about."

"I too was more than impressed by your reaction time Sir. It seemed unbelievable." Horen piped in, back up by the rest of the men.

"I never really thought about it. I just reacted." Radon replied. Looking down at his holster, he saw the front had been ripped open by his drawing of the weapon.

"I've done some checking Sir, mostly on myself. We seem to have been improved somehow." Horen answered in a quiet tone as if conveying there was danger in his information.

"What do you mean improved?" Radon whispered, as he too became aware of the situation.

"Our vital signs are now different. My blood pressure is down as is my heartbeat. I can lift a weight that before I'd not even try. When I was at the village helping Benjamin's mother, I could hear clearly, even though before this mission, my left ear gave me a little trouble. I'll have to carry out more tests, but surely others here have felt the changes." Horen put forward.

"I have noticed one thing, Horen. No one here is sick or tired, yet we've been through a major battle, after waking from an imposed deep sleep. From experience, we should all be dead on our feet." Radon pointed out.

"It would be wise Sir if Horen carried out a wide range of tests on everyone here; we have no way of knowing what is going on," Jabo suggested, his voice sounding concerned.

"Get started, Horen. Whatever has been done seems to have helped us, let's make sure it doesn't have a downside." Radon ordered, as his men moved off to get some rest.

Captain Ryan looked over the damaged ship with its new Captain. The ship was for all-intense and purpose was finished. Its new commander, Captain Stuart, had hoped to at least get it airborne, but it wasn't to be.

"Any suggestions?" Stuart asked, looking over his shoulder as Ryan examined a laser turret on the forward gun position.

"No nothing. That's one of command's little perks, you're stuck with the big decisions." Ryan answered moving back. "That was some uncanny shooting from the Katherine you know. They hit all our weapons platforms in the first volley."

"Great, I'm sure when I'm being led out to be shot for losing this ship; the Junta will be overjoyed to learn that." Stuart angrily responded, before breaking into laughter. "What a mess, if I go back, I might be executed. If I don't, I'll be hunted down and executed along with the crew. It's not much of a choice."

"If you go back the crew will be safe." Ryan pointed out.

"Yes, there is that," Stuart answered becoming withdrawn, thinking about it.

"At least you have one. I, on the other hand, have none." Ryan smiled.

"What are you going to do?"

"Leave with them I'm afraid, it's my only option," Ryan admitted, pointing at the Katherine.

"They're not as we were told, are they?"

"No, despite my misgivings I find Simon Hayes rather an enigma. At least I won't be bored." Ryan chuckled as in the distance he saw Steiger and Branson talking to several members of the crew. "Watch those two Stuart. Whatever they're up to, someone will get hurt."

"Sergeant Ross said the same thing. He suggested he take those two with him and ten men, to try and contact headquarters from the old naval base."

"Sounds like a plan. Although I'm not sure why the Sergeant needs those two?"

"I think he was worried they could be attacked by rebels. Steiger and Branson will be out in front." Stuart smiled, Ryan nodding.

"Yes, I can see sense in it now. You should send them off immediately." Ryan put forward, as Stuart called Ross over.

Sergeant Ross returned an hour later running. Of Steiger and Branson, there was no sign, and no one asked.

"Why are you in such a big hurry Sergeant?" Stuart yelled as he approached, wondering why he hadn't used his Comm's gear to contact him.

"We found a transmitter at the base, Sir. General Wordsworth is on his way here now. He's bringing every ship we have on the planet, might be best if we all move to the base."

"Pass the order, Sergeant Ross. I want everyone away from here as soon as possible."

The hurried evacuation of the crew of the Atlanta didn't go unnoticed. Johan having been told by one of his men, who'd been left, to keep watch over the ship's crew. Gathering the villagers, Johan discussed the developments. They all decided to warn the Katherine.

On board the Katherine, Simon was woken by the scream of the Klaxon. Running to the bridge, he found Radon and his men at their stations.

"Sir we have over forty ships coming in from the east. The crew of the downed ship below us have moved with haste to the abandoned base near the coast. Also, the villagers have lit a beacon; I'd say they are trying to signal or warn us." Jabo, his Intel officer, informed him.

"Thank you, Jabo for your report. Anyone else got anything." Simon asked. Silence followed as the crew searched for anything that would reveal the enemy's intentions. Radon studying the long-range sensors was the first to speak.

"The villagers may bear the brunt of an enemy attack. It may be better to move between the approaching forces and the village." Simon studying the topography nodded his agreement thinking of a plan.

"Move us directly above the village. Once we're in position, deploy our shield, so it covers not only our ship but the village below."

"Even with our ships power, we'll have to be no higher than 500metres above the village. That will expose us to fire from the village." Radon pointed out.

"I'm sure the villagers can be trusted Radon. On the other hand, I've been wrong before, so have a few men travel down in the shuttle; they can monitor the situation there for us."

"Good thinking," Kate whispered in his ear, as she sat down beside him. Tense minutes passed as the Katherine lost altitude stopping just above the village. The shield was then deployed.

Johan and the other villagers watched the Katherine halt above their homes. Almost immediately a shuttle left the ship landing next to them. As the side door opened, several alien soldiers spilled out, taking up positions around the shuttle. One Johan had met earlier named Horen came over to him.

"There is a large group of aircraft heading toward us. Simon has deployed the ships shield around the village. You must warn your villagers not to try and leave."

"Why didn't you just leave?" Johan asked him.

"Simon thinks they might mean you harm. He would not leave you to be punished."

"Thank him for us, Horen. I'll warn the others." Johan told him. As Johan made to leave, he suddenly stopped, turning back to Horen. "Isn't he leaving the ship vulnerable to fire from us?"

"Yes, he is. Although for some reason he trusts you." Horen answered. Johan could see Horen didn't share his blind faith, as he drew his weapon, moving back to his men's position. Johan seeing Benjamin watching called him over. Explaining what was happening, he had him tell all the villagers to remain inside their homes.

The streets empty swiftly as unsure of the Katherine's intention, families went to their homes securing themselves inside. Benjamin finished alerting everyone, arrived back outside their home. Johan waiting for him saw Cob and his father head for the storage sheds.

"Why are they going there instead of to their home?" Johan said out loud.

"Yeah, you think the storeman would stay home with his wife and their two other young sons, instead of going to work with Cob," Benjamin answered. His father at first hesitated having not been aware he'd spoken out loud.

"Sorry, son I was talking out loud. Tell me, does the foreman keep any weapons at the storage sheds?"

"Yes, the spare weapons we took from the crew of the Atlanta are all there. The foreman thought it would be better to lock them away."

"Yes, he's every helpful lately. Stay with your mum son, I'll be right back." Johan told him, walking back to the shuttle. Horen, still setting up their position, saw him coming.

"Is there a problem Johan?"

"I'm not sure. The foreman at the storage facility over there just entered it. The spare weapons seised from the downed ship are stored there. It might be nothing, but Cob, the foreman's son, was going on the raid my son's friends were killed on. He at the last minute didn't go.' Horen stood there at first wondering what he was getting at when it came to him.

"You think they are spies and your son's group was betrayed?"

"It makes sense. My son's friends were clever in evading detection. It worries me, how the Overmen knew they were going to the base and then after the raid failed, they came straight to our home?" Horen nodding his understanding whispered into his mike, four soldiers moved to him, all readied their weapons, waiting.

"Take these men with you, Johan. Let's hope you're wrong." Without another word, Johan drew his pistol leading the soldiers towards the storage area. 'What if I'm wrong?' Johan asked himself as he led the four soldiers into the facility. He could get two innocent people killed here he realised, as the soldiers spread out advancing beside him.

Silently the five of them moved forward as a noise above them made them freeze. There on a platform on one of the silos, they watched as Cob and his father, manhandled a heavy laser cannon onto its bipod. Johan realised they were preparing to fire on the Katherine.

"They're going for the engines." Johan yelled to the Horen's men, they all without hesitation opened fire. Cob and his father became instant candles, as with uncanny accuracy the four soldiers racked them with laser blasts.

Johan didn't even have time to raise his weapon, as the father and son fell to the ground in front of him. Running forward the four soldiers quickly covered the two dead men with hessian sacks, smothering the flames that started to spring up from their burning clothing. As the soldiers secured the area, Johan having made sure there were no other fires in the grain storage area, walked back to the shuttle.

"I'm sorry they had to die, Johan, although I'm glad you stopped them," Horen admitted, having already heard from his men.

"They chose their fate, and they deserved what they got. While we're talking about their deaths, that was impressive shooting by your men, Horen. I have never seen such fast reflexes, are all your soldiers that swift?" Horen at first was surprised by the question. It took him a moment to reply.

"I suppose it's their training. As a medic, I was trained differently." Horen lied. Johan, accepting the answer left.

Walking home, Johan thought again of the shoot out.

"What will I tell Benjamin?" He asked himself, as he spotted Benjamin waiting for him near the front door.

"We heard the shooting, what happened?" Benjamin exclaimed, as Johan sat down and waited for Benjamin to sit down next to him. He then explained what had taken place. Benjamin at first was saddened by Cob's death; this was soon replaced by disbelief, then anger.

"He betrayed us all dad, why would he do that?" Benjamin cried.

"Cob and his father were either loyal to the Junta or saw a gain in betraying you and your friends. This attempt on the Katherine could've killed us all son. If it hadn't been for their earlier betrayal of you, they would've succeeded."

"But they were part of this village we shared everything with them."

"There's no explanation for it son. As you grow older you will learn that trust is a double-edged sword, it can cut both ways." Benjamin confused excused himself, walking away from his father into the afternoon's dimming light.

On board the Katherine, everyone took the foiling of the attack, as a good sign. Radon ever cautious wanted to send more men down to the village, Simon suggested they wait and see what happened first. Since then they had watched the approach of the swarm of ships. It had surged like a giant

wave towards the coast appearing unstoppable. As they
broached the coast and approached firing range, the ships
stopped.

As one they landed near the naval base seeming
unconcerned by the Katherine's presence. Darkness
descended over the countryside as Radon in disbelief,
watched the fleet of enemy ships set up camp along the coast.

"What are they doing? Why don't they attack?" Radon
exploded, unsure of what was going on.

"I'd say someone with infinite patience is waiting to see
what we do, while he questions the crew of the Atlanta." Simon
smiled, visibly relaxing.

"Are you sure?" Radon replied.

"It makes sense. I suggest we leave a skeleton shift to keep
watch, while the rest of us turn in for the night." Simon
ordered, leading Kate back to their room. Behind him, Radon
chose men for the first shift, before following him. Simon and
Kate had just entered their room when a knock sounded on
their door. Opening it, Simon found Radon standing there.

"We need to talk?" He whispered entering.

"What's wrong?" Kate asked, closing the door.

"What's going on Simon? I want to know what the voices in
the void told you." Radon demanded. Kate at first smiled, till
she saw Simon's face.

"I thought you said you'd blacked out?" Kate asked.

"Look I remember talking to them and then being woken up
by them just before you awoke. I wasn't going to worry you two
unless I'd just imagined it. "

"Right from the start Simon, tell us everything you
remember," Radon demanded, sitting down.

"And that's it. All I know is they sent us here to stop
something bad happening to our friends, nothing else." Simon
confessed, leaving out what they'd showed him.

"You're right it doesn't help us much, but you could've told
us." Kate pointed out, unhappy with him keeping secrets,
Radon just sat there watching Simon.

"To what end? Does it make the mystery any less strange
by knowing what I remembered?"

"No not really, but it does point to a reason for all the trouble out there. Obviously, there's more going on here than just a rebellion on this one planet. We need more information?" Radon pointed out. "There's something else to Simon. We've been changed somehow. Our speed and strength and reflexes have been improved, Horen our medical officers, looking into it." The room went silent as everyone thought about what this meant.

"Let's get through this confrontation with the enemy fleet first, and then we'll look into it." Simon put forward.

"You're not telling us everything are you?" Radon smiled, knowing Simon had held something back. Kate beside him crossed her arms unhappily. Simon looked at his two closest friends who stood waiting.

"They revealed something to me, to be used in an emergency. I can't tell, or it might change the way we act. For now, it's my secret." Kate and Radon looked at each other, nodding a silent agreement to let him keep his little surprise for now.

"We all have our secrets Simon; you'll tell us when you're ready." Radon smiled leaving.

Captain Stuart waited quietly as the Overmen ship landed next to the base. His men lined up behind him, waited with an air of defeatism, wafting from them. The Junta had never handled failure well, and this defeat would have to be one of the worst suffered since the attack on Salvation. The most horrid part was it involved the same adversary.

Personally, he had found Simon Hayes totally different, from the bloodthirsty mad animal from their historical records. Stuart knew that Hayes could've inflicted much greater causalities in the first encounter, the fact he hadn't, showed their historical records were far from accurate.

"Sir, General Wordsworth is here in person." Sergeant Ross whispered from behind him, as turning towards the landed ship, Stuart saw a group of senior officers coming towards him.

"Shit they're not even taking me back to face a firing squad." He whispered to himself, as he shouted for his men to stand at attention. The General moved along his men's silent lines asking questions randomly appearing to be in a good mood. Arriving opposite Stuart, he returned his salute as the General stood watching him.

"I'm not here to shoot you, Captain. Loosen up a bit and follow me." The General chuckled, as Sergeant Ross and two of his men, followed several steps behind the group. The General seeing them following started to laugh. "Sergeant you're not planning to assassinate my staff and me, are you?" the General smiled watching Ross, as his staff unnerved looked back at Stuart's men.

"No Sir he's not. Sergeant, you and your men returned to the others thank you." Stuart ordered as Ross with his guards stopped in their tracks, watching their Captain continued on with the others.

"Your men appear to have a certain loyalty too you already Stuart. I find that rather rare in our arm forces these days." A Colonel walking behind him pointed out.

"Yes it's a good sign when the men support their commander, but let's move on." the General suggested. "What is your opinion of the enemy and their ship?"

"Quite a formidable Sir. After the battle Captain Hayes asked us aboard his ship too." Was all Stuart got out?

"You've been aboard his ship, and Simon Hayes still commands!" The General shouted.

"Yes Sir and he is still the same age as when there was the incident on Salvation."

"That's impossible, I shot him!" Wordsworth replied, clearly perplexed by this information.

"Captain Ryan was surprised too. He too was on the ship, along with the village leader Johan." Stuart told him, weighing up what the General had just revealed.

"From the start Captain, tell me everything that's occurred since you spotted the Katherine." The General ordered.

After twenty minutes the General silent through the whole report stood looking towards the Katherine, as it floated above the village, silhouetted by the village lights.

"Where's Captain Ryan?" He asked.

"He stayed behind in the village. He intends to leave aboard the Katherine." This information shocked the gathered staff.

"He knows a great deal about our weaponry General. It could be a problem." The Colonel pointed out.

"Ryan's not going to betray us; he's just looking after himself." The General chuckled. "Let's all turn in for the night gentlemen; it's going to be an interesting tomorrow." He smiled walking back to his ship.

THE MEETING

0600 saw the fleet go to battle stations, as their General called a meeting with his commanding officers.

"Gentlemen to tell you the truth, I'm not sure we'll be victorious today." The room quiet before, turned into a morgue, as everyone there wondered what he was going to say next. "Like a few of you, I've seen the Katherine in action before, and I don't think we've advanced enough in weapons and shields to take her, even with the combined fleets."

"But Sir!" Colonel Thompson started to say, as the General's hand rose stopping him.

"I intend to go aboard the Katherine under a flag of truce and find out why they're here. Who wants to come with me?" He asked, to a sea of shocked faces. "How about you Colonel Thompson, care to enter the enemy's lair with me?"

"Of course Sir," Thompson gulped out clearly not keen.

"I'll go, Sir." Stuart volunteered, as the rest of the officers, slowly chorused their enforced willingness.

"Thompson, Stuart and I, should be enough. The rest of you return to your ships and be ready if things go downhill. And one more thing gentlemen, don't shoot until I order you to, is that clear?" Getting a multitude of nods, the General signalled for Thompson and Stuart to follow him.

Taking three hover cycles from his ship, Wordsworth led the way towards the village. Just short of the first home, an alien soldier appeared. Walking out into their path, he raised his pistol, signalling for them to stop. Coming to a halt, the General got off his cycle. Carrying a white flag, he walked confidently up to the soldier.

"Good morning, I'm General Wordsworth. I'd like a word with Captain Hayes, your leader."

"Put out your hand." The soldier replied.

At first, the General seemed confused by the soldier's response. In the end, he put out his hand. It instantly struck the shield.

"That's why you stopped us? Good thinking soldier."
Wordsworth smiled, the soldier smiling as well. "You're from
the Flax Federation aren't you?" This took the smile off the
soldier's face.

"How could you know that?" He asked Wordsworth.

"I was on Salvation last time the Katherine was there,
although I was much younger and thinner." He smiled, happy
to see the soldier caught off guard.

"Follow me. Captain Simon has told me to bring you to the
ship." He told them. Not waiting for an answer he turned
walking towards the shuttle.

"They're not much for small talk are they?" Wordsworth said
to Thompson and Stuart, as putting out their hands and seeing
the shield was down, they followed the soldier.

"No. But they have great respect for Simon Hayes Sir."
Stuart warned the General.

"Then wait till they find out I was the one who shot him?"
Wordsworth chuckled, as Stuart missed a step, tripping.
Straightening up, he fearfully looked from the General to the
alien soldier. He too had stopped. In his hand he held his
weapon; it was pointed at the General's head.

"That was an incredibly fast draw soldier. And remember I
am here under a white flag."

"Our race and the Oregarthian's do not recognise white
flags. Luckily for you, Captain Simon does." He growled, as
slamming his revolver back into his holster, he continued
walking.

"That was close General," Thompson whispered beside
him, wiping sweat from his forehead.

"Nonsense! I just wanted to know how safe we'll be aboard
their ship."

"I'd say you got your answer," Stuart replied, as the General
happily continued on.

When they reached the shuttle, they found Ryan waiting
near the entry with four alien soldiers.

"Good morning General." Ryan smiled giving him a salute.

"There's no need for that Ryan, let's face it you're a traitor
now."

"Force of habit Sir. Horen, who is in command here, won't let you aboard carrying weapons."

"Fair enough, Captain, Colonel, drop your weapons." The General ordered. Taking off his sidearm, he immediately walked on board the shuttle, sitting down next to the pilot. "I've always wanted to be aboard one of your shuttles. We've copied the shape and design but never managed to get the same performance. How do you control it?" He asked as if going on a joyride. While the pilot gave him a rundown on the shuttle, Ryan sat down next to Horen.

Before the General had arrived, Ryan had asked to see Simon, to discuss going with them. Horen at first was suspicious of his motives. Ryan had only just got permission to go up to the Katherine when the General's group had arrived. The General's admission that he'd been the one who'd shot him, nearly caused all their deaths. Simon listening in had told the soldiers not to shoot. Intrigued he'd asked them all to be brought to the ship. Now Ryan sat watching his ex-General, carrying on as if he was in complete control.

"Horen the white flag is a sign of a truce, we can't touch the General," Ryan said softly as Horen beside him watched the General silently.

"We honour any meeting discussing a truce Ryan. But after it is over we will hunt him down." Horen coldly informed him.

On board the Katherine, Kate wanted the General killed. Furious she stormed off the bridge when Simon told her there'd be no killing. Radon stood to the side, his face a mask. Whatever he was thinking remained hidden.

"There will be no harm to these men while under a flag of truce. Is that understood?" Simon shouted.

"We obey Simon, but this man can't be trusted," Radon answered.

"He was just a soldier back then, following orders. I was the one shot if I can forgive I expect you to honour my decision." Simon pleaded.

"We will not dishonour a truce Simon. Afterwards is a different matter." Radon replied leaving.

When the shuttle docked, Horen followed by the General proceeded to the bridge. Arriving there even the General seemed wary. Spotting Simon, he seemed at first surprised expecting to see some sort of injury.

"You mend well? I was sure that was it was a kill shot."

"It was. An alien race far more advanced than any other we have met, healed me."

"Just like that?" the General smirked.

"You're right they wanted something in return."

"And what was that?"

"We don't know yet. Although by your arrival, another piece of the puzzle has fallen into place."

"Look at the time I was following orders. You, I was told, were the bad guys. It was only much later after the attack that I found out the truth." The General confessed.

"Why are you here?"

"I could ask the same thing, but I'll start. The Junta thinks you have come to help the aliens, who are massing near one of our outer planets. Are they right?"

"It's the first I've heard of an alien force. Who are they?"

"That we don't know. So you know nothing of them?"

"No. Although the aliens who healed me told me we were being sent here to save millions of lives. If it is to do with these aliens, I'm not sure."

"So what Stuart tells me about you know nothing about what is going on, is correct?"

"Yes, we didn't know what was going on. Since arriving here, we have learnt a great deal about you, none of it good."

"Look I'd be the first to admit the Junta's been in power too long, but there were reason for it." The General admitted as Thompson beside him blinked in surprise. Simon's response was cut off, as Kate appeared pointing a small pistol at Wordsworth.

"You tried to kill the man I love, and your President killed my parents." Kate spat out, as she moved closer her weapon coming to a stop, next to the General's head. Stuart and Thompson noticed that none of the aliens tried to stop her.

"And who are you?" Wordsworth asked, for the first time showing a hint of fear.

"My name is Katherine Jamison, and I was born on New America. My parents carried a letter from your President to Simon when we came back to Salvation. Instead of a treaty, it was a bomb meant to kill him. My parents died when it exploded in their cabin on board this ship."

"So that's how the Katherine was damaged. I've always wondered about that." Wordsworth answered. "Look back then I was just following orders. I personally arrested the President when we found out the truth. I know it's not much, but he was executed for that attack, and destroying the portal."

"Kate, lower the weapon please," Simon said softly. When she continued to stand there frozen, he walked over taking the weapon from her. "This is not the answer Kate. I know it's hard; I felt like this when the Roax killed my grandfather and took you. Let it go, or you'll become like them." Breaking down she started to sob, as Simon held her. After a time, two of Simon's crewmembers came forward. Taking her from Simon, they led her away to her cabin. Simon for a long time stood looking at the door, until Radon who had just entered, cleared his throat, making him turn back to the three men.

"I warn you now gentlemen. Kate has great sway here amongst the crew. She will not leave this planet till her people are free."

"Our planet's future is for us to decide not yours." Wordsworth firmly told him.

"Good we will stay until free elections are held. And I can assure you General they will take place." Simon assured him, a cold smile on his lips.

Taking a break, Wordsworth and Thompson were taken on a tour of the Katherine, while Ryan and Stuart had refreshments. Simon went to check on Kate, so Radon seeing the men sitting silently, sat down with them.

"This General Wordsworth has got guts; I'll say that for him." Radon started.

"Yes, he's always been that way. It hasn't made him popular." Ryan answered.

"Is he part of the Junta?" Radon asked.

"He was at first. He got demoted after the coup attempt. He wanted the two members responsible for the murderous response punished. The others saw it differently." Stuart informed him, watching the door.

"You have no need to fear him here Captain," Radon told Stuart after seeing his reaction.

"I won't always be here Radon." Stuart smiled back.

"I will." Ryan chuckled.

"You want to stay with us. I thought you viewed us, as how they'd say it, mad dogs?"

"If I go with the General I'll be shot as a traitor. I'd rather take my chances with mad dogs." Ryan replied smiling, as Radon burst into gravelly laughter. After he'd stopped laughing, he became serious.

"What can you two tell me about this alien race?"

"Not a great deal and unfortunately Stuart can't say anything," Ryan answered.

"Why not?"

"He is still under the General's command. To say something to an enemy commander without his permission would have him branded a traitor like me." Ryan smiled.

"Why don't you come with us too?" Radon suggested.

"As much as I would like to, my crew would suffer, and I have a family. There might be repercussions against them."

"Yet you serve them, and we are the mad dogs." Radon pointed out, leaving.

"You know despite their looks, I find Radon and his men quite likeable," Ryan whispered. Seeing the General arrive, he left Stuart walking over to Radon. Stuart silently wished he could too.

"What were you talking about?" Wordsworth asked, sitting down.

"Radon wanted to know about the problem at G10. I told him I couldn't say anything." He answered. The General stared at Stuart, picking up the undercurrent of hostility.

"That was the correct answer Captain. Don't be fooled by their friendliness Captain. They aren't like us." Colonel Thompson added.

"I'm well aware of that Sir," Stuart replied, excusing himself and moving to the restrooms.

"Do you think Colonel that the Junta will accept free elections?" the General asked, watching Stuart sit down with Ryan.

"Not a chance Sir."

"So tread carefully Colonel, the last thing we need is our own Officers turning on us." The General whispered as Simon reappeared. "Let's get this over with?"

This time the meeting focused on the enemy near G10. Lacking any good Intel on what was happening, Simon asked for the planet's co ordinates. The General was none too happy with giving them to him. In the end, Simon promised to do a recon of the Galaxy around G10 on the assurance the General's men kept well away from Johan's village. Reluctantly Wordsworth agreed promising to send word that they were coming in peace to their forces there.

On a handshake, Simon sealed the deal. Both sides knew the consequences if either side doublecrossed the other.

Johan was none too happy with the departure of the Katherine. Still, after hearing Simon's explanation, he saw the merits in their recognisance. As a guarantee of their safety, Simon left the shuttle with Horen and ten soldiers to make sure the village remained safe. It wasn't much, but with Radon's promise that they'd be only gone a short time, helped reassure them. The General for his part informed the fleets near G10 of Katherine's approach. This was greeted with shock and hostility.

Three of the six Junta members were there with the fleets. At first, they were against having anything to do with the Katherine. Wordsworth convinced them that it was better to send the Katherine to investigate, instead of their own forces. If things went bad then at least there were two fleets to oppose the Katherine. The part about the free election the General decided to leave out.

Secretly he knew they'd never agree, so he decided to spring it on them after he found out who the enemy was. He knew he could get executed for this, but it was worth the risk he hoped.

"You're taking a big chance General." Colonel Thompson told him once the three of them had reached their ships.

"Yes, but this way I could save our fleets. It's worth the chance if the Katherine can find a peaceful solution out there."

"What happens after that?"

"That will be up to the Junta I'm afraid." He answered sounding unsure.

THE ENEMY RACE

Simon having briefed the crew, prepared to enter the coordinates the General had supplied. Radon unsure, reminded him of Duelong. This was the planet, where the Roax had marooned his parents. At the time they had been about to target the portal base on Salvation after the Roax had fired on their submarine. The Roax, pretending to surrender, had opened a portal right in front of their sub, sucking them in. Unable to turn, they'd ended up on Duelong, a planet with a poisonous atmosphere. Having no way of returning they had all perished.

"I think the General is on the level with the address. It's returning here where things will be different." Simon replied, pushing in the numbers.

On board the General's fleet of ships and in the village, the people gathered stared awestruck, as a circle of water rotated above them. They then watched in utter amazement as the Katherine roared into it.

"I never knew you could make a portal accept underwater?" the General remarked, his crew silent as they all watched. For most, it was the first time they'd ever seen a portal.

"Nothing surprises me after meeting Simon Hayes." Captain Stuart to the side answered absentmindedly, causing many including the General to look his way.

"Be careful Captain." The General reminded him, as Stuart self-consciously left the bridge.

"Keep an eye on him," Wordsworth whispered to Thompson.

"Yes, Sir."

Two days and a lot of deep thinking by Simon saw the Katherine burst from the portal. Hundreds of cruisers in two groups silently greeted their arrival. Radon cautiously ordered the crew to battle stations, as Simon sitting patiently in his Captain's chair waited.

"They're taking their time to hail us aren't they?" Kate whispered beside him, her voice resonating, as fear made it tremble.

"It's not often a nightmare creature from your past, suddenly appears in front of you. I'd say despite his orders the Commander out there is weighing up whether to obey orders and let us pass, or try to blow us out of the sky.

"How can you be so calm?" Kate spat out, angry with him.

"I'm not calm Kate. I'm just tired of our so-called fellow human's complete lack of trust in us. Ever since we brought peace to the Galaxy, every human we've met has in one way or another, tried to kill us. The Oregarthians trust us, as do the Flax Federation, yet our own people don't. It makes me want to scream." Simon yelled, making the whole bridge look his way.

"All races have fought change, Simon. I warned you when you first talked to my people that some would not be happy with your view of peace through co-existence. Yet you did bring change, and millions throughout our Galaxies are grateful that wars that consumed their everyday lives are finally over. The price you pay with your own people is small, compared to what we achieved." Radon reminded him.

Looking around the room, Simon watched the men nod their approval. It was clear despite all that had happened; they all thought their sacrifice had been well worth it. Simon was just about to reply to Radon when a transmission was intercepted.

"Sir, one of the New America ships is hailing us."

"Open the channel," Simon ordered.

"I would like to speak to Captain Hayes." A blunt voice informed them. Many on the bridge took this as a bad sign.

"I am Captain Hayes, who is it I'm talking to?" Simon answered.

"This is Commander Abbott, commander of the Second fleet and a member of the Junta. General Wordsworth has asked us to assist you, and we shall honour his decision for the moment. Why he agreed to it is beyond us, but we will allow it. The enemy fleet is in the Galaxy to the west of your position, at grid reference 280 degrees by 267 degrees by 219 degrees. It seems to be their rally point."

"Thank you, Commander, we appreciate your help."

"If it were up to me, I'd blow you out of the sky. You're a traitor to your race, anyone who sides with aliens over his own, can't be trusted." Simon was just preparing a response when the Comm's officer told him Commander Abbotts was offline.

"Well, that was pleasant." Simon smiled, some of the crew chuckling in response.

"Unfortunately some of our people have trouble understanding that we aren't the dominant race and need friends." Ryan put in feeling a little embarrassed by his countrymen. Since coming aboard, Ryan like everyone aboard had to earn his place. At the moment he was manning the navigation console.

"Yes, for some it's hard to come to grips with the fact that you're not the biggest bully boy on the block. Let's move on people. Plot a course to the position close to where our friend Commander Abbott told us the enemy was. Let's find out whom these mysterious ships belong to?" Simon ordered as Ryan entered the new position.

"Stay at Battle stations, everyone. When we exit the portal, the reception might make this one seem friendly." Radon chuckled, as the crew joined in.

THE HEDRED

The gap this time between entry and exit was nearly instantaneous, as the Katherine exited the portal. Facing them sat a huge fleet of ships, dwarfing the New American fleet they had just left. Without warning, one of the weapons platforms on one of the strange ships opened fire. The sonic laser though powerful failed to penetrate their shield. Ignoring the unprovoked attack, Simon studied the unusual ships. Looking like long round black pipes, their design was one of adding on. All the ships seemed to have undergone continuous shape changing as pieces were added on ad hoc.

"Does anyone recognise the ships?" Simon asked. Silence followed his question as all the crew stared at the armada.

"Makes the Flax Home fleet look small doesn't it?" Radon murmured, studying the ships.

"I don't think it's an invasion fleet, Sir," Jabo spoke up, moving to stand next to Simon.

"Why would you say that?" Simon answered.

"If you look at the ships Sir, you'll see that the larger ones are transport ships. They're armed, but not as heavily as the outer ships which are moving towards us. I'd hazard a guess and say this is a colonisation fleet. The smaller ships which number about two hundred must be its escort." Jabo concluded.

"We'll know soon enough. Be ready men." Simon ordered, as the enemy ships, formed up in front of them. A stalemate then developed as each side tried to assess the opposing force. In the end, Simon opened a line of communications. After transmitting on several frequencies, all he got in return was high-pitched squaws.

"Are we transmitting and receiving properly?" Simon asked his Comm's officer.

"Yes, Sir. All I'm getting is this interference."

"Are you sure its interference? Could it be their language?" Kate suggested.

"Have one of our computers send their computers our binary code. That should give us a means of communicating directly." Simon ordered, as the room silently waited. For the next hour the Katherine's computer ran a series of programs, the opposing fleet's computers responding. In the meantime Radon had the ships scanned to study their shields. Amazed at the difference he signalled to Simon and Kate to come and have a look. Simon always intrigued by different technology looked over Radon's Intel.

"They're totally different. I can't even understand how they work." He admitted lost in the data.

"Their shields seemed to work by some sort of compressed energy similar to sound. They project the noise out around their ships using the energy somehow to form a shield." Radon explained.

"Seems to work though? They gave a good account of themselves against our ships in the first encounter." Ryan pointed out.

"Sir, we're receiving a message through the main data console." One of the Katherine's crew shouted from the side of the room. This surprised Simon like the others, thinking the aliens would adapt their language to match their own, and then transmit through the Comm's array. After reading the first text, Simon realised it wasn't possible for them to communicate, other than the screeching noise they had heard earlier.

"Ryan, can you rig something to convert what we hear into words?" Ryan already ahead of him told him to transmit. He'd converted it through the computer to speak the binary code that the computer used. "Can you understand me?" Simon asked silence followed. "I repeat. Can you understand me?" Simon was just about to suggest another means of communicating when a hesitant voice stuttered through the speakers.

"Yes, we hear you. Why have you come here?" The voice asked.

"You are attempting to approach a planet settled by another race. We are here to try and prevent needless bloodshed."

"We are the Hedred when our vanguard approached the planet Goren as we call it, they came under attack. We lost two ships and outnumbered we retreated. We have travelled through several Galaxies to reach this planet it was to be our new homeworld as our own was destroyed."

"The race, that occupies it has assembled a large force similar in size to your own. It would be futile to try to take it by force." Simon argued.

"We lack fuel and supplies to reach an alternative planet. What choice do we have than to fight?"

"Could you coexist?" Simon asked, causing a lapse in a reply.

"The Race we encountered on Goren, does not seem the type to share anything freely. We suggest you move away, or prepare to fight, we will not surrender our only chance of survival."

"Just give me some time to talk to my crew, I'll be back soon," Simon told him.

"We will wait for a short time only." The voice warned.

"Has anyone got an idea?" Simon asked looking around the bridge seeking a solution.

"The Junta won't let them share the planet I can assure you. How far is their alternative planet? Maybe we can help them out with supplies and fuel." Ryan suggested.

"Why don't we take them there through the portal? They must know its location." Kate put forward.

"We would be revealing an advance method of travelling. Is that wise?" Radon exclaimed.

"It's better than war isn't it?" Kate shot back. Radon thinking about it, reluctantly agreed.

"Okay, I'll put it to them." Simon smiled, calling the Hedred.

To say the least, the Hedred were sceptical at being able to reach their alternative planet, was an understatement. Simon explaining how the Katherine travelled only seemed to confuse them. In the end, Simon suggested they send a group over to his ship to observe how it worked. Three hours passed when a small dart-like ship approached the Katherine.

"Lower the shield Radon. Tell them our shield is down Ryan." Simon commanded, as the Hedred ship slowly advanced, entering the cargo bay area in the side of the ship.

Once the small ship had touched down, Simon had the ship pressurised, before deploying the shield. Tense minutes passed as Simon waited with Radon and several of his men for the door to open.

"How do we know they even breathe oxygen?" One crewmember whispered getting compressed sniggers from his companions.

"They were heading for a planet which the humans from New America had colonised. They must inhabit the same type of environment or why go there." Radon answered, trying to locate the crewmember that had made the remark. Whoever it was decided to remain silent.

A squeal of metal on metal put them all on alert, as the side of the small shuttle opened. Little green men like creatures, jumped into Simon's mind, as he like everyone else stared at the short little creatures that appeared to hop down out of their ship. Amazingly they were green, although unlike the early version of Martians visualised by the people of Earth, these small creatures had facial features. Their eyes were overlarge, dominating their faces. While their ears, nose and mouth appeared undersized.

Coming forward, one carrying a small box squawked into it. After a brief delay, a voice was heard.

"Greetings I am Ceb, I rule the Hedred."

"Greeting Ceb my name is Simon. I command the Katherine." Simon replied using a similar type of translator.

"Your ship is similar to the races that attacked us near Goren." The Elder Hedred told them, his voice laced with uncertainty.

"Their design, like ours, came from another race who shared their design. This ship was one of their original designs. I can assure you we're not playing favourites here." Simon replied. Squawking broke out from behind the leader.

"They want to know about the circle you came through. Is it really water?" Ceb asked.

"No that's just illusion to pacify the more primitive races. It hides the pure energy, which is used to power the portal device. The Portal is usually used between planets, coming out on the surface." Simon explained.

"Yes, I could see how its appearance could cause confusion. So Captain Hayes from what you said earlier, if I supply the co-ordinates, you can transport us to our alternative homeland."

"If you have the known position it shouldn't be a problem."

"And I'm to trust you, after just talking to you for a couple of hours? Do you really expect me to risk my fleet and my people on your word?"

"Yes, I do Ceb. When I came out of the portal and my ship was fired upon, I could've fatally hurt the ship responsible and your fleet. I didn't because we are here to help."

"You are one ship."

"It is more than just a ship Ceb. Your engineers would've told you that." Simon smiled. A stalemate developed as Ceb weighed up his options. Ceb was no fool. Even if they were victorious against the enemy fleet, he knew the battles would go on. The alternative planet Sallong had always been his first choice. They'd come to this planet purely because of the extreme distance to Sallong. Now with this young Captain's help, his people had a chance.

"Can you show me how your transporter machine works?" Ceb asked breaking the silence.

"Of course, if you follow me, I'll take you to the bridge."

Simon true to his word used a portable voice translator to explain the workings of the Portal to Ceb's engineers. They were the best in his fleet, but he could see their eyes shining with wonder, as Simon explained the Portal machine. Ceb still wasn't entirely sure of this Simon Hayes, but he seemed honest enough and open. His second in command Radon was another matter.

He seemed off guard by Simon's openness in revealing how everything worked. Ceb gauged him to be a warrior from his own race, not used to sharing information with a potential enemy. When Ceb had first seen the circle open, showing a surface of water he'd been dumb-struck. Like the rest of the fleet, he'd stood staring at it until without warning the strange ship had appeared.

One of his ships involved in the first battle near Goren had immediately opened fire on the ship with no shields. To his fleet's amazement, the sonic beam had just disappeared causing no damage to what appeared to be a defenceless ship. Ordering his ships to ceasefire, he'd tried to scan the mysterious ship, while his Comm's people tried to communicate.

In both cases, all efforts had failed to tell them anything, when his computer suddenly started warning him that it was communicating with the enemy ship. How this Simon had known to do this worried him. That was not more than seven standard hours ago, yet here he stood on the enemy ship, being instructed on how a new means of space travel worked. He knew the survival of his race depended on him finding out more about this Captain Hayes and his mixed-race crew.

"You are a different race than this Simon Hayes, Radon. Why is it you serve him?" Ceb asked Radon.

"Sometimes I wonder that myself," Radon answered, as those in hearing chuckled. This noise to Ceb sounded like they were near death. Radon went on to give Ceb a brief history lesson on how he'd come to work with Simon. Ceb many times during the story thought he was making it up. Looking around the room, he saw many in the crew were held spellbound by the story, showing they not only believed but also held Simon in awe.

"You can understand how I find this all a bit unbelievable Radon. I'm trusting, the lives of all my people in accepting your help. Many would find my actions in even coming here as foolish." Ceb confessed. Radon stood there thinking over what Ceb had said. It suddenly came to him how they could prove it.

"How about we give you a small demonstration Ceb? We need to report back to the Commander of the forces occupying the planet you call Goren. Why don't you and your men come with us?" Radon suggested.

Ceb at first didn't answer; instead, he turned off his translator before speaking to his crewmen. After what appeared to be a heated conversation, he turned his machine back on.

"Okay I'll go with you, but several of my men need to return to the fleet. I must warn though, if I don't return in two of this planet days, my fleet will attack." Ceb warned.

"We should be able to travel there and back in a matter of hours Ceb. I'll tell Simon." Radon smiled. Walking over to Simon, Radon realised he'd gone further to appease Ceb, than Kate had in revealing the Portal. 'Maybe what Simon's got is catching' he mused, informing Simon of his idea.

Ceb and his men stood opened mouth as the Katherine roared out of the Portal. Slowing down he saw in the distance a line of warships floating in two large formations.

"Battle stations!" Radon shouted, galvanising the crew.

"I thought these were your friends?" Ceb asked.

"Far from it," Simon muttered as the Katherine applied its reverse thrusters, stopping.

"How were your negotiations?" A voice sounded through their speakers, indicating the New America Commander was on the line.

"We've convinced their Commander to travel to another planet. We have brought him here to prove the Portal works." Simon answered.

"He should be imprisoned for attacking our ships, not given a tour." At the Commander's words, Ceb looked sideways at Simon.

"He is here as my guest commander, and the actual details of the attack seem different from their side," Simon replied.

"He threatened our ships here then attacked us. It seems clear to me!" the Commander shouted back.

"How did he threaten your forces, when his race can't speak our language at all?" Simon pointed out.

"I won't argue with you, Hayes. Just do what you will and leave this area." The Commander replied cutting contact.

Looking around the room, Ceb saw the anger on many of the crew's faces at Simon's treatment.

"That Commander is a fool. There is always someone bigger and smarter than you out there somewhere; his race will someday get what they deserve." Ceb exclaimed. Many of the crew silently nodded their support. Remembering Radon's story, Ceb suddenly realised who the race was. "This is not Simon's race is it?"

"Yes they are, and you're quite correct. " A female, Ceb had met earlier answered. She moved to stand beside the seated Simon, placing her hand on his shoulder.

"I didn't intend to insult you, Simon." Ceb apologised.

"You have said nothing wrong Ceb. You're right about my race. We're just putting off the inevitable today. Someday the Katherine won't be around to stop this self-destructive madness. We've become like another race called the Roax they too thought they were indestructible until they all but wiped-out." Simon saddened replied.

"They have not been destroyed, Simon. They are the reason why we left our home world, they destroyed it." Ceb answered as Simon in shock stood up. Kate looking scared rushed into his arms sobbing. The realisation that the Roax were out there stunned the crew. Radon trying to calm everyone down pointed out the facts.

"Look, they could just be a separate group that broke away after my race attacked their planet over a thousand years ago." Radon suggested as Ceb started his story.

Tens of years ago, which was about fifteen Earth years; the Roax had arrived at their planet. They had asked for the Hedred to pay tribute for their guaranteed protection. Ceb and the other leaders of their world refused. At first, many thought the Roax were bluffing until the first meteor was spotted approaching their world.

Despite their forces attacking the meteors as they came in range, some got through. Many cities on their world were obliterated. Deciding the best course was to surrender, the Hedred paid tribute in raw materials and precious metals. Unfortunately, the planet hit by numerous meteors had become unstable. It was then that Ceb gathered his people and planned an escape to another Galaxy.

Secretly, all over the planet, fleets of ships were constructed, as the Hedred prepared for the day when an alternative planet was located. Several in the next year were found, in the end, the decision came down to two. One named Goren was within reach, while the other named Sallong was outside their fleet's range. Ceb liked the planet Sallong, as it was well away from any other known races. Unfortunately, fuel proved the deciding factor and Goren was chosen.

Ceb meeting with the planets council members, urging all the leaders to order their fleets to sail immediately, before the Roax returned, for their next tribute. Some did, many hesitated, wanting more time to prepare. Ceb group left two days later. Accelerating into space, his ship flew away from their intended destination. When they'd travelled far enough to confuse anyone tracking them, they turned onto another course towards Goren.

Four days after his ships left, the Roax returned early. Finding some of the population was missing; they'd resumed their bombardment of the planet. Already damaged by the earlier barrage the planet's core exploded, incinerating the remaining population. The Roax, angry with the Hedred for fleeing, hunted many of the survivors down. A trickle made it, joining Ceb's group. By the time they ran into the forces protecting Goren, Ceb had estimated, they had ten percent of the original population of their home planet.

Simon and Kate like many of the crew were moved by Ceb's story. Radon listening became more and more suspicious of the Roax forces.

"Ceb did you ever meet any of the Roax?" Radon enquired.

"Yes at the meeting to discuss the tribute I met two of their leader's," Ceb answered.

"Can you remember their names?"

"No, they used no names. They only instructed us on what they wanted."

"So you can't be sure they were even the Roax race, they might have been just a displaced race, using their name to hide their own identity?" Ryan suggested.

"Yes they could've been impersonating them, but why would they bother?" Simon answered for Ceb.

"Either way they're not our concern at the moment. Let's get the Hedred to Sallong." Kate put forward, the others agreeing.

Sitting in his cabin, Simon thought again of the Roax leaders who had once manned the Portal base on Salvation. His mother and father had been murdered by these superior monsters, who thought of themselves as Gods. He'd captured them on Salvation after they'd kidnapped Kate. He'd been forced in the end by the people of Salvation to show them leniency. Agreeing to send them through the portal to start a new life, he'd instead sent them to the same planet they'd marooned his parents on named Duelong.

Duelong had a poisonous atmosphere, and by right they should all have perished. Could they have escaped was the question? They'd been in a submarine with their followers numbering about a thousand, so how had they survived?

"I should have killed them all!" Simon growled, furious at their possible survival. He made a mistake he realised in underestimating their cunningness and intelligence. 'They might have sent out a call for help, and some poor unknowing Good Samaritan had rescued them. It was a long shot, but it fitted and now they again preying on the defenceless, by using their advanced weaponry and shields to subjugate whole planets.

"They don't have the Katherine though. Once I'm finished resettling the Hedred, I'll look for them." He promised himself as Kate entered.

"You're not sure it's them Simon, don't worry about it, my love." She whispered reassuring him, guessing what he was thinking about. Hugging him tightly, she undid his clothing, then hers. While she continued to undress, Simon remained frozen, his mind already in a distant Galaxy looking for them. Her hands running over his body brought him back. Seeing her naked, he picked her up carrying her to the bed. The Roax could wait he smiled, as kissing Kate he put his anger away, for another day.

With the return of their leader Ceb, the Hedred fleet prepared to leave. Ceb had decided to remain on the Katherine as a sign of good faith and because he'd become something, bordering a friend with this strange group of mixed races. Handing the planets Sallong co-ordinates to Simon, he watched him enter them into the portal controls.

"Is your fleet ready?" Simon asked abruptly. Ceb had noticed a change in Simon since he'd told them of the Roax.

"Yes Simon whenever you're ready, they will follow us through."

"Then let's go," Simon ordered as the swirling circle of water came into existence in front of the Katherine. Without any hesitation, Ryan at the helm accelerated the ship forward, followed by a fleet of nervous Hedreds.

Sallong was a lot further out than Simon had realised. When travelling over massive distances between Galaxies, the trips had taken days. This trip took over a week, meaning Sallong, was in a totally unknown section of the Universe. Simon could see why Ceb had chosen Goren instead of Sallong; it was half the distance from his original planet.

When Ceb learned that Simon and the others had a history with the Roax he had gladly given them the co-ordinates of his homeworld, plus three other planets in his Galaxy. This gave Simon the ability to travel there at his discretion. Secretly he hoped Simon would go after the Roax, who'd destroyed his planet. If anyone could bring his people justice for what had happened, he believed it would be this crew.

Exiting the Portal above Sallong, Simon immediately scanned the planet for signs of life. It teamed with animal life but showed no signs of intelligent life forms. Using Ceb's shuttle, Simon travelled down to the planet for a closer look. In many ways, it reminded him of Salvation, although while Salvation had only a small land mass, Sallong had only forty percent of its surface, covered by water.

"It is more than I hoped for Simon. We can't thank you enough." Ceb squawked through his translator, his excitement evident.

"You are welcome Ceb. I hope you and your people spend the rest of your lives in peace." Ceb looked at Simon, seeing him as the Oregarthians and the Flax saw him.

"Simon, don't go after the Roax. I know you intend to, and I secretly hoped you would, but now like us, you need to find peace."

"We will Ceb. It's just I can't rest knowing those monsters are out there somewhere inflicting their twisted beliefs on some unsuspecting race."

"In that case, I have something for you. One of my engineers at a meeting with the Roax to arrange shipment of raw materials to their ship secretly took a photo. It shows two of them boarding one of their ships. Always remember Simon, we are here if you need us." Ceb whispered, turning away to hide his misgivings.

"Thank you Ceb. I hope you can all live in peace here." Simon smiled, although Ceb saw his eyes settle on the photo.

Because of the speed of the Katherine, the Hedred fleet took another day to exit the Portal. By this time Ceb had with the help of Radon and several members of the crew, mapped out suitable landing sites for their fleet. Simon couldn't remember seeing such an astounding sight, as the fleet of hundreds of ships swarming down to the surface, landing at predetermined sites. Simon waited a further two days making sure there were no problems, before leaving. As a parting gift, Simon downloaded his data on alternative fuels and farming from his experiences on Salvation. It was warmly received. Promising to return, Simon and the crew reluctantly departed. They had in a way bonded with this mysterious race.

"No matter what else happens that was a good deed." Kate smiled, kissing Simon lightly on the cheek, as the Katherine re-entered the Portal.

"Yes, we seem to have a gift for helping other races. It's our own people we have trouble with." Simon answered checking the power reading one more time, as they entered the portal. Jabo's appearance made him look up.

"How did you go?" Simon asked.

"I have analysed the photo Ceb gave you. Although the quality was poor, I have managed to improve the photo to about an eighty percent recognition level." Radon, Kate and Simon stared at the photo without a sound, their thoughts masked.

"Is it the Roax?" Jabo enquired, as Simon without another word, left the bridge followed by Kate, leaving Jabo dumbfounded.

"It's not your fault Jabo." Radon explained. "Unfortunately, the photo shows they're not only the Roax, my friend, but they're also Elena and Rile. Those two were the leaders of the ones we sent to Duelong."

Simon stared out their bedroom view screen at the multi coloured walls of the portal, which they were travelling through.

"This is my entire fault, Kate. I should've killed them all. Instead, I sent them to Duelong, taking the coward's way out."

"You did what was right at the time. Stop blaming yourself. I like the others on Salvation, thought they shouldn't be killed but exiled. The past is the past."

"But look what's happened. They destroyed the Hedred's home planet, and who knows who else has paid for my leniency."

"Then make sure it doesn't happen again. Find them and bring them to justice, but for now, enjoy the moment. You just stopped a full-scale war and with luck will free my people, concentrate on that, the Roax can wait." Kate pointed out, hugging him.

"You're right, what we achieved here is a miracle. I know I should be overjoyed, it's just I have a bad feeling about the Roax."

"Do you think it is really Elena and Rile? By rights, they should be, if not dead, at least in their nineties."

"I think what we saw are hybrids, manufactured from their DNA. Let's face it; they were light years ahead of us, cloning wouldn't be that hard for them."

"Well, it will take us at least a week to reach New America. I'm sure in between keeping me happy, you'll work out something." She smiled, dropping her clothes as she entered the shower. Smiling, Simon undressed as well, deciding to think about it later.

THE VILLAGE

A day after the Katherine left New America, Johan the village's defacto leader, detected the first sign of trouble. General Wordsworth and the majority of the fleet had left leaving four ships near the old base. In the pre-morning light, a patrol from one of the ships came within a hundred metres of the village. Stopping, it set up an observation post, digging in. Horen, curious, sent four soldiers, to watch them, with instructions not to get too close.

The patrol after staying all day, bugged out as the sun was going down. Horen's four soldiers returned, reporting nothing out of the ordinary.

"Just doing a recon I'd say." Kallong one of Horen's men suggested.

"Maybe, just be careful Kallong. They weren't supposed to approach the village at all, although it could be just training. On the other hand, they might be watching how we respond?" Horen answered, sounding as he felt, worried.

A week passed, with the patrol from the ship carrying out the same routine. Each time Horen responded by sending men, changing the approach route and number of men each time. Johan who was with Horen on the last patrol aired his concern.

"They're getting ready for something Horen. In the coup attempt many years ago, I saw them use this tactic. They call it the sucker punch. You get so used to the boring nature of the patrol, you don't see the real attack coming." Johan whispered as if the soldiers could hear him.

"You could be right. Kallong was saying how tiresome it is going out each time and shadowing them. What do you suggest?"

"How about tonight you and I take a little walk?" He smiled, Horen understanding, nodded.

After the patrol like usual had departed, Horen and Johan put their plan into action. Heavily camouflaged, they waited till dark, before moving out of the village into the surrounding darkness. Johan had warned Horen, that the Overmen would have infrared and movement sensors, so as soon as they reached vegetation, they got down and crawled.

It was slow going through the scrub on your belly. Johan keeping track of the time and their position worked out they'd taken over an hour to infiltrate behind the patrols observation post. Looking around nothing seemed out of place. All the soldiers seemed to have done was dig out several pits for cover. A muffled clang to their right made them both freeze. Backtracking they moved further away from the village. Johan whispered to Horen that an abandoned road ran in a gully in the area where the noise had come from.

Climbing a slight rise, they looked down onto where the old road used to be. There just visible, were four armoured vehicles. Johan sensing he was being watched immediately pulled Horen back below the rise.

"We'd better get back." He whispered in his ear, leading the way. Three hours of slow crawling found them back at the village. Sitting down resting, Horen gathered his men.

"They are going to try and rush us. While your men are sitting opposite their patrol, those four vehicles are going to cut them off from the village. Even if the shield is deployed, your men are outside." Johan explained nervously.

"Kallong, take two men and deploy the shield now," Horen ordered, before turning back to Johan. "Johan, why did you pull me down out there?"

"I felt someone was watching us. It saved me before." Johan confessed, hoping he hadn't overreacted. Horen nodding his understanding continued.

"If we don't send a patrol, they will know we are onto them. On the other hand, if we send men out there they'll be exposed. Anyone got a suggestion?"

"I have one," Benjamin answered from the rear, surprising them all.

"Where did you come from?" Johan barked, shocked by his sudden appearance. Even Horen and his men jumped up, many drawing weapons, before sitting back down.

"I saw you and Horen sneak out, so I put my camouflage gear on and followed you. I figure you must've seen me when you suddenly headed back."

"You could've been killed you fool!" His father chastised him.

"I think Benjamin can look after himself, Johan. We didn't even pick up his approach now, and our hearing is much better than yours." Horen pointed out, impressed. "What's your idea, Benjamin?"

"Well I was ears dropping on Kallong the other day, and I heard him mention you have a personal shield. Is that true?" Horen surprised by the question, took several seconds to answer."

"That is something I wanted to be kept secret, Benjamin," Horen replied sharply. "Have you told anyone else?"

"No, I figured you wanted it kept a secret." Benjamin squeaked out, as some of Horen's men tried not to laugh.

"Okay, let's say we have one. What's your idea?" Horen asked silencing his men with a look.

"Well if you send someone out, and they're wearing the shield, they should be safe." He suggested as Horen looked at Johan.

"That is brilliant," Horen admitted as Kallong arrived back from the shuttle.

"The shields deployed Horen." Kallong started noticing everyone was watching him. "Is there a problem?"

"Not now, I just picked a volunteer, big mouth." Horen smiled, as laughter erupted.

The next morning like usual the patrol set up in their position, watching the village. As usual, Horen sent a four-man team out, taking up position opposite them. Kallong stood on the rise watching the patrol, as his men like usual found cover. After an hour of watching each other Kallong was just about to sit down when the patrol got up, moving towards him.

"You are not supposed to approach this village. Your General assured our Commander that you'd respect the neutrality of this village." Kallong shouted out, as to his right the armoured vehicles crested a hill racing for the village.

"The Junta controls this planet demon. We go where we like." An arrogant voice responded as laser beam screamed towards him. Kallong, of course, was shocked as it hit him but received no injury.

"Now it's our turn." He shouted as he and the other three soldiers returned fire, on the surprised soldiers. It was over quickly as the survivors of the patrol hastily retreated, some running. Kallong shaken by the exchange, slowly walked towards the downed soldiers, while his men covered him. Checking each soldier, he found two still alive. Administering first aid, he quickly bandaged them up. Waving his men forward they carried the wounded soldiers back towards the village.

In his firefight with the platoon, he hadn't seen or heard, what happened to the four armoured vehicles. As he approached the shield, he found the four vehicles burning fiercely, crushed up against the shield. Most of the crews he saw had survived and were beating a hasty retreat away from the village and him.

Tapping on the shield with his rifle, Horen soon appeared and the shield where he stood opened enough to let his patrol and the wounded enemy prisoners in.

"What happened? Surely they saw the shield?" Kallong was mystified.

"Johan suggested throwing smoke grenades out, once they opened fire on you. They drove right into it at full speed." Horen smirked.

"You know I'm glad those two are on our side Horen. I wouldn't want them as enemies." Kallong smiled handing Heron the shield.

"Yes, they are the first two humans who remind me of Simon. They have the same way of grasping a problem and solving it." Horen admitted as they both walked back to the village.

"This is just the start, Johan. Are your villagers with us?" Horen asked.

"Yes of course we are, and by the way, how did Kallong go?"

"Good your son's plan worked perfectly."

"I know it is a secret Horen, but where did you get it?" Johan whispered intrigued.

"Simon gave it to me. It was his personal shield, one of his friends made it for him, for his wedding on Salvation. When both of them were ambushed on Salvation, Kate, his wife to be, was wearing it. It saved her life. Unfortunately, Simon wasn't wearing it when he was hit. I gave it to Kallong when he volunteered to go." Heron smiled.

"I never heard of personal shields."

"It is a prototype, only one exists. Now you must get the villagers to arm themselves, we will need to prepare."

"What chance have we got against their fleet?"

"You didn't think Simon left us defenceless did you?"

"Will that shield protect us?"

"It's not as strong as the Katherine's shield that's a different type. This one is similar to your fleet's shields. It will hold for a while, enough to load all your people aboard the shuttle and flee if necessary."

"I hope it doesn't come to that Horen?" Johan confessed.

"So do I my friend."

General Wordsworth read the report of the action, his face resembling stone.

"Who gave permission to try and enter the village?" He asked his voice-suppressed anger.

"General Rowling's ordered it, Sir." Colonel Thompson informed him. Wordsworth stared at Thompson wondering how much he could trust him. Rowlings was a member of the Junta, one of the men who had ordered the murderous response by the fleet on New America, during the rebellion. His third fleet was now on its way to New America, to await the return of the Katherine.

"He's a dammed fool. What does he hope to gain by causing trouble with that small village?"

"He outranks you, Sir. It's his way of showing you that." Wordsworth blinked at Thompson's words. He had just committed himself to him, by his statement.

"I'm worried Colonel. When the Katherine returns Rowling is sure to engage her. It could be a bloodbath."

"Then we've got to make sure it doesn't happen, Sir. The problem is how we stop a member of the Junta."

"With the utmost care my friend. Unless of course, you want to stand beside me at my very own firing squad." Wordsworth smiled; as the two men sat down to plan their next move.

After the initial assault, a lull developed as more Overmen ships returned. Unlike the Katherine's shield, this one was visible. Controlled by the shuttle's computers, it gave the defenders the option of dropping the shield in selected positions to allow them to fire at attackers. General Rowling, who was still over two weeks away, was fuming over his men's failure to take the village. Ordering more forces deployed there, he demanded they take the village immediately; he promised vengeance on all who failed him.

Four days passed before the next attack materialised. Both hover ships and ground forces launched a pre-morning assault. Johan awoke to the hear- stopping crump of weapons fire, colliding with the shield. The pounding continued for the next four hours as the villagers fearful the shield would collapse, ran to the shuttle. Horen unfazed by the bombardment at first refused entry to the shuttle, causing panic to spread amongst the women and children.

Johan pointing out that they'd be better on board than standing outside panicking swayed him. Swiftly loading all the women and children, the men then deployed with the Alien soldiers. Kallong in the meantime, having watched the enemy movements, suggested to Horen that they move most of their forces to the side facing the old army base. He pointed out for some reason unknown; the enemy units seem to be readying a ground attack from there.

"They think being alien's monsters, we'll just fold and run to our ship, abandoning the humans in the village." Horen smiled.

"A couple of days ago I would've suggested it. Now after living with them, I think they have worth." Kallong responded.

"You're not getting soft, are you Kallong?"

"Tell that to the soldiers about to attack us. I'm sure they'll tell you a different story." Kallong answered, heading towards the forward positions.

When the first wave of infantry approached the shield, Horen dropped it, allowing them forward. Once inside he redeployed it, trapping the soldiers, with their backs against the shield. Caught in the open those that didn't surrender were mowed down by the villagers and Horen's troops. Twice more they allowed enemy troops in before the enemy commander wised up.

This time the attacking troops lobbed smoke bombs shielding them from the defenders. Pulling the village men back, Horen went forward with his men. Moving with impossible burst of speed, they fought the fifty soldiers inside the barrier. With limited vision, they used their enhanced hearing to locate the enemy. Then using their superior reflexes and speed they rapidly overwhelmed the soldiers, most were taken, prisoner.

Once this force was subdued, Horen concentrated on the Overman's ships. With shields themselves, he could do little to stop them, but by firing accurately at the ships, made them back off enough, to lower their impact on the shield. By day's end, with no gains made and a high loss in ground forces, the enemy retreated. Their ships still fired on the village, but except for a lot of noise, the shields held.

On and off for the next two weeks, the enemy tried to breakthrough the shield barrier. Horen saw each retreat as a success hiding his misgivings. The ships attacking though powerful lacked the heavy weapons a cruiser carried. He knew it was only a matter of time till the enemy fleet arrived. Then he would have to judge the right time to run before their concentrated firepower destroyed his shuttle and the village. His earpiece chirping made him look up.

"What is it Kallong?" He asked, recognising his voice.

"There are two men at the shield carrying a white flag."

"Open the shield and let them in, but be careful." He ordered moving down the hill from the shuttle. Arriving, he found General Wordsworth and the Colonel from the first visit there waiting for him.

"We have come in peace soldier. Hey aren't you the one who nearly shot me last time?" the General asked Kallong, recognising him.

"Yes, I regret it now."

"Hey, it's not me calling the shots here soldier. I've come to offer a solution before the fleet arrives and blows you all to hell."

"I'm listening," Horen answered, arriving as Wordsworth turned to face him.

"For my own reasons, I'd rather you all survive. So here's what I suggest we do." General Wordsworth then told Horen what he planned. For the next hour, Horen listened to the General's plan, only interjecting to clarify some minor points. Kallong in the meantime, moved to the shuttle to watch for any sign of trickery. Horen, in the end, admitted the plan was feasible.

"It sounds good General, but for it to work, I must trust you with all our lives," Horen answered.

"Sometimes you've got to throw the dice son, have you ever heard that saying?"

"No, but Captain Hayes has one I know. An eye for an eye. If you betray us, General Wordsworth, my brothers in arms will avenge me, by levelling this planet." Horen promised, before calling his men.

Colonel Thompson had remained silent during Wordsworth's explanation of his plan. The alien soldier worried him. Thompson had the feeling he wasn't kidding about his friends coming for revenge if anything went wrong.

"Sir, do you think this is wise?"

"No, it isn't Colonel. So many things can go wrong here that the chances are we'll all end up dead. That aside, I'm through with killing people just for the sake of it. Hayes is right, it's time we had elections our people deserve to live free again."

Horen smiled, having heard the exchange between the two men. His vastly improved hearing enabled him to listen, even though, he was a good ten paces ahead of them. The General's plan was brilliant; he himself couldn't have planned it better. Calling his men, he had them instruct Johan and the other village men, to gather their families and what possessions they could carry and load them on the ship. It would be a tight fit, but with luck, they'd make it. Signalling to Kallong, he called him over.

"Watch what you say on the Comm's gear." He warned him, as both removed their headsets. "Okay it could be nothing but the General thinks they could be listening to our transmissions."

"What's up?" Kallong whispered, picking up his squad leader's concern.

"Bring our backup power unit out of the ship. When it's running, disconnect the portable shield from the ship and reconnect it to the backup. Once you've set it up, program a hole in the shield, in front of the ship's position, we're leaving."

"We've no protection without that shield Horen." Kallong pointed out.

"With luck, we won't need it, or as the humans say, sometimes you have to throw the dice." Horen smiled.

"What does that mean?"

"It means we're counting on our own luck to survive."

"You have been here too long Horen," Kallong replied, confused by Horen's explanation, causing him to burst into suppressed laughter. Walking back to where Wordsworth was waiting, Horen signalled him to follow him. Arriving at a large shed, he approached the door. Tapping twice, the door was opened by two villagers.

"How are the prisoners?" Horen asked.

"Quiet, but that's to be expected after you told them you'd eat anyone who talked." One of the guards chuckled.

"Yes, they really do believe all those stories don't they?"

"We did too till you turned up and explained what really happened, even though some do have reservations." The other villager chimed in. Horen could see a lifetime of fear wouldn't just wash away.

"Okay then, let's get them ready to move. We can no longer feed them, so one of their Generals has arrived to escort them back to their lines." Horen lied, indicating General

Wordsworth and the Colonel Thompson. A cheer erupted from the prisoners as Wordsworth entered.

"You okay men?" He shouted, shaking a few of their hands.

"Yes general, we're sorry we didn't succeed with our mission." One young Officer embarrassed told him.

"You did your best men. You should never have been committed to this folly. Attacking aliens defending our own people, it is insanity." Wordsworth told them, some appearing upset.

"We thought you ordered it, Sir." The same Officer exclaimed.

"No, it wasn't my order men. Anyway, let's get you all back to our lines. I might even shout some drinks." He smiled, leading his men away from the village.

Four hours after the shield was connected to the backup generator, Kallong at the shuttle's controls, spotted the fleet entering the outer reaches of New America's atmosphere. With everyone aboard, Horen signalled for everyone to brace themselves. Twenty minutes passed before a voice resonated through their headsets.

"We know you can hear us, this is General Rowling. I command the fleet orbiting this planet. Unless you surrender immediately, in ten minutes, you will be exterminated."

"We have been ordered by Captain Hayes to protect the villagers. Have we your guarantee no harm will come to them if we surrender?" Horen asked, silence followed, broken again by the same voice.

"You now have nine minutes."

Horen looked around the room, seeing Johan watching him.

"Do you wish to surrender?"

"They would shoot us as traitors. We go where you go Horen." Johan spoke out as his fellow villagers in hearing range, shouted their support.

"Well, in that case, let's go." Horen smiled, signalling to Kallong to power up the ship.

Captain Rowling stared at his viewing screen showing the shield over the village. From space it appeared a small white circle, sitting sedately in the countryside, beside the sea. No movement could be seen meaning they weren't surrendering.

"Open fire!" The General ordered.

"Sir we still have three minutes to go." His second in Command Captain Howard piped in.

"Fire Captain, I've waited long enough." The General growled as Captain Howard instructed his weapons officer and the fleet to open fire.

As if the Gods of Ancient Greece had been plotting the village's demise, sheets of lighting like bolts, roared down from the heavens, impacting with the shield. Covering his eyes, Kallong edged the ship forward before accelerating. Clearing the shield Horen beside him expected at any moment to feel the sickening impact of laser fire. Instead, the ship continued on racing for the ocean.

Their miracle hovered above them, as General Wordsworth's ship with great daring used its shield to protect the shuttle below them. Behind them, unable to maintain the shield any longer, the generator collapsed imploding. The resulting explosion levelled the area for a mile, obliterating the village and the surrounding countryside. Blinded by the laser discharge and the explosion the shield generator caused, the watching Fleet and the Overmen ships saw nothing, only whiteness.

Over the Ocean, Kallong seeing Wordsworth's plan had worked, cut power, letting his ship dive into the Ocean as General Wordsworth's ship continued on. Shutting down everything but life support, the shuttle came to rest on the Ocean floor.

"Keep noise to a minimum." A relieved Kallong whispered; as they settled down to wait for the return of the Katherine.

THE SURPRISE

General Rowling watched the circle of water form near one of New America's moons. His moment had arrived he told himself snugly, looking forward to the coming battle. His crew around him didn't share his blind faith. Many saw the circle as

a bad omen. They thought it heralded the return of an ancient
curse that would wreak its vengeance on the human race.

For over a week they'd waited, as the fleet manoeuvred,
trying to obtain the best position for the coming confrontation.
In that time old fears had again surfaced.

"Sir we have movement in the portal!" Howard, his second
in command, shouted, galvanising the crew.

"How many objects can you detect?"

"Just one Sir, I'd say it's the Katherine."

"Go to Battle stations!" Rowling screamed, as his men
unenthusiastically prepared for battle.

"Sir, General Wordsworth asked permission to come up to
the bridge."

"Tell him yes, I see no reason why he shouldn't watch."
Rowling smiled wanting the fallen Junta member to see his
triumph. He'd been surprised when Wordsworth and Colonel
Thompson had come on board. During the reprisals for the
failed coup, Rowling had felt the heat from Wordsworth's
accusations. Luckily the other Junta members had come down
on his side; otherwise, things would've been much different.

"He's here to worm his way back in." Rowling murmured to
himself, as Wordsworth appeared at the entrance to the
bridge. "Let him try, I'll deal with him later." Rowling smiled.

"Sir the object is clearing the circle," Howard screamed, the
sound of real fear in his voice.

"Fire everything we've got," Rowling shouted, as the whole
fleet, saturated the target with laser blasts. On board, his
flagship Rowling covered his eyes from the glare produced by
the weapons fire. In seconds the glow receded as the object
torn apart by the bombardment, ceased to exist.

"Well, that's the end of that. Give the men a well done
Captain Howard." General Rowling chuckled, watching
Wordsworth stare out the front viewing screen. "Well
Wordsworth, why couldn't your ground forces do that, when
the Katherine first appeared?" He smirked, enjoying the
moment. General Wordsworth at first seemed at a loss to
answer when the ship's Klaxon screamed out a warning.

"Sir another circle has opened behind the fleet. A cruiser
type warship is exiting the circle, it's charging its weapons."

Captain Howard warned. The fleet caught facing the wrong way started to come apart as laser blast impacted with the fleet's cruisers. One by one mayday calls screamed out as ships were crippled, the flagship's communications becoming jammed "What will we do Sir?" Howard asked as Rowling stood paralysed.

"Cease fire immediately!" General Wordsworth shouted. "I'm taking command. Open a channel to the Katherine while we still have a fleet."

Captain Howard looked from Wordsworth to Rowling, who still hadn't reacted.

"Do as he commands," Howard yelled, as the fleet slowly stop firing.

Simon stared out at the New America's first fleet. Of over a hundred cruisers, twenty were dead in the water, their engines disabled.

"They've stopped firing Simon. What are your orders?" Radon asked.

"What of the people we left at the village?" Simon replied.

"The village where we left the shuttle is totally destroyed. There is no sign of our shuttle or the villagers." Ryan at the scanner console reported.

"Try to raise Horen and prepare to fire," Simon ordered his anger building.

"We're receiving a transmission from the fleet's commander." Radon informed him, his eyes never leaving the fleet.

"Good prepare to target that ship next." Simon smiled at the enemy's mistake in transmitting.

"It is General Wordsworth. He said to tell you the villagers are safe."

"Put him on speaker Radon," Simon ordered.

"Captain Hayes, you're a source of constant amazement."

"Thank you, General. I decided to send a meteor through the first portal, just in case. Now, where are my people?"

"They're sitting on the ocean seabed. I arranged with your commander there Horen to exit the shield, as the fleet started to attack. They are waiting for your return."

"Who attacked my people?"

"General Rowling he's part of the Junta. He's under arrest aboard this ship. I have taken command." Wordsworth informed him.

"Good, we will talk again once I speak with my people. I suggest you arrange to repair your damaged ships. We targeted their engine only; they should be able with some minor adjustments to restore their manoeuvrability."

"Thank you, Captain Hayes, don't go too far, the Junta won't be happy with my taking command, I may need you." Radon listening to the conversation immediately tried to raise the shuttle. After several different attempts on different frequencies, they found them on one of their backup channels. Finding they were all safe, Radon suggested they stay put until they'd worked out what was going on.

While Radon was contacting the shuttle, General Wordsworth and Colonel Thompson put their plain into action. Using the pretext of repairing the damaged ships, Wordsworth started rounding up commanders loyal to the Junta. Using small shuttle-like cargo ships, he moved troops from his headquarters on New America onto the fleet ships. In just over four hours, he'd achieved complete control of the third fleet, without a shot being fired. Many on board guessed what was occurring, like most they just wanted a return to democracy.

His next step was to arrest the two Junta members still on New America. This, unfortunately, wasn't without bloodshed. Both Junta members kept a sizable force of loyal troops at hand in case of another coup. When Wordsworth's Overmen ship started taking up positions around their command centre, they called the fleet. Finding out Rowling had been relieved of command, warned them of Wordsworth's move against them.

Telling their men to hold the command centre, they sent an urgent message to the other two fleets, ordering them to return and restore order. That done they secretly prepared to leave.

Captain Stuart sat on his ship's bridge watching the other overman ships move into position. After his cold reception from General Wordsworth at the old naval base, he'd expected to lose his ship. Instead here he was in command of a raid on the Junta's headquarters. They all knew that the General now controlled the fleet above them; this move would give him control of New America.

Wordsworth in private had filled him in on the coup, making sure he was with him. Like many, Stuart was tired of this constant state of Marshall Law, the Junta exploited to keep in power. After today he hoped that some sort of peace could be put in place.

"Captain we're receiving fire from the Junta headquarters." Sergeant Ross warned him.

"Order all ships to target their heavy weapons first. Let's persuade them to surrender." Stuart ordered, as the ship shuddered, their return fire screaming down towards the base. After twenty minutes of intense exchange of fire the command centre's weapons ceased firing. "Search for enemy troops, let's make it easy for our infantry." Stuart smiled, thinking how quickly the Junta's loyal troops had become the enemy.

"Sir our ground forces are entering the base. They report light resistance. It seems the Junta leaders have fled."

"They can't be far Sergeant, look for anything out of the usual."

"There is one thing Sir. An emergency shuttle carrying wounded is leaving the area. I didn't bring it to your attention earlier; because there are many such shuttles in use at the moment. This one, however, is heading away from the area where hospitals are located."

"Good work Sergeant. Crew plot a course to intercept the shuttle. Tell the other ships what we're doing.'" Stuart ordered as the New Atlanta gave chase. It didn't take long to overhaul the small shuttle. Coming alongside, Captain Stuart hailed the shuttle ordering it to stop. Instead, it turned firing on his ship. This surprised Stuart, as shuttles weren't usually armed. Luckily their shields were deployed, or the heavy laser blast would've finished them.

"Fire on her engines, let's stop her," Stuart yelled as his own weapons returned fire. To everyone's surprise, the shuttle continued on unharmed.

"Sir they have Cruiser type shields, I don't know how, but we can't touch them," Ross informed him.

"Contact General Wordsworth. Tell him what's happening, ask him what he wants us to do." Minutes passed as the New Atlanta's shield started to buckle under the relentless fire of their small opponent.

"Sir the Katherine is approaching rapidly from the west." Sergeant Ross shouted, obviously surprised.

"Helmsmen, drop back a little, I think this encounter isn't going to go well for the shuttle." Stuart pointed out, as the gap between the shuttle and the New Atlanta increased.

Major General O'Connor watched the Overmen ship drop back. It must've come as a surprise to them, when their weapons fire, was repulsed by their shields. When O'Connor and his friend General Bligh the other Junta leader had decided to leave, they had opted to use this specially prepared craft. Always planning ahead, they'd had several of these special shuttles assembled for the Junta leadership. They were kept hidden, as a backup plan in case of another coup attempt.

Now as they travelled towards a secret cruiser base known only to the Junta, their precautions seemed well justified. Once there, they would transfer to a space-going warship and join the approaching fleets. The Overman ship had been an annoyance having somehow detected their movement away from the base. Now as they dropped back, obviously damaged by their return fire O'Connor looked forward to punishing all the traitors, starting with General Wordsworth.

Rowling had warned them about Wordsworth. He had wanted him taken care of, after trying to have Abbott and Rowling charged over their heavy-handedness during the last coup. O'Connor's and Bligh's votes at that meeting had swayed the Junta against Wordsworth. Apparently, he had waited for his chance to seize power for himself. O'Connor promised himself that the General Wordsworth death would be painful.

"General O'Connor, we have a cruiser coming towards us from the west!" Captain Twain informed him.

"What! Why would Wordsworth send a cruiser into the atmosphere?" O'Connor asked Bligh.

"The man is a fool to risk a cruiser. It won't be able to manoeuvre fast enough to catch us anyway." Bligh replied.

"The sensors are reporting that it's not one of our cruisers Sir. It's the Katherine I'd say?" Twain interrupted, startling both Junta members.

"Can you outrun her Captain?" Bligh shouted, sounding near breaking.

"Not a chance Sir. She's nearly on top of us." Twain replied neutrally.

"Fight to the last Captain. We'll use an escape pod and drop to the surface." O'Connor commanded. The crew on the bridge stared at the two Generals; all realised they were sentencing them to death.

"Why not surrender Sir? The fleet is on its way." Captain Twain suggested.

"Do your duty, that's an order!" O'Connor screeched, as both Generals moved to the escape module.

"Not this time General," Twain shouted back, pulling his pistol free, he pointed it at his former commanders.

"This is treason Captain. I'll have you and all your crew shot!" Bligh shouted, going for his sidearm. It was a stupid thing to do, as several crewmembers drew their own weapons and fired. A silence settled over the bridge, as Twain and his men took in what they'd done.

"Captain we're being hailed by the Katherine. They have ordered us to stop." One of his crewmen informed him.

"Stop the ship immediately and drop our shield. There's been enough killing already." Twain ordered, his crew obeying.

On board the Third fleet's flagship Wordsworth was told of the death of the two Junta leaders.

"Well, we now control New America and one out of three of our fleets. Not bad for the loss of just over two hundred men on both sides."

"I regret even one death General." Colonel Thompson admitted saddened by the loss of life.

"Yes, it's strange when both sides were once the same side. That aside Colonel, it could've been far worse. If Captain Hayes had returned and found the villagers and his men dead, there's no telling how many would've died. Sometimes casualties can't be avoided, although your right, the loss of life is regrettable."

"So what happens now?"

"That depends on Simon Hayes, Colonel. It's about time I found out how much we can really trust him." Wordsworth smiled. Leaving Colonel Thompson as the new Commander of the Third fleet, the general had his shuttle take him to the Katherine.

Horen had been overjoyed when the Katherine told him it was safe to return to the Katherine. Although they had plenty of air, the shuttle was hopelessly overcrowded causing some hygiene problems for the villagers. He'd just left the ocean floor when the Katherine had told him to take his time, having to deal with a problem. When he finally arrived at the Katherine to dock, he found a small shuttle already inside. Squeezing beside it he found a small group of New America soldiers sitting next to it.

"Radon what's going on?" Horen asked after landing. Radon was in the dock area, talking to the New America soldiers.

"We intercepted two of the Junta members fleeing in this shuttle. The crew decided that dying for their two leaders wasn't in their futures." He smiled.

"How is everything going?"

"Good. This General Wordsworth seems to be helping free his people. Your escape and now securing one of their fleets and this planet shows at least he's committed to some type of change."

"Yes, it was touch and go back there, if we'd make it. Without him we wouldn't be here."

"Do you trust him?" Radon asked. Horen could see Radon was unsure.

"That's a hard question. Yes, he saved us and yes he stopped the attack. If it's to free his people or take over himself is another matter." Horen answered, he too wasn't convinced.

"It's funny we automatically trust Simon and Kate, but can't bring ourselves to see any good in others of his race. I of one hope he can be trusted, it would help reassure me that Simon's race is worth saving." Radon admitted.

"I trust Johan and Benjamin Radon. During the defence of the village, they proved themselves to me more than once." Horen smiled.

"Tell me what happened as we walk," Radon answered as they headed for the bridge, to give Horen's report to Simon.

Captain Twain sat beside his shuttle watching the aliens talk freely. He'd been pleasantly surprised by their reception. Sure they'd disarmed them, but now they sat waiting to meet this Captain Hayes after being given refreshments. From what he'd been taught about these monsters from the past, he'd expected to be shot out of the sky; instead, they'd been allowed to dock.

Since then, no one seemed overly worried by their presence, so until he had his meeting with Captain Hayes he waited. His moment of contemplation was cut short as yet another shuttle squeezed into the already overcrowded hangar to their right. To Twain's shock, out of the airlock walked General Wordsworth, appearing as if he was out for a stroll.

"How are you, men? Have they treated you okay?" the General shouted, as twain and his men jumped to their feet. "Forget that men relax." He smiled, signalling twain to come with him.

"You made the right decision son those two men were responsible for helping General Abbott and Rowling getting away with murder, during the failed coup attempt. If they'd surrender, I'd have either imprisoned them or hung them for what they did." The General confessed as they approached the bridge. "Watch what you say in here Captain, they're a bit touchy at the moment." The General warned marching straight in.

Simon and Kate at that moment were giving Horon a hug, welcoming him back aboard. Both looked up surprised by the General's appearance.

"How did the trip go? Did you avoid any trouble with the fleets?" The General began as if the near war with the Third fleet hadn't occurred.

"Good to see you too General. As to how it went, yes we did manage to avoid any confrontation with your two fleets, although it was far from friendly."

"And the Alien race?"

"We moved them to a different Galaxy, using the Portal."

"Was that wise?"

"Radon said the same thing, although it did prevent a costly war for both sides." Kate chimed in. "Are you going to introduce us to the officer with you General?" She smiled.

"Oh I'm sorry, this is Captain Twain. He was in command of the shuttle you intercepted. He, unfortunately, was forced to kill the two Junta members on board." Wordsworth answered. Simon coming forward introduced himself and the others to Twain.

"You made the right choice Captain. Your shields although a surprise, wouldn't have protected you." Simon informed him, knowing how he felt.

"Thank you, Sir." Twain smiled.

"I judge you were surprised when we didn't eat you?" Radon chuckled, shaking his hand.

"Yes, it was a pleasant surprise." He replied smiling. 'This is not what we were told' He said to himself finding himself liking the alien.

"Enough of introductions Simon, are you going to help us?" The General asked.

"That depends on you General. What are your plans now that you hold New America?" Simon wanted to know if the General was doing this for the people or for himself.

"That depends on the two fleets heading here. If it's possible, I'll tell them the Junta is finished, and it's time to return this planet and the planets we control, back to a democratic system of Government."

"What if they won't listen?"

"Then it will be a second shortest lived coup attempt in our history. They're heading here at the moment, so either way, I'll have my answer soon." Wordsworth smiled.

"Will you fight them?" Radon enquired, up till now he had remained silent.

"Unfortunately I have no choice. We've gone too far to turn back now. The Junta would not be happy with just my scalp; they'd want vengeance on all involved. That, I can't let happen."

"Will you seek nomination as the new President?" Kate spoke out; she had no faith in the man who shot Simon.

"Is that what you are worried about, that I've done this just to take over?" Wordsworth exploded before continuing. "When this is finished I will retire if I'm still alive. I've got to much blood on my hands already. You can believe that or shove it!" A quiet settled in the room as many there thought of the blood on their own hands.

"There's no point in waiting for the fight to come to us General. I suggest we take your fleet and the Katherine and meet them halfway?" Simon suggested, wanting to move on.

"So you will help?"

"Of course we will General, as long as our presence doesn't hurt your plans." Simon was still worried by the rumours the people had been told about him and the ship.

"Thank you. I was thinking the same thing. I thought till the battle actually starts, it would be advisable to keep your involvement low-keyed."

"And how would we do that?"

"By pretending to be just what you aren't." Wordsworth chuckled filling them in.

FRIEND AGAINST FRIEND

For four days General Wordsworth's fleet travelled towards G10. Stopping in a Galaxy with a small collection of planets, they waited. There was no reason to believe the two fleets approaching New America would do anything other than head directly straight for the home planet. Forming a battle formation the third fleet manoeuvred using the planet cluster to give them some type of advantage over the approaching much larger fleet.

"Sir, we're detecting the First and Second fleet's approach. They're coming in on the course we suspected they'd use.

"Good work men, bring the fleet to battle stations Commander," Wordsworth ordered as Colonel Thompson gave the order. For the last four days, the General had spent nearly all his time, transmitting to the incoming fleets, without receiving an answer. He knew they could hear him, but no one answered his pleads for peace. Most he knew wouldn't answer, for fear of the reprisals it would bring on their crews and families. Still, he'd hoped someone would've had the guts to at least reply.

Fear started to eat at him. 'Was he doing the right thing, in bringing the fleet out to confront a much larger enemy force?' This worried him more than anything, the thought of his men fighting their once friends on the other ships. Most onboard knew the crews of the ships heading for them. It was one thing to fire on an enemy, it was quite another to fire on people who were your friends.

Commander Abbott, the commander of the first and second fleets, stood on the bridge of the New York, studying the fleet ahead. Beside him, standing to the side were the other two remaining Junta members.

"If we'd have dealt with the Katherine when it had come to G10, we wouldn't have this rebellion." He growled remembering how he'd had to follow the Junta member's orders and let the Katherine go.

"That problem has gone now commander. Be glad they're not here with the rebels." General Baker answered.

"Does anyone know where it went?" General Blumberg nervously asked.

"Back, to the pit of hell where they came from." Abbott snarled, unhappy with having these two fellow members aboard.

"That's not much of an answer commander. I'd be a lot happier if I knew what that ship was up to." Baker shot back unhappy with this whole operation. Both Baker and Blumberg were the moderates of the Junta. They both liked General Wordsworth and thought secretly that he was correct in trying to dissolve the Junta. Abbott saw it differently. He like General Rowling was involved in the heavy reprisal against the first coup attempt. He knew unlike the other two that he'd sooner or later be brought to justice by a democratic government.

As long as he remained in control, no one could touch him. That is why the two men were on board with him now. He knew they'd sell him down the river in return for their freedom.

"Maybe we should open a channel to the third fleet and try to talk to them," Blumberg suggested out loud, making some of the crew look in his direction. Abbott had dreaded this moment. He knew many in his fleet's supported General Wordsworth. His constant chatter over the last four days, telling the fleet's ships that he wanted peace was spreading uncertainty, amongst his men.

"We will talk to him alright! Abbott exploded. "When we're in position, I'll call on him to surrender and face his punishment for treason. That is all the talking we'll be doing. Is that understood?" He bellowed, crushing the two men.

"Sir, the third fleet is holding a defensive position, based on this Galaxies planet cluster ahead of our course." Abbott's Intelligence officer Captain Dominic informed them, which caused Blumberg and Baker to retreat to the viewing area of the bridge. There they both looked ahead trying to spot the rebel fleet and avoid Abbott.

"They're rebels now Captain Dominic. Don't call them the third fleet again." Abbott shouted, taking his anger out on the Captain.

"Yes, Sir. Are we going to ask for their surrender first before we attack?" Dominic answered ignoring his commander's anger.

"For the sake of the crews held captive by General Wordsworth and forced to oppose us, I think it advisable to offer them a chance. For now, have the fleets go to battle stations and prepare to engage." Abbott ordered. Across from him Baker and Blomberg stared at the first fleet, which had just come into viewing range. Baker could see they'd taken up tactical positions around the planets, to help protect them from the vastly numerical fleets coming into range with them.

"What is Wordsworth playing at? Even with the cover, his fleet doesn't have a chance against us." Baker whispered.

"He's fighting here to distance himself from New America. He must know he can't win." Blomberg softly answered.

"I'd have thought he'd try to enlist the Katherine to help him. It would've made a big difference, even though the crews would've been more likely to fight the alien ship." Baker confessed.

"How do you know he hasn't?" Blomberg suddenly said out loud. "Any of those cruisers could be the Katherine in disguise. Let's face it, the only difference is the shield and weaponry, they could be using one of our shields." Baker beside him, showed real fear as he too came to a conclusion, that this meeting was a trap.

"We've got to get off this ship Blomberg. Wordsworth knows Abbott; he'll wait for this arrogant fool to ask him to surrender giving away his flagship position. It will be the first targeted."

"He's not letting us out of his sight my friend, any ideas?" Blomberg asked, back to whispering.

"Yes, let me do the talking." Baker smiled. Turning he walked back to Abbott.

"How confident are you that the second fleet will back the first if fighting starts?" Baker asked him, keeping his voice down.

"They'll do as they are told General. Why do you ask?"

"I was going to suggest either Blomberg or I go over to the second fleet's flagship and encourage them to do their duty," Baker suggested. Abbott at first was suspicious of Baker's motives. On the other hand, he was secretly worried about what effect Wordsworth's messages were having on the second fleet. Making a decision, he decided to send both Junta members over to the second fleet's flagship. That way he'd be able to make decisions without worrying about their interference.

"Good riddance!" He exclaimed, after the two men had left, making his crew chuckle. "Okay, men lets finish this rebellion."

On board the Katherine, General Wordsworth watched the two fleets form into battle formations. 'So much for peace,' he mused. Secretly he'd hoped his broadcast would've worked, sparing many lives.

"Prepare for the worst Colonel and good luck." Wordsworth radioed Colonel Thompson, on the New Chicago the third fleet's flagship.

"You too Sir. For what it's worth, you did the right thing." The Colonel replied the transmission ending. Simon beside him had been expecting the General's order, ever since Abbott's fleet's arrival in this Galaxy. It was clear from their formation that they've come to fight.

"I judge it's not good news General?" Simon asked, after hearing the General's voice.

"No, they're going to attack us. I'm expecting at any minute to be called.

"Helmsman, move us out ahead of the fleet," Simon instructed Jabo, who was taking his turn at piloting the ship.

"Moving forward Sir." He replied, feeling the power of the ship through his controls.

"You've really fitted in here haven't you?" Wordsworth smiled, watching Ryan monitoring the long-range scanners.

"Yes Sir, even though you've got to watch these mad dogs constantly." Ryan answered. His reply caused an outbreak of hilarity amongst the crew.

"Get serious men!" Radon piped in, hiding a smile, as he settled the crew down, the ship edging forward.

"Once this is over Captain, you could return," Wordsworth whispered.

"I'll think about it General, but here I have a certain freedom, it's refreshing," Ryan answered happily at being part of the crew.

On board Abbott's ship, their commander watched the single cruiser move out of formation accelerating towards them.

"What do you make of that Captain? Why is one ship moving out ahead of the rest?" Abbott asked.

"It could be General Wordsworth's flagship Sir. He might want to parley with you before hostilities breakout." Dominic answered. He too had been watching the cruiser.

"Fat chance of that. Target that ship first, if it is Wordsworth we could end this rebellion with the loss of just that ship." Abbott chuckled. "Now it's time for my broadcast?" He continued, picking up his transmitter. Getting the 'we're ready' signal, from the Comm's Officer, he sent his message.

"This is General Abbott you are in violation of the Junta's orders. Cease all hostilities and drop your shields." He demanded. Several minutes passed when suddenly one of his crewmembers shouted out that the cruiser moving towards them had dropped its shield.

"Well at least one of them has his head screwed on. That's why he moved out ahead of the other ships; he's changing side's right." Abbott suggested as the cruiser continued to close the gap with them.

"Sir the cruiser moving towards us is giving off a different reading to the others." A crewmember shouted.

"In what way?" Abbott asked.

"Its energy readings are all wrong or somehow shielded from our scanners."

"That's impossible none of our ships have that ability."

"Sir I can see writing on her bow. It's the Katherine! And she's charging her weapons!" Captain Dominic hollered. Abbott looked around his bridge and saw real fear at the mention of the Katherine. He knew if he didn't do something positive, the crews of his fleets would panic. His thoughts were suddenly interrupted by a shout.

"General Abbott, we're receiving a message from the Katherine."

"What's it say?"

"We are about to target your flagship, lower your shields or be destroyed."

"General! The second fleet has dropped their shields; they're turning away from the battle." Captain Dominic warned as the crew looked at each other, wondering what was happening.

"We'll deal with those traitors after we finish with these alien monsters. Tell the fleet to open fire on the Katherine, let's finish her than deal with the third fleet." Abbott shouted.

Confusion reigned, as some ships fired, while others hesitated. Still, the combined firepower of even half the fleet was more than impressive. Shielding his eyes, Abbott stared at the brilliant whiteness that was forming where the lasers were concentrated on the last position of the Katherine.

"Burn in Hell you bastards!" He screamed as around him his crew tried to evaluate the damage to the Katherine.

"Sir the enemy is continuing to charge its weapons!" Dominic screamed, as multiple laser blast impacted on his ship.

"Keep firing Captain!" Abbott shouted sweat, making him wipe his brow.

"With what Sir, our laser cannons have all been destroyed, we're sitting ducks!" The bridge grew as silent as the grave, as Abbott unable to make a decision, found himself thrown to the floor as their engines were hit. Trying to climb to his feet, he felt someone kick his legs out from under him. Looking up he saw several figures standing over him, as his sidearm was removed.

"It's over Sir. Stay on the floor, or I'll shoot you." Captain Dominic told his ex-commander, signalling for two guards to come forward. "Watch him, men." He ordered, moving to the Communications controls. "All ships ceasefire immediately Commander Abbott is under arrest." He broadcast to the fleet and the Katherine.

"We can't surrender Dominic they'll hang me for what happened at the last coup attempt." Abbott pleaded.

"That's the problem General. Everyone knows that should've been done years ago." Dominic answered, signalling the guards to take him away, as he picked up the General's discarded Comm's gear. "Can you hear me, General Wordsworth?" He broadcast.

"Yes, Captain we can. I judge you have General Abbott under arrest, what of the other two Junta members?"

"They are on board the second fleet's flagship Sir. I judge by their shields being down they've made their position quite clear."

"Thank you, Captain, you've saved a great many lives today. Let's all head back to New America, we've got a lot of work to do."

"What of the Colonies?" Dominic asked.

"Once democracies has been restored, we will let them decide to be part of New America, or govern themselves. It will be their choice."

"It sounds reasonable Sir. We will now need time to attend to our injured and then repairs to our ship. Did you suffer any casualties?"

"No Captain, but the Katherine certainly shook the shit out of me, I can tell you." The General chuckled, as the three fleets, turned towards home.

THE TRUE MISSION

"Thank you, Captain Hayes. You have helped change the course of our planet's history. If it's for the best, only we can decide, but that's the whole point of freedom isn't it?" General Wordsworth pointed out smiling.

"Despite my misgivings General, you pulled it off and without a major loss of life. For a man who once tried to kill me, I find myself impressed by what you've done."

"Thank you, Captain Hayes. Does that mean Radon and his men, won't hunt me down, for attempting to shoot you?" He chuckled, having heard from Ryan about the vendetta.

"We'll see what happens once there has been an election." Radon replied he too was smiling if you could call it that.

"Well, I take that as a positive sign anyway. What do you plan to do now Simon?" The crew noticed this was the first time Wordsworth had used his name.

"I'm not sure? These events though important, didn't seem to warrant our intervention. True you might've gone to war with the Hedred, but one way or another I couldn't see it affecting the Universe."

"What did your benefactors actually say to you?" Radon and Kate both looked to Simon at Wordsworth's question. Up until this point, none of the crew knew Simon had conversed with the race called The Chosen. Simon not worried about keeping it a secret answered.

"They said we were sent here to save our friends." Some of the crew stood opened mouth being the first time they'd been told that Simon talked to the First.

"A strange message, you'd think they'd have known that we were exactly friends." Wordsworth put forward, as Simon as if struck by lightning, jumped to his feet.

"My God, you're dead right; you're not our friends. Kate, we've misread the message from them. This isn't the reason why we were sent, it is just a small piece of the puzzle."

Then who are our friends?" Radon asked thinking it could be anyone of millions upon millions of Flax Federation and Oregarthian settlements.

"Our families on Oregarth, are our true friends?" Heron admitted, dread in his voice.

"He's right, it makes sense, but there is also Salvation, it has a great many friends of all of us there as well." Simon thundered, angry with himself, wondering which one to travel to first.

"We must open a Portal to Oregarth first. If they're safe there, we can then travel straight to Salvation." Kate suggested sounding worried. Simon saw the fear on his crew's faces. Even though fifty years had passed, the crew's first concern was for their families and friends left behind.

"Then let's not talk about it. General we'll drop you at the village where Johan is rebuilding. We'll say our goodbyes quickly and leave, but remember, we will return to check that your word was honoured and the people live in peace."

"Sounds good Simon, although you must remember, that no one controls the future, even your benefactors, must know that?"

"Set a course for New America, Ryan. We've no time to lose." Simon ordered, as the Katherine rapidly entered a portal leaving the three fleets to continue on their own.

The villager having started to rebuild along the coast from their first village, turned out to see the Katherine leave. Johan made a small speech thanking them for all they'd done. Even Wordsworth echoed Johan's sediment admitting they had saved their planet. Finished their goodbyes Kate and Simon moved to the shuttle to find Benjamin waiting with a bag.

"Mum's much better and dad said it was okay to go if you'll have me."

"Are you sure Benjamin? We may not return for some time, if at all?" Kate pointed out.

"Here I'm just a farmer's son. Out there I'm part of something unimaginable. I want to go."

"Are you okay with that Johan?" Simon asked.

"He's a grown man now. He makes his own way, although his family will miss him." Johan choked out, hugging his son.

"Then let's go then. Time is everything at the moment." Radom reminded them, as with a quick wave to their friends, the shuttle roared into the sky towards the Katherine. On the shuttle, Radon saw Ryan was at the controls.

"You could've stayed Ryan. No one sees you as a traitor now."

"What and miss your constant merriment, no way." Ryan answered, the crew trying hard not to laugh.

"I can be funny?" Radon perplexed replied, causing everyone to muffle their laughter.

OREGARTH

To avoid causing a panic when they exited the portal, Simon opened the portal out in space away from Oregarth. The trip through the portal usually would've taken a week from New America's galaxy. Radon apprehensive insisted that they travel at the ship's maximum speed, ignoring safety concerns. So in just over three days, the Katherine exploded out of the mirror of water, continuing to travel for thousands of miles, before they could slow down.

Turning the Katherine, Simon set a course back to the planet, while the crew scanned the planet. By the time they'd established an orbit, the crew knew the awful truth.

"Oh my God!" Kate sobbed, trying to keep her emotions in check, as many of the crew rushed to the observation deck, to see for themselves what the ship's instruments were already telling them. Below them, belching poisonous gas was the burnt out lifeless husk of Oregarth. Many of the crew joined Kate in shared agony, as they silently stared down at the once thriving peaceful planet.

"What happened here?" Ryan asked as Benjamin stood with him noiselessly, unable to share what their friends were going through.

"I suggest we find out. Everyone, back to your stations now!" Radon ordered, as the crew, coming to their senses, resumed their duties.

"See if you can locate any life forms," Simon ordered getting the crew back to functioning.

"The planet is deserted, Simon. Whatever occurred here, has made the entire population abandon the planet." Radon concluded, although no one knew for sure if the people they left behind even managed to leave.

"I'm getting an energy reading Sir," Ryan shouted, the crew looking his way as if he had given them a glimmer of hope. Swiftly moving to Ryan's console, Simon, Kate and Radon, looked at the power reading flickering across the screen.

"It's the shield we left over the portal base." Radon smiled; hope lighting up his face, where just seconds ago his hard eyes had looked like death.

"We have to get down there Radon. We'll take the shuttle; the Katherine can keep watch, while we're away." Simon suggested as the crew sprang into action.

Horen flew the shuttle, as its small crew waited. Radon had insisted Kate stay aboard in charge, while Simon and Ryan joined Horen and himself on the trip to the old portal base. Many had wanted to come, and some were upset with missing out. Horen had been chosen, because of his medical background, Ryan because he was not emotionally compromised like the others.

"There is still a breathable atmosphere inside the shield Simon. Outside it's poisonous." Ryan informed them, as Horen landed next to the shield. Donning spacesuits the four pressurised them before leaving the shuttle. Walking to the access part in the shield, Simon entered the access code on the pad located there. To his surprise, it opened showing the code hadn't been changed in fifty years.

"Is that a good sign or a bad one?" Radon whispered, as Simon unsure, entered the shielded area. Once inside and the shield door was again closed, they removed their space suits. Looking around they found the portal base had been completely destroyed, yet the shield still functioned.

"Whatever happened here, we know whoever destroyed the base, did it deliberately or the shield too, would be destroyed. That, of course, means that some of our people at least left here alive." Simon exclaimed, feeling if not relieved at least optimistic. Moving further into the base, the four came upon a small park area, with a statue of three figures standing together.

"I don't believe it?" Radon smiled, "That's Simon in the middle, me on the right side and Jeddah on the left."

"You made an impact that's for sure. Who's this Jeddah?" Ryan asked.

"He was the leader of a group of Flax Federation freedom fighters who came to live here with my people. We helped him

overthrow the tyrannical leaders of his race and set his people
free. After elections, he returned his race to democracies,
then returned here to Oregarth to co-exist with my people.
Jeddah was a brave man and one of my closest friends."
Radon admitted out loud, his voice full of emotion.

"Why would you destroy the portal base and leave the
shield intact?" Simon said out loud, walking around the statue.

"Maybe they sought to deny the attackers the portal
technology, yet still shelter here," Horen suggested.

"Well at least we know someone survived, the problem is
where did they go to?" Radon pointed out as across from him
he saw Ryan smiling. "What's so funny Ryan?" Radon clearly
saw nothing funny about what had occurred.

"It's just whoever sculpted this statue must have never seen
Simon. Look at his left ear, it's twice as big as his right and
pointed. Makes him look lopsided?"

"Jeddah knew what Simon looked like. He would never
have allowed that mistake." Radon snapped, as he too looked
up. Seeing the ears were uneven, he was just about to agree
with Ryan, when an idea came to him. Climbing up onto the
statue he peered at Simon's ears before turning the larger
one. Behind them, towards where the portal base had once
stood, the ground caved in revealing a set of stairs. Waking
over to it they found they disappeared down into the darkness.

"Ryan, contact the ship and tell them what we have found.
Don't build their hopes up too much yet." Simon told him,
unsure what they'd find.

"Okay, they received the message. Kate's said to be careful
Simon." Ryan answered, after talking to the ship.

"I always am," Simon replied, the others raising their
eyebrows. Before Simon could take the lead, Radon pushed
past him, followed by Ryan. Simon found himself third, with
Horen watching his back. "You know the Captain usually
leads?" he muttered the others ignoring him.

The passage led down into a dark tunnel. Halting Radon
looked for something to light the way, when without warning
the passageway was bathed in light, causing everyone to draw
their weapons.

"Some type of sensor system," Ryan said nervously out loud, getting smiles from the others, for stating the obvious. Moving in single file, the group continued down for over an hour all the time wondering where the hell they were going. Coming at last to a door the group halted. Radon with great care examined the door.

"There is something familiar about the door'?" He said out loud, looking for any signs of a booby trap. "It's definitely a vacuum sealed door, similar to spaceships airlock," Radon concluded when it him. "I don't believe it? It is the outer door of an Oregarthian battleship!" He gasped, as he searched for the secret release switch that all their battleships had. "What in the Seven Pillars is it doing here?" he exclaimed, mystified by the door, as he continued to search for the latch.

"What are the Seven Pillars?" Ryan asked, watching Radon search.

"It's a large group of mountains on a planet in a Galaxy several thousand light years from here. When we trained to be commanders, we would go there to learn to work as a team, in solving problems. While there we must also try to conquer the heights of the seven mountain ranges located there." Radon answered

"You wouldn't want to be scared of heights?" Ryan answered.

"I have never heard of that problem. Is it common in humans?" Radon asked, wondering if Ryan was having him on.

"Yes, it is. When I was young, it took me many years to get over it." Simon confessed, as Horen, burst into laughter.

"You are scared of heights, yet you command a ship in space? From now on you, humans aren't piloting the ship." Horen exploded, the others joining in. The laughter soon stopped, as with a faint, barely audible click, the door began to slowly slide open.

"Be ready, that door opened far too easily. It must've been opened not too long ago." Radon whispered, leading the group inside.

To Radon and Horen's surprise, it was indeed an Oregarthian battleship. The question was how did it end up underground? Walking down a corridor, which Radon knew from past experience, would lead to the control room, the group kept noise to a minimum. Horen behind Simon had his weapon out covering him when he noticed a light flashing on a small wall display as they passed. Signalling for everyone to stop he examined the console.

"We've triggered some sort of security system," Horen informed them, showing an elevated level of stress.

"I didn't know we had internal security," Radon whispered, watching the passage ahead.

"I have never heard of any of our fleet ever needing one, but we have been gone for a while. Maybe it has something to do with the ship being buried?"

"What do you think the response will be?" Simon enquired, as a feeling of being watched settled over the group.

"Keep moving there's no point in staying here," Horen said softly from the rear, watching behind them. Taking his advice, the group continued forward. They'd been moving for just over twenty earth minutes, when the sound of running feet could be heard approaching, from both in front and behind them.

"Take a defensive position!" Radon barked, shepherding them all into a dead end hallway of the corridor they were following. As if their pursuers were aware of their position, the sound of running feet, stopped.

"Identify yourself!" A guttural voice demanded as everyone remained silent. Radon and Simon stood facing their weapons down the hallway in the direction they were travelling, while Ryan and Horen faced down the hallway behind them. "This is your last chance lay down your weapons, you are vastly outnumbered." The voice repeated its warning. Radon beside Simon suddenly pulled him back behind the wall, as if in shock. Looking at Simon, he suddenly smiled.

"That's not you is it Jeddah?" Radon shouted as an intake of breath could be heard down the corridor.

"Radon is that you?"

"Yes, Jeddah it's me. What's going on, why are you here underground?" Radon yelled back.

"When did you last see me?" A suspicious Jeddah shot back.

"You tried to talk me out of hiding on the Katherine. In hindsight you were right. We were in the Katherine's loading dock." Radon shouted, as one set of feet could be heard hurrying towards them. Walking out into the open, Radon looked down the hallway to see an older version of his friend approach. Both men stood frozen before moving forward giving each other a bear hug.

"You haven't aged at all my friend. Where have you been?" Jeddah asked his emotions bare. Pulled away, Jeddah looked beyond Radon, seeing Simon standing behind him. The shock made him nearly fall backwards. "Simon by all the Gods, I never thought I'd see you again." He confessed rushing forward hugging him too. The group of thirty soldiers behind Jeddah lowered their weapons and approached, as the ones behind Simon's group did the same. To Simon's surprise the soldiers when they saw him, dropped to the floor bowing to him.

"Get up, I am just a man, maybe a strange and young one, but still just a man." Simon angrily exclaimed. Seeing their reaction to his harsh words, he explained "I'm sorry men, it's just I had enough of races pretending to be Gods. I expect to be treated as you would Jeddah." Slowly the soldiers stood, even though their eyes shone with fanatical obedience.

"What is going on here Jeddah why are you hiding?" Radon asked, smiling at Simon's antic.

"We both have much to explain, and most of my men have just left their hibernation chambers, let's move to the bridge," Jeddah suggested as the group moved off, in the direction they'd be travelling in.

Once everyone was in the command centre, Jeddah explained their situation. After the Katherine entered the void, Jeddah's fleet returned to Oregarth. For forty years they lived in peace slowly expanding their settlements. During that time while exploring an underground mineral deposit, one of his mining groups discovered this vast system of tunnels. Lava tubes from prehistoric times had carried liquid magma below the surface. Over hundreds of years, the tubes had cooled leaving enormous perfectly round tunnels.

At the time of course the tunnels were nothing more than a curiosity, but Jeddah had decided to map them for future use as storage areas. They had over the years been forgotten until the first meteor hit. It at first was considered a fluke, a rare happenstance, until a second and third meteor struck, a week and two weeks later. Jarob, still their lead scientist, considered it too exact to be an accident. Knowing the Portal base position was the most protected, he had a tunnel built down to the lava tubes.

Fearing the planet was under attack from an enemy unknown and with only ten armed spaceships, Jeddah called on the Flax Federation for help. Their allies as expected swiftly sent a fleet of a hundred ships to help their neighbours. They remained on station for several months reporting nothing out of the usual. With no enemy activity, the Flax's seeing no reason to maintain the fleet's presence, recalled it, promising to send assistance if it was needed again. Four days after their departure, several meteors were spotted approaching.

Loading everyone aboard three warships for safety, the other ships scrambled to intercept the incoming objects. The meteors were massive, far larger than the first ones encountered. One, unfortunately, got through, severely damaging the planet. It hit a fault line in the planet's crust, punching a hole, deep into the planet's core. This released poisonous gases into the atmosphere. Seeing the planet could no longer support life, Jeddah decided to abandon the planet and move to another location.

Jarob suspicious of the enemy's motives, thinking they might be walking into a trap, suggested an alternative plan. Taking one of the Oregarthian battleships, he had it flown down a Lava tunnel. Once inside and below the Portal base, he had the tunnel entrance blocked. He then had the population secretly moved down into the buried ship via a tunnel from the Portal shielded area.

Adrian now over seventy, volunteered to command the fleet, pretending they were leaving with the whole population on board. Jeddah had wanted to command the ships himself, but Adrian insisted he stay with the people to keep order. The plan was to travel for three days away from the planet, if they encounter no trouble, they would return and pick up the population.

Clearing the planet, the fleet headed out into space. Two days into the journey a fleet of unknown ships overhauled them. Even with skeleton crews aboard, the nine ships fought well, destroying twenty enemy ships. In the end, outnumbered three to one, they were overwhelmed, all nine ships were destroyed. The victorious enemy fleet had then prepared to land near the Portal base and seize it.

Jeddah, having laid charges, remotely detonated the portal base. This to the enemy appeared to have been planned by the departing ships before they left. With the shield still in place the enemy could look in at the damage, but without the code, they couldn't enter. The deception seemed to work, as the ships left, to take up station above the planet. Jeddah now faced the real threat that the enemy ships might detect their presence.

Having a limited amount of food and no alternative transport, the population of nearly six thousand was forced to enter hibernation chambers onboard the buried ship. There they waited for a sign that the enemy ships had left and it was clear to leave.

Jeddah believed the Flax Federation had sent ships several times to find out what had occurred. From their observation post in the shielded area on the surface, they'd seen an exchange of weapons fire. Who won remained a mystery, and to show themselves would give away their position so they'd continued to remain hidden. Jeddah, in the end, had with Jarob's help constructed an early warning system, which allowed them to sense intruders inside their ship. With this in place, the whole crew had entered hibernation, leaving their chambers only to do scheduled maintenance or in an emergency. It was Radon's group's entry, which had awoken them.

"Why wait so long Jeddah? You've been here nearly ten years." Simon wanted to know why they hadn't left.

"That was because of me." A voice answered behind them, as Jarob entered the bridge. Simon noticed that Jarob had aged quite a bit since last he'd seen him. After greetings were exchanged Jarob explained. "Like you Simon, a voice told me to remain hidden. It didn't say you would return, but it promised if we remained hidden we'd be found in time. Like you I was sceptical, but it also mentioned the trap, so when Adrian was ambushed, I knew the voice was real."

"So now you know what happened here, what is your story, Simon?" Jeddah asked, his crew behind him silently waiting to hear where Simon had been. He then spent over an hour telling them what had occurred since leaving them at the border of the void.

"That's it? You were healed and slept for fifty years; until you were awoken in time to stop an Alien race and the planet New America from going to war? It doesn't sound like much for fifty years?" Jeddah pointed out, his crew smiling at his downplaying of their adventure.

"There was one other thing, the Hedred race left their original planet, after being attacked by meteors," Simon told him.

"Did they know who the enemy was?" Jeddah growled, knowing it was too much of a coincidence.

"They called themselves the Roax!" Radon answered as a storm of noise erupted.

"This cannot be! You sent the rebel Roax to their deaths on Duelong." Jeddah exclaimed, having heard it from Radon.

"We're not completely sure yet, although a photo we obtained from the Hedred though not perfect, showed a young version of Elena and Rile, two of the Roax leaders we sent to Duelong. This could be a deliberate attempt to deceive us by another group, but I doubt it." Simon himself was convinced.

"It's them, Simon. The use of meteors could be just a coincidence, but the Roax hate us for destroying their rebellion on Salvation. I'd say these attacks against Oregarth, are reprisals, that's why there is no communications or threats from them." Jeddah too was convinced that their old enemy had returned.

"We must find them and this time make sure they are never a threat again." Radon spat out, the others agreeing.

While Jeddah started the process of waking his people, Simon returned to the Katherine. News that most of the population had survived the attack was greeted with jubilation. The confirmation that the Roax were most probably the enemy responsible was met with disbelief. The first priority was to move the people to a safe planet. After discussions with Radon and Jeddah, it was decided to move the people to Pathalong.

This was the planet, where Simon had first encountered Radon's people. They'd crossed a Galaxy to return Radon to his race, after being trapped on Salvation. While looking for them, they had been discovered by a fleet from the Flax Federation. At the time the Flax and Oregarthians were deadly enemies. The Oregarthians having taken massive losses were at the time in the process of leaving the known Universe. With support from Simon, the Oregarthians managed to defeat the Flax Federation fleet, causing it to retreat.

The Oregarthians unsure if another fleet would arrive continued with their plans leaving the Universe. Radon with a group of his supporters, stayed behind to continue with Simon on the Katherine. They were just about to leave when a Flax cruiser contacted them. Jeddah, a Flax Federation Captain at the time had disobeyed orders and stayed behind to rescue stranded crews. Having limited resources, he had asked Simon for help in saving the trapped crews. Although still not trusting them, Simon's crews with Radon's help had freed them. From then on Radon and Jeddah had been firm friends.

The planet although not as hospitable as Oregarth, had several oceans and a breathable atmosphere. Simon remembered it had some savage creatures, but he figured they'd cope. By using the portal, Simon calculated they could move six thousand people in three trips, the Katherine, of course, being much smaller than the battleship. Jeddah was dead against leaving anyone behind.

He was convinced the Roax were still watching the planet and might know the Katherine had returned. Simon throwing the discussion over to the whole crew, asked did anyone have an idea? Strangely Benjamin came up with it. Looking at the planet while in orbit, Benjamin had used the microwave transmitters array, to locate the buried Battleship. The array was usually used for communications, but he had adapted it to scan the surface.

Going over the footage, he noticed a fissure in the planet's crust behind the ship. Although it was still buried the amount of soil between the rear of the ship and this new fissure was only a few hundred metres thick. He suggested with the use of its weapons a hole might be pushed through to the fissure allowing the ship to break free. The room at first hearing his idea remained quiet until Radon jumping from his chair lifted Benjamin above his head laughing.

"One thing I'll say about you humans, you can just about solve anything!" He roared as the others joined in.

"I hate to burst your bubble people, but our guns face forward, and to the side, they don't shoot backwards." Jeddah pointed out, silencing the celebration.

"They don't have to," Simon explained. "We fly the Katherine down and vaporise the soil behind her while her shields are deployed. We should be able to monitor the battleship's shield, so we don't penetrate her hull."

"Okay, it's worth a try. Let's get moving we don't know if we're going to have company." Radon insisted, picking up Jeddah's unease.

After considering Benjamin's idea Simon brought the Katherine down beside the portal base. He had at first thought to fly down inside the fissure and fire horizontally. The chances were the Katherine's power laser might this way destroy the battleship before they could stop it. Instead, he lined the Katherine up above the fissure cutting sections from behind the ship, like slices of cake.

It was slow work, as with each vertical slash the Katherine would then have to move slightly to fire back at the cut piece, which would cause it to collapse. Three hours had passed, and of the three hundred metres to cut, one hundred still remained.

"Simon we've got something coming towards the planet!" Kate warned. She had volunteered to watch the long-range scanner while they worked on the cutting. Tense seconds followed as they all waited for Kate to identify the object.

"It's a large meteor. I calculate it will impact with the portal base!" She warned.

"Can we stop it with our weapons?" Radon shouted watching Simon cut another slice away.

"No it's massive. The computer has calculated it's two thousand metres across." Kate sounded scared.

"How long till it impacts?" Simon yelled, his eyes never leaving the laser.

"One hundred and forty-two Earth minutes."

"How far have we got to go?" Radon whispered to Simon.

"Should we evacuate who we can Simon?" Horan asked relaying what was happening to Jeddah, who was on board the battleship. Simon kept cutting while everyone waited for him to answer. Pointing to Radon, he had him take over.

"We haven't got the time to evacuate and keep cutting. If we go for the people, we won't rescue them all. On the other hand, if we keep cutting, I don't think we'll make it in time. I'm open to suggestions." Some looked to Benjamin.

"How strong is the battleship? Can it help push its way out?" He asked.

"It's risky, and before your idea of cutting it out, I had thought about it. Maybe a combination of both is what we need?" Simon considered. Horen passing on what they had discussed to Jeddah waited.

On board, Jeddah was just getting over the news that a meteor was coming when Horen told him what they wanted to try. Looking around at the gathered people he knew they had no choice.

"Captain, prepare to get under way, fire the forward thrusters, back us up." He ordered.

On the bridge of the Katherine, Benjamin watched the battleship push into the earthen wall that entombed it. Although it had deployed its shield, it had little effect, as it was crushed between the ship and the soil that held it tightly. Since Kate's announcement that the meteor was on its way, half the time had passed.

"For God's sakes come on," Benjamin said out loud, as Simon dropped another piece of the barrier into the fissure.

"How many metres remain?" Radon asked Simon. Benjamin for the first time heard a hint of fear in Radon's voice.

"Less than fifty metres Radon. Tell Jeddah there's no time, push harder. Simon confessed, moving the laser to just behind the ship's position. This time he cut a much larger piece, trying to loosen it just behind the sub.

Jeddah felt the groan shudder through the battleship as he told the Captain to give it everything, as they all looked at the clock.

"It's going to be close. Bring the ship to battle stations." Jeddah roared above the groan of metal, galvanising the crew. 'Did it just move?' Jeddah said to himself, wondering if he just imagined it, as a change in the engine heralded movement. "It's working!" He screamed relaying it to Horen.

"Jeddah just confirmed they're moving!" Horen shouted as a scream went up from the crew. Simon nodding he'd heard, ran to the Portal controls. He was in the process of entering the co-ordinates of Pathalong, when the proximity warning sensors sounded a collision warning, as the meteor came into plain sight above the planet.

"Go, we can't wait," Simon yelled, ordering Radon at the helm to enter the forming portal. Fear gripped them all as the ship began to tremble. This was caused by shock waves from the meteor striking the atmosphere, reverberated through the hull. Radon at the controls didn't hesitate. Ramming the power control forward the Katherine leapt forward into the portal.

On the battleship, Jeddah felt the shudder. His ship was already at full power pushing thousands of tons of soil and debris into the fissure, as the ship free, accelerated. Blinded by the cloud of dust, Jeddah felt the ship break free, its speed rapidly increasing. Holding his breath, knowing the Katherine was gone, fear touched him as shockwaves of the meteors, impact with the planet's surface, throwing everyone to the deck.

The ship's shield took the first shockwave, although the ship still rolled over onto its left side. This caused the disorientated crew and passengers to be catapulted into a tangled pile, on the side of the vessel.

"This is it." Jeddah murmured to himself, wishing his wife and children were with him on the bridge. He'd wanted them here with him, but so did every member of the crew. He'd set an example and had them wait in the cabin, till they'd broken free of the tunnel. He'd then ordered everyone else to do the same. Now with death upon them, he'd have given anything to have them with him. Closing his eyes, he prayed that Simon would bring them revenge preparing for the end, as screams filled the air.

Opening his eyes, startled by the screaming, he brushed aside his misgivings. Looking around the slanted ship, he tried to think of something that would instil some sense of order.

"Be brave men! Remember what we stand for!" He shouted, as the panic that had gripped the crew subsided. Many he saw were hurt in the violent scramble to save themselves from what they saw as certain death. Now after his words the crew focused on their training, helping the injured and returning to their stations. 'Good now what' he smiled to himself, when it occurred to him, that they were all still be alive. 'We should be dead' he realised, as the ship continued to turn over, bucking wildly.

Getting to his feet, he saw the Captain was at the controls, steadying the ship. As he brought the ship back onto an even keel, Jeddah seeing the debris had gone from the scanners, looked backwards out the front of the ship. There through a watery hole, Jeddah watched Oregarth, disintegrate into a burning ball of flames.

"My God we're in the portal." He exclaimed, as his crew gathered to stare out the front of their ship.

"Jeddah how is it possible?" His captain asked, many falling to their knees, seeing it as a miracle.

"Simon deployed the Portal right behind us. When we reversed out of the tunnel, we went straight into it." Jeddah laughed, still having trouble believing he was alive.

"Can we turn the ship in a portal?" His Captain asked.

"I'm not sure, I know you can't change your direction once you've entered. But then again, I've never heard of anyone entering backwards, so let's give it a try." Jeddah smiled, leaving the bridge to find his family.

Simon with the rest of the crew stood watching the portal. They'd been in orbit around Pathalong for three days, and like everyone else he was worried.

"They should've been here by now?" Radon whispered beside him, his voice becoming gravelly as his emotions made his speech hard to understand through his two rows of teeth.

"They went in backwards. If they couldn't turn around, it would be a slow trip with just reverse thrusters." Simon pointed out.

"We could've waited a little longer?" Kate suggested upset at abandoning them.

"No Kate, Simon was right to leave, if we'd have waited, both ships would've collided as we entered the portal." Radon explained, still, a sense of guilt hung over the crew.

"Captain, there's something moving at high speed in the portal, it should be visible shortly, but I'd say it's a ship," Horen yelled from his station, as the crew sprung to battle stations.

"Raise the shield just in case," Radon ordered as Simon moved to stand behind Horen looking at the image.

"It's an Oregarthian battleship! Jeddah's made it!" Simon yelled, the crew joining in. To their front with a flurry of debris the battleship came into view.

"Hope you all haven't been waiting long?" Jeddah's voice boomed out of their communication speakers.

"We're glad to hear from you Jeddah. Now how about taking us down to our new home?" Radon replied, his voice again calm and controlled.

"I know just the place," Jeddah answered leading the two ships down.

They landed now in the valley, where the once invincible Flax fleet's survivors, had landed their crippled ships. The undamaged ships had fled, leaving Jeddah to rescue the doomed crews and land them here. With Simon's help at the time they'd managed to rebuild twenty ships and head home.

Once the two ships had found suitable landing sites, Radon had ordered a complete sweep of the area to make sure no unfriendly surprises awaited them. Except for the occasional local inhabitant, nothing too dangerous was discovered so with Simon's approval the people crowded aboard Jeddah's ship were allowed to disembark. Housing in the meantime was easy as there were over thirty damaged Flax warships on the surface.

Food, of course, was scarce, so the first task was for groups of volunteers to go out hunting. Game was in great numbers, and it wasn't long before cooking fires appeared all over the area. At a service held that first night for the fallen, Radon and Jeddah noticed Simon seemed withdrawn. After the celebrations had got into full swing, they approached Simon.

"You don't seem happy Simon? Is everything okay?" Radon asked as Kate joined them.

"He's worried the Roax will follow us here," Kate said softly, not wanting the others to hear.

"Do you think they have a portal like we do?" Radon asked, as both men inadvertently looked to the sky.

"Yes, it would explain a great deal. Remember how I explained, how I sent a meteor through a portal to confuse a New America fleet. I also wanted to know if it was possible. These attacks on planets would mean someone steered meteors, in a direction he wanted them to go. With a portal, all you do is line up the meteor and open the portal on a path to the target. It would also explain how no one has seen the enemy ships."

"Then we are not safe here." Jeddah put forward, looking at his people.

"Unless they follow us through our own portal, they would have to find this planet first. I'd suggest no radio chatter from this location, it could help them track us." Simon pointed out.

"So what do we do?" Kate whispered.

"First we check Salvation. If they're safe, we will try to get a portal going for them. Once they're secure, we will find a planet and set a trap for the Roax. It's about time we settled with them!"

PLANET SALVATION

The trip through the portal to Salvation was clouded with a sense of pessimism. Radon kept his thoughts to himself, but Simon could see guilt in his eyes for going to Oregarth first. Many had concluded that Salvation would've been the Roax's first target, now they knew Elena and Rile were the suspected leaders of the enemy forces. The two had been humiliated on Salvation during their failed coup attempt, and they were not the type to forgive and forget.

The crew knew their loyalties to their families on Oregarth had made them travel there first, at the expense of Salvation. Accompanying them on this trip, were Jeddah and 500 of his troops. Simon had wanted him to stay on Pathalong in case there was trouble, but he'd hear none of it. Instead, Jarob had been put in command, having orders to flee in the battleship, if anything came in range.

Before they'd left, Radon had sent a message to the Flax Federation asking for help. Although no answer was received, Jeddah was confident his people would come to their aid.

"Captain Simon Hayes, we're approaching the portal exit point." One of Jeddah's men manning the sensor array formally told him. Despite Simon's best efforts to make them part of the crew they still treated him as a saviour, making Jeddah and the other smirk at his discomfort.

"Captain will do soldier or even better Simon." He reminded him, turning to Radon. "Battle stations let's be ready." He ordered as the crew manned their weapons. Like on Oregarth they exited above the planet, this time coming to a stop without overshooting.

"Any sign of life?" Simon asked watching the monitor.

"No Sir. Although my sensors are picking up low levels of radiation over the whole planet."

"That doesn't sound good." Kate whispered beside Simon, as a hush fell over the bridge.

"The land surface shows no structures at all. The computer has compared the landscape against its historical files. It believes that huge tidal waves have crossed the entire land continent." Radon explained.

"Keep searching people I won't leave to we're sure no one is down there. And let's find out when all this occurred if we can." Simon requested, his voice betraying his concern.

After hours of analysing the data, Simon's crew had worked out what had occurred. As Wordsworth had told them, his president had exploded a nuke inside the portal base's shield. Not only did it destroy the base, but it also triggered meltdown in its thermal reactor, causing a massive underwater explosion. As the planet only had a small percentage of land, the blast caused huge tidal waves that swamped the landmass. All agreed that no one could've survived those waves.

The only glimmer of hope that anyone survived was a sign of agriculture around the old port of New Vancouver. The wreckage of several submarines could be seen at the port showing someone might have survived the tidal waves at sea. If the radiation occurred from the portal explosion or later would remain a mystery, as no one could be certain. The only good news was the Roax hadn't been responsible, for this disaster.

"I see no reason to stay any longer. Best we leave." Simon suggested. Seeing everyone was in agreement, he moved to the portal control. Punching in the coordinates of their next destination, he watched the portal form in front of the ship. Simon was just about to give the command to proceed when Ryan shouted from the Comm's station.

"Simon I've got something!" Simon in response shut down the portal.

"What have you got?"

"I just picked up a weak signal from under the ocean on the opposite side of the planet to us. I wouldn't have heard it, except I was listening to see if any sea life survived. I've got a thing for whales, I'd heard there were some on Salvation, New America has none."

"Are you sure it wasn't just background noise or some sort of sea creature?" Radon asked hiding a smile, at Ryan's search for the mammals.

"No it was two, I say humans talking. One a male said, 'They're leaving through a portal'. The other, a female, told him to 'shut up and remain silent'. That's definitely an intelligent life form." Ryan explained.

"Why are they hiding from us?" Simon wondered.

"Let's go ask them." Kate smiled, as Radon headed for their coordinates.

Arriving right at the stop where the transmissions had been picked up, the ship's sensors spotted two old earth submarines sitting on the ocean floor. They were giving off no radiation or electronic signatures, meaning everything was turned off on board.

"What do we do now? Apparently they're hiding from us." Ryan pointed out.

"Try calling them on the same frequency, they must be monitoring each other," Jeddah suggested.

"My name is Captain Simon Hayes. I am on board the Katherine above your position, can you hear me?" Simon broadcast then waited. Five minutes passed before he retransmitted. Another five minutes passed with no answer.

"Look if I meant you harm, I would've acted by now. Surely you have heard of the Katherine, even though we've been away for fifty years."

"What was the name of your father's best friend when you lived on Salvation?" A female voice sounded, through their Comms gear.

"My father died when I was young. I lived with my grandfather, his name was Mike, and his best friend was named John."

"Is it really you Captain Hayes?" Came an excited voice, as the two subs powered up, rising to the surface.

"Yes, it is. Who is this?"

"My name is Katy, my father named me after Kate, your wife. Simon looked to Kate, knowing they hadn't still got around to getting married.

"How have you survived so long?"

"We exist on a diet of seafood and seaweed. We refresh our air supply through special filters, although we're nearly out of them."

"Why are you hiding?"

"That's a long story. Have you a means of transporting us aboard. The air outside although it wouldn't kill us is far from safe."

"We have a couple of shuttles; we'll send them down immediately," Simon told her, as Radon, already moving ordered his men to help.

Although both subs could've held ten thousand people, there were only five hundred on each. Katy who was in command was brought straight to the bridge, while room was found for the survivors.

"My God it's beautiful." Katy smiled, looking out into space from the ship's observation deck. Moving closer, she looked down at the two tiny subs, sitting forlornly on the ocean surface. "I'd thought we'd all die aboard those two tombs." She confessed wiping her eyes. Simon noticed how undernourished she looked. Signalling to Horen, he told him to check out the others and make sure they had something to eat immediately.

Going to a small food locker, Simon brought her what they called an energy bar. Without a word, she gobbled it down.

"Thank you. Where is Captain Hayes?" She asked.

"I am Captain Hayes."

"You can't be him; he's an old man by now." She replied.

"That too is a long story. Now how about telling me your story Katy?" Simon asked, sitting down with her.

About fifty years ago, her father John, and Ileana were preparing to visit New Russia. With the trouble with New America, the UN wanted to explain why they were locking New America out of the portal system. For safety, an escort ship was also going. Having the new shields that Simon had given them, made them slightly superior to the other planet's ships, meaning two subs was sufficient. They had just left port when an explosion rocked the two subs.

Deploying their shields, both subs dived to the bottom till they found out what the explosion was. When they came to the surface four hours later, it was all over. Going to the surface, they tried to contact their base at New Vancouver. Receiving nothing from the base, they instead received several transmissions from damaged and crippled subs.

Ordering everyone who could hear them to either meet back at their base or stay where they were, they sailed for home. Arriving back at New Vancouver their homeport, they found total devastation. Everyone who had been on land was gone there were no survivors. While there searching five other subs had limped into port.

Since the trouble with the other Gun Barrel planets, the naval forces of the UN on Salvation had been greatly increased. This meant there was a chance that many other subs may have survived. Suspending rescue efforts on land, knowing it was pointless; John instead sent out all the seaworthy subs to look for the other submarines. Thirty were known to be at sea at any time giving some hope that many may have survived. Four were known to have been guarding the portal entry point near the portal base. Since the explosion originated there, the chances were they hadn't survived.

Splitting up John's two subs and two others from the group that had arrived, they started a grid search along the known subs' patrol routes. For two weeks they searched, finding four more boats with crews still alive. All had to be rescued from the ocean floor, their engines gone. The others were never found. They stopped searching after that, as air supplies after two weeks without power, would've been exhausted. In the end, they had nine subs and four thousand people.

The great majority of the crews were young although like John the senior staff were older. The first line of business was to find food and water and treat the injured. With the oceans again settled, rain supplied their water requirements. Food was plentiful in the sea, though all land-based food except birds had ceased to exist.

For the next year, they cleared land, planting crops from the seeds they gathered from all over the land, and seed stocks carried on the subs. Vegetables and fruit had up until then, been supplemented with seaweed and other ocean growing plants. Now as the crops grew, they went back to eating them. For forty years they built from scratch never giving up, hoping one of the other worlds would find them.

Worried by the blast that caused the initial damage, John searched for a place to fortify in case another attack was launched. One of the subs by accident found a suitable base. While searching for seaweed and other plant life along the southern shoreline, the sub discovered an underground base. From the equipment found there, it was believed that the New Russia Planet's naval forces had built it. Constructed of concrete with a submerged entrance, it had survived the tidal waves unscratched.

Why they'd built, it would remain a secret, but to John, it was their panic room. With room for four subs and a massive storage area, it became their fall back in case of attack. Over the years that followed, silos for food and water were constructed, and the excess food was stored there. All sub commanders were given the location verbally; there were no maps to indicate its existence.

John decreed that no one should discuss the base over open lines, only in coded messages was it mentioned. To all intense and purpose, New Vancouver was there home and always would be. John and Ileana in this time had two children Simon and Katy. Both John and Ileana passed away about twenty years ago, leaving Simon, her brother in charge.

Six years ago, one of their subs was patrolling, the southern ocean, when it spotted a portal. Rushing to the site, they excitedly transmitted the information to New Vancouver. It was the last message sent by the sub, it was never heard from again. Suspecting foul play, Simon ordered all the ships to stock up on supplies, sending two subs to investigate. While the two boats searched, the other six subs loaded all food and water they could carry.Then along with all their people, they moved to the base.

His caution proved warranted when the two subs found wreckage from the first sub. It had been destroyed by laser fire it was no accident. While there, the subs encountered a huge spacecraft about to enter a portal. Becoming aware of the subs, it immediately attacked. Both subs' shields were up this time and proved more than a match for the ship. Although they seriously damaged the spaceship, it fled, escaping back into a portal.

After six months in hiding, the people tired of living underground, insisted they be allowed to return to New Vancouver. Against Simon's better judgment, he accepted the majority's decision and ferried them back to New Vancouver. To be safe, he left two subs on guard near where the portal had opened. Life over the next few months returned to normal.

Katy a year later was in command of two subs, on watch, where the portal had opened. They'd been there only three days when a distress call was sent from New Vancouver. The message stated that they were under attack from space. Rushing back at full speed they arrived seven hours too late. The entire area was aflame. Every sub there had been destroyed at the docks, no one in them survived. The only other sub out at sea was on a fishing expedition. When it transmitted it was under attack, Katy ordered her two ships to dive and head for the base, observing radio silence.

For another month the alien ships scoured the planet looking for survivors. In the hidden base, the remaining two crews waited. Desperate for information, Katy in command, travelled back to New Vancouver in one sub. Remaining submerged a small party waded ashore to search. To her amazement she found hundreds hiding in the ruins. Near starving and many needing medical care, she had the sub nose into the docks and pick them up. In was a tense time as to avoid detection, the sub was running on minimum power, and could not deploy its shield.

Luckily the alien ships had left, so with another quick look around for survivors, they departed. The reason why so many survived was because of her brother Simon. He was on board one of the subs when their sensors picked up a fleet of ships entering Salvation atmosphere. Raising the shield, he ordered all weapons to fire. This alerted the people on land to flee. Several of the alien ships were hit in the exchange, one crashing. Simon's action caused the spaceships to concentrate their fire on the subs, giving some others a chance to escape.

One survivor remembered looking back and seeing all the subs being bombarded, till with a gigantic flash the subs vanished below the surface. By the time they arrived back at the base, the population had gone from around nine thousand to one thousand. Despair, anger and grief filled the hidden base, as they came to grips with what had occurred.

They had remained in hiding fearing to leave the base in case the aliens returned. In the end, another problem forced them out. The last sub to be destroyed had ruptured its reactor. A cloud of deadly radiation had been released into the atmosphere. Picking up the rise in radiation levels as the wind carried it towards the base, Katy ordered all food stocks and the remaining people aboard the two subs.

Deciding to give the radiation a year to disperse, they'd taken the subs down deep, sitting on the bottom, hoping in time to return to the base. It was then that Simon's portal had opened. Expecting the worst, they turned off all equipment and played dead, hoping they'd remain hidden. Unfortunately or luckily someone seeing the portal open again had broadcast to Katy's boat that the aliens were leaving, both a mistake and a blessing.

"Any idea, what race the alien ships belonged too?" Simon enquired after she was finished.

"No, but they were huge, far bigger than this ship, maybe ten times larger." Simon worked out that would make them larger than Ceb's ships. "Now I've finished, can you explain why the woman I am named after, is younger than me," Katy asked, seeing Kate sitting across from Simon.

"Are you kidding you've all been asleep!" Katy exploded.

"It's a bit more complicated than that, but yes," Simon answered sheepishly.

"Dad said you were most probably dead. He also said he wouldn't believe it till he saw your body. I for one thought you were a ghost sent to scare people, to keep them on the straight and narrow. You didn't even get married, and that's part of the legend."

"Well, that's something we will have to change." Kate giggled from the side, watching Simon go red.

"You're lucky Simon. In our culture copulating without being bonded together is shameful." Jeddah explained, causing the whole room to go silent. "Did I say something wrong?"

"I think it's the same with their race too Jeddah." Radon replied chuckling at his friend's mistake, as Katy, for so long she couldn't remember, burst into uncontrollable laughter.

Simon curious and cautious at the same time had the Katherine remain in orbit, while he with Radon, Jeddah, Ryan and Katy took the shuttle back down to New Vancouver. Simon wanted to look at the crashed alien ship. Following Katy's directions, they found the ship hidden to the north of the destroyed port. When it had crashed, the ship had dived into a deep canyon, making it hard to locate. As she had said, the ship was enormous, by far the largest spaceship Simon had encountered. The damage to the ship was extensive giving no clue to the race's identity.

Radiation levels were fractionally too high, negating a more detailed physical search. This meant, for now, the mystery of Katy's people's attackers remained unknown. Knowing staying any longer was fruitless, they returned to the Katherine.

"Did you find anything useful?" Kate asked upon their return.

"No, although we know the ships were huge and of an advanced design, we know little else about them," Simon answered.

"Where to now?"

"Back to Pathalong, I don't think that planet's safe."

Despite his misgivings, when they returned to Pathalong, they found no sign of trouble. Meeting with Jeddah, his officers and the Katy's and her officers, Simon with his team, discussed their next move. Jeddah, like Simon, thought it more than a coincidence that the Roax attacked as soon as Simon arrived. If they had been watching the planet Oregarth, surely they would've spotted them leaving before the planet was destroyed. The next question was, did they know they'd travelled to Pathalong?

After debating the problem for some time, Simon put forward the idea that Jeddah's people should travel to the Flax Federation for protection. By travelling there by ordinary propulsion instead of using the portal, they would take about two months. Since there were many routes they could take, their course would be near impossible to follow or intercept, giving Simon a chance to find the Roax.

"Wouldn't it be better to just stay here and keep alert?" One of Jeddah's officers asked.

"Even if you keep the ship button up and ready to fly, the Roax could still surprise you. By opening a portal in a neighbouring Galaxy, they could send the meteor there first. Then by opening another portal to this planet, they could send it here, giving you no advanced warning at all. To launch, let alone load your people aboard, would further delay you. No, as much as it's a major discomfort, I would still suggest moving. Even now we risk an attack." Simon explained many nodding.

Putting it to a vote, the group unanimously decided to leave Pathalong. Jeddah reluctantly volunteered to captain the ship, as long as Simon took a contingent of his troops aboard the Katherine for training.

"At least this time the population of Oregarth won't have to enter hibernation chambers, as food, water and oxygen supplies are now sufficient for several months of space travel," Jeddah confessed, accepting his captaincy, but still wanting to go with his friends.

"Our time apart will go quickly Jeddah. A lot faster than our last trip." Radon assured him.

"Let us hope so Radon. And this time keep awake and out of trouble." Jeddah smiled the group breaking up.

Loading began immediately, while lots were drawn for positions on the Katherine. Jeddah wanting the experience of travelling on the Katherine passed on to all his men, allowed them to hold a ballot, to rotate his men aboard Simon's ship. Katy's people, most who needed care, would travel with Jeddah's on his ship with his people.

Only Katy and twenty of her senior military people would remain aboard. Many were unhappy with leaving, but the Katherine was not a large ship and had limited accommodation. In the end, just over a thousand travelled aboard, and space was tight.

"You and Jeddah always want as many soldiers as we can carry Radon. I'm amazed you didn't bring armour vehicles as well?" Simon smiled.

"We would've, except the shuttle bay has two shuttles in it, unlike when we went to Salvation, and that time we were right. Let's face it Simon, where you go there is always action. Someday we'll need a bigger ship." Radon chuckled.

"Maybe you're right Radon; maybe we do need a bigger ship. I'll see what I can do." Simon answered smiling. Radon was momentarily caught off guard by Simon's answer. Simon usually wasn't cryptic in his answers. Getting over it, he moved on.

"What is your plan for the Roax?"

"We find another planet and set a trap. Then we follow these monsters home."

THE TRAP

Simon stood on the bridge staring out at the endlessness of the portal. They'd been travelling for over a week, leaving Pathalong, to travel to the other side of the Universe. The Hedred's home planet was situated in a Galaxy with several hospitable planets. Although they had colonised some, the arrival of the Roax had made them look further afield for a new home. Ceb had given Simon several addresses, one, in particular, he found attractive.

Colinar was a moon the size of earth, orbiting a large waterless planet in a neighbouring solar system, with a dwarf Sun. Although it wasn't perfect, it suited Simon's needs being completely isolated. The Hedred had built an underground city completely run by solar energy. When the first meteor attacks had been launched by the Roax, this moon had remained silent, avoiding detection.

Ceb had during the years of servitude that followed with the treaty with the Roax, moved many of his people here. Hiding them below ground, they were kept hidden, while he readied his fleet. They were his backup plan, in case the Roax decided to exterminate them all before they had time to leave the home planet. Luck was with them, and once the exodus of the Hedred main planet began, Ceb had dispatch ships to pick them up.

Abandoning the underground city, they joined their kin leaving for a new life in a distant Universe. During Simon's trip to Sallong, with Ceb, the Hedred leader had told them that the city could sustain a population of twenty thousand people. It would've been the perfect place for Jeddah's people to hide from the Roax, or so Simon hoped it would appear.

Landing the Katherine next to the abandoned city, Radon swiftly sent search teams throughout the city, making sure it was truly deserted. Finding no signs of intelligent life, Simon put his plan into action. While the crew busied themselves turning on every electric appliance they could find, Simon set up a powerful transmitter. Sending out a coded message twice a day, in every direction, he added his name in clear into each.

It took the crew over a week to turn on enough lights and electric devices to make a heat signature that would indicate a large population was living there. Satisfied he then had everyone reboard the Katherine. Moving to the main dead planet that Colinar orbited, Simon hid the ship in a deep canyon. Deploying their shield, which electronically made them invisible, they waited.

For over a month, they remained in hiding, many finding it hard to combat boredom. Simon and Kate kept busy always together, enjoying the time in a way the other single members couldn't. The crew gave them their space letting them have this special time, while they drilled. Radon knew that many of the crewmembers especially Benjamin and Ryan and Katy's men hadn't been in combat with them. Ryan he knew had experience, but not on the Katherine.

Because of their increased crew numbers, Radon made a suggestion. It was to train each member to have a working knowledge of all areas of the ship. Getting permission from Simon he had all the new members put through a rigorous training program.

While Radon put the crew through their paces, Horen watched from the sidelines. He had never seen such high levels of fitness and stamina in either Flax or Oregarthian crews. When the Katherine had sailed into the void, Radon and thirty men had hidden aboard. On New America, he had seen the difference in these men in combat. Now with a crew of over a thousand members from Jeddah's group, he watched for the differences.

When they first entered the portal leaving Pathalong he'd seen how sluggish Jeddah's men were compared to the originals. After a time they had reached parity before returning to Pathalong. Those soldiers had now left, replaced by new soldiers. Now they were the same, as were Ryan, Benjamin and Katy's men. He knew there could only be one conclusion, whatever was affecting them, was here on the ship, not as they thought carried out in the void.

On New America when he and his men had held the village, their heightened strength and speed had allowed them to outfight and outperform the enemy troops. Towards the end of the siege, he'd noticed he was slowing down as if he was being drained of his strength. Once back on board his health had bounced back, making him feel all-powerful.

He found it in some ways worrying that the ship itself affected them making them more than they were. Yet despite his misgivings their strength and fitness had made them fighting machines, saving them from having casualties. That wouldn't always be the case, sometimes casualties occurred no matter how good you were, but it was something positive to think about he mused.

Simon rolled over awakening from a sound sleep. Through his half-opened eyes, he watched the rise and fall of Kate's breast as she lay next to him. 'How much more could a man love a woman,' he smiled thanking God for giving him a life with Kate. Aroused he felt the need to wake her when in the distance the sound of a klaxon horn belched out it's warning. His needs forgotten, Simon surged out of bed swiftly dressing. Kate too made to dress, but Simon told her to rest.

Lately, she'd been, to say the least rather irritable when it was time to get out of bed. She complained of stomach cramps and being nauseous, which left Simon in the dark as to what was wrong. Horen had checked her over finding nothing out of the ordinary. To be safe he'd taken a blood sample, he promised to check it as soon as he could.

Running to the bridge, he arrived to find the crew at battle stations. Walking up to Radon sitting in the Captain's chair he tried to discreetly find out what was going on.

"Something big is coming in fast." Radon volunteered seeing Simon looking at the instruments.

"Do you think it's a meteor?"

"It's as large as a fleet of battleships. If it's not a meteor, it's one giant ship." Radon smiled.

"Will it hit the city?"

"That's what we're waiting for. Jabo is checking its trajectory." Looking to the Intel officer's station Simon watched

Jabo check his computer before hesitating and checking it again. 'He's found something' Simon realised watching him frantically recheck the data.

"Captain, we've got get out of here now," Jabo screamed startling everyone.

"What's wrong?" Radon demanded.

"It's going to miss the moon. It's going to hit this planet."

"Engines full ahead!" Radon shouted as Simon rushed to the Portal controls, swiftly entering co-ordinates into it. Without warning the ship started to shake, as the meteor impacted with the planet's atmosphere. The portal was barely open, as the Katherine accelerated forward entering the horizon. Behind them the meteor hit the planet's surface, sending a massive shockwave through the portal. Caught by the blast, the ship rolled over doing a complete 360-degree turn to the left, throwing everyone into the walls.

Shocked and disorientated the crew hung on to anything solid as the ship swung back and forward unable to stabilise. Tense seconds passed as Radon wrestled with the controls, trying to right the ship, onto its original course. To everyone's relief, the ship slowly responded, finally regaining its stability.

Once calm had been restored the injured were moved to the infirmary. Kate arrived with a nasty cut on her forehead. Horen quickly bandaged it, promising to return. Nodding her understanding, Kate knew that he'd have more urgent injuries to attend to than hers. Jabo moving to Simon's side seemed wary of something.

"What's wrong?" Simon whispered.

"Move to the observation deck." He softly replied, leading the way.

"That was close. Too close" Radon growled, as Kate and Jabo entered.

"What happening?" She asked as Simon signalled to keep her voice down.

"That meteor wasn't aimed at the moon. It was heading straight for us." Jabo said softly, watching the door. The room became unnaturally still as they all pondered his statement.

"Do you suspect we've got a spy onboard?" Kate asked, breaking the silence.

"I'm not sure Kate, but it fits," Jabo answered sounding far from sure.

"It can't be our people from Oregarth surely?" Radon pointed out.

"I wouldn't think so. That then leaves only Katy and her men, plus Ryan and Benjamin." Simon put forward, finding it hard to believe.

"I find it hard to believe any of them betrayed us," Kate exclaimed, Simon, signalling her to keep her voice down.

"Then how else did they know we were here?" Jabo countered.

"Could there be a bug, I mean a tracking device," Simon suggested.

"There could be, although we have pretty sophisticated frequency monitoring equipment, for detecting planted devices. Next time we stop though, we'll do a more thorough search?" Jabo assured them.

"Still we can't take the chance that maybe we have a spy aboard, who could sabotage the ship. For now, we must secure Katy and her people, plus Ryan and Benjamin." Simon ordered.

To say the two new crewmembers from New America were surprised was an understatement. When Jabo first walked into the bridge area, he found them discussing the meteor's path with Horen. Both Benjamin and Ryan thought the meteor's path to their position was no accident. Jabo stealing himself drew his weapon. Ordering two of his men to escort them from the bridge, he had them secured in one of the storage rooms. The rest of the crew looked on in disbelief, though most saw the meteor coming after them as a sign that the enemy knew they were here.

As they passed Simon on their way to detention, Ryan stopped.

"Simon, both Benjamin and I have done everything to show we want to belong, that aside I can see your point," Ryan told him, clearly upset at the lack of trust, but understanding their position. Most of the crew who had remained silent since their arrest spoke out now in their defence. Simon was forced to raise his arm to silence them.

"I too have my doubts of their guilt men, but we must be sure. Until they are proved innocent, they must be held." This seemed to satisfy them, although having accepted them as crewmembers; it was hard to believe they had then betrayed them.

"I for one know they are innocent," Horen spoke up getting a smile from Benjamin, as they disappeared from sight, beginning their forced isolation. Katy and her officers were far impressed by their arrest many voiced their anger until they arrived and found Ryan and Benjamin there.

"You're here too?" Katy asked surprised, knowing they'd been part of the crew for quite a while.

"What would you have done? It's quite clear someone told the Roax we were on that planet?" Ryan pointed out offering her a seat.

"Thank you." She replied, sitting down.

"How long do you think we will be here?" Benjamin asked Ryan, seeing the guards appeared less than worried by their captors. He figured that they like Horen found the idea of spies hard to believe.

"Who knows? I for one will enjoy this time with our kindred from Salvation." Ryan smiled, Katy returning it, as the others made themselves comfortable. On the bridge the case for letting them return to duty continued. Radon who was usually the most suspicious aired his views.

"I must admit, I too find it hard to believe that any of the humans are guilty. Unfortunately, until we have evidence that proves otherwise they must remain secured." Radon confessed.

"Yes, like you I think they're innocent. In that case, we must find an answer to how the Roax knew. Until then we have a problem." Jeddah suggested sounding unsure.

"Where are we headed anyway?" Horen asked knowing they were in the portal still.

"Only to the next Galaxy, we'll drop out soon. That should be far enough, for us to check the ship over for damage. We can also try to find out how they knew we were there." Simon told them.

Two days found Simon and his staff on the observation deck, discussing their options.

"Anything new on the search?" Jeddah asked for the second time, clearly not believing that Ryan and Benjamin were involved.

"Everything checks out. There seems nothing out of the normal." Jabo had ripped the ship apart trying to locate the source.

"What about the humans' gear? Maybe something was planted on them." Horen suggested.

"That was the first thing we checked. We even scanned their bodies and found nothing." Radon admitted sounding tired. The room lapsed into self-imposed stillness, as everyone turned to their own thoughts. Kate smiling made them all refocus, as she burst into the room.

"I might have the answer." She beamed, motioning them to follow her to the bridge. Once there, she moved to the Portal console and waited, for them to all be present. "It occurred to me when we arrived here on Collinar, that it took a while for them to attack us when you would've thought they'd been right behind us. It then occurred to me that after we escaped from Oregarth, they must have retreated to their fleet or home planet, or they would've appeared out of our own portal behind us.

When we jumped to Pathalong to Salvation and back again and then moved on again to Collinar, it occurred to me that they might just be waiting for us to stop for a set period of time so they could plan an attack. That would explain why they didn't attack Jeddah's people when we left them on Pathalong. When they did attack us here after waiting some time, it struck me that maybe we weren't the main target, that they were busy elsewhere?"

"That sounds reasonable, but that would mean they had some way of knowing where we are going when we activate the portal." Simon smiled, watching her look at the console.

"No one's tampered with it, Kate. We'd detect it." Jabo pointed out. He too was watching her.

"Would we? What if it was a new alien device we hadn't seen before?" Kate answered, as her hand came away holding a small fingernail sized object. The gathered group stood spellbound as Kate handed the device to Jabo.

"It occurred to me that this device not only betrayed our position but was designed to remain invisible to our scanning equipment. It was only by touch that I found it."

"That doesn't explain how it got there. Someone must have placed it there." Horen pointed out.

"There's only one group of aliens that have been on this ship that might use this type of technology," Kate answered.

"The Hedred!" Radon growled, as the realisation that the Hedred engineers had examined the Portal device when aboard with Simon.

"I trust Ceb, Radon. But it did occur to me when Ceb was telling his stories of escaping the Roax, that the Roax had returned early and discovered them leaving. How did they know?" Kate put forward.

"My God they must be either attacking the Hedred now or preparing to, that explains why we haven't seen them here yet," Jeddah exclaimed.

"Prepare the ship; we have no time to lose," Simon shouted as everyone rushed out, to mobilise the crew. Simon walking up to Kate gave her a kiss smiling.

"That was good detective work my love. You constantly surprise me." He told her as she held his hands. Jabo clearing his throat beside them brought their private moment to an end.

"What is it?" Simon asked.

"We have another problem." He whispered leading Kate and Simon, back out onto the observation platform. He then signalled for Radon and Jeddah to join them.

"What it is Jabo?" Radon softly replied, picking up Jabo's concern.

"I've checked the ship not only for the bugging device but also for its structural integrity. Although the shield and weapons are faultless, the superstructure of this ship is approaching the end of its life. The Roax built this ship thousands of years ago, it can't take much more of the pounding it's been getting from not only fighting but travelling in the portal constantly."

"Is there a danger?" Simon asked.

"Not yet, although a major engagement could cause a breach in the ship's outer hull. Damage could be extensive; we will have to be careful." Jabo warned, causing Radon to scoff.

"We're heading for a battle right now, and Simon usually ends up leading the attack! How are we going to be careful?" He smiled.

"Look I have a solution. Let's get through this situation first, and then we'll worry about the ship." Simon suggested as they hurried to the bridge to get underway. Radon behind him rubbed his chin.

"He's got more secrets than a female." Radon chuckled, as beside him Kate snigger.

A week of mind-numbing speed saw the Katherine exploded from the portal. To avoid detection, they were in an adjoining Galaxy. Simon had noticed this system when they were waiting for the Hedred fleet to exit the portal and rendezvous with them above Sallong. Although the Galaxies' sun had long ago burnt out, a strange magnetic field radiated from the sun's old position. Every planet in this system was dead, devoid of life, yet this strange field held them in their orbits around the dead sun's core. It was the perfect place to arrive unannounced, as the magnetic field nullified sensor arrays on most spaceships.

Moving to the very edge of the system, Simon had Radon scan the surrounding systems. As they feared the Hedred's new homeworld was under attack. To the west of their position, the Hedred fleet was deployed, facing off against a steady stream of meteors. It was an impressive display of firepower as the Hedred did their best to either turn or destroy the incoming huge fast-moving mountains of rock. Studying the planet, Simon saw clearly where at least two meteors had gotten through. Damage was widespread, though fortunately, it was away from where the Hedred had settled. As yet the planet had weathered the impact of these missiles, but it only took one to hit a fault line, and they have another Oregarth.

Looking around the bridge, he saw most of the crew was close to exhaustion. You couldn't keep constantly travelling in the portal at high speed without having side effects. 'How far can I push them?' Simon asked himself readying himself.

"Battle stations!" He shouted, the crew's exhaustion forgotten, as they moved swiftly to their positions. Calculating where the enemy portal was positioned, Simon worked out where to exit the next portal. Punching in the co-ordinates he tried to think of something to lift the crew, nothing came. "Fire as soon as we exit men." He said instead, Radon to his right, nodding his head, knowing how he felt.

When the portal opened, Horen at the helm pressed the thrusters' controls, slamming the Katherine forward. No sooner had they entered than they exited to find twenty warships turning to face them. Before this moment, Simon had always thought the Flax Federation cruisers, and the Oregarthian battleships were the giant ships of space. True the Hedred transport's vessels were larger, though they were not purpose-built warships. These monsters in front of them now bristled with guns, dwarfing their cruiser.

Like Simon, most of the crew just stared at the ships, Radon who was a battle-hardened commander reacted.

"What are you all waiting for? Fire everything!" He screamed, making even Simon jump. It did the trick though, as the crew swung into action, opening fire.

The Katherine had eight batteries of double laser cannons. Targeting eight different ships, at the same time, required amazing discipline. Radon over the last week while they travelled through the portal, had continually drilled them on this form of warfare, honing their skills. Ryan and Benjamin during this time had proved their efficiency with the lasers. They now manned one of the two forward batteries.

One of the first things they all had done after finding the Hedred homing device was to free Ryan and Benjamin and the others.

"It's about time!" Ryan had shouted, smiling at the same time, as the silent, embarrassed group, begged their forgiveness. "I'd have done the same, my friends," Ryan confessed glad he was in the clear. Benjamin at first wasn't as forgiving feeling slighted and hurt. A hug and a kiss from Kate brightened him up, before going red. The crew to a man had welcomed Katy and her crew back, many including Radon admitting they always knew they were innocent and was sorry. Now, their troubles were forgotten, as they all faced a major action, wondering if they'd survive it.

"Their shields are more advanced than the ones New America ships use. I wonder how our weapons will fare." Benjamin warned Ryan, who was watching his weapon's sensor console. A red light flashing indicated their weapons were fully charged.

"We'll know soon enough," Ryan replied pulling the trigger. Both men watched the twin beams strike towards the centre ship. Ryan secretly hoped it was the command ship; it would certainly help to eliminate the people in charge of these death machines.

As their laser hit the first enemy ship, their doubts were forgotten. Despite the enemy's size, their lasers cut deeply into the enemy ships, straight through their shields. The eight ships hit were immediately crippled, seven exploding. By this time, however, the enemy had turned enough to bring their weapons online. Despite the Katherine's advanced shield, the Roax lasers managed in some places, to penetrate, causing damage to the hull. Many of the crew were thrown to the deck as the ship tumbled sideways rocking violently.

"Is that all they've got?" Radon laughed, many nervously at first joining him, as their weapons crews recovering, switched targets racking the next eight ships. As before the juggernauts couldn't take the pounding disintegrating under the relentless barrage. Now with only three ships left Simon ordered a ceasefire.

"Contact them Jabo. See if you can convince them to surrender." Simon ordered as their ship received another round of fire from the remaining ships. After several tries to contact them failed, and they continued firing, Simon ordered his crew to reacquire the targets. Most of the crew had expected the enemy ships to surrender. When this failed, they reluctantly finished the ships off. This left just one ship, the one that in the first opening volley had been immobilised.

"Scan her for life and check for damage," Simon ordered as his crew still at battle stations, visibly relaxed.

"Stay focused." Radon barked, as he continued to watch the enemy ship. "Remember, we don't know anything about them men, so stay sharp." Jabo and Katy seated beside Radon, scanned the enemy ship and their own.

"The air seals are gone. There is no sign of life or power, Captain." Jabo informed Simon, who stood looking out the front viewing screen at the ship.

"Our ship has received minor damage to the hull. Our emergency crews have already repaired the damage, although a more detailed inspection of the outside hull might be needed." Katy informed Simon, who still stood staring at the Roax ship.

"Thank you, both. Give the crew especially the repairmen a well done." Simon answered studying the Roax ship.

"You think someone would've survived. Surely their weapons batteries had their own life support?" Radon answered, always expecting the unexpected.

"Well they could be shielded, hiding somewhere, but with no power, it would be hard to survive. It should be safe to visit it?" Simon mused. Everyone there could see he wanted to board the ship.

"Just like you thought the Portal controls couldn't be bugged." Kate piped in, playfully tugging his ear.

"That was different. There was power everywhere to hide the signal."

"If you say so, it must be right." She giggled, slipping away, as he tried to grab her.

"It might be possible for me to visit the Roax ship? I might find a clue to their origin?" Simon put forward.

"Not a chance." Kate thundered.

"You're too important Simon; for all, we know the ship could be a trap," Radon warned. Simon looked to the others, seeing no support.

"Okay, we'll send a group of volunteers first. If they report everything is okay, I'll go across for a more detailed inspection.

How's that sound?" He asked her, getting a nod of approval in return. "Okay, who wants to go first?" Simon asked as a room full of hands exploded into the air.

Picking who could go, Simon was just about to leave the bridge when Katy entered, her face white as a sheet.

"It's them, Simon. It's the same type of ship that attacked Salvation." She sobbed, as Ryan ran to her, holding her so she wouldn't collapse. Simon in all the excitement hadn't yet compared the damaged ship to the spaceship, which crashed on Salvation, near New Vancouver. Looking out the viewport, Simon took in the ship's lines and her size.

"You're right Katy it is the same type. That means the Roax did attack Salvation as well as Oregarth." He concluded feeling crestfallen.

"I'm not blaming you Simon; it's just opened old wounds for me," Katy explained, seeing his guilty expression.

"Well, we stop them here," Radon growled. "Now let's move on!"

Jabo, Ryan and Benjamin guided the shuttle next to the Roax's crippled ship. Simon in a sign of trust had sent Ryan and Benjamin with Jabo. They, to all intense and purposes, were just to watch over Jabo, while he carried out tests on the ship. Docking was the first problem, as the ship had taken several hits where the airlock, used to be. Benjamin, in the end, solved the problem. He suggested driving the shuttle into the laser's blast point. This was where the laser had cut into the ship, melting a large hole in the superstructure, causing a massive explosion. The crater in the ship's side was now the perfect spot to gain entry.

Because the ship had vented its air supply, the three visitors donned spacesuits, exiting through the airlock. It was not as simple as it sounded, as gagged pieces of metal protruded from what once was the infrastructure and walls of the ship. Moving with extreme care to prevent puncturing their suits, Ryan with the help of an industrial laser knife, carried on the ship for rescue work, cleared a path to an internal passageway. Jabo now took over the lead, heading for the bridge.

Since the docking port was towards the front of the ship, Jabo estimated, that it would take them only about ten minutes to reach the bridge area. Unlike the Katherine or for that matter any ship Jabo had been aboard; the main passageway they were walking on had no side corridors. This meant there were no areas for the crew to sleep or eat; the ship seemed completely full of equipment.

Stopping, Jabo intrigued by the lack of corridors, moved to an inspection hole covered in the side of the passageway. Attempting to open it, he found it was sealed with a locked door.

"Now would be a good time to use that laser knife." Jabo smiled, knowing they'd left it behind because of its weight.

"Move to the side, I've got an idea," Benjamin suggested, pulling out his laser pistol.

"Is that a good idea?" Jabo asked as Benjamin pointed the pistol at the lock.

"Most probably not, but let's see what's in there shall we." Ryan smiled, giving Benjamin the go ahead.

Benjamin was no fool and used his experience with the weapon to give just a small burst, just enough to melt the internal workings of the lock. This he followed up with a swift kick. Jabo a little rattled by his fellow crewmember's lack of caution, had to admit it had worked. He knew his race the Oregarthians would have hesitated and gone back for the laser knife. 'Maybe that's what makes these humans so dangerous, their ability to react swiftly,' he mused. On the other hand, it could've caused an explosion. 'What's done is done' he smiled, remembering Simon using that phrase, as he peered inside. What he saw both amazed and worried him, as he swiftly resealed the door.

"Let's get going! We need to get to the bridge immediately!" Jabo told Ryan and Benjamin, moving off at a quick jog.

"What's the problem?" Ryan asked from behind him keeping pace.

"I don't think there is a crew aboard this ship, it appears to be some sort of remote-controlled platform."

"But if that was so, how'd it turn to fight us, whoever was controlling it wouldn't have known we were coming," Benjamin replied.

"Did you notice in the battle how all the enemy ships were turning at the same time when we exited the portal? It's hard to believe that all the ships would be facing exactly the same way unless they were linked."

"We'll know soon enough." Benjamin pointed out as they arrived at a blast door.

"This is it, the control room or as you call it the bridge is on the other side," Jabo announced as the three came to a halt, breathing heavily from their jogging. Seeing the door was locked Benjamin drew his pistol.

"Wait! Not this time." Jabo warned. Moving forward he examined the door. Although he found nothing, Jabo had a bad feeling about opening it. "Back down the hallway about twenty metres, I saw another inspection door. Let's see if we can enter through that point." The others without a word followed. As before Benjamin with his laser pistol gained entry. Squeezing inside Jabo leading, the three crawled forward, their spacesuits making the trip all that more difficult.

Benjamin bringing up the rear, edged forward, behind Ryan, who followed Jabo's feet in front. They'd been crawling for close to thirty minutes, and Benjamin started to develop a case of claustrophobia. The electrical cables that filled the service duct they were in, seemed to be deliberately ensnaring him trying sinisterly to suffocate him.

"Is it much further?" Benjamin suddenly bellowed out, startling Ryan and Jabo.

"Take it easy Benjamin," Ryan answered using a reassuring calm voice. "It can't be far, just try to relax."

"Is there a problem?" Jabo enquired, his race having no conception of what Benjamin was going through.

"On Earth, Jabo, we have a fear of enclosed spaces," Ryan explained, wondering if Jabo's race had any problems.

"I have heard of these things. Simon, it is said had a problem with heights, now your race has another problem. How did you ever learn to travel in Spaceships?" Jabo sounded confused, as he reached another service door. "I have found another door, do you feel better?" Both Benjamin and Ryan burst into laughter at Jabo's statement, confusing him more.

Using the internal handle, which luckily wasn't locked from this side, Jabo cautiously slid out onto the floor of the bridge. Once he was clear, he whispered for the other two to follow him and stay on the floor. Looking around the room he saw one panel still was functioning.

"It has some sort of security system. Do not move." He ordered sliding forward to the console. It was a dead man system he realised, installed in case the ship was disabled. Slowing raising himself off the floor, he saw it had a digital clock imbedded in the console; it was counting down towards zero. Studying it, he worked out he had a good three hours before it reached its objective. Reaching into his pack attached to his suit he withdrew a screwdriver type device. With great care, he began dismantling the console.

For over an hour he worked with the minimum of movement, while behind him, Benjamin and Ryan waited silently. Taking a break, Jabo loosened his shoulders trying to relax.

"It's okay to talk; I see no sign of an audio detection system," Jabo whispered, showing he wasn't a hundred percent sure.

"How long will it take to disarm it?" Ryan softly asked.

"No idea. But I'm closer now than I was an hour ago." Jabo smiled.

"You're kidding aren't you?" Benjamin nervously replied, wondering if Jabo had developed a sense of humour.

"No, I am not as you say 'having you on'. The console is now dismantled, I won't know if I can stop the detonation until I examine the system's wiring." Both Ryan and Benjamin looked at each other. Both smiled realising sometimes nothing made sense with an alien race.

"Should we head back to the ship then?" Ryan suggested.

"We would not make it. Better to stay and solve the problem, than die trying to run away from it." Jabo chuckled. "Now I make a joke."

"Shit you need practice," Ryan answered, his guts in a knot, as Jabo with a shrug of his shoulders, went back to the console. Twenty minutes of nail-biting tension passed before Jabo stood up stretching.

"It is done." He announced moving to the main control panel. It was as Jabo had earlier pointed out; the ship was an unmanned drone. He spent another hour pouring over each piece of equipment before after looking at his suit's oxygen gauge; he'd decided to call it a day. Moving to the door, he overrode the locking system pushing one of the two entry doors open. Signalling to Ryan and Benjamin to follow, they started their walk back to the shuttle.

Once aboard they pressurised the ship getting out of their suits. After checking and cleaning them, they stored them in special containers, before moving to the shuttle's bridge. Once clear of the Roax ship, Jabo called the Katherine. This was the first time since arriving that he'd used the radio equipment. Radon had given strict instructions that only in an emergency were they to transmit. He too had feared some sort of explosive device would be on board the ship.

Telling Radon briefly of what he had found, he put forward the opinion that coming aboard this ship could be still dangerous. Radon acknowledged his advice admitting he wasn't too keen on anyone else going aboard but would wait first for his report once they'd docked. Signing off, the three men thankful to be going back to the ship, blasted off. Behind them, the seemingly dead ship picked up the close proximity of the radio transmission. Turning on a shielded reserve power unit, it activated its failsafe backup system.

On board, Jabo, Ryan and Benjamin after a brief rest, met with Simon in the meeting room of the bridge. Simon of course, was keen to go back aboard the Roax ship. He hoped from examining the ship's data logs to work out where the ship had come from. Radon was dead against it. He was worried by the apparent lack of an internal defence system. He received support from Jabo. He had been a little suspicious of how easy it was to disable the dead man switch.

He knew the Roax were advanced, so why leave their ships to be dissected by anyone lucky enough to get on board. There was also he had observed, an energy reading briefly after they'd left, its source unknown.

"You people make these Roax seem invincible, yet you beat them on Salvation when they launched their coup," Benjamin spoke out.

"They are to be feared, Benjamin. They were light years ahead of our human civilisation. Those ships prove that." Simon answered.

"But we defeated them like you did on Salvation." Benjamin pointed out.

"This ship and the knowledge the people of the void gave us to beat them Benjamin, not any of us. Even with that advantage, our ship took damage where before, we were invincible. If we run into more of their ships, we mightn't be as lucky next time. That's the problem with being part of a myth; everyone expects great things from us as if we were immortal." Simon answered remembering Jeddah's men bowing to him.

"That could explain something," Horen exclaimed. "I wondered why we have been altered by the ship. We don't really need to be super fast or incredibly strong, to fight on this ship, so why do it? I believe the Ancients wanted us to appear unbeatable to our enemies."

"That might explain it, although the action your men saw on New America shows that it came in handy." Radon pointed out.

"Then we can use these special abilities to investigate the ship?" Simon suggested, trying to get around their ban on him going.

"There's not a chance in hell you're going over there so forget it." Kate spat out, ending Simon's argument and the meeting. As the group was in the process of leaving, Katy appeared at the door. She informed Simon, that Ceb's fleet was approaching. This came as no surprise, as his crew who had been monitoring their movement towards their position for several days.

Simon decided to take the ships shuttle and visit Ceb on board his flagship. Informing Radon of his plan, he then asked

Kate to accompany him, with several crewmembers, including Benjamin and Katy.

Radon after talking with Simon pulled Jabo aside for a discreet talk. Despite Radon's pessimism and their blunt opposition to Simon going, he still wanted to search the ship for data. Knowing there could be a trap in a way, helped as the two conspirators prepared for another visit. Secretly gathering a team that included Ryan, Horen and two of Jeddah's soldiers, they waited till Simon had departed. Once he'd left, they would take the New America shuttle reluctantly gifted from General Wordsworth.

When they prepared to leave New America, Radon curious had commandeered the shuttle. The General was far from impressed, wanting it for himself. In the end, instead of causing a confrontation, he'd laughed it off, telling them they could have it as a present. He then had its crew return with him on his shuttle that he'd arrived on. General Wordsworth secretly wasn't too worried. He knew he'd find someone who could explain how it worked, once he was back on New America.

When they left New America and entered the portal for Oregarth, Radon had his men strip the shuttle down. It took three days with Simon's help, to work out how it produced the massive amount of power required, to deploy the cruiser strength shield. It proved to be far more advanced than anything any of them, had seen before. Although not up to the Chosen's level of advancement, it was a great leap forward in technology for the humans.

Radon knew if they'd used this type of power unit on their cruisers they'd have been ten times more powerful. Maybe not enough to take on the Katherine singularly, but with overwhelming numbers, it might make the difference. At the time he had wondered why the Junta hadn't equipped their cruisers with it. Ryan believed they'd kept it to themselves to give them an edge in any future coups.

Radon concluded he was right, but with the near confrontation with the Hedred and later the Katherine, not to give their fleets every advantage was just dim-witted.

"We're ready Sir," Ryan shouted to him from the docking port of the Katherine, interrupting his thoughts.

"Good, just give Simon another twenty minutes, and we'll leave, using the Katherine to hide our movements."

"Do you think that's wise, to deceive Simon?" Horen asked, having heard the exchange.

"No it's not, but he'd wanted to come, and he's too important." Radon pointed out.

"What about us?" Ryan smiled.

"Welcome to the crew of the Katherine Ryan," Radon answered, chuckling.

"See, I told you he had a sense of humour." Horen laughed.

"He too needs a little improvement." Ryan pointed out, his smile gone.

TRUSTING ALLIES

Simon, having signalled Ceb his intentions, piloted the shuttle himself across to Ceb's flagship. When the meteors had suddenly stopped, one of Ceb's ships had tracked the source of the meteors to this Galaxy, finding the tell-tale signs of a battle in progress. They had rushed here at their maximum speed to find the Katherine and the remains of a massive enemy ship. Contact had been established, and Simon had briefly told Ceb of the battle and of sending a team across to investigate the remaining Roax ship.

Ceb cautiously had kept his fleet at a distance, just in case the disabled ship somehow picked up its presence. Now the danger had passed, they rendezvoused with the Katherine. Benjamin was one of the crew of the shuttle travelling with Simon. The excitement of meeting another race made him fidgety, as their shuttle locked onto Ceb's flagship. Benjamin watched in amazement, as the Hedred people welcomed Simon like he was a Hedred hero, not another alien.

No one bowed, but Benjamin saw the attentiveness this race showed to an unknown man, who had saved them, yet again. It suddenly dawned on him what Simon meant about expecting him to move mountains.

"What if we fail them in the future, what then?" Benjamin whispered, seeing Kate beside him turn towards him, he could see she too understood and worried about it.

"We haven't yet, but you're right, we can't stay here forever, and without us, they are vulnerable." She softly replied.

"Simon will think of something." Benjamin automatically answered, getting a small smile from Kate and Katy, before he could stop himself. He too it seemed, expected him to save them no matter what.

"So if they have no crew, what is their purpose?" Ceb asked.

"I believe one of the ships was crewed. The others were drone systems, responding to commands from the manned ship. They were here I believe, to correct the meteor's flight path to your planet and secondly, to protect the exit point of the portal. Once your planet was destroyed, they would take care of any survivors." Simon replied.

"But surely they must have someone on each ship controlling them?"

"Ceb we're dealing with an advanced race. As I pointed out, when we were spotted emerging from our portal, all the ships turned at the same time in the same direction. It had to be controlled by a single person on one of the ships. A portal link, no matter how advanced, would take days to reach this Galaxy."

"Then what do we do Simon? I know you can't stay and protect us. Do we run or stay?" Ceb exclaimed, upset by the situation.

"No this is your home, running will achieve nothing. There is one thing though. How did they know you were here? The only answer is someone told them. We also found this on the portal control of the Katherine. The technology is unknown to me, do you recognise it?" Simon asked, keeping his voice down.

"Yes, it is a concealable tracking device, very advanced. Only our top engineers have access to them." Ceb conceded crestfallen. "I am so sorry Simon. It appears that one of my people has betrayed not only his race but yours as well."

"My race tried to kill me for having aliens as my friends, it happens. Let's move on, we must find this man."

"How can that be done? At least forty of my engineers visited your ship. It could be any one of them?"

"Yes, it won't be easy, although I do have an idea." Simon smiled.

Calling a meeting of all Ceb's top engineers and commanders, Simon outlined his next move. He intended to take the great bulk of the Hedred fleet and launch an attack on the position where the enemy was holding up. Using information obtained on the enemy ship, they would end the Roax raids forever. Cheers had broken out as Ceb told the Commanders and their engineers to return to their ships and prepare to leave.

"Now we wait." Ceb growled, as his most trusted officers manned their transmission detection devices. With over three hundred ships, Benjamin, who had been made aware of the operation, compared it to finding a needle in a haystack. Airing his doubts to Simon, he was surprised when he smiled.

"Each ship has one engineer or scientist, as we would've called them. Only forty ships have one of the Hedron's top engineers aboard who visited our ship. They were all at the meeting, which included several engineers from ships that weren't on the Katherine. By adding the other engineers, we should alleviate any suspicions that the meeting was a trap. Right now the traitor is trying to warn the Roax of the coming attack. Once he transmits, Ceb's men will have him."

"That's brilliant," Benjamin exclaimed.

"No, it's just mathematics. We just divided forty up into single numbers, it couldn't be simpler."

Twenty Earth minutes after the meeting broke up; two transmissions were picked up from two separate ships, surprising everyone.

"My God, there are two of them." Ceb exploded, ordering his men to arrest them both.

"Makes sense, if you catch one and turn him, the other informs his masters," Benjamin replied, seeing how Simon's plan still worked perfectly, as long as there weren't too many spies.

"Now Ceb since the threat has been neutralised, I have two gifts for you in private," Simon said softly, as Ceb picking up the secrecy pointed to a room beside the bridge where they were. Entering Simon found it was Ceb's private quarters.

"That's a good idea, having the Captain's cabin near the bridge," Simon admitted looking around.

"It has its drawbacks as you are always on call." Ceb pointed out, waiting.

Looking around seeing no one was paying attention, Simon handed Ceb two sets of plans. Taking the first, seeing it was the plan for an advance form of power plant, Ceb gasped.

"This will make our weapons and shields vastly superior. Why are you doing this for us?" Ceb answered, seemingly overcome by the gesture.

"Your race needs this to survive Ceb. You are a man of peace, forced to fight to protect your race. I trust you to use this wisely." Simon conveyed an air of respect for Ceb that humbled him. Ceb unable to answer nodded his acceptance. Looking at the second plan, his eyes bulged, as he sort words. Signalling to remain silent, Simon pulled him aside.

"When I call, be ready." He whispered into his translator. Nodding again, Ceb wiped tears from his eyes, as he hugged Simon.

"Never doubt it." He softly replied, his translator having trouble translating his slurred words.

While Simon held talks with Ceb, Radon's raiding party arrived alongside the Roax ship.

"She really is a monster isn't she?" Horen whispered nervously, caught up in the tension of approaching this ship.

"Yes, it's impressive alright. Jabo bring us around to the front next to the bridge." Radon ordered. This time they wouldn't be entering through the blasted entry port. Radon had decided to anchor the shuttle right next to the bridge and using a laser lance, cut a hole, straight into the control centre. It was tricky, but if the ship was aware of their last entry through the entry hatch, it might be taken by surprise if they cut into the hull instead.

Using a magnetic collar, Jabo with Ryan's help, made a rough connection between the shuttle and the Roax ship. By this stage, the shuttle had depressurised, and the entire crew was suited up and ready.

"Well, at least there's very little chance of fire, with no oxygen," Jabo muttered, starting up the lance and applying its flame to the enemy ship's hull.

"Of course the ship might pick up the heat and self-destruct." Ryan pointed out, causing everyone to look at him. "Hey, I was only joking." He added.

"And you think I have no sense of humour?" Radon said softly behind him, the others remaining silent.

Two hours of slow, meticulous work found Jabo pulling a large piece of hull out of the Roax ship onto the shuttle. It left a doorway, big enough to crawl through. Jabo lowering the lance signalled for everyone to remain quiet, as he edged inside. Ryan like the others held his breath waiting to see what happened, as Jabo disappeared inside. The hole they'd cut came out in the electrical duct. It was the same one they'd used on their first expedition to the enemy ship's bridge.

Moving silently along the duct, Jabo hesitantly deployed a tiny remote camera. Resembling a small insect-like creature, it crawled forward, while Jabo watched its progress on a small screen. Reaching the bridge, the creature crawled up the side of the security panel Jabo had worked on earlier. From on top Jabo scanned the room. All seemed the same as the tiny creature turned clockwise, Jabo stopping it every now and then to examine individual pieces of equipment.

After doing two scans of the bridge, Jabo relaxed letting his tension go, made to move into the room. He was just starting to move forward when a muffled crack like lighting sound came from ahead of him. Looking down at the monitor he saw nothing but static. 'It had been destroyed by a laser' he concluded, as he lay frozen by what had occurred. Quickly recovering, he started to back up, as a humming sound started in the bridge area. Forgetting caution, he rushed back towards the shuttle. The humming behind him grew louder, seeming to now radiate through the ship, as the entire superstructure started to vibrate.

Reaching the hole cut in the Roax ship's side, he dived through, cutting open his space suit in the process, on the jagged edges. Barrelling into Ryan, Jabo gripped his ripped suit with his hands. Ryan had been in the process of climbing through the hole himself, to search for the overdue Jabo and was taken completely by surprise.

"What's wrong?" Ryan exclaimed shaken.

"We've got no time. Close the door, Ryan. Radon if you can hear me, launch immediately!" Jabo screamed into his headset. Ryan in response jumped past him, slamming the door, before rushing back to him, helping seal his suit. Radon who had moved back into the cockpit to monitor for any transmissions from the Roax ship jumped into the pilot's seat at Jabo's shout. Engaging the engines, he swiftly moved the throttle to maximum burn, while at the same time deploying the shield.

"What's wrong?" Horen yelled, as seating himself down beside Radon, he pressurised the ship, inadvertently saving Jabo's life.

No answer came as the ship catapulted forward, throwing Ryan, Jabo and the rest of the crew not belted in, into a pile of twisted arms and legs against the shuttle's docking door. Ignoring Horen, Radon contacted the Katherine breaking radio silence.

"Katherine, engage your shield now!" He screamed into the radio, as behind him the Roax ship exploded. On board the Katherine, it looked like the Galaxy burnt out sun had suddenly ignited, as dark red cloud mushroomed towards them, before impacting on their just raised shield.

Simon was just about to transfer to his shuttle when the blast hit Ceb's fleet. Being some distance from the enemy ship, Ceb's fleet had time to deploy their shields. Still, the impact was considerable as the whole fleet staggered sideways, as the shock waves passed them.

"My God, what was that?" Kate moaned having been thrown from her feet. Katy rushed to her side, helping her to her feet. No one answered as they watched Ceb confer with his command centre.

"The Katherine is okay Simon, her shields were deployed. The shuttle you sent to the Roax ship appears to be in trouble. Do you want us to approach it?" Ceb asked.

"No we can reach it just as quick with this shuttle and if they need assistance it will be easier to dock with a shuttle." Simon answered.

"I thought you said you weren't going back to the Roax ship?" Ceb pointed out.

"I wasn't. I'd say in my absence Radon secretly decided to sneak over there and have a look around."

"A secret no longer." Ceb smiled, before continuing. "My Comm's officer has just told me the shuttle's crew has signalled that they are all okay, though some have minor injuries. Till we meet again my friend." Ceb held out his hand like he'd seen Simon do. Simon, smiling at the gesture, gripped his hand.

"Goodbye for now." Was all Simon said, as he helped Benjamin get Kate who was having trouble standing, onto the shuttle.

Coming to a stop beside the New America shuttle, Simon looked over the damage. The total surface area of the shuttle was pitted with impact marks, where objects, most probably from the Roax ship, had penetrated the shield, striking the shuttle.

"Boy, it's going to need a shitload of paint." Benjamin sniggered from behind Kate and Simon, trying to lighten their mood. Both turned and stared, making him lose his smile.

"I see nothing funny Benjamin." Katy scolded him. She was angry with Ryan for going with Radon, without her. After they had been released, Katy had mooted going with Ryan to secretly look over the Roax ship. It appeared he had gone with Radon instead.

"But they're all okay Katy and let's face it; we all secretly wanted to go."

"He's right Katy, although they should've told Simon," Kate added.

"Yes, I might've been able to defuse the booby-trap and gain some Intel on the Roax if I'd have gone." Simon pointed out.

"You also might've been blown up, and let's face it, Jabo is our Intel officer. If he couldn't defuse it, I don't think you would have done any better." Kate shot back. Simon made to answer; when it dawned on him that she was right. His ego was getting in the way of his decisions.

"You're dead right Kate. Let's move on." Simon grudgingly admitted, giving her a forced smile.

"Now that didn't hurt, did it?" She giggled, hugging him. Katy too looked happier, making Benjamin's smile return.

Radon looked truly embarrassed, as he and the other conspirators in this failed raid, trooped onto Simon's shuttle.

The New America shuttle propulsion system had been severely damaged in the explosion; meaning Simon's shuttle would have to tow it back to the Katherine. He'd decided to move it like he'd thought about moving the sub on the ocean floor back on Salvation when they'd first found the Portal base. Once he had transferred the crew to his ship, he enclosed it in an expanded shield from his ship.

Although the shield on this shuttle had only a fraction of the other shuttle's power, it would do. Then they could limp slowly back to the Katherine and dock both in the storage compartment which was now known as the shuttle bay.

"I'm sorry Simon. We should've told you, but we thought you would want to come and it was too dangerous." Radon stuttered out, pleading his case.

"You were right Radon. Let's be glad no one was hurt." Simon smiled, seeing Radon and the other guilty members of his group look stunned. "That doesn't mean you get off without some sort of punishment. I want that shuttle back in working order straight away. And your group of commandoes will see it's done on your own." Simon ordered, turning the ship towards home.

"Thank you for understanding." Jabo quickly added, disappearing with the others, leaving Benjamin, Kate and Simon in the cockpit, trying hard to look angry.

"It was worth admitting I was wrong just to see Radon's face," Simon whispered, as his companions tried not to laugh.

Radon feeling they'd got off lightly, drove his ex-commandoes to get the shuttle back in working order. They found after a thorough examination, most of the major damage was at the rear. The rest was just superficial, needing only a grind and a little paint. Ryan cursing he'd gone in the first place, welded a new section on the rear of the ship. He was on the tail fin, which had been bent severely in the explosion. This piece would finish the welding and Ryan couldn't wait to get his next backbreaking assignment from Radon. Still, he forced a smile; despite a few broken bones and scratches, they'd got away with it.

Horen who like usual studied everything; put their escape down to their improved reflexes. Ryan, when he'd first come aboard, had been told of Horen's theory, that everyone aboard was being changed. He'd put it down to the voodoo scientist, meaning he thought it was bullshit. Now looking back, he remembered Jabo barrelling into the ship at an unimaginable speed. Even so, he had managed to get up off the deck and lock the airlock door in the blink of an eye, before helping Jabo up.

He had to admit, he felt stronger, and his mind solved problems, which back on New America he would've struggled with. Of course, there was always a downside, what happened when they decided to call it a day and leave? Sure Horen had assured them there would be no side effects, but he'd pointed out one problem. During the battle at the village on New America, he'd felt drained towards the end of the conflict, having trouble with fatigue.

If that occurred when you were away a few weeks, what happened when you went cold turkey and didn't come back? It made staying seem rather attractive; maybe that was the true reason for the supposed gift. The true test would be when they again joined Jeddah and the first group of his soldiers from the last trip. They had been aboard and then left, so it should now be possible to see what side effects occurred when you didn't return.

"How's it going hero?" Katy yelled from the hanger floor, making Ryan look down. Seeing it was Katy, he decided to take a break and climb down. Since their confinement together, the two had become close. The mess up with not taking her to the Roax ship, was in the past now, although she still made him feel guilty.

"Looks like you're nearly finished?" She smiled looking at his work.

"Yeah, it hasn't been easy, especially with Captain Bligh in charge," Ryan answered, indicating Radon.

"You know Ryan I'd be one of the only ones who would understand that joke, makes you think doesn't it?"

"We're a long way from both our planets Katy. Makes you marvel at how big the Universe is and how small mankind's part is in it all."

"Simon's human and he has made a big difference," Radon said from behind them, having heard.

"Yes, he has Radon. Unfortunately, there aren't many like him." Ryan answered.

"You are wrong, you are all like him," Radon answered, seeing their expressions he continued. "True some of your leaders have deceived you and fought us, yet the everyday humans I have met, have shown an unreserved ability to welcome myself and my men as friends. That is despite our obvious differences as unknown alien races."

"I could never be another Simon, Radon. He has done things I can't even understand let alone do." Ryan answered.

"I didn't mean it that way Ryan, what I meant is you all have made a difference. Katy here saved her people with the help of her crew. You stood up for your men and paid the price for saving them. You then became part of this ship's crew helping us where many would not have. Both deeds are of worth, don't underestimate yourselves." Radon told them, before walking away.

"That guy is something else?" Katy whispered, watching Radon check over the work being carried out.

"Yes, I can see why Simon trusts him like a brother." Ryan smiled, as feeling confident he reached across holding Katy's hand.

"I was wondering when you would make your move." She sniggered, gripping his hand as well. Ryan, his confidence overflowing pulled her to him, kissing her. Someone clearing his throat made them break apart.

"I hate to interrupt your moment, but you're both wanted on the bridge," Benjamin informed them, looking slightly embarrassed.

"Do you know where we're headed?" Katy asked, squeezing Ryan's hand before releasing it.

"Not really. Horen told me we're heading for a planet called Craigure, wherever that is?"

"That's the Capital of the Flax Federation, isn't it?" Katy asked having overheard Simon and Radon talking about it.

"Yes, it is." Ryan answered, trying to work out why they were going there, when all he could think about was that kiss.

"One thing about being on this ship, it's not boring?" Benjamin smiled.

"I could use some boring right now?" Katy giggled, leaving Benjamin confused.

OLD ALLIES

It took over a week to reach Craigure, the Capital of the Flax Federation. Simon had deliberately opened it in the same place where Jeddah had launched his attack on the ruling council, who once dominated the Federation.

"Shield up," Simon ordered as the Katherine emerged from the tell-tale circle of water. He knew that since a week had passed since the circle of water had appeared that a warm welcome could be expected. Whether it would be laser fire or a cordial greeting remained to be seen. As before they found an armada of warships floating before them, as for the Planet Craigsure there was no sign.

The Flax Federation ships seemed to Simon to have been completely overhauled. Their size and triangle shape was still prominent in the design, but the acute angles had been softened, giving the ships a more sleek shape. The shields and weapons too appeared to be of a new design. Radon, to his side, viewed data on the ships trying to gauge their strengths and weaknesses.

"Simon they're charging their weapons," Ryan informed him from his station, trying to remain calm.

"Open a channel Horen, they're your people. Try to explain to them that we come in peace." Simon suggested. Switching to his native tongue, Horen repeated several times that they came in peace. A standoff then developed, as the ships remain motionless as if they were waiting for the inevitable order to fire.

"I'm receiving a reply," Horen exclaimed.

"Have it translated." Simon ordered, as a deep voice echoed through the bridge.

"Identify yourselves."

"This is Captain Simon Hayes commander of the Katherine, who am I talking too?" Silence lasted for several seconds before a reply boomed through their radio receivers.

"Captain Hayes and the Katherine have not been heard of
since they entered the void over seventy of our years ago.
How can this be?"

"It's a long story. Who rules the Council now, when we were
here last, Commander Hague and Captain Tarwin were
arranging free elections."

"President Hague led our people for several years before
Tarwin's opposition party was elected. Since then we have
had many different leaders. Five years ago, unfortunately,
Marshall Law was introduced when our Capital planet was
destroyed. My name is Admiral Radom Hague; I am President
Hague's son." Everyone on the bridge looked towards Radon
who stood opened mouthed, his two rows of teeth visible.

"You're named after Radon an Oregarthian Captain; he is
my second in command and here with me now." Silence
followed before the voice again sounded.

"We ask of you to indulge us with another sign of proof. I
would like one of my ships to fire on you. My father told me
that even though your ship shows no shield, it is
impenetrable."

"Go ahead have several ships fire if it allays your fears,"
Simon answered turning to Radon. "How strong are the Flax's
new ships?"

"Hard to say, they've had some major improvements.
Anyway, we should know in a moment." Radon smiled, truly
unfriendly looking with his teeth exposed. Taking his advice,
Admiral Hayes opened fire with two ships. Although the
weapons were far more powerful than the old Flax Federation
ships, they weren't as deadly as the Roax ships. Still, except
for the shuddering as the lasers impacted with the shields,
they still failed to penetrate. After ten minutes of throwing
everything they had at the Katherine, the barrage ended, and
communications were re-established.

"It seems the legend still holds true Captain Hayes. The
question still is though, why have you come here?"

"We face an enemy from old, the Roax have returned,"
Simon told him.

"How do you know?"

"A race called the Hedred were forced to flee after a race that identified themselves as the Roax, destroyed their planet with meteors."

"That explains much Captain Hayes. With your permission I would like to visit your ship."

"Very well Admiral. I will have one of our shuttles orbit our ship, to allow your shuttle to dock in our shuttle bay." Simon informed him. Turning to Radon, he instructed him to have Horen take the New America shuttle for a run, telling him to make sure the shield was deployed.

On board Admiral Hague's flagship his Captains gathered. Many of course weren't happy with their leader going aboard an impregnable ship.

"We must know for sure if it is Simon Hayes. I don't want them aboard our ships until we know they can be trusted." Hague bristled with the situation. In the past, he'd just have gone. Now he had to get a majority decision from his fleet commanders.

"The talk about the meteors fits with the destruction of Craigure. We know something big impacted with the planet, now we have proof it was no accident." Commander Droid commander of the Home fleet, pointed out, as many officers nodded their support of his idea.

"Yes, but who arranged it, the Roax or this Simon Hayes? I suggest caution in dealing with these people until we know." Captain Dane, one of Admiral Hague's squadron leaders, interjected, not liking his Admiral visiting the ship.

"Why would they bother? That ship could take this fleet apart if half the stories are true. I say we take a chance and have the Admiral meet with them. We've got nothing to lose, except the Admiral." Jeddar, Radom's second in Command and brother jokingly replied, causing many to smile.

"Yes I think my learned brother is correct and to show how confident I am, I'll take him with me." Radom Hague smiled his officer's chuckling.

It had worked Radom admitted, watching the gathered Officers. Up until this meeting he'd had serious doubts he was still in command. The loss of Craigsure had hit his people hard. For years they'd searched for the people responsible, having lost one of their fleets in an attempt to reach Jeddah and his people on Oregarth.

Many including Dane and Droid, although showing signs of having different views, had formed an alliance. Between them, they held nearly two-thirds of the votes needed to rescind the Marshall Law proclamation and disband the fleet. Like his brother, Radom saw a plan in the attack on Craigure, which was contrary to the others who believed it was an unforeseen, but natural catastrophe. Up until now, he'd get no proof, now this.

"Prepare my shuttle, we leave once the officers have returned to their ships. Just remember no one fires while I'm on that ship." Radom Hague added, as the commanders their thoughts hidden, left.

"You worry too much brother," Jeddar whispered, giving a wave or nod to the leaving officers.

"There is a lot at stake here Jeddar. Watch what you say when we reach the Katherine." Radom warned.

Radom and Jeddar looked out at the New America shuttle gliding through space beside them.

"Are you telling me that little shuttle has a battleship size shield?" Radom asked his shuttle co-pilot, who was monitoring the shuttle.

"Yes, Sir. It should be impossible, but the power readings on that small ship are unbelievable." The Co-Pilot replied nervously.

"Yet we can scan this one, while the Katherine's remains invisible?" Jeddar added, getting a nod from the Co-pilot.

"I can't believe it. That small ship, although its shield isn't as advanced as our fleets, could put up a good fight against our biggest ships. I find this worrying." Radom exclaimed. Looking at the Katherine's docking port Radom spotted an old shuttle once used by the Oregarthians. "Well, that explains it. This ship was either a gift or a prize taken from another race. That's why she is so different, and they still have the old shuttle from their last visit." Radom smiled, feeling better.

"I see nothing to be cocky about Radom. We are approaching a ship, not seen for seventy of our years, yet the crew is the same, and by voice, analysis points out no ageing in Simon Hayes's voice, from his last visit." Jeddar softly replied, as their shuttle docked.

Stepping out of the shuttle, Radom and Jeddar were greeted by two lines of soldiers. On one side were Flax Federation troopers. On the other side were Oregarthian soldiers with several humans at the end of the line. Walking down the lines, Radom couldn't believe how fit they looked. Coming to the end of the lines after having an occasional chat with a soldier, they came at last to Simon Hayes, Kate and Radon. Radom stood looking at the Oregarthian he was named after. He looked every bit the formable commander his father had told him about.

After introductions, Simon led the way to the Command centre. Giving them a brief tour of the bridge, he suggested they move to the conference area, they had much to discuss. Simon started off with what had happened to him and the crew before moving on to what had occurred since they reappeared. To say Radom and Jeddar were sceptical was an understatement.

"So after all that's taken place you decided to come here to bring us up to speed on what is occurring all over the Universe?" Jeddar scoffed.

"We have come here to find out if you have had contact with these Roax pirates. At first, I thought the Flax Federation was too big for them to target. By what happened to Craigsure, we now have our proof." Simon answered.

"You could've done that for all we know!" Jeddar shouted out.

"How dare you accuse us of such a thing." Kate spat out, defending Simon.

"I will say what I like woman!" Jeddar shouted, jumping to his feet. Standing up he found two pistols held by two of the Katherine's crew against his forehead. The room went silent, as Jeddar clearly surprised by the soldier's reflexes, sat back down. Radom who had remained silent during Jeddar's outburst now asked for calm.

"Be quiet Jeddar and I'd suggest not jumping around so much. Radom smiled "Okay let's say I believe you. Why would they attack us and then leave?"

"I'm not sure. The Hedred were blackmailed into supplying raw materials. The Roax even planted spies inside their command structure. What else has occurred here?" Simon enquired. Radom hesitant at first, explained what had taken place.

After the loss of Craigure, Radom after taking command had become worried by another call for help from Oregarth. Dispatching the same fleet that had travelled to Oregarth earlier to check on the meteor situation, he waited for their answer. What they received instead was a call for help from their own fleet. This surprised Radom, who knew the fleet of ships sent, though old, numbered over a hundred vessels.

Taking their most powerful battle group, the Home fleet, Radom in command travelled to Oregarth. Although they found signs of a recent battle, nothing was found of their fleet. Oregarth was uninhabitable, and no population could be found. Thinking the worst and knowing the fleet might be needed back in the Federation, Radom returned to protect his people.

Since those first two contacts with the enemy, if it was the same enemy, they'd had no other incidents with this unknown force. Now the people feeling the danger had passed, wanted military rule dissolved, returning to normal government rule.

"Are there many pushing for the disbanding of the fleets?" Radon asked, watching Radom, the man named after him.

"Yes, it is growing amongst the commanding officers who must make the final decision," Radom replied.

"Why they attacked you, then left you alone is interesting. Maybe with the trouble with the Hedred and the re-emergence of the Katherine, they found themselves spread too thin? Whatever it is, I can assure you they will return." Simon warned.

"We have much to think about Captain Hayes. With your leave, we will return to our ship and discuss our talks with the ship's commanders. They, in the end, will decide if the military law is dissolved. One thing though, before we go, how does your shuttle power such impressive shields?" Radom asked.

"Yes, they're quite impressive. The design comes from a human planet called New America. I too was amazed at the power unit's ability. As a sign of good faith, I will give you a copy of its design. It could help you improve your shields and weaponry if the enemy returns." Simon pointed out.

"That is a generous gesture Captain Hayes. You must realise it will make our shields and weapons more powerful against you as well." Radom answered, surprised by the gesture.

"Yes, and with greater numbers, you may be able to overpower us. Unfortunately, I feel you will need them so we will take the chance. We will await your decision." Simon smiled, as Radon escorted them back to their ship.

"They do not trust us, Simon. Is it wise to give them advanced technology?" Kate whispered as Radom and Jeddar left.

"Most probably not, but we must prove to them that we will help them. I fear like the Hedred, there is a reason for the Roax leaving them alone."

"You suspect the Roax have people in the Federation's military?"

"Yes I laid the seed of suspicion; let's hope they come to the same conclusion."

Jeddar and Radom sat quietly as they travelled back to their ship. Both thought over what they had been told dissecting the information to try to find any signs of treachery from Simon Hayes.

"You push your luck testing them Jeddar. I thought for a second, they were going to shoot you." Radom smiled.

"Yes, they're protective of Simon's woman. I couldn't believe how fast those soldiers reacted." He chuckled.

"There is more to this crew than meets the eye, although, he seems genuine in his willingness to help us," Radom admitted.

"He was also trying to tell us something, but didn't want it to be obvious."

"Did you think Jeddar, that when he brought up the Hedred having traitors in their command structure, that he was warning us, we could have the same?"

"It fits. If he'd suggested that straight out, we would've rejected it out of hand."

"When we get back, see if any of the fleet ships have picked up anything being broadcasted, especially codes which aren't Federation fleet ones."

"Do you think they would've warned the Roax of our meeting?"

"If I were them, I would've."

Once Radom's shuttle had touched down, he called a meeting of his commanders. Jeddar in the meantime hurried to the Comm's room to see if anything had been picked up. Radom at the meeting outlined what he had discussed with Captain Hayes and the threat they believed the Federation would soon face. Like they had been, many were sceptical.

"All this could just be a fantasy, made up by someone who looks like Captain Hayes. I think we should stick to the plan and revert back to Civilian rule. The people should decide what to do." Commander Droid put forward many agreeing.

"I too have a problem believing this Captain Hayes, but on the other hand what if he's right. I think we should think on it and meet back here tomorrow." Captain Dane suggested, for once not backing Droid on surrendering Marshal Law. The great majority nodded their agreement, as Jeddar entered the room. Walking over to Radom, his face blank as he kept his emotions in check, he showed Radom a piece of paper. For several seconds he stared at it, as several guards slipped into the room behind the gathered officers.

"Why wait another day, Captain Dane? Surely we can decide now?" Radom snarled, surprising the gathered commanders with his tone.

"We don't want to rush a decision here when so much is a stake." Captain Dane smiled back; despite Radom's outburst, he knew Droid and himself, still held the majority of support in the room.

"It wouldn't be so your friends can launch an attack against the Federation would it?" Radom growled. The officers gathered stood silently, taken aback by the question and Radom's anger.

"How dare you take advantage of a meeting to attack an officer of your own fleet!" Commander Droid answered, shocked by Radom's obvious manipulation of the meeting.

"Silence all of you! Guards secure Captain Dane now!" Radom ordered as soldier-drawing weapons seized Captain Dane, much to the horror of the gathered Officers. To all appearances, Captain Dane seemed calm looking like an innocent man. Radom then held up the piece of paper.

"This is a message intercepted while I was on the Katherine. Captain Dane sent it supposedly to his wife. If that was the case, why did he use a code not used by the Federation?" Radom asked. Jeddar looked around to see astonishment on the Officers' faces, slowly replaced by anger.

"Are you saying Captain Dane betrayed the Federation and is helping the enemy?" Commander Droid stammered out, clearly not believing the allegations.

"Yes, I am. I further believe one of our homeworlds is about to be attacked while we are here. Isn't that right Captain?" Dane slowly lost his composure, his eyes taking on a malevolence expression.

"You can't prove a thing Radom. Anyway, it's too late, you'll soon wish you were dead." He sniggered, the Officers around him horrified by his answer, moved away from him. Any doubt in the gathered Officers' minds about him being guilty, died with these two sentences.

"Take him away for questioning." Radom spat out, before continuing. "Gentlemen we will soon be under attack has anyone an idea where they will strike first. I myself don't think they'll attack the fleet, we're too strong?" Radom pointed out.

"My God it's got to be the Home planet Crytstan." Commander Droid answered, looking worried. Seeing the looks from the crowd around him, he continued. "I had a report just before I came to this meeting. One of the ships left to keep watch over the planets near Crytstan, reported seeing a huge ship in the Galaxy adjacent to it. When it went to investigate it, they found nothing. I thought it might have been a supply ship of course. Now I believe it must have been there to recon off the area and the only planet in that area of any worth is Crytstan."

"What can we do? The travelling time to the homeworld from here is over two days. The fourth fleet is the closest, although it would take over twelve hours." Jeddar pointed out.

"What about the Katherine? Doesn't she trek through space in some type of advanced travelling system?" One junior officer put forward, as the room looked at Radom.

"Prepare your ships, I'll go back to the Katherine and ask for their help. Be ready to leave in a moment's notice!" He ordered. Signalling to Jeddar to come with him, he ran to the shuttle bay. Once away from the room Radom pulled Jeddar aside.

"Take command of the flagship. I will stay aboard the Katherine and watch for any sign of treachery. I'll stay in contact and command, but you are in charge if anything happens to me." He confided in him.

"I could go in," Jeddar started to say, when Radom stopped him.

"No I must do this Jeddar. Don't worry; I'm sure I can trust Captain Hayes."

"What if we are too late?"

"Then billions will die and the Federation might fall. Have faith my friend. In the meantime alert the ships we left behind. Although not numerous, they should put up a good fight till we arrive. Till we meet again." Radom smiled hugging his brother, before entering his shuttle

THE ENEMY OF MY ENEMY IS MY FRIEND

On board the Katherine, Simon watched as their scanners indicated the Federation fleet was preparing to leave. They hadn't received an answer to their treaty proposal, and the fact they were leaving didn't fill him with confidence.

"Simon, Radom is returning on the same shuttle. He is asking permission to come aboard." Radon informed him.

"Tell him he has permission."

"What do you think is going on?" Kate asked beside him.

"I'm not sure, but we will soon know. In the meantime, prepare the ship to leave, and raise the shields as soon as Radom's aboard." Simon ordered.

"I find it confusing he shares the same name with me?" Radon put in.

"It could be worse, Jeddah could be here too. Then we have to put up with double the amount of confusion." Ryan pointed out, realising Katy's names was close to Kate's as well.

No one had to be told something was wrong, when Radom rushed in, causing some to move their hands towards their weapons.

"What's wrong?" Simon asked.

"We did what you hinted at and found a spy aboard our ships. He'd tried to delay us leaving for another day, while we discussed the situation. We believe that the enemy intends to attack the birthplace of our race, the home planet of Crytstan. A strange ship was reported in a neighbouring Galaxy."

"Do you have the co ordinates of the Galaxy where the ship was spotted and your home planet Crystan?" Simon requested.

"Yes I have them here. But aren't you going to ask for something in return for helping us?" Radom was taken aback by Simon's gesture.

"We have no time Radom. Order your ships to follow us and tell them to prepare to open fire once we leave the portal."

"How will they know we are leaving the portal?" Radom exclaimed.

"They'll know all right." Ryan smiled, as Simon feed in the portal co-ordinates.

On board, the Federation flagship, Jeddar like everyone else stared at the revolving circle of water.

"My God that's unbelievable." One of his crew murmured beside him. Watching the Katherine shoot forward into the circle, Jeddar realising everyone was still watching, broke the spell.

"Order the fleet to follow the Katherine and go to battle stations!" He shouted galvanising the crew, as one by one the Federation's ships roared into the circle.

Between Crytstan and the neighbouring Galaxy, thirty Federation ships formed a wall between the coming attack and the unknown enemy. Commander Tubler on board the improvised command ship, watched with a growing sense of futility, as forty huge enemy vessels, headed straight towards him. Behind them, just coming into view, three gigantic meteors could be seen.

"They're going to try and divert our fire-power to fighting off the ships, while the meteors pulverise the Homeworld." He said out loud.

"What are your orders, Sir?" His second in command, Captain Polen asked.

"Tell Captain Dorgan to take his squadron of five ships and target the meteors, while the rest of us engage the enemy ships.

"We will be outnumbered two to one Sir, is that wise?"

"A wise man would run away my friend. Just pray help arrives. In the meantime, send a message to Crytstan, have them evacuate as many people as they can."

"Yes, Sir. Although on the outside they only have another two hours."

"Any we save will be worth our sacrifice Captain. Now order the fleet forward, the sooner we engage them, the better." Tubler confessed, secretly praying for a miracle.

On board the enemy ship, their commander watched the five ships break away.

"Contact the base. Inform them the planet is defenceless." Commander Brugger smiled. "Prepare all weapons and fire as soon as the Flax ships come into range." He ordered. This is it he mused; the Federation had always been the key. With their huge resources, there will be nothing to stop them from conquering all of space. All they needed was the fleet disbanded. The reappearance of the Katherine he knew had rattled the Roax council. This action would prove to the Federation, that one ship, no matter how advanced, couldn't protect them from random attacks.

To his left, out of the corner of his eye, he saw one of his ships open fire. The range was extreme, but his men were confident. A flash in the distance indicated a hit. At this distance damaging one of the Federation's ships he knew would be near impossible, although it did show the accuracy of their weapon systems. A slight tremor through his chair indicated his ship had fired, as pinpricks of light could be seen approaching from the enemy ships.

A loud thump shook the bridge, forcing him to grip the side rest of his chair to stop from being thrown out. Smiling he remembered the council's warning about being overconfident. The Flax Federation he knew had updated their ships, shields and weapons, making them although impressive, still not their equal. It this battle though, it didn't matter much, he concluded.

Numbers counted here, and with forty ships to their twenty, this battle wouldn't last long. Already he could see distant explosions as the firepower from his ships overpowered the incoming ships' shields. Once they had been eliminated, he would turn his fleet's attention on the five ships sent to attack the meteors. True they might in the meantime destroy the three incoming meteors, but there were plenty more waiting to be sent, once these ships were taken care of.

"Commander Brugger, a portal is opening to our right." His second in command warned.

"Is it one of ours?"

"I don't think so, Sir. The long-range scanner is now picking up hundreds of objects travelling in the portal. They will be here in ten minutes Sir."

"But the Flax Federation doesn't have portal technology?"

"Does it matter at the moment, Sir?" His Captain warned.

"Tell all ships to disengage and open a portal now Captain!" Brugger ordered, ignoring his Captain's tone, his confidence gone by the approach of an unknown enemy. Swiftly pushing in the co-ordinates, the Roax opened their own portal. "Okay have the ships form up and leave immediately." He shouted, his ship rocketing forward entering first. Behind him, the Katherine roared out of the circle of water.

Simon taking in the situation ordered the emerging Flax Federation's fleet to engage the enemy ships. Radom taking in what was happening didn't hesitate, immediately passing on the order to his fleet to open fire. It was a massacre, as hundreds of Flax ships racked the enemy with a burst of laser fire as they exited the portal. Of the forty Roax ships, only ten made it into the portal, the others being destroyed as they lined up to enter.

Simon in the meantime ordered his crew to intercept and help the five Flax ships that were targeting the meteors. He could see that despite their best efforts the three meteors were just too big.

"Okay men. First of all, we change their direction before we try to destroy them. We can't have even house size pieces impacting on Crytstan, so first divert them away from the planet." Simon explained, as his weapons crews opened fire.

Captain Polen stood with his crew staring at a legend. They'd been told the fleet had arrived to help, but the sight of the Katherine, first roaring up beside them and then pounding the meteors had spellbound his crews.

"Keep firing; don't let them get all the glory." He shouted, his crew responding. Twenty minutes of unrelenting bursts of energy saw the last of the three destroyed. "Cease fire men and well done." Captain Polen ordered, his men, in turn, shouting out victory chants. Opening a Comm's line he contacted the Katherine thanking them. You're welcome came back, as the group headed back to the fleet's position.

"Radom signalling to Jeddar that they had destroyed the threat was greeted by the news that one of the Flax Federation ships had entered the Roax portal. It was a brave act by that ship, as once it exited the portal the Roax would spot it.

"Why didn't Jeddar stop them?" Simon asked Radom.

"As you said, we must find their base. The crew of that ship knew what they were doing when they entered. Their sacrifice will not be forgotten."

After a wait of over four hours, a signal was received. The ship sending its co-ordinates, spoke of hundreds of ships massing, before going off the air. Simon standing with Radom and Radon had no doubts the ship was destroyed.

"They were brave men." Simon admitted, admiring their bravery and sacrifice."

"They will be avenged; do we now travel to the location?" Radom asked.

"No, they will be ready. I suggest we send the Katherine first, to see what we're up against. Then we can act." Radon put forward Simon agreeing.

"But my fleet is here now we could end this," Radom argued.

"Their ships are more than a match for yours Radom. We beat them this time because of our vast numbers. Use the data I gave you and update your power units, then you will be ready. In the meantime spread your older and unarmed spaceships throughout your Federation. Chances are they'll try again to hurt you. Also watch the portal where the meteor's exited, more may come through." Simon warned. Radom at first fought to argue further about going after them. Looking at Radon, the alien he was named after, he saw a warrior who knew his stuff.

"Okay, I will return to my ship and await your call, and thank you both for saving my people." Radom bowed slightly before walking towards the hangar. He was just about to board when Radon came up behind him.

"Radom, wait a minute."

"What is it?" Radom asked.

"Here take this; Simon thinks you might need it when the call comes." Mystified Radom looked at the data his eyes bulging.

"Is this what I think it is?"

"Yes, against my advice, Simon said you will need it, now go and be ready," Radon warned turning and leaving. Radom stood frozen. They hadn't known him for more than a day and yet they trusted him. Climbing aboard his shuttle, he told his pilot to immediately take off and head to the flagship.

Jeddar was waiting along with the Captains of all the Federation ships when Radom arrived. Cheers broke out at the victory Radom had delivered.

"What did Simon Hayes demand for his help?" Jeddar asked the room going silent.

"Nothing," Radom answered as the room stood still.

"Then why did he help us?"

"Because he is our friend gentlemen like he was my father's. To him, that's enough." Radom confessed, handing Jeddar the data. At first, Jeddar just stared at it, wondering if Radom was joking, when looking at his brother he saw tears in his eyes.

"My God why has he done this?" Jeddar choked up, looked to Radom.

"So we'd be ready to answer his call. Gather all our forces, we prepare for war!" Radom shouted as the room exploded into cheers.

On board, the Katherine Simon and Radon convened a meeting. Every crewmember on board was there.

"We are all friends here, and I wanted you all here for this discussion. We now know where we think the Roax are based and I intend to go after them. The ship isn't what it once was and unlike before, we may face serious damage this time, even our destruction. Before we attack, I want to give everyone the chance to make a decision if they want to stay aboard. We have one stop to make before we commence our attack; I would suggest if anyone doesn't want to come with us, when we stop there they can leave no questions asked." Simon put forward.

"Katy, you and your people, are new to the ship, it isn't your fight, and you have been through enough." Ryan pointed out, secretly wanting her safe.

"Hey, the Roax attacked us long before you knew they were back. I speak for all my men when I say we will see this through or die trying." She snapped back, knowing why Ryan wanted her safe.

"Where are we going first anyway?" Benjamin asked seeing no one was going to leave.

"Back to New America, we may need their help," Simon admitted.

"Then let's get going, we're wasting time." Radon pointed out, knowing no one would leave.

"Maybe Kate would like to leave?" Horen said distantly going over his medical records.

"Why in Hell would I leave?" Kate exploded, causing Horen to become attentive.

"Well, it's just your pregnant, and I thought,' was all he got out.

"Pregnant are you sure?" Simon and Kate answered, both sounding slightly rattled.

"Why yes it's nothing out of the ordinary, I have known for several weeks," Horen replied, wondering what the fuss was about.

"Horen, to humans this is a big thing, especially as they are unmarried." Radon explained as nods of understanding flowed through the room, making both Simon and Kate go red.

"Their colour is changing, is that something to do with the pregnancy?" One of Jeddah's men asked as the humans in the room started to giggle.

"Is this another human joke?" Jabo smiled, seeing the confusion on the non-human crewmembers.

After Horen's news, the meeting broke up, as they all prepared to enter the portal to travel to New America. Once underway and in the Portal, Simon and Kate left the bridge. Arriving at their room, they silently entered sitting down.

"That was a surprise?" Simon muttered.

"Well we have been sleeping together for some time; sooner or later it was going to happen," Kate answered, knowing this explained her sickness in the mornings.

"I know we've always talked about it, but when we stop on New America we could get married?" Simon suggested.

"That would be nice to marry on my home planet, but we have no time. We must attack the Roax as soon as we can before they leave." Kate whispered her parent's death appearing in front of her."

You know being pregnant, maybe it's better if you stay there till I return?" Simon started to put forward as Kate came alive.

"Don't even think about it. I'm coming with you that's the end of it."

"Just thought I'd put the idea past you that's all?"

"Well forget it, Simon, it isn't happening," Kate growled the discussion over.

Arriving at New America caused quite a stir. All three fleets were still there having waited till after the elections to redeploy. Simon noticed as soon as they exited the portal, that the fleet's crews had been busy. All the ships had incorporated the new power systems from the prototype shuttle.

"Welcome back Simon. Come to see if I kept my word?" General Wordsworth's voice boomed through their Comm's gear.

"No not really, but how did it go anyway?" Simon replied.

"You'll never guess who's President?" Wordsworth chuckled.

"Okay, we give up, who?"

"Remember Captain Stuart, Ryan's second in command. Well after things settled down after the coup, he became a bit of a hero. I suggested he make a difference and run for

President. He did and was elected. He even made me commander of the first fleet, although he could be just trying to get rid of me."

"That sounds like good news. Unfortunately, we're not here to celebrate. Can you arrange a meeting with him with us immediately?" Simon requested.

"All arranged. When the circle opened, he prepared a special welcome for you. One of our shuttles will guide you down to the planets new capital, New York."

"Thank you General and one other thing, watch for portals. Not all of them are made by us anymore." Simon warned.

"I will be at the reception we can talk there." The General answered his voice sounding worried.

As the Katherine descended toward New America's, new Capital, Radon like usual, ordered the crew to go to battle stations.

"Stand down men, it won't be necessary Radon." Simon smiled, his friend always pessimistic when meeting Simon's race.

"We've been through this before Simon. Radon's right the shield stays up." Kate chastised him, the crew siding with her and Radon, moving to their positions, deploying the shield.

"Can you see where we are headed?" Simon asked Ryan at the helm, changing the subject.

"There seems to be a space cruiser base built beside the city. There's a lot of activity on the ground there." He warned. Simon after digesting this information started to feel less confident about what was waiting for them.

"My god I don't believe it!" Ryan suddenly spoke out his eyes on the view screen.

"What is it?" Radon barked, his fear of a trap heightened.

"Sorry, there's no danger, it's just the activity I've never seen so many people in one place," Ryan exclaimed. Everyone who could, rushed to the observation deck, the argument over going to battle stations forgotten.

"Why are they all here? I thought we were feared?" Simon whispered, Kate beside him gripping his hand.

"I'd say someone has told them the truth," Kate answered holding him.

"Horen have the men breakout their dress uniforms," Radon ordered. "And stand down from battle stations." He added, noticing that most already had.

"I can't even remember where they are Radon. We only have a few for greeting guests. It's been a long time since we were welcomed by anyone." Horen replied, some of the crew chuckling.

"Well, we can't go out there looking like we're here to fight. Ditch the heavy weapons, side arms only." Radon suggested.

"I think I can help." Jabo interrupted. "Jeddar loaded uniforms from his stock on his battleship, just in case we needed them. They were to be used when we rendezvoused with his people when they reach the Flax Federation."

"You can always count on that man. Break them out immediately. Anyone who wants to leaves this ship had better have one on! And that includes the humans." Radon warned as the crew rushed out to find a uniform that fitted.

President Stuart stood with his wife and children on a podium as the Katherine touchdown. In the morning light, the Katherine shone reddish white, looking every bit an invincible warship, as she glided into land. The gathered crowd hushed till now, broke into a roar, welcoming the once feared ship. New America had gone through a process of shame, shock and anger when the truth was told about what happened on Salvation and their part in it.

Many didn't believe it until General Wordsworth appeared on TV telling them the whole story. It was a lot for the people to take in. Stuart on his maiden speech had promised his people that they would find the other Gun Barrel planets and try to rectify the disgrace they felt at what their leaders had once done. It was met with universal support.

Soldiers wearing no weapons, cordoned off an area around the Katherine, as the side of the ship housing the space shuttles, slid open. Once it was fully lowered an honour guard of the Katherine's crew numbering 500 hundred marched out, under the watchful eye of Radon. Lining up in four rows they stood silently listening to the roar of the crowd, awaiting Simon and Kate's arrival. The crowd sensing something special was about to happen went mute holding their breaths.

Simon feeling slightly embarrassed waited in the hanger for Kate. Jeddah as a sign of respect had given him a High Commander's uniform, which had once been worn by the Commander of the Flax Federation. Jet-black with silver epaulettes on his shoulders, with a dragon-like creature on his black peak cap, made him uncomfortable. Feeling he should change into something more relaxed, he turned to the doorway to see Kate staring at him.

"Simon you look so much like a leader. " She murmured looking impressed. Simon took a moment to reply as he stared at her. She was dressed in a silver coloured dress, which shimmered as she moved covered with crystals it reflected thousands of colours all around her. On her head, she wore a small black hat with some type of feather the colour of pearl.

"You are beautiful Kate." Simon got out overwhelmed. Moving forward she kissed him lightly on the cheek.

"Let's go my love. We have a planet to impress." She smiled, as hand in hand, they walked down the ramp. As they emerged into the light the crowd seeing them went wild.

Across from the Katherine, waiting on a hastily built grandstand, stood President Stuart. Pulling at his collar he tried to get some more room for his neck. He felt like killing General Wordsworth, for suggesting he run for President. He won and went from at one stage waiting to be shot, to having people pander to him, while he wore a suit with ties trying to look casual.

"Stop fidgeting Bill." His wife Anna whispered beside him, as looking across he saw Simon emerge from the Katherine to a huge roar. "My God I'd kill for that dress." Anna said softly her eyes glued to the young couple walking down to stand in front of his crew.

"Well General what do we do now?" Stuart asked Wordsworth.

"Protocol would suggest that Simon approach you. Under the circumstances, I would suggest we walk over there and review his guard of honour."

"I wouldn't do that Sir, it's too risky." His head of security whispered from behind him. Turning he found Sergeant Ross dressed in a suit looking as uncomfortable as he felt.

"Relax Sergeant I think we're safe. You can walk behind me if you feel better." Stuart smiled, thinking Ross would never change.

"Of course Mr President." Ross shot back, hiding a smile, knowing Stuart hated it.

"Okay people, let's go," Stuart ordered as Anna, General Wordsworth and Ross and himself walked across to the Katherine, as the crowds' cheering grew even louder.

Walking up and down the lines, Stuart started to relax enjoying talking to the soldiers lined up for inspection. They were soldiers like he had been and he felt a bond with them, as General Wordsworth and Ross did. Anna not into the warrior show stood with Kate talking. Reaching the last row, Stuart noticed humans made up this row. His old Captain Ryan was there with the kid from the village who went with him, but who were the others? Approaching a woman in a naval Captain's uniform he stopped.

"Good morning Captain. I wasn't aware the Katherine had some humans aboard?" Stuart smiled seeing some hostility in some of the human's faces.

"I should have warned you, Mr President, they are from Salvation. We rescued what was left of the population several months ago." Simon interrupted. A dark silence settled over the group as Sergeant Ross fingered his weapon.

"Relax my friend we know you weren't responsible," Katy said softly seeing Ross' movement.

"I speak for all my people when I tell you how sorry I am for all the suffering you have been through." Stuart apologised sounding and acting like a true President.

"What happened?" Wordsworth asked Katy.

"How about you all come aboard, a lot has occurred Simon confessed, President Stuart agreeing.

Two hours of shame later, President Stuart stood up and walked around the observation deck, deep in thought.

"My God a tidal wave was bad enough. Then you had to endure the Roax try to annihilate the rest of you, is something our planet will always feel responsible for." General Wordsworth confessed, truly sorry for his part in this mess.

"What's done is done General. I for one will call the debt you owe us cancelled if you help us get the Roax murderers responsible." Katy put forward, her officers agreeing.

"That is not enough we would do that anyway." Stuart interrupted. "When this is all over, the people of New America would gladly welcome you here or assist in re-establishing your people on Salvation. That I promise you." Stuart declared his voice full of emotion.

"We thank you for your offer, Mr President. But first, we must assist Captain Hayes to defeat this enemy.

"You can have every ship we have Captain Simon, just tell us where and we'll join you." Stuart pledged offering his hand to Simon. Shaking it, Simon knew Stuart was a hundred percent with them.

"If everyone could leave us I have a matter to discuss with General Wordsworth and President Stuart in private," Simon announced the others sensing something big was coming, left the three men. Sergeant Ross like usual, hesitated until Stuart waved him outside.

"Okay, what is it?" Wordsworth asked thinking Simon wanted something from them.

"I judge you've fitted your ships with power supplies similar to the one on that Junta shuttle?" Simon softly asked.

"Yes, it seemed the right thing to do," Wordsworth replied.

"Do you have a problem with us updating our defences?" Stuart snapped back.

"Quite the opposite Mr President. I think you will need them for the coming battles and defence of your homeworlds."

"Then why asked?" Stuart enquired.

"In the coming battles and there maybe more than one, firepower and shields will mean the difference between defeat and victory. The fact your ships are fitted with them makes your ships the most battle ready of all the races I have met.

There is only one thing you lack, that's speed." Simon pointed out handing Stuart a set of plans.

Looking at the plans, Stuart wasn't sure what he was really looking at, Wordsworth beside him who was also looking gasped in surprise.

"Good God Simon, why give this to us? Let's face it you don't really know us that well." Wordsworth humbled by Simon's gesture.

"What is it General?" Stuart spoke out, worried by Wordsworth's expression.

"It's how to construct your own portals, Mr President. You are now the third race I have trusted with this data. Keep it a secret as long as you can, we don't know if the Roax, have people here or not." Simon answered. Like Wordsworth, Stuart couldn't find the words. With this, his people could expand into the surrounding Galaxies and search for the other Gun Barrel Planets.

"I don't know what to say." Stuart got out in the end.

"Don't say anything just be ready when I call," Simon replied.

Kate, while Simon was talking business, had taken Anna for a tour of the ship. The dress Kate was wearing had intrigued her. Explaining about Jeddah's people and the Flax Federation led to Anna talking about trading with them. After working out a plan to influence their husbands, the talking changed to the slight bump in the front of Kate's dress. Explaining how they'd tried to get married on Salvation over fifty years ago and it hadn't occurred led Anna to make a suggestion.

A state wedding on New America would help cement peaceful relations with Simon's other friends across the Universe. And as Anna pointed out, it was her homeplanet. Unsure and with a coming battle, Kate agreed to think about it.

"Don't leave it too long?" Anna smiled as Kate self-consciously touched her belly.

For the cameras outside, the President posed with Simon. With great fanfare, they signed a formal treaty between Radon's people, the Oregarthians and New America. Although no one mentioned they were at the moment in transit with Jeddah or outside the known Universe. The President then surprised the gathering by announcing that General Wordsworth had volunteered to travel with Simon as an ambassador for New America.

This caused the people in the crowd to shout his name. To say the General was speechless, didn't quite describe the look on his face, as forcing a smile, he waved to the excited crowd. Simon also too stunned, to reply, instead he shook his hand, welcoming him aboard. Radon chuckling behind them realised Stuart would make a fine President.

To a roar from the crowd Simon, Kate and his crew marched aboard the Katherine. As the shuttle bay doors closed, the Katherine slowly rose into the air. Hovering two hundred metres above the ground, Simon opened the portal right above the landing field. The crowd who had never seen anything like the portal, were instantly hushed as the Katherine roared into the circle of water.

"You've got to get one of them husband. The crowd love it." Anna suggested to her husband, as in answer the crowd went wild, cheering long after the Katherine had disappeared.

"I'll work on it." Stuart smiled, as Ross beside him gave a rare grin. "Moving on Ross, call a meeting of the General staff immediately, I have to make an announcement to the people about what's going on." He explained his face turning serious.

On board the Katherine, the crew made a room available for the New America's Ambassador. General Wordsworth was, to say the least unimpressed with his hasty departure from New America. True he could see the President's motives, in wanting to know what was going on in the Galaxies around them, he just wished he had had more time to gather his personal gear before leaving.

There was also the issue of once trying to kill Captain Hayes. Many on board this ship, practically worshipped the guy, it made him very uncomfortable. At that moment a knock rang out from his door making him jump.

"Who is it?" Wordsworth shouted.

"It is Radon. I need to talk to you." Radon replied. Wordsworth opened the door to find him standing in the hallway holding a large bag." Simon has asked me to invite you to dinner. We have much to discuss."

"Sounds good, although Radon, I have a problem. I have no shaving gear or spare clothing." Radon smiling passed him the bag. Inside Wordsworth saw shaving gear, toothbrushes and several pairs of uniforms. "You're way ahead of me aren't you?" Wordsworth smiled.

"I have always been a commander. Allowing for even the smallest details is the way to victory."

"Yes although I didn't expect the second in command to bring them." The General chuckled. "Now, how do I find the dinner area?"

"One of our men will escort you in an hour's time if that is okay?"

"Good I will be ready, and the name's John," Wordsworth answered, watching Radon nod and turn away.

"That man scares me." The General admitted to himself, walking to his shower.

At dinner, the General was introduced to a room full of officers. Katy's group were all officers, her soldiers staying with their families on Jeddah's battleship. The rest were mainly Jeddah's troops or from the crew of the Katherine. After a cordial, if reserved introduction, dinner was eaten in silence. Simon and Kate broke the silence with questions about life on New America. The others just sat there listening. In the end, Simon aware of the quiet reception Wordsworth was getting, spoke out.

"General Wordsworth is our guest people. I expect him to be treated as you would Kate or me. Am I understood?" Many nodded their understanding, although no one spoke up. In the end, Simon and Kate stood up and left both angry. The room, which before was silent, became a tomb as Wordsworth continued to eat his meal appearing unaware of the problem. Finishing his meal, he wiped his mouth looking over the gathered group.

"Wake up to yourselves. I have always been a soldier; I follow orders, as do you. Don't hold me responsible for what happened in the past. Grow up or let's have it out now." Wordsworth challenged.

"You shot Captain Hayes." One of Jeddah's officer's accused, jumping to his feet, many stamping their hands on their tables.

"Big deal. I was following orders or don't you soldiers do that?" He snarled, causing many to go quiet thinking over what he said.

"You destroyed our planet and my entire family, with an atomic bomb." One of Katy's officers cried out, his voice full of emotion.

"The people responsible for that are long dead; they were executed when we found out what they did. The people of New America are ashamed of our past, but they weren't responsible for that cowardly act. I know you got a shit deal, but you must move on. Our President promised to help you all rebuild or let you live on New America with us, but you must for yourselves, move on." Wordsworth answered, his voice sounding sorrowful.

"I might remind you, people, that General Wordsworth at great personal risk led a coup which toppled the Military Junta controlling New America. He saved thousands of lives and brought peace and democracy to his people. I at one stage wanted this man dead for what he did to Simon, my friend. That was before I saw his true metal. We have an enemy out there who if they get the chance will enslave us all. Only by working together can we defeat this foe." Radon growled, "Now all of you leave and get to your stations, there is work to be done."

Many as they left passed Wordsworth nodding or offering their hand, which he gladly shook, in the end only Radon remained.

"Feel like a drink?" Radon smiled.

"I didn't know your race drank."

"It, not something I brag about, but Simon's grandfather and I often shared a shot of whisky many years ago, when we were living on Salvation. The taste stayed with me."

"Where do you get it from?"

"One of my men is a scientist of sorts. You've met him, his name is Horen. He built a device which makes a close match to it." Producing a flask, Radon handed it to Wordsworth. Taking a swig, Wordsworth broke into a fit of savage coughing.

"He's got a little way to go yet." Wordsworth wheezed, wiping his eyes where tears started forming.

"Welcome aboard John." Radon chuckled.

FACE OFF

Unlike in the past, when the Katherine had roared out of the portal, this time it emerged drifting. With only enough power for steerage, the Katherine crawled along, barely moving. When going to the aid of the Hedred, they had hidden in an adjoining Galaxy. This time having no option, Simon opened the portal in the same area as the ill-fated Flax Federation ship.

Radon had suggested the slow approach, as with their low power, it reduced their silhouette, reducing the enemy's chances of knowing quite when the Katherine would emerge from the obvious portal ring. Their precautions seemed unnecessary, as the galaxy they'd entered showed no signs of the enemy fleet.

"Keep alert people, we don't know anything about this location." Simon reminded the crew, as the Katherine increased speed moving forward. The Galaxy they'd entered consisted of two suns and thirty planets. As they moved between the two solar giants, the crew scanned each planet, searching for anything to give them a clue as to the enemy's intentions. Chances were they'd find no indigenous life as the orbits around the two suns produce both extremes of heat and cold.

"Captain there is wreckage ahead." Ryan at the forward detection scanner warned. All eyes turned to the forward viewing screen as the debris came into view.

"Looks like the remains of four ships." Radon to Simon's side pointed out, his sadness for the loss of the brave Flax crew in his voice.

"They took three with them!" Jabo exclaimed the crew stamping their feet.

"Yes, they were brave soldiers. Move on people concentrate on your instruments." Radon warned.

"Sir I'm picking up a weak signal from the last planet in this system. Its orbit suggests that the temperature, although lower than most habitable planets our races are used to, would support life, as it has a breathable atmosphere.

"Stop engines." Simon ordered looking at the planet. "Why transmit as we're approaching?" He asked himself out loud.

"Could be a random signal or a call for help?" Ryan suggested.

"It could also be a trap." Wordsworth pointed out, Radon beside him agreeing, as the room grew quiet.

"Prepare for action, man all weapons," Simon commanded, having already deployed the shield.

"I'm getting a visual of some type of base on the planet surface Sir. There appear to be two towers pointed up into space." Benjamin reported staring at the picture. In two steps Radon was beside him, studying the picture.

"Horen turn the ship! Maximum speed, get us away from here!" He shouted. He voice had only stopped when the ship banked to its left side shuddering as it accelerated. Without warning the ship was slammed sideways klaxon horns screaming out their warnings.

"Damage report!" Simon yelled, above the noise.

"Ship's hull has been breached forward of engineering. There's extensive damage." Jabo reported.

"Fire everything we've got at that base," Simon ordered as small shudders indicated his order had been received. Again the ship was struck this time knocking everyone not secured to the deck.

"Simon we're hitting the base, but it has heavy shielding, we're just not getting through to the weapons," Jabo shouted from his station.

"What if we got closer?" Simon asked.

"We're taking too much damage, the superstructures being hammered by that space gun. Maybe if we come around behind the planet. Jabo suggested." Simon was just thinking of over a route to do that when Ryan shouted a warning.

"Enemy ships are closing on us from several portals behind us!" he screamed, several crewmembers looking back at the rear wall as if expecting to see something.

"How many?" Simon softly asked, trying to keep everyone calm.

"At least a hundred ships Sir. They've just opened fire." Simon was just about to answer when he was thrown to the ground. Radon running to him pulled him back into the Captain's chair.

"Sir, the shields are holding, but the enemy concentrated weapons fire is too powerful. It's breaking through; several areas are reporting fires and hull breaches. The ships can't take much more." Radon softly told Simon. The fact he'd called him Sir showed the seriousness of the situation. The crew were all now watching him. Making a decision, Simon ran to the portal controls. Without thinking he entered a set of co-ordinates, as the ship lurched onto its side. The Katherine staggering forward, one engine destroyed, entered the portal, firing as it went.

"All sections report. Engine room, what's your situation first." Simon called over the intercom, as the firing ceased and the ship quietened down.

"We've got steering only Sir, the remaining engine is only producing ten percent of its power."

"Ryan. Can you organise teams to search for fires and leaks in the superstructure? Anyone not at a working weapon or working on the bridge is to help." Simon ordered, as the room swiftly emptied. Kate appearing at the door, made Simon breathe a sigh of relief. During the engagement, her safety had flashed through his mind but was unable to look for her.

"Are you okay?" He whispered as she came close.

"Yes, Katy and several of her men helped me. The accommodation section is all but destroyed. We've lost a lot of people, many others are trapped in different areas of the ship." She informed him.

"I'm sorry Kate, but they are going to have to wait. Our main priorities at the moment are first fires then the hull's integrity. Once they're secure, we'll look for trapped crew. If we don't stop the fires or stop our air supply venting we're all finished." Beside him Radon nodded, backing his decision.

"I'll organise some of the lightly injured to help me that won't use up able body crewmembers." She smiled running off.

"You've got a good female there," Radon whispered, giving a quick smile.

"Yes, without her I wouldn't have got this far," Simon replied as Ryan interrupted.

"Sir, there is movement in the portal behind us." He Ryan warned.

"Can you tell how many vessels?"

"Four I say Sir and they're gaining on us fast. I estimate twenty minutes till they open fire."

"Any ideas people?"

"Can we turn and fire? Jeddah managed to turn his ship in the portal when he left Oregarth." Benjamin suggested.

"We have too much battle damage. If we turn the ship, we may break in half. Only the shield is keeping us intact." Jabo informed them. This shocked the crew, who thought the ship was invincible.

"What about the New America shuttle? It's shielded and has weapons, it could give them a surprise." Radon smiled.

"Good idea, but why not use both?" Horen added telling him his plan.

Commander Brugger watched his ships close the gap on the Katherine. His defeat by the Flax Federation had been blamed on his overconfidence, something his leaders had warned him about. Even so, their main aim had been achieved, the destruction of the Katherine. Elena had planned this trap as soon as she heard the Katherine had returned. Every mission they went on returned through this Galaxy, before proceeding onto their base.

It was a brilliant strategy, and the Katherine had fallen for it. They had also planned on the Flax Federation fleet arriving with them. That had not occurred, meaning the Katherine's Captain had been overconfident had come alone to scout out the enemy. Now badly damaged, with her engines nearly totally destroyed, the Katherine limped ahead of them, practically defenceless. True she still had her shields and some weapons, but they were no use to her unless she could turn.

"We are approaching firing range, Sir." Brugger's, second in command informed him, startling him from his thoughts.

"Prepare to fire, victory is ours." He shouted his crew joining in.

"Sir we have two small craft possibly shuttles, coming towards our position." One of Brugger's crewmembers warned.

"I thought you couldn't change direction in a portal," Brugger asked his second in command Captain Mackenzie.

"You can't Sir. I'd say they are stopped and facing towards us. It appears they are moving towards us by our forward movement towards them." Mackenzie explained. 'What is Captain Hayes planning?' Brugger mused. He knew from experience the man was clever, but why did he deploy the shuttles?

"Are their shuttles armed?" he asked out loud, his crew looking at each other, no one answered. "Inform the other ships to target them first, just in case. We'll target the Katherine." He ordered his ship and the other three opening fire. After several minutes of firing, Brugger started to get worried.

"Why is it taking so long to take care of those shuttles? We need the firepower of all four ships to finish the Katherine" Brugger snapped at Mackenzie.

"The first shuttle has cruiser size shields. It should be impossible, but she is holding her own against our laser fire, even at this range. The second shuttle 's behind the first, she hasn't got shields, but the first shuttle is protecting her."

"Wait there, what did you say the range was?" Brugger barked.

"We're nearly right on top of the two shuttles Sir. The range is only a kilometre at the most." Mackenzie replied wondering why his Captain hadn't been paying attention.

"No, it can't be!" Brugger screamed. "Scan the shuttles for life," Brugger shouted, startling Mackenzie. Several seconds passed before a nervous Brugger received an answer.

"Sir, both the shuttles are unmanned. Also our gunner's report the first shuttle has been disabled. They are now concentrating on the second." Mackenzie answered smiling.

"Tell them to cease fire immediately. The second ship is a bomb!" He shouted, the future rushing towards him, as he stared now at the stricken ship receiving blast after blast of laser fire. He was too late, as the shuttle mushroomed towards them, an all-consuming ball of fire.

On board the Katherine, the destruction of the enemy ships
went unnoticed. The whole crew were busy fighting fires,
which had sprung up all over the ships. The fire from Brugger's
ship had finished the main engines, causing fires throughout
the rear of the ship. Feeling he was losing control, Simon
asked Radon for his opinion.

"We've no choice, Simon. We have to seal of the rear
compartments and vent the air, or we'll lose her." Radon put
forward, his eyes betraying, that he knew what he was
suggesting.

"You're right, I just wanted some backup for what I must
do." Simon swallowed readying himself. "Horen, can you hear
me?" Simon spoke into his headset.

"Yes, Simon."

"Recall all crews from the rear of the ship. Tell them we will
vent the ship in one hour, from the centre shuttle bay to the
rear engine room." Simon ordered.

"The Engineers at the rear are trapped they cannot
evacuate," Horen answered unsurely.

"Give the order Horen, we have no choice." Simon
reiterated, signing off. Heading back to the bridge, Simon was
met by Kate and Katy. They'd had some success in rescuing
trapped crewmembers. When the fire teams had been set up,
half of Katy's men went with Jabo to engineering to assist.

"Simon," Kate begun, tears in her eyes.

"Don't ask it, Kate. I know Katy's men are trapped with Jabo
along with who knows how many men. If I don't act now, we
are all lost." Simon trailed off, moving past them both.

"It is the right decision, Katy," Radon said softly, as Kate
held Katy. "Don't give up on them just yet," Radon reassured
them.

In the engineering section of the engine section, the
announcement was met with disbelief. The fires in their area
were under control. Jabo in charge tried to think of a solution.

"Are there any exits we can take?" Benjamin asked,
watching the clock, they had fifty minutes.

"No, moving forward is impossible, all the passageways are blocked or on fire. We're trapped I'm afraid." Jabo confessed.

"Well, what about the other way?" Ryan spluttered, having breathed in too much smoke.

"There isn't much in that direction, except non-essential stores." Jabo pointed out.

"But the rooms are airtight aren't they Jabo?"

"Not many, maybe the freezer sections. I believe they are airtight."

"Where there is air, we have a chance, let's go." Ryan smiled, lifting the room.

It was a perilous journey through blackened and smoke filled hallways. Amazingly along the way, they met others coming towards them. Explaining what they planned the word was passed around by mostly shouting and yelling as all the communications equipment had failed.

Reaching the storage area groups split up searching for anything that would help them survive. In one room they found stores of clothing another they found spacesuits for working outside on the ship. The number of suits was low, but they did have oxygen bottles and refills. Carrying everything they could they all met outside a meat locker.

The clock read fifteen minutes till venting, as the men worked as if possessed, tossing food outside to make room for crewmen. Jabo then with the help of a pistol shot out the temperature control, which slowly raised the temperature. Looking at his watch, Ryan saw time had run out.

"That's it men, everyone inside." He shouted, as on mass the group moved inside. Looking around outside, Ryan and Jabo shouted out, making sure all in the hearing were inside. Hearing no answer, they sealed the doors.

"Vent the ship," Simon ordered as the bridge crew opened the outer shuttle doors and exit doors along the rear of the ship. "Close off all air supplies to the rear sections of the ship." He ordered the bridge becoming as silent as a tomb.

"The ships completely vented Sir," Horen replied his voice sounding as if he'd sentenced the men trapped there to death himself.

"Are the fires contained?" Radon barked, snapping the men out of their depression.

"Yes Sir, all fires have been eliminated," Katy announced, her face downcast.

"Close the outer doors and turn the air supply back on," Simon commanded. "How many crewmembers are unaccounted for?" he asked Radon.

"Three hundred and twelve missing Sir, roughly a third of the crew," Radon told him, the whole bridge speechless.

"Some may have survived in pockets of air," Kate suggested, putting some hope into the room.

"She's right. Redeploy the fire teams Radon. Let's find our people." Simon ordered, as again everyone who could leave the bridge to search left.

In the first couple of hours, no one was found alive just bodies. Then when hope was fading twenty men several of Katy's missing people were discovered clinging to life in an old decompression chamber. Why it was onboard, no one knew, in the end, no one cared, as long as it had helped. Further, towards the back, ten men were found in an area used for exiting the ship for repair work on the hull. Having five spacesuits, they'd buddied up, sharing the oxygen with companions, through a tube connected to the suits.

Thirty, out of three hundred and twelve, wasn't too impressive, as the search neared the end of the ship. Many had already given up on finding any more crewmembers alive. Reaching the storage area the search found no one. The search party was just about to move on when one member noticed meat thrown all over the floor. Walking to the meat freezer, he tapped on the door, getting a faint tapping in reply.

The team reacting to the noise forced the door open. Inside huddled in groups for warmth, they found one hundred and ten survivors. Near frozen close to death they were dragged out, collapsing onto the meat littered floor.

News that so many had survived spread like wildfire. Every able body crewmember rushed to the storage area. The accommodations area had been destroyed, so the injured were carried to the observation deck area. It was a tight fit, although this helped with the shared body heat, to rejuvenate the ones suffering from hypothermia. Still, over two hundred had died, over one-fifth of the crew.

Two weeks, with food running out and the air supplies getting dangerously low, the Katherine cleared the portal. The trip would've usually taken four days under power; instead, they had drifted through it. When the Katherine had entered the portal, she was travelling at twenty percent of her cruising speed. Exiting she had the same velocity, as when she had entered. Drifting aimlessly, Simon at the helm, steered her using the side thrusters, towards a distant planet.

"I know this area," Radon said out loud before realising it. "I just can't put my finger on it?" He continued, staring at the planet, which had come into view.

"We met here a long time ago Radon. You were helping Jeddah free his people, and I was delayed while Kate recovered."

"I remember. You arrived through the portal, dazzling the Flax Federation's ships that had joined us. You made us fire on this ship, to show its unbeatable power. Times have changed, we no longer dominate the battlefield." Radon sadly admitted.

"We'll see Radon, we'll see," Simon mumbled watching the planet grow larger.

"Horen, can we land on the planet?" Simon asked. Horen checking his calculation weighed up the data before him.

"We can land Simon, but we will not be able to take off again. Better that we call one of our allies for help."

"Too risky, the enemy may well be on their way here now. Let's take her in, I want to bury my friends and fellow crewmembers with dignity." Simon responded, the crew nodding their support.

"Simon I know you blame yourself, but we may never leave this planet if we land," Kate interjected.

"Remember I told you the voices in the void told me something special that I couldn't reveal. It's here Kate." Simon confessed. As Radon hearing him raced to the forward sensor console.

"I knew you had something up your sleeve. Why now? Why didn't we come here earlier?" Radon asked sounding puzzled.

"They told me not to come here till the need was great. I would've come straight here if I'd have known what was going to occur." Simon confessed.

"Nothing is showing on the scanners, Simon. Are you sure this is the right planet?" Radon sounded sceptical.

"Take us down, Horen." Simon smiled "Battle stations everyone, this could be rough." He continued. Horen checking his console found the ship already had plotted a course to the planet."

"Simon, the ship is taking us into a prearranged location. Have you been here before?

"No, we met in orbit near this planet, we didn't land."

"Do you want to override it?"

"No, let the ship proceed."

"Are you sure you haven't landed here before?" Kate whispered.

"No never. Let's have faith everyone, we're here for a reason." Simon raising his voice told them all.

"We will follow you anywhere Captain Hayes." One of Jeddah's men shouted out, the room exploding with support for him.

"Well, who am I to argue with a legend." Radon scoffed, causing cheers from the crew.

"Approaching the atmosphere reverse thrusters are firing," Horen warned as the ship groaned the stress on the hull mounting. The cheering now stopped as the crew weighed up the ship's condition against a voice Simon had heard. Radon to the side softly chuckled at the crew's sobering.

The ship severely damaged took the full force of the planet's gravitational field, yawning sideways shuddering as the outside temperature rose. The shield that had once held back a bombardment from two of the Flax Federation's strongest fleets now seemed paper-thin barely protecting the hull, from the extreme outside heat.

"Sir the ship is having trouble slowing down. The outside temperature is causing the superstructure to buckle." Ryan informed him. He was monitoring the ship's hull's integrity. He didn't know how it was holding together.

"Drop what's left of the shields. All power to the reverse engines now!" Simon ordered, as with an audible scream of metal the Katherine rolled onto its side throwing Simon, Kate and Radon into a pile. Getting back up, Simon secured Kate to a seat on the ship's side. Then he and Radon with great difficulty moved back to and stood beside the Captain's chair.

"Take your seat Captain." Radon smiled.

"Thanks for everything Radon," Simon told him clearly worried.

"We're not dead yet legend." Radon smiled, moving away, making Simon grin.

"I'm having trouble controlling the roll." Horen volunteered from the helm.

"No kidding!" Benjamin yelled from behind him producing smiles from members of the crew, who before showed the first signs of fear.

"Would you like to take over?" Horen asked thinking Benjamin was serious.

"It was a joke. You're doing great." Benjamin apologised.

"I find the human's sense of humour unfathomable." Jabo put in, not understanding.

"That's what makes it funny," Benjamin told them, smiling. Most of the crew although they smiled back, had a look that said they didn't quite understand.

Simon ignoring the conversation watched the land surface ahead of the ship. He had expected the ship to come in on one of the planet's flat desert areas; instead, they seemed to be heading towards a mountainous part of the planet.

"Is that where the ship is heading?" Simon shouted above the noise to Horen, the ship vibration becoming extremely loud and rather frightening.

"Yes, we seemed to be programmed to land in a small valley surrounded by jagged peaks. Do you want me to override it?" Horen answered as the crew held on silently listening.

"No, they sent us here for a reason. Just try to keep the ship flying straight."

"Is that another human joke?" Jabo asked thinking how else could you fly a ship, making the human members of the crew start sniggering. A giant snapping noise made the crew jump, many murmured to themselves, many thought it was the end.

'Sir, the hull is breached where the shuttle bay is located. A hole the length of the bay is venting our remaining air supply." Ryan shouted.

"Can we slow down anymore Horen?" Simon yelled above the noise, knowing the loss of air at the moment wasn't important. Horen instead of answering shook his head, signalling no. Standing there, Simon watched the valley fill the front viewing screen as the Katherine fatally wounded approached it. A hand in his made him look beside him. Kate had unstrapped herself and made the dangerous crossing from the room's side to stand with him at the captain's chair.

"I love you, Kate," Simon told her, his voice a whisper in the noise, as he held her.

"Sir the ship is slowing." Horen bellowed out, sounding jubilant. By this time the ship was travelling parallel to the ground entering the valley. All the crew shouted with joy, as the ship stopped its shuddering, flying level.

"We haven't got enough room to stop," Radon yelled. "Everyone prepare for impact." He told them. Rushing to a spare seat Radon strapped himself in, as Simon making room for Kate put the safety strap over them both. Although the thrusters continued to fire, the walls of the valley the ship was travelling in, started to narrow becoming a steep-sided canyon. All eyes watched the front viewing screen as the end of the canyon came into view. It was a flat vertical cliff a black stone.

"We aren't going to stop in time Simon. There's just enough room." Radon warned the ship shuddering with the effort to stop the thousands of tons of spaceship.

"Everyone brace for collision!" Simon instructed as Benjamin at the Communication's console, passed the order to the rest of the ship. The canyon wall now loomed above them as the jagged rocks beckoned to the ship. Holding onto Kate, Simon increased his grip on her, as the cliff filled the whole screen and he prayed for a miracle, closing his eyes. Feeling

the ship finally ground to a halt, Simon opened his eyes to see
a giant cave in front of him.

"What happened?" He asked looking around the room
seeing most of the crew stood frozen.

"I don't believe it? The cliff face, was an illusion, we passed
right through it. We're now in a giant cave." Horen at the helm
told them all.

"It's not a cave Horen, it's a base." Radon pointed out,
staring out into the darkness.

"Why would you say that?" Ryan asked.

"Put on the outside lights," Simon commanded as Horen
switched on their navigation lights, illuminating the area.
Simon looking to their right saw the image he'd been shown.

"My God is that a spaceship?" Kate shouted, climbing of
Simon and moving to the screen.

"It's the one I was shown in the void. Beautiful isn't?" He
answered smiling. Five times as large as the Katherine, the
ship was silver in colour. Its shape reminded Kate of the eagle
on her Planet's flag. Like it, the ship had a smooth, sleek body
with two wings, angling back giving it a look like a bird diving
from a height into water. There was something else,
something intangible about the ship, a shimmering as if it was
a mirage or haunted.

"And they said it was yours." Kate smiled, as Simon came
up to stand beside her.

"Yes, although they didn't explain why."

"I don't understand Simon. Why if they knew we'd have
problems, didn't they give this to us first?" Radon interrupted.

"They believe in free will. They seemed to only interfere
when a problem that affects the whole Universe comes along."
Simon tried to explain, even though he had doubts about their
benefactor's true motives.

"What now?" Ryan asked his gaze locked onto the silver
ship.

"We bury our dead and visit our new ship," Simon told
them, as the whole room continued to stare out at the ghost
ship.

The dead crewmembers were buried together in the canyon outside the base. In four long lines, like on a parade ground, they faced outwards from the base, silently guarding the approach. Simon as Captain led the service, thanking them for their bravery and friendships. Each man or woman who had been killed in action, had a friend say something about their past. Most were of bravery or friendship; sometimes they were humorous as their crewmates remembered better times. Simon saddened by their loss, knew this moment would stay with him forever.

Finished, they moved back to their ship. Most preparing for the next day, when they would enter the ghost ship, as it was now known. The crew after a sombre dinner turned in early their thoughts with their comrades. Simon after he finished his meal, asked Horen, Radon, Katy, Jabo, Ryan and Kate to meet him on the observation deck to discuss their next move.

Simon knew that after they'd exited the portal, that the scanners had picked up debris from the Roax ships exiting the portal behind them. He believed that there was a good chance the Roax might have the co-ordinates of this Galaxy.

"Do you think they'll come looking?" Ryan whispered as if they might hear him.

"I would. They must know their ships were destroyed, they'll want to know if the Katherine was too." Radon admitted.

"I think we should give them something to find. Once we know that the other ship is functional, we will move the Katherine out into the open and destroy her." Simon suggested.

"Do you think that's wise? We don't know anything about this new ship, and the Katherine is still the most advanced ship in space." Jabo pointed out.

"It's sad, and I love this ship, but the Katherine's beyond repair. It would be better to destroy her than leave her behind to be discovered by our enemies." Simon explained, the others sadly agreeing. "With luck, the Roax will take several days to follow. Let's see what the new ship's like before we make a decision." He continued, the meeting breaking up.

Early the next day, Simon with a group of forty soldiers and technicians, walked across the open ground towards the ghost ship as the crew now called it. The shimmering became more obvious as the group drew closer, some suspecting rightly, that it was a shield of some kind. Ryan leading the group, reached out his hand as they neared the shimmer, as suspected he came up against a barrier.

"Well this is great, how do we get in?" Benjamin asked, running his hands over the shield as if expecting to find a doorway. Simon approaching put out his hand walking forward like the others, but instead of being stopped by the barrier, he passed right through. Looking back he saw the others hitting the wall trying to attract his attention, as Radon walked through next to him.

"Why us?" He asked as Horen too walked through.

"We were all in the void together," Simon suggested the others nodding. Walking back out, they found the group trying to work out what was going on.

"Simon thinks somehow it knows us from our time in the void," Horen explained.

"Then what about the rest of us?" Katy asked.

"Let's try something," Radon spoke out. Holding Benjamin, he walked forward, half dragging the reluctant volunteer with him. To everyone's amazement, they both passed through. Letting go of him, Radon walked back out followed by Benjamin. "Now try it on your own," Radon said pointing him back inside. Not sure Benjamin walked forward passing through unaided. Turning to wave at the others, he walked back out.

"That's fantastic, any idea how it works?" Ryan asked Simon.

"It seems to remember a person's DNA. You must pass through with someone known to the shield. Once you're in the system, it will let you through. It makes sense, although I don't understand how it works." Simon confessed.

After a couple of minutes, the whole group gained entry. Walking towards the ship, a quiet settled over the group at they looked over their new ship.

"She's stunning. Until this moment I thought the Katherine was the most beautiful ship I'd ever seen, but this one leaves her far behind." Benjamin declared, his eyes shining at being one of the first to see her. "I can't wait to see the inside." he continued, the others smiling at his boyish enthusiasm.

"I hate to burst your bubble, Benjamin. Does anyone see a way in?" Radon asked, as they reached the ship, which floated several hundred metres above them.

"You'd think after letting us in, it would've landed and allowed us to enter." Simon pointed out. He too showed signs of eager anticipation at boarding their new ship. The group stood for several minutes, uncertain about what to do next when Benjamin overeager approached what they took to be a landing light. The ship was projecting two lights straight down, about ten metres apart, as if marking a spot on the ground to land on. Walking out into one of the lights Benjamin looked back to say something when with a flash of light he was gone.

"Benjamin!" Ryan screamed running forward as Radon, too late, yelled for him to stop. Ryan also entered the same lit area, only like Benjamin to disappear. The rest of the group stunned, stopped just outside the light beam area.

"What do you think happened? " Radon asked Simon, who stood studying the glowing area.

"I think Benjamin has found the doorway to the ship?" He smiled, walking forward, as Radon tried to stop him. Both inadvertently entered. One minute Radon was holding Simon on the planet's surface, the next they were both on the deck of the ghost ship. Looking around they saw Benjamin and Ryan to the side looking over a console. Seeing Simon, they hurried over.

"We think that console controls whatever brought us up to the ship," Ryan suggested.

"You could be right, although I think it's simpler than that," Simon answered looking back at where they'd appeared. There he noticed a circle engraved on the deck. Moving further along what appeared to be a hold of some type, Simon found another circle. Stepping into it, he appeared again, back on the planet across from the rest of the group they'd left behind. Walking over to them he told them to enter the first circle of light. Once everyone had travelled up to the ship and back down, fascinated by the device, they decided to search the ship.

Far larger than the Katherine, the ship took Simon's breath away. By comparison, the Katherine seemed like an antique compared to this ship. Fully automated the ship Simon realised practically ran itself. Reaching the bridge, they found four tubes, which looked like hibernation chambers. Studying the tubes, Simon theorised, that the ship ran on impulses from the four crewmembers that entered the tubes.

Radon in the meantime had gone searching the ship itself. In one huge bay, he found two shuttles towards the rear of the ship. Far larger than the Katherine's shuttle, these were also armed and equipped with shields. He too had found tubes on board both ships, but no controls.

"Thought control, is it even possible?" Radon enquired when Simon explained how he thought the ship worked.

"It would appear not only is it possible but on this ship already in use." Simon grinned excitedly.

"How do we know for sure?"

"Let's take it for a spin. I'm sure the others won't mind." Simon put forward the others happily agreeing.

Kate aboard the Katherine watched the ghost ship shimmer. Like usual Simon had again gone beyond what he planned. He was supposed to just visit the ship, not go joy riding. Secretly she had to admit she was a bit jealous of Simon's new passion. Since finding she was pregnant, she'd become more emotional, crying at nothing and like now getting upset over practically nothing.

"Why couldn't we all go?" Jabo asked behind her making her smile. He like most of the others left behind felt slighted by missing out.

"Okay everybody, monitor the flight carefully. You're all important; Simon's just playing it safe that's all." She told them secretly hiding a grin sharing their pain.

"Kate the ghost ship's gone!" Jabo shouted, galvanising the crew.

"Can you follow their course?" she asked.

"No Kate, I mean the ship is gone, it's invisible both visually and to our sensors," Jabo replied. Like many of the crew, Kate moved to the viewing deck, as Jabo had said the ghost ship was gone.

"Simon, can you hear me?" Kate transmitted, hoping the signal got through.

"Yes, of course, I can, why the urgency?" He answered, picking up the stress level in her voice.

"Your ship has disappeared off our screens, and we can no longer see you at all." Simon looked around the bridge of the ghost ship. He was in the commander's tube, while Horen was in the helmsman's tube. Radon and Ryan occupied the other two that were believed to be weapons and engineering.

"Did you all hear that?" Simon asked, his three companions in their tubes voices answering in his head. "Any ideas as to how we did it?" he continued.

"That may have been me, Simon," Ryan answered. "When I powered up the engines, the computer or whatever I'm talking to, asked if I wanted the stealth and shields deployed. I answered yes. I thought it was just a strange way it activated the shield, although it would appear it's something far better."

"Did you hear that Kate?" Simon asked getting a yes in reply. "It looks like you won't be monitoring this flight after all. We'll take her out for a few hours and return. Just keep radio silence; we'll warn you when we approach." Simon explained.

"Okay, just don't be too long," Kate replied as Simon told the ship to get underway. It took some time to get used to mental communications. Being in contact with the other three tube members meant the computer, or the Artificial intelligence, which ran the ship sometimes became confused with whom the tube members were talking to.

"Give it a name." Radon suggested as the ship climbed out of the planet's atmosphere, accelerating out into space.

"Any suggestions?" Simon replied.

"Well it's got to be something different and easy to say, so we don't get confused." Ryan pointed out.

"How about Erd?" Radon put forward.

"A bit weird Radon, whose name was that," Ryan asked smiling.

"My father's," Radon answered, sounding slighted, as Ryan lost his smile.

"I'm sure it was a good name Radon." Ryan apologised, the others going silent.

"I think we should call it what it is, an advanced computer or just computer." Horen put in, everyone agreeing, although Radon still mentally mumbled about his father's names. It did the trick though and as time passed the crew became more adept at controlling the ship. They were just about to return to the base when the computer's voice sounded a warning.

"Ten ships, they are bearing three one four degrees." Chirped out the computer, as Simon commanded it, too close on their position.

"Radon battle stations," Simon said out loud, knowing Radon had already heard his thought command and acted. 'This could be very confusing' Simon mused, hearing three answers to his unasked question.

Simon, they're Roax warships. They appear to be scanning the whole Galaxy." Horen informed him. Benjamin and the others although not in the tubes, stood and listened in the viewing deck area, watching the enemy ships take shape as they closed on the fleet. Horen bring the ship within spitting range; turn the ghost ship following the enemy fleet.

"That's amazing. They have no idea we're right behind them." Ryan whispered his thoughts still loud and clear. Simon remained silent. He knew the Roax ships were advanced, he wondered if they were just luring them in, pretending not to see them. Twenty minutes passed as they shadowed the enemy fleet, waiting for any sign they'd detected them. When Simon was convinced they couldn't see them, he ordered the ship to return to the base.

"Aren't we going to destroy those bastards?" Ryan thoughts erupted through their link.

"No, not yet Ryan. I want them to think we've been destroyed. It's no good just killing a small fleet, I want them all." Simon growled as the ship withdrew heading back to the base.

Kate heard Simon out as he laid out his plan. Like the others she wanted the Roax gone. When Simon's ghost ship had suddenly appeared next to theirs, she felt momentarily that the Roax had found them. Touching her belly without realising it, she felt a growing sense of fear that the Roax were hunting them. For her unborn child's future, she knew they had to be eliminated.

Jabo, Kate noticed lately, always seemed to be shadowing her. If not him, she'd noticed there were always at least two soldiers trailing her. Grinning she came to the conclusion that like many of Jeddah's men, he viewed the child as something spiritual, as if a future mighty being was forming in her womb, rather than a defenceless human baby. This in a way worried her, as, like most mums, she wanted her child to grow up having had a normal upbringing.

"Is that even possible?" She said out loud, causing the gathered crewmembers to turn in her direction.

"Is everything okay Kate?" Simon asked sounding concerned. Lately, he had trouble talking to Kate, finding her distant and snappy. He'd assigned Jabo and some men to watch over her in secret, scared that this life they were leading was affecting her wellbeing. He'd found that the crew were already on the sly watching over her. He too sensed they thought the child was somehow special.

"No, I'm okay. I just want this business over with, that's all."

"We all do Kate. Despite our past, all of us want peace, it just someone must always pay the price." Radon answered.

"So let's make sure this time it's the Roax who pay!" Simon called out, the crew cheering.

It was sad looking down from space at the Katherine. She lay with her back broken across a small mountain, in a desert area on the planet, where Radon had crashed her. He had volunteered to fly her to her doom knowing no one else wanted the job. Once the ship was down, he'd set the explosive chargers, before flying one of the ghost ship's shuttles to safety.

The explosion gutted her and Simon like many other crewmembers felt tears form in his eyes, at the destruction of their once invincible ship. Radon once he'd secured the shuttle met the others on the viewing platform.

"I checked the scanners; the Roax will pass by here tomorrow. By then the fire will be out, and there'll be no way of telling how long she's been sitting there." Simon told the others his eyes still locked on the doomed ship. "She was a beautiful ship. I will miss her." He continued.

"We all will Simon. Just remember, her crew still live, and we will make sure, that what she achieved is always remembered." Radon told them all, as the ghost ship returned to their base.

Just to be sure their presence went unnoticed; Simon had the ghost ship power down. Only life support and essential systems were left running, leaving a nonexistent power signature.

"You're overreacting Simon. This ship is a hole in space, nothing can spot us." Jabo smirked, knowing how over protective Simon was.

"Simon is right. We underestimated the Roax and were nearly all destroyed, by that planet based space gun. We must never again be so over confident with our technology." Radon pointed out.

"Captain, the Roax are orbiting the planet!' Ryan in one of the tubes warned them. A still settled over the ship as they all waited. "They're sending a small ship; I'd say a shuttle, down to the planet near the wreck of the Katherine."

"What are the other ships doing?" Simon asked, his voice communicating, with the crewmembers in the tubes.

"The others are orbiting the planet; they're continuing to scan. One has already passed directly over us, I'd hazard a guess and say they can't detect us." Ryan added.

"Okay, it seems to be working. The crewmembers in the tubes can now change to the next shift." Simon had made a decision to give as many crewmembers a chance in the tubes as possible to find the ones who had the best connection with the computer. So far the computer seemed comfortable with all the crew, making Simon wonder if the DNA scanning when a new member entered, did more than just allow entry and exit.

For the rest of the day or eight Earth hours, the Roax examined the burnt out Katherine, before returning to their ship. Once their shuttle had docked, the Roax opened a portal, accelerating into it leaving.

"What now?" Kate asked.

"We follow them. Helmsman launch immediately, follow the Roax." Simon ordered, as the crew prepared for battle.

THE ENEMY BASE

Entering the portal, Simon had the helmsmen keep a respectable distance behind the enemy fleet. The one problem Jabo had pointed out about being completely invisible was they could be hit by another ship purely by accident. If that occurred, the ship's cloaking device could be damaged, making them visible. Radon argued that the chances of a collision were slim, although in battle he admitted that anything was possible. Simon coming down on the side of caution decided on keeping a safe distance.

Two days of shadowing the Roax saw them clear the portal. Simon recognised the same system where the planet based space gun was located. He surmised that for safety, the Roax ships passed through this system, before moving on to their home base. Passing the area where they'd been attacked before, the whole crew held their breath hoping they truly were invisible. With great relief, Simon, saw the Roax fleet deploy another portal entering it.

"Follow them," Simon ordered, as again they entered an enemy portal.

Only an earth day after they entered, the nine enemy ships and their shadow emerged from the portal.

"Where are we?" Simon asked, not recognising the system.

"We're on the border of the Flax Feceration and an area of space where Pathalong is located." Katy at the helm answered.

"There is nothing of any worth in this area of space, why did they come here?" Radon asked.

"What are the enemy ships doing Katy?" Simon asked.

"They are all deploying near the third planet from this system's sun. It has a heavy metallic atmosphere, making their signatures hard to read."

"Is the planet habitable?" Simon enquired.

"No, it's poisonous. Of the seven planets in this system, only one would support life, and it's the sixth one from the sun."

"Then they're waiting to ambush someone, it's the only thing that makes sense." Radon put forward, Simon beside him thinking, suddenly came to life.

"Do a sweep of the surrounding galaxies. See if you can spot anything. Sound battle stations and prepare to target those ships." Simon shouted, looking worried.

"What's wrong?" Kate asked, moving to stand beside him.

"There's only one target I can think of in this area they'd be interested in," Simon replied as Katy's voice rang out.

"Simon, sensors show an Oregarthian battleship coming towards this system. They will be here in less than twenty minutes."

"Even with her new shields and weapon, compliments of New America, she won't have a chance against a fleet of Roax ships," Radon warned.

"How long, until we are in range?" Simon barked.

"Ten minutes Sir." One of Katy's men nervously answered, picking up on Simon's agitation.

"Send a message to Jeddah, warn him," Simon ordered.

"They will detect our approach if you do," Radon warned.

"So be it. Fire when we are in range, Katy." Simon commanded. Katy didn't need any urging. Sending a message to her gun crews, she told them to wait till she gave the order.

"They destroyed our people, they've got it coming!" She growled, her headset passing on her thoughts to her men and Simon.

"Every ship must be completely destroyed, Katy. We cannot let them inform their commanders we still exist." Simon explained.

"We are now in range Sir. All weapons fire." Katy shouted, the response immediate.

When the enemy ships exit the portal, they as planned took up station in the shadow of the third planet. After the destruction of the Katherine, the council had decided to search for the Oregarthian battleship seen leaving Oregarth. The

Roax had always had a deep hate and fear of the Oregarthians. The council knew that the Oregarthian race had left the known Universe and this group was all that remained of their race. Worried that they might attempt to contact their people, the council had decided to act.

Knowing the Flax Federation were their only ally in this Universe, the council had deployed detection devices in a wide arc to monitor spaceship movement towards The Flax Federation. They'd got lucky, one of their buoys picking the ship up at extreme range. Taking no chances, a fleet of nine ships had been ordered to lay in wait and capture the battleship if possible or destroy it. The commander didn't care either way.

He was still upset with missing out on the destruction of the Katherine, and now with another major battle looming, his unit had been assigned to the Home fleet in reserve. This ambush of a hated enemy he hoped might get his small fleet deployed to their main force in the coming attack.

"Captain Prossio, we have an unknown transmission being broadcast from the area where the portal opened." His Comm's officer screeched from his station. Prossio knew it wasn't from any of his ships, as they all were ordered to keep radio silence.

"Can you verify the source?"

"No captain, our sensors show nothing whatsoever."

"Well, something must have transmitted. Send two ships to investigate. We must now go on the assumption that, whoever sent the signal, warned the Oregarthian ship. Order the rest of the fleet to follow us, we will take the fight to them. Bring the ship to battle stations. Helmsmen, plot a course to intercept the Oregarthian's" Captain Prossio ordered, upset his plan had been betrayed.

No sooner had the fleet left, when they received a panicked message from the two ships left behind to find the transmission's source. They reported they were under attack, before going silent.

"Can our sensors tell us who are attacking them and where they are?" Prossio snapped becoming slightly rattled by what was occurring.

"No Sir our ships have been destroyed. Maybe we should open a portal and withdraw or at least contact the council." His second in command argued.

"We need more information. All ships turn back towards the last position of the two ships." Prossio ordered as all hell broke loose.

After destroying the two ships sent to look for them, Simon ordered his ship forward. It was all too easy he thought. The enemy had no chance whatsoever, they couldn't see them or detect them.

"This is murder, Simon. Shouldn't they be given a chance to surrender?" Kate beside him whispered.

"I can't Kate. If they broadcast that we're still alive to their base, they will scatter. We can't afford to let any of them escape.

"We're in range Captain," Katy called out, she too sounded upset by the slaughter.

"Fire all weapons. Target the one issuing orders first." He commanded as the Ghost ship fired its deadly lasers. Ten minutes was all it took to destroy the remaining seven ships.

"I know we had no choice Simon, but that was not a battle, it was an execution," Radon admitted, he too was troubled by the ease at which they had destroyed the enemy.

"How do you feel Katy?" Simon enquired.

"I thought I would feel better having avenged my people. Instead, I have done what the enemy did and killed knowing the enemy couldn't defend themselves."

"The loss of life in this conflict is sickening. And although I feel like you all do, it is necessary. As Captain, I gave the order and I would again for the greater good. Yes, we are at the moment invincible, but it won't always be like this. The loss of the Katherine shows how advanced our enemies have become. Just give thanks we saved Jeddah's people from either death or slavery. There will be many more deaths people I can assure you of that. Live with it, that's what this is all about, living!" Simon declared, before moving on. "Where is Jeddah's ship?"

"It's coming up on us now Captain," Katy informed him, her emotions hidden.

"Good, warn them where we are and drop our invisibility we don't want them to hit us." Simon forced a smile, before continuing. "Right Benjamin I want you to send four messages." Benjamin approaching Simon took the data from Simon.

"I'll send them immediately Sir." He softly replied he too was shaken by the action.

"Good now stand down from battle stations. I'll be in my room. Contact me when Jeddah arrives." Simon told them, before leaving the bridge, followed by Kate.

Once in his cabin, Simon collapsed, sobbing. He had just murdered thousands of men giving them no chance. Kate, hurrying to him held him, crying as well.

"I had no choice Kate. It had to be done."

"I know my love."

"I'm tired of the killing Kate; I just want to be with you and our child."

"When this is over, we will get away on our own for a while, just the two of us."

"Do you think it will ever be really over Kate?" Unable to answer, Kate just held him.

Jeddah on his battleship, looked out at the wreckage, floating peacefully past them, many pieces colliding with their shield.

"Good God what a massacre." He said out loud, his crew like him looking at the wreckage. "Can anyone tell me where the Katherine is?" He asked his crew.

"We have nothing on our sensors, but she must be around somewhere, the battle just took place." His Second in Command replied.

"Sir we're receiving a message."

"What's it say?"

"Stop engines we are next to you."

"Well do as Simon asked. He's here somewhere." Jeddah scoffed, the crew laughing. Without warning to their right, the

Ghost ship suddenly appeared. Jeddah like most of the crew stood frozen wandering what was going on.

"Give me Comm's and stay at battle stations!" Jeddah yelled.

"Lines open Sir."

"Simon, can you hear me?" Jeddah began, suspicious of this demon looking ship.

"It's Radon, Jeddah. I suppose you're wondering about the new ship. Sorry about that, I should've warned you."

"It would've been nice what happened?"

"The Katherine was destroyed; we lost a lot of good men. The Chosen gave us this ship as a replacement."

"I'm coming over." Jeddah declared turning to his crew. Asking that his shuttle be made ready, he left the bridge. Travelling across to this new ship, Jeddah was worried. Radon sounded strange as if under a lot of stress. What had occurred to depress him, after such an impressive victory? Docking with the ghost ship, Jeddah made to enter but found his way blocked by a shield. At that moment Radon appeared. Walking straight up to him he hugged him, Jeddah thought he looked ten years older.

"Everyone hold hands. Even though we dropped the main shield, the ship won't allow people it doesn't know on the ship." Radon told them his speech slurred. This time Jeddah felt no barrier as they all moved onto the ship. Pulling Radon into a side room, Jeddah told everyone else to wait outside.

"What is wrong my friend?" Jeddah whispered.

"I thought I would never say it, but I'm tired of killing in the name of freedom, Jeddah. This ship, unlike the Katherine, is only meant to kill. We slaughtered those men they had no chance. I felt like we were killing defenceless children." Radon sobbed. Without warning Jeddah slapped Radon across the face, knocking him backwards. Tripping over a table, he ended up on the floor. Angry he sprang to his feet going for his weapon.

"That's better. That's the Radon I know." Jeddah chuckled, as Radon shaking himself let go of his laser. "You saved our lives from certain death you fool. Wake up! Death comes to us all. To stop evil, you must fight it with everything you've got."

Radon still angry at the slap tried to think of an argument to prove his point. In the end, he knew he'd been stupid.

"You're right Jeddah, although I owe you for that slap."

"I didn't come off too well either." Jeddah smiled, showing his badly cut hand, where he'd hit Radon's two rows of teeth. Taking out his handkerchief Radon wrapped it around Jeddah's hand.

"We'll call it even." Radon smiled back, hugging his friend.

"Where's Simon?"

"He went to his cabin. He showed no emotion at all."

"Like a true Captain. Let's go find him." Jeddah suggested knowing what he'd find.

Rushing to Simon's cabin, Jeddah knocked on the door.

"Come back later," Kate's voice whispered through the door.

"Open the door, or I'll kick it in!" Jeddah yelled as voices could be heard softly talking inside."

"Right, I'm over this," Jeddah growled, putting his foot to the door. With a splintering of metal and moulded plastic, the door folded in.

"Are you okay Simon?" Jeddah asked hugging both Simon and Kate.

"We are Jeddah, and yes I've gotten over it with Kate's help. I was going to open the door once I got dressed." Simon smiled looking at Kate.

"She is a good woman, its time you both bonded in a relationship," Jeddah admitted thinking.

"We were going to wait till things settled down first, then get married."

"That is no excuse. Everyone to the bridge, this is just what you all need." Jeddah proclaimed as the group moved out into the hallway, followed by Jeddah.

On the way there, Jeddah was brought up to speed on what had occurred. Telling Simon to enter the co-ordinates of the system where the space gun was, he called his ship instructing them to follow. Once in the portal, Jeddah ordered the whole crew to the bridge.

"Where is General Wordsworth?" Jeddah asked.

"I'm here." The General replied stepping forward.

"You're a lucky man. I would've killed you." Jeddah started out. "That aside do you have this book called the bible?"

"Yes. Although I'm not really religious, I carry one."

"Go get it now," Jeddah instructed as a slighted General Wordsworth hurried off. "You Horen get the clothes Kate and Simon wore on New America."

"Yes, Sir," Horen answered he knew Jeddah all too well to argue.

"Right, everyone you are here to watch these two get, what is the word, married. If you wish to change do it now, you have ten minutes or until that General returns." Jeddah informed them. Many of the humans ran off to change, while the Oregarthians and the Flax Federation crewmembers wondered what the fuss was about. On both their planets, when you found a mate, you formed a partnership for life, simple.

Simon and Kate through all this had remained quiet happy to go along with it. Simon wondering if they should wait voiced his concerns.

"Jeddah, do you think we should wait for a better time.

"Kate is with child isn't she?" Jeddah asked as the room dropped into an enforced silence.

"Well yes but," Was all he got out before Jeddah cut him off.

"The time to wait is over Simon, you must do the right thing," Jeddah warned, the crewmembers stamping their feet in support. Simon seeing any sign of support was gone turned to Kate.

"Will you marry me?"

"Yes, Simon, of course, I will." She replied as Simon overjoyed kissed her.

Wordsworth in time returned with his bible. Kate and Simon swiftly dressed behind a line of soldiers, Jeddah refused to let them leave till the service was over. Both dressed, Wordsworth, having married crewmembers before as a Captain in the fleet, led the service. Afterwards, Horen worked overtime, producing alcoholic refreshments, while the kitchen did its best turning rations into a banquet. It was a good wedding all agreed, although many had never seen one before.

The celebrations finished found Kate and Simon Hayes, escorted to their cabin by Jeddah; the door had been hastily fixed.

"Enjoy your time together; we will come for you in four Earth hours." Jeddah declared marching off.

"Who'd have thought Jeddah would play cupid?" Kate laughed, carefully taking off her only dress.

"He is clever beyond his years. In one move he turned a sorrowful crew into a close-knit group again, supporting each other."

"Do you think when this is over we can find another Oregarth?"

"I hope so Kate, I hope so."

After Simon's short honeymoon, he met the others on the bridge. Jeddah suggested that the only way to find the enemies' base was to flush them out. Exiting the portal they immediately opened another portal. Jeddah's ordered his ship to enter wishing them good luck. To keep them safe, Simon had sent the ship to a small planet inside the Flax Federation. It was to contact Radom and wait there until they came for them. He had tried to convince Kate to go, but like usual it hadn't worked.

"You need me as much as I need you, so forget!" She bluntly told him. Giving up, he accepted her decision. Now as they cruised towards the planet where the space gun was positioned everyone held their breath.

"Sir we have a portal opening near the base." Ryan at the sensor array warned.

"Okay, gentlemen let's move the ship close to the planet and wait," Simon ordered, the ship's crew responding.

An hour afterwards movement was spotted in the portal.

"Sir, we have at least forty hostiles inbound," Ryan shouted.

"Battle stations people. Watch out for ships getting too close?" He cautioned knowing they couldn't see them. Once the forty ships had exited, they moved towards the two portals.

The one Simon had arrived through and the other, they sent Jeddah's battleship through.

"They don't know who made them. It could be just one of their fleet's ships entering and exiting this system." Simon without thinking said out loud.

"Yes, their base would've seen the Oregarthian battleship enter and exit alone. I'd doubt they'll send anyone through after them, they'll think it's a trap." Jeddah pointed out. For the next four hours, Simon and his crew watched the enemy fleet slowly cruise back and forward between the two portals as if waiting for some telltale sign of what was going on. Finding nothing of interest, the fleet suddenly turned moving back to the portal they'd exited from. Sure they were alone the ships entered disappearing.

"After them helmsman, let's find out where they're going?" Simon smiled, as the ship surged forward, following them.

The travelling time this time was much longer, taking four days. As they exited this time, they came face to face with the enemy's true size. Hundreds of ships were gathered in what appeared to be five distinct groups. In the centre was a planet the same size as Oregarth. Scanning the surface revealed four continents with at least twenty major cities.

"The computer reports a population of around thirty million. They appear to be quite an advanced civilisation." Kate informed Simon, as he sat with Radon, Jabot, Horen, Ryan, Katy and Benjamin discussing this development.

"They can't be the Roax left on Duelong, they're just too many, unless they cloned thousands?" Horen pointed out.

"I'd say they have enslaved a population, as well as cloned themselves. It would explain the huge numbers of ships and people on that planet." Benjamin put forward. Even though he was young, Simon found Benjamin highly intuitive in problem-solving, that's why he was included in this group. Radon beside him nodded his support for Benjamin's theory.

"You could be right Benjamin. Somehow we must get down there to find out what's going on." Kate suggested Simon agreeing.

"The shuttles have the same cloaking devices as the ship. I suggest a small group go down and observe." Radon added.

"They are either humanoid or Roax in appearance meaning only Ryan, Benjamin, Katy and her crewmen can mix in amongst the population. I suggest we send a group of ten plus a backup force of twenty of my men." Radon put forward.

"There is also Kate and myself." Simon put in, looking keen to go.

"There is no chance that either of you will be going, Simon. Kate is pregnant, and you are the Captain and too important for this mission. That's why you two were deliberately left out." Radon forcibly answered, already anticipating Simon would attempt to go.

"Okay, it was just a suggestion that's all." He replied sheepishly.

"Good, then we'll proceed with planning the mission." Jabo jumped in, stopping any further attempt from Simon to go.

"You know I am the Captain." Simon spluttered out, feeling slighted.

"Sure you are." Kate smiled hugging him, tne others trying not to laugh.

"Sir the computer has worked out which planet it is."
One of Jeddah's men informed Simon.

"That was quick, which one is it?"

"The computer from listening to radio transmissions has heard the name New Europe mentioned many times. It has come to the conclusion it is the planet's name." He told him, seeing his face go white.

"My God those monsters have enslaved a planet belonging to the Gun Barrel planets, they're my people." Simon groaned as the group moved off leaving Simon and Kate alone.

FINDING THE TRUTH

Travelling down to the planet, Ryan looked over his group. General Wordsworth had on this mission taken Radon's spot as leader. Like Simon the others had decided that Radon was too important to come on the mission, much to his obvious displeasure. Kate had pointed out to him that because he was an alien, he wouldn't be able to leave the shuttle anyway, placating him to a degree. Still, he got over it, assisting with the planning.

Jabo of all of them had grave doubts about this mission. He worried that even though English was the planet's universal language, they had no idea of what laws and regulations were enforced on the planet, now the Roax held sway. He insisted that some if not all members carried weapons, even though the population didn't. General Wordsworth too supported this move. He pointed out that if trouble started and the deployment of alien troops was discovered, the Roax's would know their enemies had discovered the planet.

Ryan and Katy who would be the ones going amongst the locals didn't want firearms, worried their discovery, and their origin would label them as spies. Simon after thinking about it sided with Jabo. He gave all of them the option to carry protection but insisted at least every third person should carry a concealed weapon. Both sides weren't overjoyed with what they saw as a compromise, in the end, both sides accepted it.

Gliding into a forestry area bordering one of the main cities, Horen made sure to avoid any sign of life. Invisible or not, the engines still roared, and the ship's wake could be felt for quite a distance. Cutting the engines, leaving the cloak and shield up, the group moved to the air lock. Like all spaceships, there was an internal door and an outer door. On this shuttle opening the outer door automatically deployed a staircase to the ground, as the shuttle's entry door was at least thirty metres to the ground this saved a lot of trouble.

The planet's orbit here was similar to Salvation, having ten hours of day and ten of night. To allay any suspicions they had landed in the late afternoon. As they prepared to leave the ship, they all watched the sun start to set.

"Be careful," Jabo whispered, his soft voice sounding out his concern at their mission.

"We'll be right back, stop worrying," Ryan assured him, as with Katy and Benjamin they moved off through the trees.

"They'll be okay?" Wordsworth reassured him, watching another group of Katy's men scurry off through the scrub towards the distant lights.

"I hope so General. Like Simon would say, I have a bad feeling about this."

"Well, we can't do anything out here. Let's go back and monitor their transmissions." Wordsworth suggested, as closing the door, the stairs retracted.

The plan was for the three groups of three, to enter the city from different points. Ryan's group would travel to the far side of the wooded area, before merging into the outer city area. The other two groups made up of Katy's men would enter by two closer routes in case of trouble. Radio silence would be maintained for the next two hours, after that, an hourly report from each group would be sent. Having scanned the frequencies in use, Jabo had piggybacked their frequency onto a local radio station, so anyone monitoring would only hear garbled background noise.

Two hours passed and all groups reported in giving little in the way of Intel, as the streets were near empty. The thought that something wasn't quite right nagged at Jabo as a klaxon horn sounded over the local radio station announcing sixteen hundred hours, which was when the small sun the planet orbit moved behind the planet.

"Why would they announce the time with a klaxon horn?" Wordsworth asked, as Jabo as if waking from a nightmare jumped to the microphone.

"All groups return immediately you're in danger!" Jabo shouted into the Comm's gear startling the other crewmembers. Getting three confirmations from the three groups, he ordered the crew to battle stations.

"What's wrong?" Wordsworth asked climbing into one of the two tubes on the shuttle.

"There's a curfew on this planet. It means that it's under Marshall Law and all this planet's citizens must be off the street by sixteen hundred. I should've known." Jabo castigated himself, as he entered the other tube.

The klaxon horn Jabo heard on the radio also sounded in the city. Ryan had already guessed what it meant when Jabo sent his recall.

"What's happening?" Katy asked beside Ryan, seeing him talk on into his headset. Benjamin on the opposite side of the street seeing them stop did the same.

"We've been recalled, I'd say that klaxon is some sort of curfew. Jabo must have figured it out and tried to warn us." Ryan told her, as he signalled to Benjamin to head back to the ship. Understanding, Benjamin immediately turned moving back the way they'd come. To Ryan, it started to make sense. They'd noticed on the outskirts that someone had scrawled messages of defiance, mostly saying 'Stop the War'.

Staying calm, trying to act like a couple out for a stroll Ryan and Katy walked along the sidewalk, the forest trees appearing at the end of the block. Ahead of them Benjamin far quicker entered the trees, looking back as he moved out of sight.

"Not far now." Ryan smiled, holding Katy, enjoying it.

"Halt!" A shout erupted to their side, as out of a side alley appeared two men. Both were dressed in long dark overcoats, with matching black boots. Ryan didn't have to be psychic to known cops when he saw them. Stopping, knowing running was futile, Ryan waited, as the two men weapons drawn, moved to block their path. Up close, Ryan noticed that one's of the men's coats had silver pins on its shoulder pads.

"Why are you out after curfew?" Silver pins barked at them, Ryan could see he enjoyed his job.

"I'm sorry Sir, we just went for a walk and forgot the time." Ryan apologised, he didn't have to fake being scared.

"You know you could be imprisoned for breaking the curfew," the officer without the silver pins warned them.

"It won't happen again we promise." Katy cried sounding genuinely scared. The silver pinned officer continued to stare at them, as a deadly quiet settled over the street.

"Okay, you can go. But next time you two are caught, you will regret it." The silver pinned officer growled, as both Katy and Ryan slowly started moving past them. "By the way where do you both live?" The other officer asked, as Ryan again stopped.

"Katy lives just around the corner in the next block, opposite the forest. We're both staying at her parent's place tonight." Ryan lied.

"You live in Forrest Parade your parents must be doing okay?" The Officer with no pins asked Katy a small grin appearing on his lips.

"Yes, they have been lucky." Katy smiled back turning to go.

"Unfortunately you aren't. Forrest Parade is not on this side of this city." The officer with no pins laughed pointing his weapon at Ryan and Katy.

"Good work Lieutenant looks like we bagged another two terrorists." Silver pins chuckled. "Both of you, on the ground now!" He ordered as Ryan fear written on his face lay down next to Katy. A sob escaped Katy as the officers swiftly searched them, being very thorough with Katy.

"Get your hands off her." Ryan barked, feeling a gun touch his forehead.

"We do what we like with prisoners. She'll get a real good time in the cells" Silver pins chuckled, his partner joining in. When they'd first left the shuttle, Ryan against carrying weapons had given their only weapon to Benjamin, now he'd wished he'd listened to Jabo and had them all carry one.

"What is this?" Silver pin snarled, pulling Ryan's Comm's gear from his ear and neck. Ryan not having an answer remained silent. "I'd talk if I was you, or your girlfriend here is going to get a good going over right now." Silver pins sniggered kicking Ryan in the ribs making him fold up in pain.

"What's going on here?" A voice boomed out of the dark, making the two officers jump back.

"Identify yourself?" Silver pins shouted as Benjamin walked straight towards them smiling. "I won't warn you again young man stop or we'll shoot you." Silver pins commanded as he and the other Officer took aim on Benjamin.

"What type of scum hurt a defenceless woman?"
Benjamin's voice boomed. To the surprise of both officers,
Benjamin too raised a pistol, pointing it at silver pins as he
continued to approach. Ryan felt like laughing at Benjamin's
bravado, as both officers hesitated. It occurred to Ryan that
these two men had never come face to face with an armed
man.

"For the last time, stop and raise your hands." Silver pin
stuttered out, as his companion opened fire.

Ryan and Katy both screamed expecting Benjamin to be
cut in half. Instead, he stood there untouched, much to the
surprise of the two officers.

"Now it's my turn." He informed them, shooting silver pin in
the chest. The other officer, too stunned to do anything,
continued to stand there as Benjamin came forward pistol-
whipping him across the head.

"Quickly you two grab the guy I shot," Benjamin
commanded, as Katy and Ryan got to their feet.

"How are you alive?" Katy sobbed, in a state of shock.

"Oh that. Kate made me bring Simon's personal shield.
Looks like she was right, we did need it." Benjamin pointed
out. "We better call Jabo. He'll want to question this other guy."
Benjamin continued, picking up the Comm's gear.

Jabo upon receiving Benjamin's message swiftly sent one
of his units through the forest to retrieve the two officers, as
well as assist Ryan, Katy and Benjamin. Jabo greeted
Benjamin with a bear hug, nearly crushing him.

"You never fail to amaze me. For one so young you are as
brave as a Malian tree climber."

"Well, thanks, Jabo although I'll have to take your word on
the tree climber." He smiled.

"Yes, that was good work back there; I thought we'd had it,"
Ryan confessed still holding onto to Katy.

"You have done the same for me," Benjamin replied as the
three of them hugged each other.

Once airborne Silver pins was jettisoned. The officer who
was still out cold was thrown in the airlock. A guard placed on
the internal door just in case. Jabo despite his doubts had to

admit they'd gotten their Intel in the form of the police officer. Hearing how he'd roughed up Katy and Ryan, gave Jabo something to look forward to during his interrogation. Discussing the best way to break him, Ryan came up with a great idea.

Once back aboard the ghost ship, Simon moved the ship away from the planet. Explaining what had occurred and what they planned, Radon had the prisoner who was blindfolded led out onto the observation deck. Now conscious, the officer stood defiantly in the middle of the room.

"Okay, take his blindfold off," Simon commanded, as one of Horen's men removed it.

What inner strength the officer had, fled at the sight of the Oregarthians. Unlike the Flax Federation soldiers who appeared close to human, the Oregarthian two rows of teeth, made them look anything but friendly.

"Do we eat him like the other one?" Radon growled, turning towards Simon to hide his smile, as a sob leaked out of the officer.

"I'll tell you nothing!" He shouted, fears making a wet stain spread over the front of his pants.

"We don't need to know anything from you, whoever you are. What is your name anyway?" Simon asked.

"Romus, my name is Romus." He answered, forgetting to say nothing.

"Look Romus, we are above your planet with the Roax fleet surrounding us, yet they don't know we're here. What can you possibly tell us that we don't already know?"

"Who are you?" Romus replied, starting to shake. Signalling to one of the crew, Simon had them give him a blanket. Taking it, he wrapped it around himself hiding his wet pants.

"I am Captain Simon Hayes, and you are aboard the Katherine."

"That cannot be, we have just celebrated your ships destruction."

"It appears the celebrations, are a bit premature." Ryan put in, some of the crew chuckling.

"You are a traitor to the human race. You sided with aliens against your own kind." Romus shot back, his eyes becoming wild and fanatical.

"You are slaves and serve the Roax, and you have the hide to call Simon a traitor. That's a good one." Katy put in, her hate for the man obvious.

"Well, you don't know everything. We are not their slaves, the Roax serve us!" Romus laughed.

Romus' statement brought an abrupt end to all chatter on the viewing deck. Simon found himself unable to reply, so sickened was he by what his own people had done. Kate beside him, unable to get what she wanted to say out, left. Pulling himself together Simon continued, as General Wordsworth took his place beside Radon.

"Are you telling me that the people of New Europe are responsible for the death of millions, if not billions of people?"

"They are not people. They are inferior animals to be enslaved or eliminated. It has always been this way. The strong always dominate the weak." Romus explained as if reading a prepared statement.

"I'm glad your race believes in that principal Romus. For we are about to teach them a lesson, they'll never forget." Radon smiled, his double rows of teeth, making it look more like a threat than a friendly gesture. Romus sensing the mood of the room wisely didn't answer.

"You insolent little pup! My planet has spent years trying to find your planet and restore communications. We hoped that we could make up for the wrong we did when we destroyed the portal. You have shamed all the planets of the human race." Wordsworth spat out.

"What planet are you from?" Romus asked.

"New America, a planet a lot more civilised than yours," Wordsworth answered preparing to leave, he had clearly seen enough.

"Not for long?" Romus smirked, before looking visibly shaken realising he'd said more than he should have.

"What did you mean by that?" Radon snarled, as Simon, who'd been studying Romus, weighed up what he'd said.

"They must be going after New America." Simon put forward.

"How would they even know where our planet is?" Wordsworth asked sounding confused.

"They may have tailed your fleet after the run-in with the Hedred." Radon suggested.

"My God, I've got to warn them," Wordsworth exclaimed.

"Prepare to leave!" Simon ordered, the crew moving to their stations.

"What about the enemy ships and this planet?" Katy barked, wanting retribution.

"They can wait Katy. Once we make sure New America is safe we'll return, I promise you. Lock our friend away he's been more than helpful." Simon smiled, as Romus crestfallen was led away.

"We have a problem, Simon. If we open a portal, they'll know an undetectable ship was here." Radon whispered beside him.

"Good point. Helmsmen, take us away from this planet at full speed. Once we reach a suitable distance we'll deploy a portal. In the meantime send New America a warning. It might take longer than us to get there but you never know." Simon instructed. Following his instructions, the ship started to accelerate when Ryan shouted a warning.

"One of the ships to our right is opening a portal."

"Helmsmen stop engines," Simon yelled, as in response the ship's engines died. "Okay, now steer the ship towards the portal." He ordered as the ship that deployed the shield entered it. Simon was just about to order his helmsman to follow when two more enemy ships formed up entering the portal as well. Waiting, making sure no other ships were moving into position, Simon ordered his ship into the portal.

"They mightn't be going in the direction we want to go." Radon pointed out, as their ship entered.

"You're right, but we keep our departure a secret this way, it's worth the risk," Simon answered.

"What are we going to do when we exit the portal? They'll know we exited with them if we open a portal." Ryan asked.

"Once we're clear of the portal, we target their three ships. That way no one can report anything." Simon bluntly told them. Silence followed as no one could suggest another way.

"Battle stations people!" Radon yelled giving the crew something else to think about.

"What if we exit near that space gun?" Kate whispered beside him.

"Then we deal with it too. Sooner or later we will have to; it may as well be now." Simon murmured, as Kate grabbed his hand squeezing it.

"Don't give up Simon. Too many people need you." She said softly.

"Exiting the portal found them near the planet G10 where the first confrontation between the Hedred and the planet New America took place. Radon in one of the tubes was talking to the computer.

"Simon, the computer thinks the Roax might be here to eliminate the New Americans left here. It reports that there is a small population of around five hundred on the surface in one village, with two warships orbiting above. As if the enemy ships had heard him, they formed up into an attack formation raising their shields and heading straight for the planet.

"Maximum speed. Fire when you're in range." Simon barked, as the Ghost ship whipped forward making several crewmembers reach for something to brace themselves.

"In range Captain, weapons firing," Horen shouted.

It was over in seconds, the three ships not even returning fire. The two New America ships had in the meantime moved towards the incoming ships. Now they swerved away wondering what was going on.

"Open a line to them," Simon ordered. Seeing Ryan nod he began to speak. "New American warships, this is Captain Simon Hayes, can you hear me?"

"This is Captain Fortescue of the Detroit. Yes, we can hear you, although we cannot detect you." A voice answered, sounding unsure.

"Captain, we followed these ships through their own portal. We are on our way to New America and fear it is under attack. I would suggest picking up your people on the planet and moving away from here as the enemy might come looking for the three ships we destroyed."

"Sound like a good idea and again thank you. We had reported the portal opening but received no reply from New America. Without your intervention, those three ships may have wiped us out. I know it's stupid of me to check but is General Wordsworth aboard. I must confirm who you are as I can't see you and I know the General."

Simon turning to Wordsworth handed him the Comm's headset.

"Is that the same Fortescue who ran off with General Raymond's daughter?" The General chuckled, awaiting an answer.

"Yes Sir, thanks for confirming your identity. I'll load the settlement aboard immediately" An embarrassed Captain Fortescue replied.

"Good work Captain and next time a portal opens, act, don't just sit there expecting someone to save your arse." The General barked.

"Yes General, have a good trip, Sir." The Captain added cutting the transmission. Around the bridge, the crew stared at the General.

"Hey, the kid's got to learn, it's no good pampering them," Wordsworth explained Radon and Jeddah beside him agreeing.

"Shit I thought Radon was hard.' Horen whispered to Ryan using words he heard Ryan use.

"Did you say something Horen?" Radon asked his improved hearing allowing him to hear Horen's conversation.

"No, nothing Sir." Horen quickly answered, Ryan, grinning moved away.

BACK TO NEW AMERICA

"I hope this works Jeddah," Radon whispered beside him, as they neared the exit point from the portal. Knowing they might be arriving in a war zone, Jeddah had come up with a plan. Sending a transmission ahead of them, Simon had warned the New America defences that he was coming. They hadn't received a reply, although it could be because they were engaged with the enemy.

During Simon and Kate's absence, both Radon and Jeddah had pointed out that the ship needed a name, rather than ghost ship, as the crew all called it. After several names were mooted the crew overwhelmingly decided on calling it the Katherine again. As many pointed out, the Katherine was a legend, its name striking fear in the enemy. By renaming this ship the same name, meant the legend continued. Painting a name on a ship while travelling in a portal was, to say the least difficult. During their time in the portal, the crew working four-hour shifts inside the shield, had laser painted the name on the ship's bow, the same as before.

"Battle stations people. Mask the ship." Simon ordered as Radon and Jeddah took up positions either side of him. Kate experiencing morning sickness had been ordered by Horen to stay in bed, much to her regret.

"Sir Sensors are picking up multiple ships near the exit point," Ryan informed him, beside him in the next tube, Katy smiled handling communications.

"I hope we're not too late?" Wordsworth muttered standing to the side of Radon, looking worried.

"Death comes to us all General," Jeddah replied having heard him.

"Well, thanks for that Jeddah it really lifted me." Wordsworth chuckled many joining him.

"I was just pointing out the obvious," Jeddah responded, unsure why people were laughing.

"We're not as old as you my friend. Life is still before us." Radon put in, smiling at Jeddah. Jeddah was just thinking of an answer when the Katherine exited the portal, into hell itself.

All around them, New America warships fired on meteors streaking towards their home planet. The three fleets plus every other ship they could muster faced off against hundreds of incoming meteors. Chaos reigned although despite the onslaught only minor damage could be seen on the planet.

"New America forces, this is General Wordsworth, can you hear me?"

"Yes General. This is President Stuart how long till you exit."

"We are here now Mr President. Yes, I know you can't see us, but we're here."

"I should have known. The enemy asked us to surrender. They told us the Katherine had been destroyed and they were invincible. We, of course, declined asking them to prove it. This bombardment started the day after, which was three days ago. As you can see we're still here although just holding our own.

We sent twenty ships to find where the meteors were coming from, none returned. Any suggestions?" The President asked.

"President Stuart, this is Simon Hayes. Help is coming can you hold for another day?"

"Yes, although the fleet is dangerously low on power we will hold. Any timeframe on the help."

"Very soon that's all I will say at the moment. We will now scout the enemy position and return. In the meantime, I'll have General Wordsworth and Jeddah, one of my closest friends and advisors flown over to your ship. They have much to tell you." Simon informed him. "Right General, you and Jeddah get going. We'll meet up later."

"Good luck Simon and be careful. Remember the first Katherine was thought to be invincible too." Wordsworth warned, hurrying off with Jeddah.

"Jabo once the shuttle has left I want full power, then I'll open a portal," Simon informed him, as the ship leapt forward.

On board the President's flagship, the crew watched a portal open as a shuttle appeared out of nowhere right beside their ship. Getting permission to dock the shuttle swiftly entered the flagship's shuttle bay. Escorted to the bridge, the crew stood silently as Wordsworth introduced Jeddah to Stuart.

"I wish we could've given you a better welcome Jeddah, regrettably this will have to do." The President smiled, offering his hand. Shaking it Jeddah looked Stuart in the eye, liking what he saw.

"My race has a saying President Stuart. It's not the welcome, it's the friendship that follows that counts. I am glad to be here." Jeddah returned the smile, before getting down to business. "They are attacking you in the same way they did my planet. Soon they will use far larger meteors, we must be ready."

"So you manage to stop them?"

"No, we lost our planet and our fleet and many brave men." Jeddah sadly answered. All in hearing range looked like Jeddah had just told them that they were all going to die.

"Then what do you suggest?" The President asked, doubt creeping into his thinking.

"We follow one of your sayings. The best defence is offence. We also wait for Simon's return." Jeddah smiled.

"Since his ship is invisible how will we know?" Stuart asked.

"You'll know Mr President, I can assure you." Wordsworth smiled, as the group of men moved to the war room.

Travelling for two hours found the Katherine at its objective. They were in a neighbouring Galaxy away from the fighting. There, looking derelict, floated two huge fleets. Over five hundred Flax Federation ships and four hundred Hedred ships sat silently.

"Contact the two fleets and drop our masking," Simon ordered as the two fleets came to life.

"Is that really you Simon?" Ceb voice echoed through the ship.

"Yes, it's us Ceb, although the first Katherine was destroyed.

"You seem to have found another?" Radom's voice echoed as well.

"I judge you two have met?" Simon asked.

"Yes, we both arrived yesterday. Since no one greeted us, Ceb used his translator to communicate. Since then we have designed our own." Radom replied.

"Let's keep transmissions to a minimum. Radon and I are coming over to Ceb's ship, can you meet us there Radom?"

"I am on the way now." He answered as Simon and Radon with Ryan as pilot, moved to the shuttle bay.

Entering Ceb's flagship's shuttle bay, they found Radom and Jeddar already there. Exiting the new Katherine's shuttle, they found not only Radom and Jeddar staring in awe at the shuttle, but also Ceb and his engineers.

"My God is the ship like this as well?" Radom asked looking over the sleek craft.

"Yes, the Chosen sure know how to build spaceships." Radon smiled.

"Have you found out where the enemy is?" Simon changed the subject, wanting talk of the new ship's potential kept secret.

"Yes. We used an unmanned drone, which we sent in the direction the meteors were originating from. It was destroyed after entering the Galaxy there, although it did manage to send back data." Radom pointed out. Arriving at Ceb's command centre, Radom put the data up on a screen for them to examine.

"These are the captured images from the drone before it was destroyed. As you can see, they have a fleet larger than our combined fleets here. We will need the fleets of the planet under attack if we are to succeed." Radom pointed out.

"The problem is, how do we free them up to help us? Like Radom said they are defending their planet." Ceb interrupted.

"That will be our job Ceb," Simon muttered, concentrating on the image of the enemy's formation.

"How will you do that?" Radom asked.

By going where they'll least expect us." Simon answered a small grin on his lips.

"Shit no." Ryan murmured out loud, those in hearing distance nodding their agreement.

ELENA

On the New Europe's flagship, a meeting of the war council was in session. So far their mission was going to plan. Of the war council, only three of the twenty members were Roax, and this infuriated Elena. For over fifty years they'd planned and waited, their dream of domination only a few more battles away. Looking across at her supposed masters she hid a smile.

"Your time is nearly up." She whispered to herself, knowing the settling with their allies was almost ready. Glancing out at the fleet that filled the sky in all directions, she silently congratulated herself, knowing, that the Roax controlled it. So self-absorbed were the humans from New Europe in Universal domination they'd let their ships be automated by the Roax, to cut down on the size of crews.

Now only a handful of crewmembers manned the ships, some even were now fully automated. Elena knew that with a flick of a button the ships themselves would respond to their commands and not for the so-called 'Privileged of New Europe.' Only one dark cloud had hung over their schemes, and that was the Katherine.

"Why had she appeared again after fifty years and why now?" She asked herself out loud, some of the gathered leaders turning her way, at her raised voice. Smiling, nodding to some of the gathered, she regained her composure, moving to her seat. Rile, their other Roax leaders was already at his seat beside hers. As she made to sit down, he stood holding her chair for her.

"What was that all about?" He whispered having heard her speak was well.

"Just airing some thoughts. I was just pondering where the Katherine had been for fifty years?" Elena smiled.

"That is old news, my dear. She went to her death as she should, on a deserted planet, in a nowhere hole of a Galaxy." He chuckled, thinking himself quite clever.

"It just seems too much of a coincidence that our arch enemy should appear after so long at such a critical time."

"The legend the Flax Federation pedalled is that a race called 'the chosen' are keeping them safe. They don't interfere with their day to day lives, they only return in the Universe's time of need." He laughed, as the Supreme commander of the New Europe stood up, as did they all.

"Let's get through this meeting first, we'll discuss it later," Elena suggested, Rile agreeing.

Most of the meeting dealt with the meteor bombardment and the defence the planet New America was putting up. The council had been surprised by the planet's warships' strength in shields and weapons, putting them on even par with their own, if not a bit more advanced.

"Numbers speak volumes in warfare, my friends, we have nothing to fear." Rile interrupted, getting support from the room.

"That might be so Rile, but what of the gathering of ships in the adjacent Galaxy? We know they're there, but not in what strength?" The Supreme commander pointed out.

"Once we have dealt with New America, we will hunt down this rogue force. If it is part of the Flax Federation fleet, we can destroy it here, thus leaving their planets at our mercy." This brought cheers from the gathered group.

"Every good Rile. We will give you command of half the fleet once the planet falls, that should be more than enough. In the meantime, we have another problem. A small force sent to intercept the Oregarthian's remaining battleship has failed to report. All attempts to raise them go unanswered. A battle group sent to investigate found nothing but wreckage, which we now believe to be of our ships. Any suggestions?" The Supreme commander asked.

"Maybe the Flax ambushed them? They may have discovered our surveillance buoys?" Rile put forward.

"That's what the reserve home fleet commander thinks also. The loss of the ships is regrettable, and although I've asked the battle group to keep looking, I ordered the fleet to remain on station near New Europe."

"Yes, like usual Supreme commander you are right, the strategy is a good one." Elena smiled; backing him, as the room broke into applause. 'And for you supreme commander, I'll arrange something special,' Elena whispered to herself, holding her hatred in check.

Rile and Elena after the meeting, travelled back to their ship. Unlike the other fleet ships, the interior of this one was far different. On board this ship, the cloning of their race's remaining members, took place. Prolonging their lives through cloning had one unfortunate side effect. It was found over time to prevent couples producing offspring through reproduction. The females became sterile for some reason, making them unable to bare children of their own.

Males, mating with humans were found to be okay in producing offspring, although it did dilute the Roux race's gene pool. Many opted to continue cloning themselves rather than pollute the race's pure line. At the age of sixty, Rile their lead scientist had devised a way to transfer knowledge from the older clone to the new clone allowing their combined knowledge to survive. This meant that each generation would carry the race's entire cultural, historical and technical background. Rile himself, was occupying, his second clone of his line, his intelligence greatly increased by the cloning.

Other males lent towards breeding with the humans, which though disgusting to some, gave them a pool of loyal human soldiers. Elena had taken advantage of this and had secretly built up the number of these soldiers onboard their ships. Seated now in their own Roax war council, the group went over preparation for seizing power, protected by their own men.

"Rile, when you told the Supreme commander that the fleet of Flax Federation ships could be part of the mystery armada, were you guessing?" Elena asked.

"Broadcasts picked up, although scrambled, seem to have their language, so in a way you could say it's a guess, but I think I'm right."

"Then how did they get here and so quickly?"

"You're right Elena they must have their own portal, I didn't see that." He confessed.

"That means either Simon gave it to them or they somehow stumbled onto how to make one." Elena put forward.

"I would go with the first that Simon Hayes gave it to them. I can't see them suddenly inventing it at this precise time, my men there would have told me." Burgus their Intelligence officer suggested.

"Are we sure Simon's dead? I know the Katherine was destroyed, but the ship was burnt so severely their deaths couldn't be confirmed. Could he have survived?" Elena warned. She like many of the survivors who had been left to die on Deulong, had a deep fear and hatred of Simon.

"He's gone Elena, don't dwell on it! The planet he crashed on was in a remote Galaxy. If they'd survived, we would've seen them or signs of them on the surface. We know they ambushed some of our ships with their two shuttles, so they had no way to leave the planet" Rile barked. He too had a deep hatred of this troublesome human too, but facts were facts.

"He just has a way of doing the unbelievable that's all Rile. And then there's the disappearance of that ambushed squadron, what happened to them? I find it hard to believe they failed to send a warning."

"Yes although I didn't say it to the Supreme commander that is suspicious. Despites the Flax Federation's fleet's power it's hard to believe they destroyed seven of our ships and no one called for help." Rile admitted.

"One of the ships investigating the wreckage has found a communication computer from the flagship, commanded by Captain Prossio. They are looking over the system to see if they can reconstruct some data. They will send it to us when and if it is deciphered." Burgus informed them.

"Good, it's all coming together people. Once this planet is eliminated, we'll convince the Supreme commander to launch another attack on Crytstan. Once we've finished mopping up the Flax Federation fleet there, we'll take care of the New Europeans in one decisive battle. Then we'll attack the other planets at will until the whole known Universe either submits to our rule or dies!" Elena exclaimed the room breaking in to a victory chant.

Leaving the Hedred and Flax Federation fleets to prepare, Simon travelled back to the New America's fleet's position. The portal opening warned the New Americans that someone was coming just not who. Dropping their cloaking device, Simon manoeuvred the Katherine next to the President's flagship.

"Jeddah did warn us you'd appear suddenly." President Stuart's voice rang out, as Comm's were established.

"It time to attack Mr President are your forces ready?"

"Of course, but what about the meteors?"

"I'll handle that. I am sending you the co-ordinates of the enemy and the type of ship they use. Open your portals directly between them and yourselves, as you will have company. There are two friendly fleets that will be attacking at the same time from the opposite direction. The enemy ships are huge and totally different from our allies; bare that in mind when you're targeting ships." Simon warned.

"Yes Jeddah has sent copies of the friendly fleets' designs to all our ships, confusion should be kept to a minimum. So when will you launch the attack?"

"When the meteors stop coming," Simon answered.

"I don't think we will miss that." Stuart replied, "Good luck Simon," He added cutting its transmission. Turning to his crew who stood staring at the Katherine he tried to think of something to lift them.

"Let's go teach these Roax scum a lesson they'll never forget!" Jeddah screamed out, as the crew taking in what the alien had said, shouted their support.

"That'll do," President Stuart smiled, joining in.

"Battle stations!" Simon yelled, galvanising the crew as he opened a portal. "Remember our only target is the meteors, leave the enemy fleet to our friends." He ordered as the Katherine cloaking itself entered the portal.

On board Elena ship, alarms sounded as the portal appeared to their right.

"Fire at anything that appears." She yelled the crews already at battle stations. Tense minutes followed as everyone waited. "Anything moving in the portal?" Elena asked her nerves jumping.

"No there is nothing Sir." A crewmember called out, his fear evident. She was just about to say something to inspire the crew when a massive explosion shattered the sky.

"What was that?" Rile shouted the explosion appearing to have started where their meteor portal opening was.

"One of the meteors exploded as it exited the portal." A crewmember informed them.

"Why would it do that?" Elena asked, as around her blank faces greeted her question.

"I can think of no reason why it would explode. It's never happened before, and the meteors are carefully picked to make sure they traverse the portal easily." Rile answered, watching the portal.

"How long till the next meteor arrives?" Elena snapped, clearly worried.

"Another twenty minutes. I can already see it on our scanner." Burgus informed her, having taken over the long-range scanner console. Tense minutes passed, before the meteor burst from the portal, only to explode like the last one.

"Sir, the Supreme commander wants to know what's going on." Their Comm's officer informed them.

"Tell him we're working on it," Elena ordered the room going silent at her response.

For the next hour, Rile, and Burgus tried desperately to work out what was happening. Elena felt the optimistic mood of the crews dropping by this strange event. Burgus watching the meteors explode, on the computer's time-lapse data recordings, saw an anomaly.

"Rile look at this. There appears to be a beam of energy hitting the meteors, just before they explode.' Burgus reported. Rile watching the beam eyes grew wide.

"They're being destroyed by a powerful laser beam; can anyone see where it's originating from?" Rile shouted as the whole crew, not at a console rushed to the observation platform. While they were all standing there, including Elena, they saw a meteor, which was just about to leave the portal hit by a beam coming from right beside them. Several voices shouted at once, Burgus signalling all but Elena to keep quiet.

"The beam came from our right. It appeared right beside us." She informed him keeping her voice calm.

"There's nothing there, are you sure?" Burgus answered.

"Sir the Supreme commander wants to know why we're firing on the meteors?" This caused the crew to look to Rile for an answer. Grabbing the headset Rile opened a channel.

"Sir we are not firing, but I believe there is a cloaked ship next to us."

"What are you talking about Rile? No one has cloaked ships." The Supreme commander angrily responded.

"We'll soon know commander. I'm about to order our lasers to fire all around our ship in an arc, we'll soon know." Rile replied, his eyes full of hate.

"Do you think another ship is beside us?" Elena barked sounding scared.

"It's the only thing that makes sense. Burgus fire our lasers along the length of our ship, see if they encounter anything." Rile ordered.

"Maybe we should open a portal and leave," Elena shouted, the crew paralysed by her fear.

"Let's see what we find first." Rile replied coming towards her, moving her away from the crew.

"Go to the shuttle bay and prepare the shuttle." He whispered, as Elena taking his advice, moved casually out of the bridge. Once outside, she ran for the bay. Burgus, unaware of Elena's departure, continued firing laser beams randomly along the ship's side. Thinking it a waste of time, he was just about to give up, when one beam seemed to melt disappearing, as the faint outline of a ship appeared before disappearing again. Frozen it took him several seconds to sound the warning.

"Rile there's an unknown ship beside us. Our laser beam was absorbed by the ship, but it made it visible for a few seconds."

"Did you recognise it?" Rile barked.

"No, its design is unbelievable, but it had a name on the side. It's the Katherine!" Burgus cried out.

"Full power! Get us away from here!" Rile shouted, as the helmsmen reacting, pushed the ship's engine controls to their limit.

"Commander Rile we're receiving a message," Burgus informed him.

"What's it say?" Rile asked as they were nearing the portal.

"I should've done this, instead of sending you to Duelong," Burgus told him, as Rile stood frozen.

On board the Supreme Commander's flagship, the Commander was trying to work out, what Rile, and Elena were up to. They had always had their suspicions about their allies, but why they were firing on the meteors made no sense. One of the Roax soldiers had secretly told the Supreme commander in private, That Rile and Elena were planning something, but not what. It had been decided that after this campaign, Rile and Elena would be taken care of, in a supposed accident.

Now faced with betrayal, the commander was thinking of not waiting, but ordering the fleet to fire on the Roax controlled ship now. He was in the process of contacting the ship's captain when Rile's ship suddenly accelerated towards an opening portal. Angry at what he saw as a betrayal, he was just about to order his ships to open fire, when with a brilliant flash of white; Rile's ship, was blown to pieces.

"Good God he wasn't joking, there is an invisible ship out there." He said out loud, as a beam from where Riles ship had been, destroyed another meteor.

"Sir!" Came a shout from his Comm's officer.

"What is it, man?"

"Just before Commander Rile's ship exploded, we received a message from him. It says just two words, the Katherine." The Supreme commander stood silently shocked by the report, as the warning system, burst into life.

"Sir we have portals opening all around us. Hundreds of ships are exiting them, firing on our ships." His Intelligence officer warned.

"Have all ships return fire. Open a portal, we're leaving," the Supreme commander ordered, his crew open-mouthed at running away. He was just about to yell for them to hurry up when his ship came under fire. The laser cut right through their shield disabling their engines. Dead in the water, the commander looked out the viewing screen to see a ship suddenly appear.

"The Katherine!" he screamed, as his ship was vaporised.

On board the Katherine, Simon watched silently, as the combined strength of the Hedred, Flax Federation and New American's fleets, overpowered the leaderless enemy. When the Katherine had first arrived and destroyed the first meteor, they'd picked up the chatter between Rile's ship and the Supreme commanders flagship. Manoeuvring the ship next to Rile's they continued to destroy meteors under the very nose of Rile.

When Rile's ship had started firing its lasers randomly along its side, Simon knew they were onto them. The laser hit on his ship did no damage, but it did make the cloaking device waver for a few seconds, giving them away. Rile's ship accelerated away from their position and opening a portal, gave Simon a chance to correct a wrong. He knew the time had come to finish something he should've done fifty years ago.

Sending a message to Rile, let him know who was about to destroy him and his ambitions. Giving the order to fire, Radon at the weapon's controls needed no encouragement. Using their weapons' systems at full power, Rile's ship glowed pure white, before melting into nothingness.

"Try coming back from that one," Radon spoke out, the crew stomping their feet in support.

"Okay, target the flagship when you can Radon, but the priority is still the meteors." Simon reminded them, as Kate beside him squeezed his hand. Radon, seeing another meteor was due, fired on it first. With its destruction, he turned his weapons onto the flagship.

"Be careful Radon our friendlies are arriving everywhere," Ryan warned as flashes from the three fleets lit the horizons.

"No better time than now," Radon answered firing his laser at the flagship's engines. "She's crippled Simon, what now?"

"Destroy her. As long as the Supreme commanders alive, he can rally his forces. This way we've cut the enemies head off." Simon replied coldly.

"Yes, Sir," Radon answered firing everything he had. "Target is gone, Simon. Our fleets already seem to be getting the upper hand."

"Broadcast to the enemy fleet. If they transmit their intention to surrender and drop their shields, we will allow them to surrender. Those who continue to fight will all be destroyed." Simon ordered. "And make us visible; let them see who is transmitting." The enemy fleet that surrounded the Katherine gave mixed responses.

Some seeing their leaders gone and the enemy fleets overpowering them turned away lowering their shields. Others fought on targeting the Katherine, which didn't return fire, as it seemed untroubled by their attacks, it just continued to destroy meteors. This gave the three allied fleets time to target the remaining ships, while their attention was on the Katherine.

Ten hours found the victorious, if not heavily damaged allied fleets, rounding up the enemy ships that had surrendered. Only a quarter of New Europe's fleet had survived many only surrendering when they were too badly damaged to continue fighting. Jeddah, President Stuart, Radom, Jeddar and Ceb came aboard the Katherine, meeting with Simon, as the Katherine continued to destroy meteors.

Whoever was sending them through had no idea what had occurred, which caused a problem. Until those rocks ceased to come, the Katherine was grounded. It was the only ship with powerful enough weapons to stop the meteors.

"To all of you thank you. Without you, my planet would've been destroyed." President Stuart confessed.

"You have nothing to thank us for. If we hadn't come together here, we all would've been destroyed or worse been slaves to our enemies." Ceb garbled voice admitted, through his translator.

"Did any getaway?" Radon asked.

"The battle was confusing; with so many portals in use it was hard to tell." Jeddah pointed out, looking exhausted.

"My men reported seeing several enemy vessels including several shuttles entering a portal just after we exited ours," Stuart reported. Simon at first didn't reply. Instead, he went to the recorded footage of the destruction of Rile's ship. For a split second, before his ship exploded, Simon could just make out a shape leaving it.

"Damn, something left Rile's ship just as it was being destroyed." Simon barked, causing a momentary silence.

You're not sure it was a shuttle though?" Jeddah added.

"Do you want to take the chance that any Roax survived?" Simon answered, looking crestfallen.

"There's only one place they could go," Wordsworth exclaimed as he entered the bridge.

"I thought you were staying on the flagship?" Stuart asked.

"This can't wait, and I didn't want to broadcast it," Wordsworth answered, placing a disc into Simon's navigation system. "One of the enemy captains in exchange for a promise we wouldn't destroy their home planet gave me the position of several bases. One is where the meteors are coming from. The other is a facility where the Roax have been carrying out experiments on cloning.

Since Rile's ship with their reserve clones aboard is gone, the only way they can duplicate themselves is to return to their base. I thought it prudent to come in person and tell you of this Intelligence rather than broadcast it."

"Good work general. The question is what do we do about it?"

"Can I make a suggestion?" Ceb cut in.

"Of course you can Ceb," Simon replied waiting.

"You now have three targets, the Roax base; the meteor's launch platform and the New Europe planet and its Home fleet. I would suggest President Stuart and Radom send their forces to secure or destroy the home fleet and the planet New Europe. I can send my half my forces commanded by Jeddah, to the meteor area and destroy whatever is sending those rocks through. Simon with a few ships can attack the Roax base, as it is near the planet based space weapon, which destroyed the first Katherine."

The rest of my fleet can remain here with whatever you can spare from your fleets, to destroy the meteors as they exit. Our ships mightn't be a match for the Katherine weapons, but with our weapons concentrated on the portal exit, I see no danger of the meteors getting past."

"Don't you want to lead one of the attacks?" Radon asked.

"I have had my fill of war gentlemen. I will be happy and honoured to protect New America in your absence." Ceb explained, the others nodding their acceptance.

"You know Ceb the Katherine could attack the New Europe planet on its own." Simon pointed out.

"Yes you could, but this is an alliance, we must all shoulder the responsibility." Ceb smiled. "And see that justice is carried out," Ceb added.

"Are you telling me you want the Roax and the New Europeans taken alive?" Simon growled, he was intent on wiping them out.

"They must face a court of their peers. If they are found guilty, then they will die. Their guilt is not in question Simon, but justice must not only be done, but it must also be seen to be done, or we're as bad as they are." Ceb answered. Simon, his guts in a knot, tried to find an argument to challenge Ceb's logic, in the end, he admitted he was right.

"So be it Ceb, I will ask for the Roax's surrender. Although if they fire on us, that's the end of it." Simon promised, Kate beside him squeezing his hand supporting him.

"They have killed millions of not only our people but the Hedred race and the human worlds plus Oregarth. I will find it hard not to wipe them out, giving no quarter." Radom admitted.

"Ceb is right brother. Although I feel like you do, justice must be done." Jeddar confessed sounding conflicted.

"Well let's get going, although, like Radom, I want these people taken care of. That aside, when were finished, we'll meet back at New America. We can then bring everyone up to date on their actions and discuss a treaty so this problem won't happen again." President Stuart suggested, he too wanted the bloodshed over with.

"Right, let's work out what forces we have available and get moving," Radom suggested, keen to get moving. Radon beside him, watched his namesake plan the operations, feeling a touch of pride that he was named after him.

'He's a good leader', he said to himself, as the group gathered around the computer's communications console to plan the attacks.

Elena stood silently on board the New Europe spaceship that had picked up her shuttle, as they'd entered a portal. She was still shaking at how close she'd come to death. Rile was gone, along with a large percentage of her people. Again the Katherine had appeared from nowhere wrecking their life's work. Rile deserved his fate from being overconfident, but the others who had perished had done nothing but follow orders.

Now with a handful of followers, she wondered if the Roax would ever rise again.

"Elena it appears the Supreme commander has been killed. You are one of the only commanders that survived the attack, what would you suggest we do?" The ship's captain asked.

"We must warn the Home fleet, and prepare to defend New Europe until we can evacuate."

"We have only just over a hundred ships, including the few that escaped. Wouldn't it be prudent to attempt to negotiate a truce?"

"There can be no truce Captain. We have killed millions of their peoples, I'm afraid the enemy will come for blood. You must instruct your population to flee by whatever means possible."

"That would mean leaving millions to their fate?"

"It is unfortunate Captain, but we have lost, it is time to cut our losses and run."

"As you command Elena, I will send orders to prepare to defend the planet, until we've evacuated as many of the population as we can." The Captain informed her, moving away.

"Elena, can we talk?" One for her Roax soldiers whispered. Moving onto the observation platform the soldier making sure they were alone spoke.

"We can't stay with the New Europeans Elena, they are liable to surrender if the enemy arrives before they can evacuate."

"And what would you suggest?"

"Go to our base and gather the clones and equipment and escape. We can rebuild and repopulate, even Rile can be brought back."

"You're right, I forgot all about the base. Can we get control of this ship?"

"No, the crew is mostly human. One of other ships has a Roax crew of mostly clones, with some mixed blood. That one we can take without any trouble."

"Our allies won't be happy if we try to run?"

"They will let us go if they think we are returning with a new weapon. You could suggest moving the space gun to their planet. It served us well when we ambushed the Katherine. They are desperate Elena, they will believe anything you tell them." He smiled, as Elena worked it over in her head, trying to work out how she could convince their allies she was sincere.

"Yes you're right, they are desperate, but you don't know the full story. The Katherine is back."

"That's impossible. I was on one of the ships that pursued her. The wreckage was clearly the Katherine."

"Yes it was, but he has a new ship renamed the Katherine. It is five times larger and a lot more powerful. It is also invisible to both scanning and normal sight. It could be beside our ship now, and we wouldn't know it." Elena explained, her voice betraying how scared she was.

"Then this planet is doomed. We can't match his technology and may never. Best to retreat and consolidate, and await our chance in the future."

"What is your name soldier, you seem quite gifted.

"I am a clone of Burgus. He copied himself several times to make sure he survived. He sent me with the fleet to get me customised to battle." Looking at the young Burgus, she saw what a difference time could make. Burgus, the Intelligence officer, was in his late fifties and balding, while this young man was fit and in his prime, with short cut brown hair.

"That explains a great deal." Elena smiled before becoming serious. "We have no time to wait Burgus. Can you prepare my shuttle immediately? If you can, we will transfer to the other Roax controlled ship as soon as I can arrange it."

"It shouldn't be a problem. I'll gather what crewmembers are loyal as well, we may need them." Burgus suggested moving away.

"Now for the hard part, to convince the New Europeans that I'm trustworthy." Elena chuckled, walking towards the ship's Captain.

Despite his doubts, the Captain seemed excited about bringing the space weapon to New Europe. Taking the ship, which was crewed by mostly Roax personnel, made him hesitate. Explaining how she needed skilled Roax engineers to dismantle the weapon placated him, although he insisted that two New Europe ships accompany them. Elena hiding her anger thanked the Captain, promising to return as quickly as possible.

Taking her shuttle across to the Roax controlled ship, Elena once there, worked out a plan to lose their escort. Burgus in the meantime brought the Roax crewmembers up to speed on what was happening. To allay suspicions, Elena went along with the plan to dismantle the space gun, opening a portal to that gun's location. Once they had arrived there, they swiftly went to work dismantling and loading the gun into the two escorts' shuttle bays. Because Elena's ship had its own shuttle plus Elena's, they use that as an excuse to load only the escort ships with the gun.

It took two days to load the gun aboard the escorts, plus a day to travel there, which meant three days, had passed since the battle. Opening a portal back to New Europe the two escorts' lined up followed by Elena's ship. As the two escorts ships rocketed forward into the portal, Elena's ship, veered off.

"It was that easy." Elena smiled, the crew chuckling. "Now let's head for our base we have no time to lose."

Scanning the surrounding Galaxy found nothing out of the ordinary as they approached the small planet where the base was hidden. Approaching the base, they found the base personnel had seen no anomalies in the area, so they went straight in and landed inside the underground dock. Safe they quickly explained what had occurred. This brought a chorus of 'what should we do' from the apprehensive Roax survivors of Duelong.

In the end, Elena ordered everyone to pack his or her gear and board her ship. While this was happening she dispatched her crew to gather up as much equipment as possible, including everything to do with cloning. Working around the clock found the Roax ready to leave twenty-five hours later.

"Launch and prepare a portal," Elena shouted as the ship screamed into the sky, leaving the atmosphere. She was just about to open a portal when her crew shouted a warning.

"We are being hailed by the Katherine." The Captain informed her.

"Can we jump into the portal?" Elena whispered as they could hear her every thought.

"We might make it, but we don't know exactly where the Katherine is," Burgus warned.

"We can't be taken, they'll execute us! Open a portal we'll chance it!" Elena screamed out sobbing.

"Yet we will survive if you do surrender," Burgus explained, drawing his weapon. Around Elena, the clones disarmed the Roax members of the crew. Elena looked around the ship, seeing the once mighty race defeated by their clone copies.

"How dare you betray us, we gave you life," Elena screamed, backing away from them.

"You gave us life so you could take it when you needed our bodies. We are sick of your dreams of conquering, all we want to do is life." Burgus shot back stunning her. When Elena hadn't replied, Burgus took over.

"Lower the shields, stop the engines." He ordered, as beside the ship, the Katherine appeared. Many including Elena jumped back, shocked by the ghost ship appearance.

"This is Captain Hayes. I've waited a long time for this moment. Prepare to be boarded." His voice drowned out all opposition, as Elena unable to look at her brothers in arms, ran from the bridge.

Burgus knew his life swung in the balance as the Katherine's shuttle touched down in his docking bay. Most of the Roax leaders stood handcuffed and unarmed, lined up as if on parade. As the shuttle doors swung open, alien soldiers poured out. Radon, who had been dead against Simon going at all, had brought over forty soldiers with him.

Jeddah, who was commanding the force attacking the meteor launches, had told his men before he left to protect Simon with their dying breaths. Not one of them underestimated the hatred the Roax had for Simon. All feared that the Roax might do something stupid at seeing their nemesis aboard their ship.

Seeing the area was secure, Radon reluctantly signalled for Simon to come out. Looking around seeing Burgus standing in front of his men, Simon approached him first.

"I take it you're the leader."

"Yes Sir, Burgus is my the name, I am a clone for Burgus, Elena's Intelligence officer." He answered.

"Being the leader now mightn't help your future prospects, Burgus, why are you taking it on?" Radon asked.

"I am a soldier Sir. Even though we lost the war and our leaders failed us, as a soldier I must do what I think is right. Someone had to make a decision, or we would've all perished. I made that call."

"Despite what the Roax and New Europe had done, Simon saw that Burgus had gained some respect from Jeddah's men.

"Well said, commander. Did any of your leaders survive?" Radon asked.

"Yes, Elena still lives and the other leaders are here handcuffed. Elena is hiding somewhere on the ship." Burgus seemed embarrassed that one of their leaders would hide instead of accepting her fate.

"Okay, we don't have time to search. Order your crewmembers and your prisoners to assemble and prepare to board your shuttles. I don't care if they bring personal possessions, but no technology of any kind must leave this ship." Simon ordered. "You will be placed aboard several ships and transported back to New America to stand trial.

"You can't have conquered New Europe that quickly," Burgus spoke out before stopping himself. "Sorry, I apologise for my outburst."

"We're not sure what's going on there Burgus, that's someone else's responsibility, so pack up and get moving commander." Simon barked, walking back aboard his shuttle.

"Captain Hayes, can I come with you, I always wanted to see the Katherine?" Burgus asked, making Radon smile.

"You've got balls Commander; I'll say that for you." Simon smiled, waving him aboard, as around him the Roax were moved towards the other shuttle.

Walking onto the bridge of the Katherine, Burgus couldn't help staring. He hadn't really expected to be alive after surrendering as the Roax leader, yet here he was on the bridge of the Katherine.

"Cloak the ship and open a portal to New America." Simon beside him ordered, his crew responding without any hesitation. "Are you impressed Burgus?" Simon continued.

"I can't find the words Captain. This ship is so far advanced, it's hard to believe you could dream it up, let alone build it."

"We didn't build it, Burgus, it was a gift from an advanced race to stop the New Europeans and Roax takeover of the Universe," Simon explained. Burgus at first started to smile, thinking it was some sort of joke. Seeing everyone was waiting for his answer, he realized Simon was telling the truth.

"Why would they do that, why give you the means of conquering the Universe yourselves?"

"That is a question I would someday like an answer to myself. Somehow they trust us to do the right thing." Burgus was still trying to work that out when a young woman walked onto the bridge.

"Who's your new friend?" She smiled at Simon.

"This is Burgus. He's the commander of the remaining Roax people. Burgus this is my wife, Kate." Simon smiled, as Kate's happy smile evaporated.

"What is he doing on this ship?" She exploded.

"He volunteered to take the job as their commander knowing his fate if he did. The man's got guts Kate and he asked to see the ship. Until he's sent to trial, he is our prisoner and guest."

"Are you forgetting the millions of people his friends have killed?" Kate retorted.

"No Kate I am not. As the commander of this ship, I too have given orders and had my crew slaughter my enemies without remorse. Anyone, who attacks this ship, dies, they have no chance. Would you want Ryan or Katy to answer, for what I have ordered them to do?" This caused all in hearing distance to stop and look towards Simon. They had become aware lately of the burden their Captain carried.

"There is a difference Captain Hayes, your cause was just. Our leaders fought to dominate others. For a long time, many of us knew this and wanted to just be free. I, like many others, was produced to be a clone for one of our leaders. Their knowledge, their personality and their very being, was transferred into our bodies. After this process is completed, the clone's self ceases to exist. In other words, we died.

Like many I accepted my fate and went along with it, too afraid to challenge my creator's grand plan. When you defeated their fleet, we saw our chance to be free. I convinced Elena to abandon the New Europeans and flee to this base. I knew because of your history with the Roax, you would come after her. The only thing I wasn't sure of, was what you would do when you arrived. Luckily you didn't destroy this ship immediately but gave us the option to surrender.

Secretly I passed the word to the other clones that I expected you to appear at any moment and to be ready. When you contacted us, we seized the opportunity and forced the Roax to surrender. Now we are finally free, if not for a short time." Burgus confessed.

Kate stood looking at Burgus her hands still balled into a fist. All she could see was the race that had tortured her and murdered her friends. They'd been kidnapped on Oregarth and taken by their captives to Salvation, where the Roax had launched a coup against the humans there. She had spent so long demonising them that she hadn't even considered that any of the Roax wanted to just be free.

Instead, Burgus and the other clones had been used to fulfilling the Roax leader's perversion of living forever by stealing another being's life. Burgus, she now saw as just a soldier, doing the bidding of his master.

"You're right Simon. My passed experiences have blinded me to the truth. I have always seen the Roax race as evil; I didn't know men like Burgus existed." Kate confessed as Simon pulled her to him hugging her. Silence settled over the bridge as the two stood holding each other. Breaking reluctantly apart Kate left the bridge to rest.

"Sir the portal is ready." Ryan at the helm informed him.

"Burgus, are all your people off your ship and the base?" Simon asked.

"Yes Captain, all accept Elena."

"Good. Gun crews, fire on the enemy ship, full power! When the ship is gone, fire on the base." Simon ordered as a withering blast of energy roared across the gap between the Katherine and the enemy ship. Pulverized by the unrelenting discharge, the ship crumbled melting out of existence. When the ship was destroyed, the weapons changed target concentrating on the base. In seconds it was reduced to a molten mass of metal.

"That is the end of that!" Simon declared sounding relieved. "Full ahead Ryan, let's get it over with," Simon ordered as the crew felt a weight had been lifted, entered the portal.

The arrival at New America was in a way, an anti-climax. Orbiting the planet unseen, Simon observed calm had settled over the area. Ceb's ships, which had been commanded by Jeddah and sent to the meteor field had returned. Now the meteors had ceased to exit the portal, Ceb's with the other half of his fleet had rendezvoused with Jeddah.

"I judge you're here Simon?" Jeddah's voice boomed from the Communications console, having guessed by turbulence in the portal, that a ship might've exited.

"You were always clever Jeddah, and yes we are about half way between your ships and the portal," Simon replied.

"That's good news," was all Jeddah got out, as another portal opened and the ship's alarm roared into life.

"It is most probably Radom and Stuart although I suggest we stay on alert just in case," Simon suggested everyone staying put.

For two days, all of Ceb's ships and the Katherine, readied themselves, as unknown ships were picked up travelling in the portal towards them.

"Sir, the computer has identified the ships. It's Radom and President Stuart's fleets." Ryan informed Simon, the room visibly relaxing.

"How did you go Radom?" Simon asked, dropping his cloaking device as Radom's flagship and fleets emerged from the portal.

"It was a fierce battle. I will wait for President Stuart before telling it." Radom answered as another group of ships was picked up in the portal. President Stuart's fleet arrived shortly after.

"Okay now everyone's here, can Radom, if you can hear me, bring us all up to speed on what occurred at New Europe?" Simon enquired.

"As planned we opened a portal for our two fleets, to the adjoining Galaxy. Once there, we deployed the Flax Federation Fleet directly opposite the New Europe's Home fleet, while this was happening the New American fleet deployed behind them. When we first appeared, we found the enemy's Home fleet, loading some of the planet's population on board their ships. After several calls for them to surrender, a space gun located on the planet opened up, destroying several of our ships. I immediately ordered the fleet to open fire on the gun, as the New European fleet remained inactive.

After twenty minutes of sustained fire, the gun was eliminated, causing several major fires in the city where it was located. During this exchange, the Home fleet as it was called, dropped its shields and surrendered. As part of the surrender, all ships were forfeited and their crews transferred to the planet. I then asked for all members of the government and military leaders from the ship from Captains up, to be transferred aboard our ships to stand trial.

I was surprised when the soldiers on board the ships also wanted the secret police officers on their planet rounded up and taken as well. Altogether we have over fourteen thousand prisoners. I also imposed a condition on the planets for its survival. They are not allowed to build warships of any type, and a garrison of our combined forces will be permanently left on their planet. Amazingly they accepted our terms without a fuss. It seems for a long time the majority of the population has been against the war, they were just too scared to do anything." Radom reported.

"Jeddah now the others are here, can you tell them what occurred where the meteors were coming from?" Simon asked already having heard.

"When we arrived we found huge machines loading large rocks into the portal from a meteor field. Despite calls for them to surrender they engaged us. The battle was over swiftly all the enemy ships and machines destroyed, with no survivors" Jeddah told them.

"We have much to discuss, I suggest we all meet on New America and sort out what happens now." President Stuart suggested, the others agreeing.

It took weeks to work out all the details of the surrender. With the Roax prisoners thrown in, there were nearly twenty thousand prisoners. Each ship's Captain was given a chance to put forward his case, many only following orders were sent home. The others including the secret police and the Roax and New Europe leaders were exiled to a small planet once considered for colonisation by New America. It had breathable air and water plus abundant wild life and fish in the three oceans of the planet.

The prisoners would be given the means to survive, but no technology. They would all live out their lives isolated from the

Universe around them. New America took on the responsibility of monitoring the planet. The Hedred and the Flax Federation shared responsibility for monitoring the planet. They told New Europe they'd keep their distance, as long as no sign of warship building took place.

During this time the crew of the Katherine took a backseat keeping in the background. Their ship plus Radom's and Ceb's had landed at the airfield where the first Katherine had touched down. The biggest problem seemed to be crowd control, as the population of New America flocked to the field to look at the alien ships. So popular was it, that President Stuart had two of their fleet ships plus one of the captured New European ships touchdown next to the other three.

Although this proved popular, the Katherine remained the most photographed ship. Unfortunately, it didn't stop there. Hundreds of dignitaries and military personnel from all the different races all tried for a chance to visit the ghost ship. The continuing stream of tourist though was beginning to bore many of the crew. All that came to an end when Jeddah's battleship arrived.

Once hostilities had come to an end, Jeddah sent a message to his ship. He'd asked Radom if possible, could he open a portal for his ship. Radom happily had sent the message to his reserve fleet, which had opened one for them. The landing of the Oregarthian battleship completed the Katherine's stay. It was time to move on. Spreading the word to prepare to leave brought many of the crew back from visits all over the planet.

Many were just sightseeing, although Horen and several of his men, who help defend Johan's village, had returned with Benjamin for a visit. They had all crowded into Johan's new home, which had been built for him by the village for his leadership during the uprising as they called it. The recall to the ship had taken them by surprise as many had settled in becoming part of the village. Promising to return, they all left, Benjamin assuring his family he'd keep in touch.

"Is everyone aboard?" Simon asked, staring out at the millions of people there to watch their departure.

"Yes, Sir. All accounted for," One of Jeddah's new men answered, snapping to attention, making the regular crewmembers smile.

"Simon will do soldier," Simon replied, a pregnant looking Kate giggling beside him.

"Yes, Sir Simon." The soldier answered, the crew this time hiding muffled laughter.

"Okay. Ryan take us home." Simon smiled; he knew he'd have to get used to this. Ryan nodding he understood in the helmsman's tube, dialled the portal co-ordinates for Salvation. The crowd gathered hushed as the watery circle opened. Unlike last time when Simon opened it right above the field, this time it was out in space at a pre-determined position.

It had been agreed between all the allies to nominate certain areas for travelling, to and from different planets and Galaxies. This was because, now so many different races could make portals, that there could be a problem. It was suggested that was a chance, even though it was remote, that two portals might open at the same point. This might result in an unprecedented disaster. So to stop this occurring, stringent conditions for their use were put in place.

Engaging the engines, the Katherine's crew, watched the people of New America wave their goodbyes. Rising into the sky, Simon spotted the Oregarthian battleship, again commanded by Jeddah follow them out into space. There, lined up along their route to the portal, were the fleets of their allies, honouring them as they passed. Signalling his goodbyes to their friends, Simon ordered his ship into the portal leaving a chapter of their lives behind.

Jeddah's people from Oregarth had unanimously agreed to take Katy's people's offer up, of living with them on Salvation. Simon and his crew had also opted to start over on Salvation most having had their fill of war. They all knew they were starting from scratch, knowing everything on Salvation had been destroyed

Radom's people had given them a special gift. It was a system for cleaning the atmosphere of radiation. This had been caused when one of the planet's sub-cores melted down during a fight with the Roax. The planet, although only having a small landmass, still was more than enough room for the settlers to live freely, their allies promising to assist them. To Simon and Kate, it was a place to start over, to raise a family in peace.

HOME

Arriving above the planet, Simon gave the order to deploy Radom's atmospheric cleaning systems, before landing on the planet. Radiation levels were only marginally higher than normal, as the Katherine touched down where New Vancouver once stood. The wreckage of the Salvation subs was still visible at the docks, although the rest of the city had been completely destroyed. The crew all moved to the shuttle bay, as the large doors in the side of the hull were opened. Opposite their ship, Jeddah's ship, also touched down sending a cloud of dust and debris into the air.

"This is it, Kate, this is home." Simon smiled hugging Kate as they watched the dust hit their shield forming a grey horizon.

"When can we leave the ship?" Kate asked, excited at being away from it.

"We can leave now, although in your condition you can't go further than the shield. The others are free to go wherever they like." He explained, not wanting Kate exposed to the radiation.

"That will do for now." She chuckled walking down the ramp amongst the other crewmembers, all wanting to see their new home.

They'd been there for a month, before the reduction in radiation levels, made it safe for all to leave the ships. Simon and Kate had decided to build on the waterfront like Mike his grandfather had done. Accommodation would be for sometime aboard ship until a dwelling could be built. Kate spent hours working on a plan for their home, while Simon worked out where to obtain the necessary building materials.

Maps of Salvation supplied by Katy showed old cement and gravel quarries. Although they'd been destroyed during the floods, they could be repaired. Timber was easy, as huge forests had grown back since the floods. The first course of action was to get these critical works back on line before any building was started. Help poured in from their allies all willing to lend a hand. Trade between the races was now in full swing as war gave way to rebuilding. Even New Europe received help although it was limited.

Kate in her last months of pregnancy spent most of her time now just sitting at the site where their home would someday be built. She seemed happy, although she constantly looked to the skies as if expecting the Roax to reappear. Of all people, Burgus and the other clones kept her company, catering to her every need. Her acceptance of them after what had been done to her by the Roax seemed to have left the clones in debt to her.

Simon had to admit he liked Burgus, although Radon still had his doubts. Still, the majority had accepted them into their family, and that was that. Hard working, willing to earn their places, the clones soon found themselves spread out throughout the settlement. Still several of the female clones were always to be found with Kate. Of course so were a few Oregarthian, Katy's Salvation and Flax Federation women as well.

"It's dangerous for the single men when women gather in numbers." Radon suggested, seeing Simon watching Kate with the women.

"That right you're considered single now too aren't you Radon?" Simon smiled, watching him look around nervously.

"It is nothing to joke about Simon. Women outnumber men here, and I like my life as it is." Radon whispered scared they'd hear him.

"You coward Radon. Fearless in battle and scared of females." Jeddah exploded with laughter behind them, having heard their conversation.

"I will not stay and debate such silliness I have work to do." Radon scoffed hurrying off towards the ship, as Kate and Jeddah's wife approached.

"What were you three talking about?" Severage, Jeddah's wife, asked.

"Nothing my dear just discussing the ship's maintenance that's all." Jeddah lied, making Simon hide a smile.

"You know Simon, Radon looks lonely, maybe you should suggest he take another wife?" Kate put forward, taking Simon by surprise.

"I think he's happy the way he is?" Simon being evasive answered, as Jeddah beside him remained quiet.

"Nonsense! A good friend would see him married, wouldn't you agree husband?" Severage snapped, watching Jeddah.

"Of course dear you're right we'll ask him," Jeddah replied pulling Simon with him, as they both hastily left.

"God Radon was right, we should warn him," Simon whispered to Jeddah, as they neared the Katherine.

"He's on his own Simon when it comes to wives, I'd rather face the Roax," Jeddah confessed, shaken by the admission.

"I can't believe you're scared of your wife, Jeddah?" Simon laughed, making him stop.

"Then you go back there and tell Kate you aren't going to tell him to get married." Jeddah put forward, waiting his answer.

"Maybe later?" Simon softly told him.

"And I'm the coward!" Jeddah grinned before they both burst into laughter.

For the next three years, the settlement grew as many people from other planets came to make their homes on Salvation. Radon despite Simon and Jeddah's asking remained single, much to the disgust of the women. Kate had two children both boys. Mike, the oldest and John, filled their days with happiness, the outside worlds forgotten.

Despite their peaceful existence, the Katherine was kept ready, its camouflaged shield making it invisible to any unfriendly visitors. Manned day and night, the crews constantly trained, the people of Salvation remained vigilante. Always on watch, they remain alert monitoring approaching danger. Part of living on Salvation meant you had to serve part-time on one of their ships. With the growing population, Simon had procured four Roax ships, captured during the war. Gutting them, he had redesigned them to carry thousands of people or trade goods, which was their primary duty.

At anyone time, at least two of these ships, plus the Oregarthian battleship and the Katherine were on Salvation in case they needed to leave. Maybe it was being over protective, but Simon had always been worried by the

Chosen's complete absence since the end of the war. 'Surely they worried about the Katherine left sitting idle?' he mused. His question was answered, when he saw Radon running towards him.

"Simon can I have a word?" Radon asked short of breath.

"What's the problem?" Simon asked knowing it was serious.

"A portal just opened. Radom, Jeddar, Ceb and General Wordsworth, are on their way here. Kate seeing Radon came out of their house with the two boys.

"What's wrong Radon?" she asked her voice trembling.

"Kate, it could be nothing, but Radom and Ceb and some of the other war council members are on their way here. Stay here till I return." Simon asked her.

"Okay, Simon," Kate answered, looking crestfallen as gathering up the boys, she took them inside.

"She took that well?" Radon whispered.

"Did she?" Simon sadly replied, jogging with Radon to the Katherine.

Entering the ship, Simon found Ryan and Benjamin there as well, manning the tubes.

"Relax everyone, its most probably some detail of the trade treaty they forgot to get us to sign," Simon assured them smiling. Most smiled back acknowledging his idea, although they still brought the ship to battle-stations, warning their crewmembers on call, to report to the ship.

"What have you got Ryan?" Simon asked, taking the Captain's chair.

"I've got three ships coming in through the portal fast," Ryan confirmed, waiting for the computer to identify them. "One is Ceb's flagship, the other is Radom's ship. The third is an Oregarthian battleship."

"That's impossible my people left this Galaxy!" Radon exploded, moving to the viewing screen. "My apologies Ryan you are correct, although this ship is of a newer prototype of Jeddah's ship." Radon explained as Jeddah entered.

"I came as soon as I heard." Jeddah interrupted looking at Radon's expression he continued. "What is wrong my brother?"

"One of my people's ships is with Radom and Ceb's ships."

"So, they could be here to see how you are going for all you know. Let's not think the worst yet." Jeddah pointed out, as the three ships burst from the portal.

"Can you here us Simon?" Radom's voice boomed out of their Communications receiver.

"Yes Radom, why are you here and with an Oregarthian ship?"

"It's a long story, can we come down by shuttle?"

"Of course, land your ships if you want," Simon replied.

"No, we'll leave them in orbit on guard for now," Radom answered all in hearing sensing something was up.

By the time the shuttle had landed, Simon, Radon and Jeddah had walked outside the ship, to wait just inside the shield. Across from them, the shuttle's door opened, and six figures emerged. Radom, Ceb, Jeddar and General Wordsworth walked across towards them with two Oregarthian. As they grew closer Radon gasped in surprise.

"By the mountains of Gorion, what are you doing here Kargol?" He shouted, moving forward through the shield. His appearance from nowhere stunned the Oregarthians. Running up to the first Oregarthian, he grabbed both his arms, before embracing him.

"I never thought I would see you again old friend. You haven't aged a bit?" Kargol sounded wary as if Radon mightn't be Radon.

"It is I, my friend. My youthful appearance, is a long story and I am sure you didn't come all this way to talk about it?" Radon smiled, looking past him to the woman.

"You're right, let's go inside this new ship of yours and sit down, my legs aren't what they were." Kargol grinned unable to see any ship behind them. Seeing Radon was looking at his companion, he introduced them. "This is my daughter Royan. Royan, this is Radon, the leader of the Ninth." Radon bowing to her, turned back to Kargol.

"Come my friend let's get more comfortable." Radon smiled. Turning, he walked back through the shield, as Kargol and

Royan were made to follow. Of course, they both hit the shield hard, being thrown back.

"Oh sorry about that Kargol, the ship doesn't know you yet." Radon apologised, holding Kargol's hand and Royan's, he guided them through

"How does it do that?" Kargol asked amazed, the woman looking back at the shield in awe.

"We're not sure we think it records your DNA and only lets you through once it knows you." Simon volunteered, as Kargol and the woman stopped in front of him.

"You have been busy Captain Hayes if half of what these allies of yours tell me is true?" Kargol smiled hugging Simon nearly crushing him. His grip loosened, as he stared past him at the ship. "By all the Gods Simon. What a ship." He murmured, in awe.

"Yes, she's quite something," Simon answered watching Kargol's look, sensing something in it.

"We have no time to lose Captain Hayes I need your help," Kargol begged, dropping to his knees, stunning Radon and Royan.

"Get up father, you are the leader of our people, you don't have to beg," Royan exclaimed, emotionally upset with him.

"I will do anything to save my people Royan. If that means grovelling in the dirt, then so be it." He explained as Simon helped him to his feet.

"What is wrong Kargol?" Simon asked, holding up the once indomitable warrior leader of his race.

"I need to sit down," Kargol informed them as Radon and Radom carried him aboard the Katherine. Seated Kargol began his story.

"Travelling in hibernation the Oregarthian fleet travelled outside the known Galaxy for twenty years. Coming to a small solar system, they found a large planet, with a stable sun. It was paradise with other planets suitable for colonising in surrounding Galaxies. For the next few decades, we lived in peace, though always on guard in case of trouble.

Five earth years ago Kargol's first son Paycon, in command of two of their battleships, led an expedition to an outer Galaxy. Transmissions had been intercepted from this area, the source unknown. The mission was peaceful as the Oregarthians were happy with what they had, needing no new colonies. Paycon reported meeting a friendly race of beings, which had invited them to their home planet to discuss trade.

Although many of Paycon crew were worried by the strange, hostile appearance of this new race, Paycon seemed unconcerned. The Captain of the second ship as a precaution sent a picture of this new race and the analysis of their spaceships back to Kargol's command centre. It was the last time Kargol would see his son or the rest of the expedition's ship's crews. After waiting days and receiving no answer, the whole fleet sailed for Paycon's last reported position. All they found were the two ships floating lifeless in space.

Putting two crews aboard the two ships, they sailed with the fleet searching the Galaxy. Finding nothing Kargol frustrated returned to their home planet Oreigon. Despite continued searches, nothing could be found of this mysterious race. Four Earth months later, two ships patrolling the colonies' outer boundaries disappeared. This time the wreckage of the ships was found, as well as the wreckage of a third ship. Unlike Paycon's ships, these two weren't caught off guard and defended themselves. A study of the mystery wreckage showed it was the same design as the so-called friendlies, Paycon had met with. After this, the home planet and their colonies were put on alert.

Travelling in fleets of ten ships, seemed to work as no further attacks occurred. For an Earth year, the enemy kept its distance until a patrol received a distress call from an outer colony. Arriving there the patrol found the colony of ten thousand people gone. All equipment was in place although, by blood trails found, the colony had defended itself. Fearing further attacks and being unable to defend themselves, Kargol ordered the colonies abandoned and all his people to return to Oreigon.

The planet then went on a war footing as space guns were set up all over the planet. This plus the fleet of a hundred new designed ships made them all feel safer. Another year passed when without warning, a large force attacked their fleet destroying or crippling half. Casualties to the enemy fleet were double theirs, although they didn't appear worried.

At personal risk, some of Kargol's best soldiers including his daughter Royan boarded a crippled enemy ship. The enemy asked for no quarter, fighting to the end. From the information, they obtained they discovered the horrific truth. The enemy race were meat eaters, their main food supply was of other races. The Oregarthian also feed off meat, but from wild unintelligent animals. This race gorge itself on primarily intelligent life forms.

Horrified by the news, Kargol knowing there were too many people to evacuate, set up powerful shields on the planet's surface to protect his people. While doing this, the attacks on his fleet continued till only a handful of ships remained. Kargol knew that his race's destiny was sealed unless he could get help.

Taking one of the remaining ships with a volunteer crew, he decided to fight his way through to their original home planet of Oregarth. One of their leads scientists had come up with a new way of travelling. By entering a hole made from and filled with energy, he assured them they would reach Oregarth in record time. Unfortunately because of the energy involved Kargol worried about an explosion, insisted he open it in orbit above their planet. As the scientist had predicted, the large hole appeared and Kargol's ship swiftly entering it escaped the surprised enemy forces. Unfortunately, four enemy ships had also entered the hole, chasing them.

Unable to turn they had only survived by keeping ahead of their enemy who continued to fire on their ship's rear. For ten days the chase continued, until as suddenly as it started, they exited the ring of energy. Badly damaged they sent out a call for assistance to Oregarth, hoping for help. Instead, their enemy of old, the Flax Federation, appeared with over a hundred ships.

Under attack from the enemy, Kargol was shocked, when the Flax Federation ships bypassed his and attacked the enemy ships. It was a heated battle with the Flax federation losing five of their own ships. We were then stunned when the Flax ships asked us if we required help. Telling them who I was brought an instant response. They explained the truce between our two races that you Radon had engineered, with Simon and Jeddah.

I was sceptical till as a sign of trust the Flax Federation ships dropped their shields, instructing us to follow them to their Capital on Crytstan. There our ship was repaired, while we waited for Radom, their leader. Once he arrived and heard what was occurring, he sent a message to his allies, calling for them to meet on Crystan. Once they arrived, they thought it best to travel here and explain what was going on to Simon in person. And that's my story, Simon, can you help us?" Kargol asked drinking a glass of water refreshing his voice.

"This race of cannibals worries me, Simon. Their ships are more powerful than ours, and after they finish with the Oregarthians, they might head here." Radom pointed out.

"Relax Radom, of course, we'll help. First, we'll send the Katherine and have her scout out the enemy. Then we'll make a decision on either sending our fleets and fighting or evacuating Kargol's people. Either way, we need more information. In the meantime, we better bring our own people up to speed to see who wants to go and whose staying."

"I thought you ruled here," Royan interjected sounding angry.

"We are all free here Royan. We live in a democracy where everyone is equal." Radon answered seeing the warrior in this woman scoff at their system.

"Sounds unworkable to me." She continued, her father signalling her to be quiet.

"That may be so Royan, but like it or not that's the way it is." Simon forced a smile, not looking forward to explaining this to Kate.

Two weeks later, found the Katherine exiting the portal into Kargol's Universe. A fleet of strange ships sat watching the exit, as the Katherine invisible glided by unseen. Simon had mixed feelings at being here. Kate had been against him going, wanting Radom and the other allies to send their fleets as well. He'd, in the end, agreed on a compromise.

A force big enough to evacuate the Oregarthians would follow in three days' time led by Jeddar, giving Simon time to work out what was going on. The allied fleets would stand ready to follow if they were needed.

"Aren't you going to attack them?" Royan asked standing beside her father.

"Where's the fun in that?" Radon smiled, his eyes looking over the enemy ships. They were purpose built fighting ships, which unlike most of the allies' ship had only one function, to fight. Travelling to Oreigon they arrived as the enemy was starting a bombardment of a shielded area in the mountains above one of their cities.

"They are trying to breakthrough to the power generators. If they go, all the shields will collapse." Kargol warned as Simon ordered the weapons to acquire targets.

"Okay let's give them a look shall we?' Simon smiled, as Ryan dropped the cloaking device. "All guns open fire!" The enemy ships to surprise at first to respond, started to come apart as the Katherine unleashed a massive barrage of energy. Simon watching the destruction of the enemy fleet was startled when one of the Chosen finally decided to speak to him.

"Simon, gather the Oregarthians and leave as quickly as you can. This enemy is not who they appear to be."

"Then who are they?" Simon asked, as Kargol beside him, turned to see whom he was talking too.

"They are the slaves of another race, you are in great danger." The chosen warned, as in the distance four ships suddenly appeared. Unlike the Katherine, they were ugly looking ships. Black in colour, the same size as the Katherine, they radiated malice. They had similar wings, but unlike the Katherine's sleek predator bird shape, they had more tucked in design as if the bird was landed on the ground.

"Cloak the ship and turn immediately!" Simon shouted. The ship responding turned sharply, as the other ghost ship's opened fire.

TO BE CONTINUED IN...
GUN BARREL PLANETS - BOOK 3

www.ingramcontent.com/pod-product-compliance
Lightning Source LLC
Chambersburg PA
CBHW031229120726
47905CB00002B/520